P
Pam

A Young Wife

"In this compelling read, Lewis beautifully captures the essence of a place, from the lushness of the Netherlands to the wilds of Argentina to the inhospitable urban streets of New York."

—*Booklist*

"A stirring journey . . . its images are undeniably alluring."

—*BookPage*

"Minke's resilience and determination will make readers eager for a happy ending. . . . Sure to please fans of historical romance and family dramas."

—*Library Journal Express*

"In her third novel, loosely based on the life of her grandmother, Lewis (*Perfect Family*) delivers an exuberant protagonist . . . the unexpected twists in Minke's story and her feisty appeal will keep readers eager to turn the page."

—*Publishers Weekly*

Perfect Family

"Pam Lewis is the literary equivalent of a forensic scientist. In her compelling second novel, *Perfect Family,* Lewis pulls the body of a beautiful young woman from a lake, then, layer by suspenseful layer, unpeels and reveals a well-to-do family's secrets, lies, and hidden heartaches. I was riveted."

—Wally Lamb, *New York Times* bestselling author of *She's Come Undone* and *I Know This Much Is True*

"Nothing about Pam Lewis' *Perfect Family* feels clichéd. . . . Lewis' plot twists and turns to a satisfying conclusion."

—*Parade*

"In this fast-paced novel, secrets haunt an old-money Connecticut family after an accident taints their vacation home. As they attempt to understand the tragedy, the truth of their matriarch's past is revealed, spinning them into a reexamination of their identity. You'll be swept up too."

—*Hallmark Magazine*

"Lewis skillfully lures the reader through her narrative maze with plenty of plot twists."

—*Publishers Weekly*

"Lewis's thrilling and gritty novel dispels the myth of the 'perfect family.' The characters are flawed, insecure, and enmeshed in a compelling conflict that will satisfy the author's many fans."

—*Library Journal*

Speak Softly, She Can Hear

"Gripping, . . . with a freshness that sets it apart from the thriller genre. There is a queasy darkness to the novel that the reader will savor. Once begun, it's a hard book to let go of, and the writer's skill prompts re-reading of passages for their craft alone."

—*New York Post*

"This debut psychological thriller is full of promise for author Pam Lewis, who takes various familiar genre elements and gives them some fresh twists."

—*Chicago Tribune*

"Pam Lewis's novel vividly captures the hippie era of free love, pot and rock 'n' roll, developing an unsettling and mesmerizing psychological thriller."

—Ann Hellmuth, *The Orlando Sentinel*

"This psychological thriller is an excellent debut for first-time novelist Lewis. Her settings are vibrant, from the hippie culture in San Francisco to rural small-town life in Vermont. Her descriptions, especially of angst-ridden teen years and those friendships that pull us through them, are dead-on. In subtle strokes, she paints a menacing darkness around Carole, who, no matter how far she runs, can't seem to escape the threat lurking in the shadows."

—Karen Carlin, *Pittsburgh Post-Gazette*

"[A] chillingly elegant first novel."

—Joanne Sasvari, *The Calgary Herald*

"Well-written and gripping . . . Readers will stay up late to see whether beleaguered, tortured Carole can free herself from the despicable Eddie."

—*Publishers Weekly*

"Lewis, in her debut novel, tells an engrossing tale of an unlikely friend-ship, the burden of keeping secrets, and the insidiousness of lies."

—*Booklist*

"Pam Lewis will keep you guessing, she'll keep you up late at night, but most of all, she will bring you back to the friendships and betrayals of your past. Smart, clever, and emotionally involving. You'll never feel the same way about keeping a secret."

—Brad Meltzer, *New York Times* bestselling author of
The Tenth Justice and *The Zero Game*

"The very first chapter of *Speak Softly, She Can Hear* fires an electric charge that sent me racing through this sexy and suspenseful psycho-logical thriller. Pam Lewis is a sly and sure-footed storyteller whose literary tale of treachery, deception, and truth sits comfortably along-side Donna Tartt's *The Secret History* and Patricia Highsmith's *The Talented Mr. Ripley.*"

—Wally Lamb, *New York Times* bestselling author of
She's Come Undone and *I Know This Much Is True*

Also by Pam Lewis

Perfect Family

Speak Softly, She Can Hear

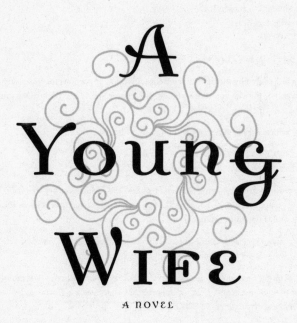

A Young Wife

A NOVEL

Pam Lewis

SIMON & SCHUSTER PAPERBACKS
New York   London   Toronto   Sydney   New Delhi

Simon & Schuster Paperbacks
A Division of Simon & Schuster, Inc.
1230 Avenue of the Americas
New York, NY 10020

First Simon & Schuster trade paperback edition June 2012

SIMON & SCHUSTER PAPERBACKS and colophon are
registered trademarks of Simon & Schuster, Inc.

For information about special discounts for bulk purchases, please contact Simon & Schuster
Special Sales at 1-866-506-1949 or business@simonandschuster.com.

The Simon & Schuster Speakers Bureau can bring authors to your live event. For more
information or to book an event contact the Simon & Schuster Speakers Bureau at 1-866-248-3049
or visit our website at www.simonspeakers.com.

Designed by Davina Mock-Maniscalco

Manufactured in the United States of America

10 9 8 7 6 5 4 3 2 1

The Library of Congress has cataloged the hardcover edition as follows:

Lewis, Pam, 1943–
    A young wife : a novel / Pam Lewis.
        p. cm.
1. Young women—Fiction. 2. Married people—Fiction. 3. Deception—Fiction.
4. Drug dealers—Fiction. 5. Kidnapping—Fiction. 6. Children—Crimes against—Fiction.
7. Netherlands—Fiction. 8. Argentina—Fiction. 9. New York (N.Y.)—Fiction. I. Title.
    PS3612.E974Y68 2011
    813'.6—dc22

                                                                    2010053374

ISBN 978-1-4516-1272-1
ISBN 978-1-4516-1273-8 (pbk)
ISBN 978-1-4516-1274-5 (ebook)

In loving memory
Eelkje van der Wal Thummler
Elly Thummler Lewis

Part One

ENKHUIZEN, THE NETHERLANDS

January 1912

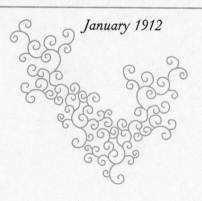

1

MINKE HEARD HIS velvety voice downstairs; the visitor from Amsterdam must have arrived. Sander DeVries was his name. A wealthy man, according to rumor, and a distant relative, although in the Netherlands everyone was a distant relative. He owned a ship or ships or something. He had children older than Minke and a wife who was dying. This was what she knew.

She lay on the floor peering down the ladder to the entry of the kitchen. Her mother's high-pitched laugh betrayed nervousness. Her older sister, Fenna, who at sixteen had the most commanding voice, asked for his coat and scarf, inviting him to sit. Her father cleared his throat. In town, everyone would be talking about this visit. A stranger in Enkhuizen was an event.

She swung her feet around and descended the ladder to the middle rung, where she hung on, leaning forward to catch a glimpse of him. She was supposed to stay out of sight because Fenna had already laid claim to the position he was expected to offer. Fenna was the thicker, stronger of the two sisters. Fenna with her certainty and coarse sense of humor had the stomach for a dying woman.

In his lovely, smooth voice, Meneer* DeVries spoke of his automobile, the icy condition of the roads, and the stale smell of the sea here in Enkhuizen and his regret that over the years their families had not been closer. In that silken voice, he explained it was his Elisabeth's idea that one of the van Aisma girls be asked to come. Elisabeth was, as they knew, of course, the daughter of Papa's much

---

* Meneer is the equivalent of the English Mr., Mevrouw is the equivalent of Mrs.

older cousin, Klara, a name Minke recognized as that of the woman whose funeral she had attended in Leeuwarden five years earlier. Meneer's voice became grave. "This is work for a person of great patience," he said.

"I'm patient," Fenna said quickly.

"And what of the other girl?" He was talking about her! She stepped quietly down the ladder to peek into the parlor. He sat at the family table, facing in her direction, his fingers drumming the wooden surface, surrounded by Fenna, Mama, and Papa.

"Well, here's the other one!" Minke realized he was talking to her, that the conversation had stopped, that he'd caught her spying. Feeling her face redden, she entered the room. He stood, his chair scraping against the floor. He was as tall as her father, who was himself the tallest man in town. But where Papa was rail-thin, Meneer DeVries had the powerful look of an athlete. He had ginger-colored hair and mustache, and a chiseled, handsome face.

Why, Minke wondered, noticing for the first time, had their mother ever allowed Fenna to wear that outgrown dress for company? The dress was so tight at the waist and the bodice that Fenna's breasts strained against the material. Fenna cared nothing for her looks. Her hair was the same white-blond as Minke's but lacked luster. Her blue eyes bulged slightly, and her skin was ruddy from sunburn. She twitched with annoyance at Minke's intrusion.

"Please." Meneer DeVries pulled his chair from the table. He stared at Minke so intently that she thought something was expected from her, but she could not think what. "Do sit down," he said, not taking his eyes from her. She glanced for permission at Mama, who shrugged in confusion. The visit was not going as Mama had expected.

"I'm going to Amsterdam with Meneer DeVries." Fenna's voice held an edge.

Mama laughed again from nerves. She badly wanted this job for Fenna, who was trouble in the household. In fact, Minke wanted her gone as well and felt guilty for it, but it had been difficult going through school in Fenna's wake. Doing anything in Fenna's wake. The boys expected Minke to be loose. The girls kept their distance. Better for Fenna to be far away in Amsterdam.

Minke slipped into the empty chair Meneer had offered, not knowing what else to do with herself.

"Thank our guest, Minke," Mama said, and Minke tipped her face to him and said in a near whisper, "Thank you, Meneer DeVries."

"So, Minke, is it?" he said. "That's a very pretty name."

She looked down at her lap. She had been told to stay out of the parlor today, and here she was drawing the attention.

"And you would be the elder sister?"

"She's younger," Fenna said.

He considered this a moment, then paced about the table, his hands locked behind his back. He stopped behind Fenna. "Fenna, you're very like my Elisabeth. Two peas in a pod." Fenna beamed. She could be cute in an impish way when she smiled. "But that is why I am now glad to meet your sister."

No one said anything. It didn't exactly make sense. Minke had nothing to do with this arrangement. Meneer DeVries shut his eyes and canted his face toward the ceiling. It was a complete change in mood, as though just the mention of his ill wife had overcome him. His massive hands landed on Fenna's shoulders. "My wife is a strong-willed woman, and I suspect that you too are strong-willed."

"I am," Fenna said, and Minke wondered how he knew that so quickly.

He shook his head. "Such a combination won't succeed. In the company of a strong-willed woman, my wife will fight, refuse medicine, disobey. In her final days, she needs a quieter soul. I see this quality in Minke; it is Minke who should come."

Fenna whipped around and gripped his hands as if laying claim. "But that's not fair," she said. "It's been decided!"

"That's precisely right," Meneer DeVries said. "I have decided."

"Mama?" Minke felt utter confusion.

"Meneer DeVries, are we to understand this correctly? That you've decided against Fenna in favor of Minke to nurse your wife?" Mama asked.

Meneer DeVries nodded and withdrew his hands from Fenna's grip.

"This wouldn't have happened if you'd stayed upstairs like you were supposed to," Fenna said.

"It's not my fault," Minke said.

"She gets everything she wants, and she always has," Fenna said to Mama. "You and Papa always favor her over me."

Oh, she could make Minke so angry with that old, utterly false complaint. Fenna had always ruled the roost with her demands and tantrums. Mama and Papa spent so much time worrying over her that Minke sometimes felt invisible.

"Fenna, we *meant* for you to have the post." Mama was as red as a beet.

"And anyway, I don't even—" Minke began but stopped herself. *Want it,* she was going to say. Taking care of a sick woman held no appeal for her. She addressed Meneer DeVries. "Fenna would do a very good job for you, Meneer."

"She's far too spirited for the work, as I suspected."

"Papa, *do* something," Fenna implored.

Papa opened his hands in resignation.

Meneer DeVries, still standing behind Fenna, patted her cheeks lightly with both hands. "There, there," he said. "I am terribly sorry this upset you, but it's such a delicate matter with Elisabeth." Fenna was quiet from then on, following Meneer with her eyes as he discussed with Mama and Papa the payment arrangements.

MINKE MADE THE journey with Meneer DeVries in his shiny yellow car. "A Spijker," he said. The car's heater blasted against her feet, which swelled painfully in her tight boots. She stared straight ahead, excited by the terrific speed, terrified when Meneer DeVries slammed on the brakes behind horses and carts. He pulled levers and adjusted knobs. He spun the wheel, and she couldn't take her eyes from his wonderful honey-colored gloves. Noticing that she was admiring them, he splayed the fingers of both hands and said, "Pigskin. The supplest of leathers."

Just then the car slid sideways, tipped sharply to the right, and came to a heaving stop, followed by utter silence.

"I'm sorry," she whispered. It was her fault for distracting him. They'd gone off the road and landed in the drainage ditch at such an angle that outside her window she could see only snow and outside his window, only sky.

He stared at the wheel as if in disbelief and, with great effort, pushed open the door, which fell back against him from gravity; he finally managed to squeeze through and trudged up the embankment, where she could see his bottom half pacing up and down the road. She never should have come. It was a mistake, and already he no doubt hated her for causing this accident. She didn't even know if she'd have the strength to climb out as he had. Fenna would have been able to. Indeed, Fenna would already be outside doing something. Running down the road for help, shouting out orders even. Meneer DeVries's face appeared in the open window. "You steer the car and I'll push."

Before she knew what was happening, he was reaching in through the window to pull her—drag her, really—from the passenger side into the driver's seat while she scrambled to get her feet under her somehow, an almost impossible task given her heavy coat, the confined space, and levers that stuck out every which way.

When she was behind the wheel, he gave her a lesson, if you could call it that. He put a gloved hand first on her right leg. The pedal under that foot was for the gas, and gas was what moved the car. Everybody knew that much, even people without cars. Then he laid his hand on her left leg. That pedal was called the clutch, and she was supposed to let it out slowly while pushing down on the gas at the same time to engage the gear so the car would go forward.

It went forward all right, with a violent lurch and a terrible grinding sound before it stopped cold. Meneer turned the crank at the front of the car so she could try again. The exertion made his face glisten with sweat.

She tried again and again, tears running down her cheeks in frustration and feeling less capable each time. But on perhaps the sixth try, something felt different. Just as her feet passed each other on the pedals, there came a feeling both soft and solid, and she knew to push on the gas pedal just a hair at first, and a split second later, to press it to the floor. The car jumped up the embankment almost to the road before coming to a stop with the same awful grinding sound as before. But they were free. She'd done it. Meneer was still in the ditch, with an exultant smile on his face, his lovely camel-hair coat splattered, his gloves blackened from wet snow. For the remainder of the trip—even though he was sloppy with mud and the car stank of wet wool—he beamed at her. "Well, well," he said. "I see I selected a very capable girl."

SHE HAD BEEN to Amsterdam once as a child but had little memory of its many converging streets, or the wide canals that threaded the city, so much deeper and darker than the canals at home. The Spijker came to a stop next to a canal at a row of stone houses, twice as high as the houses at home and all with hoisting beams and splendid facades that came to high peaks decorated in scrollwork.

At home, the houses had only a front and a back door, and the front door stayed shut except for weddings and funerals. But this house had two doors side by side at the front. The door on the right gave onto storage for his imports, Meneer explained, opening the one on the left and ushering Minke inside. She found herself at the foot of a steep, curving staircase, illuminated by gaslight. She didn't recognize the heavy odor but supposed it was the smell of illness.

She followed his broad back up to a landing where she could see quickly into a parlor before he hurried her on. The shades were pulled, the room was hot, and she had the impression of a great deal of cloth-covered furniture, too much for the room. The odor was more pronounced on the landing.

She hadn't been afraid of what was to come until now; she didn't know what illness his wife, Mevrouw DeVries, suffered from, what to expect or what to do. She'd heard stories of the grotesque deaths some people suffered, how they sometimes begged to die. When her uncle died, she'd seen him only afterward, tidy and sunken-faced in his coffin. And when her grandmother had become ill, she'd watched as Mama braided her hair and bathed her. Minke had never attended anyone except for Fenna, who took to her bed at the first sign of a cough.

Another staircase across the landing rose to a second landing, where there was a door ajar to a darkened room. Minke sensed movement inside and caught a quick glimpse of a woman's pale face. After that the house was a warren of short staircases and landings zigzagging to a large room at the top, the sickroom, from the smell of it. It had two closet beds against the right-hand wall, both with the doors drawn. A small table and chair stood next to one of the beds, and on the table were bottles of medicine. Like the rest of the house, the room was dark, cluttered, and stuffy.

Meneer DeVries, in his soft voice, announced that he'd brought a wonderful girl to help. He pulled open the door to one of the closet beds and leaned in, blocking Minke's view. When he stood back, Minke had a shock. The woman's face seemed a skull covered in the palest translucent skin. Her eyes were unnaturally large. Her hair hung in dark strands, unwashed, but her gown was pure white, bleached and starched and ironed so stiffly that its collar came to painful-looking points against her wasting neck. Minke wanted to throw open a window. She was afraid she would gag.

"Come!" Meneer DeVries motioned Minke in with the enthusiasm of a man delivering a wonderful prize. "Elisabeth, this is Minke, your relative from Enkhuizen." He patted the side of the bed, and Minke did as instructed, using the stepstool to climb up and sit on the side of the bed. She looked down on Mevrouw DeVries, whose large eyes took Minke in fully—her face, her clothing, her hands.

"I'm here to care for you."

Meneer DeVries cleared his throat, and when Minke turned, she saw that two more people had entered the room. "My son, Willem. We all call him Pim. My daughter, Griet."

Minke knew right away that Griet's had been the face in the shadow. Griet was about Minke's age, perhaps a year older. She had her father's ginger-gold hair and a well-fed look about her. Her eyes darted from Minke to her father. Pim was smaller than his sister but seemed several years older.

"So, Enkhuizen, is it?" Griet looked her over, top to toe.

Minke nodded.

"Where is that, Papa?" Griet turned to her father. "I mean"—she waved a hand as if to take in the whole country—"I just can't place it."

"The Zuiderzee," Pim answered. He had a wide forehead and stiff posture.

"Minke drove us out of a ditch!" Meneer DeVries beamed at her. "Did you hear that, Elisabeth? We veered off the road, and Minke saved the day."

"You drove Papa's car?" Griet turned to her father. "I want to drive the car. Why can't I drive the car?"

Meneer DeVries shook his head with impatience. "We were stuck," he said. He turned abruptly and pulled open the doors to the second bed, addressing Minke. "You're to sleep here with the doors open in case my wife should need you. Dinner at half past."

He ushered his children from the room, leaving Minke alone with her patient. In her whole life, she had never slept all by herself in a bed. She had shared a bed with Mama and Papa when she was little, and for the past six years, she'd shared a bed with Fenna.

"You must excuse them," Mevrouw DeVries whispered. She was sitting up taller, propped by pillows. She raised her shoulders and dropped them. "Sander has let them do what they like."

"It must be difficult for them to see you ill," Minke said.

She looked beyond Minke to the window. "They'll survive."

"I only meant—"

Mevrouw winced briefly, in pain. "I should be turned twice a day," she said quietly. "Bedsores." She drifted off, eyes half shut, then open again. "When I need my medicine—" She took a quick breath. "Bring it immediately, no matter what. Anywhere in the house. Feel." She guided Minke's hand to the side of her abdomen. Minke's hand lay on something hard and misshapen as a stone. She felt both revulsion and a determination not to take her hand away. If Elisabeth had to live with this, Minke could certainly bear to touch it. She shut her eyes, and when she opened them, Mevrouw DeVries had fallen asleep.

Very slowly, Minke removed her hand and tried to get her bearings. She missed home already. She wanted her mother. Mama would know how to proceed. Minke cracked open the window to breathe in the cold air and clear her head. Across the canal were more houses just like the one she was in—made of gray stone and with fancy carved scrolls at their peaks. She counted the stories: six. She'd never seen such tall buildings except for the Drommedaris—a large fortress—in Enkhuizen and the Westerkerk, of course. At home the houses were small, with the kitchen, parlor, and beds downstairs and storage in the attic.

She bit her lip. What would Mama do? She scanned the room. Mama would say, *First things first.* Before it grew dark, she must unpack. She slipped her few belongings into the drawers of the wardrobe and hung up her two dresses, keeping an eye on Mevrouw.

Moments after she was done, the door opened. Meneer DeVries entered carrying an oil lamp. Mevrouw DeVries did not stir. He raised the lamp to his wife's face. "She was beautiful once, like you," he said. Minke glanced quickly down at the floor, uncomfortable that he would say such a thing in front of his wife. "I've come to tell you it's time for dinner."

GASLIGHTS BURNED IN the dining room. Pim and Griet stood side by side behind their chairs at a long table, waiting. Minke marveled at the furniture, which was large and strange, not at all what they had at home. And the walls had tapestries of Chinese men scowling out. Even the table service was bizarre, with a spinning island at the center that held colorful platters and bowls. The DeVrieses used beautifully decorated metal pots in all sizes and shapes, with fabulous designs of animals and women. She wondered who had cooked the meal. Certainly not Griet, who sat with her arms folded, looking sullen.

"Papa tells us you're a nurse," Pim said, tucking a linen napkin beneath his chin.

She eyed Meneer DeVries, who astonished her by nodding in affirmation. Well, best not contradict him, although why he would fib was a mystery to her.

"She's too young to be a nurse," Griet said, as if Minke weren't present. "She'll die, you know. The doctors have said. I'm sure Papa told you."

The serving girl entered just then, and the cook came to the open door to peer from the steamy kitchen at Minke, who smiled and said hello.

"Did you hear what I said?" Griet asked.

"Of course," Minke responded.

"And?"

"I'll care for her as if she were my own mother."

"I'm very busy," Griet said, pouting. "If that's what you mean."

"I only meant what I said."

Meneer DeVries gave her an approving look that said she had passed a test of some sort. After that, the family talked with one another as if Minke weren't present, which suited her fine. What she learned of them was this: Meneer DeVries was anxious about his business. In fact, all three of them were anxious. It had something to do with new laws from The Hague, with the possibility of war, rumors about the confiscation of ships sailing under Dutch colors. Minke understood none of it, only that Meneer was worried. It was easier for her to follow when the conversation turned to the children. Pim was a student at the university, studying the law, and Griet was delaying her marriage because of her mother's illness. She was clearly unhappy about it, worried her fiancé wouldn't wait. She complained about all there was to do—the mending and washing and so on. "I hope you sew," she said to Minke after they'd finished dessert.

"I enjoy sewing a great deal," Minke said. "I made this dress." She opened her arms to show it off.

"She can help with the wedding dress, then," Griet said to her father.

"First things first," Meneer DeVries said. "Minke will have a great deal to do."

* * *

IN THE MORNING, Minke washed at the basin. Should she wake Mevrouw DeVries? No. Let her sleep. It was her own decision, and no one was there to tell her otherwise. She opened the window to air the room, which smelled of urine. The chill air woke Mevrouw DeVries. "Lovely," she said.

"Do you take breakfast, Mevrouw DeVries?"

The woman studied her. "You're very young. Please call me Elisabeth."

"I'm fifteen," Minke said, confounded by the request. To call a grown woman by her given name was improper, but she would try. "Shall I bring tea?"

Elisabeth shut her eyes.

Minke went into the hall, intending to go to the kitchen, but a tray had been left at the door. Coffee, two poached eggs. Everything was cold. Tomorrow she would wake earlier.

A knock came as Minke was trying to spoon a tiny amount of egg between Mevrouw DeVries's parched lips. "Yes?" she said.

Pim opened the door but seemed hesitant to enter.

"Ah, my sweet son, the advocate, is here," Elisabeth said, smiling.

"Not yet," Pim said, blushing. "I mean I'm not a lawyer yet. Not that I'm not here."

"You've noticed our little Minke," Elisabeth said, causing Pim to blush more deeply. Minke understood what it was that made Pim's posture seem odd. He had the start of a hunchback; his curved spine had thrust his head permanently forward.

"Good morning, Mother." Griet's voice was shrill. She kissed her mother's cheek, then picked up the bottle of morphine. "How much has she had, Minke?"

"Nothing," Minke said. "She's not had pain. When does the doctor come?"

"What can a doctor do?"

Minke was alarmed again at what this family said in front of Elisabeth, but the older woman seemed unfazed. "Who provides the morphine if not the doctor?"

"Papa gets it. We'll inject it when she can no longer swallow. Right, Mother?"

"So I understand," Elisabeth said. Minke was struck by the woman's passivity, quite the opposite of what she had expected, given Meneer DeVries's description to Fenna.

"How much do I give?" Minke asked.

"Mix it with sugar syrup, give a little. If it doesn't work, give more. You're the nurse," Griet said.

After the children left, Minke could hear Griet calling out to the housekeeper and the cook, her voice plaintive at first, then rising to a shout when they didn't come quickly enough. Elisabeth was sleeping again.

Now what to do? It was still early, and the day stretched out before her. She ran a finger along the decorative trim of the wardrobe and came up with a smudge of dust. She could hear people in the house. The bell ringing at the door, people coming and going downstairs. Visitors? But none for Elisabeth. Minke used her cloth to clean dust from tabletops and soot from the sill. She ran it over the photographs on the wall and the objects that adorned the surfaces. Such odd things Elisabeth had. Minke peeked into a small ornamental purse, dusty but colorful and thickly embroidered with the tiniest beads. Inside was a pot of rouge. On another table lay a brown object with a small opening at the top that was lined with a wide collar of dented silver. It surprised her with its lightness, and on closer inspection, she saw it was a gourd of some type, hollowed. A long silver straw with a porous silver bulb stuck out of the opening on top.

"Maté," Elisabeth said, causing Minke to fumble with the item.

"I'm sorry?"

Elisabeth motioned her to the bed, took the silver straw in her mouth, and whispered, "The *bombilla*. To drink their special tea. Their yerba maté."

"Who does?"

"Gauchos."

"What are gauchos?"

"Horsemen in Argentina. Adorned in silver. Their saddles, their horses. Oh, how they ride."

"You've *seen* them?"

"Once." Elisabeth pointed to a small wooden statue on a shelf. It was of a man, roughly carved and painted, with a slouch hat, black beard, and wide red pantaloons stuffed into high black boots. Without warning, she threw back her head and let out a terrifying groan, more animal than human.

Hands trembling, Minke immediately mixed sugar and water together in a small dish and added the morphine from its dark brown bottle, a teaspoonful, as Griet had instructed. She pulled Elisabeth up as far as she dared—the woman was light in her arms—and slipped the spoon between her lips. Elisabeth sank back against the pillow, her face vacant.

Minke sat at the bedside, shaken. What if she'd given too much? She smoothed the woman's forehead, pulled the covers over her, and was reassured by her steady breathing. She was shocked anew to see how clearly visible Elisabeth's skull was beneath her skin, how atrocious her hair, which had been braided once but had grown out and was loose at the roots. Minke undid the clasp, meaning only to rebraid it, but found it incredibly dirty. "Shall I wash it?" she whispered.

Elisabeth slept.

The task took the afternoon. Minke washed one small section of hair at a time, then dried it with a towel to keep Elisabeth's bed from becoming damp. Elisabeth's hair, which had seemed the color of lead, was jet black, threaded with silver. When the hair was mostly dry, Minke spread it over the pillow and combed it smooth, and when that was done, she braided it back into its thin rope. Through it all, Elisabeth slept.

Meneer DeVries came into the room as Minke was finishing. He watched her with a fatherly pride. She felt very pleased with herself for her ingenuity, and this only the first day.

"Aha," he said. "You've discovered the yerba maté cup!"

"It's unusual," Minke whispered.

"Then it's yours," he said.

"But it belongs to Mevrouw DeVries."

He glanced at his wife and shrugged.

"DID I HEAR Mother cry out today?" Griet said at dinner. "I thought I did." She looked from her brother to her father for corroboration.

"She had pain," Minke said. "I administered the morphine immediately."

"Do *you* have a beau?" Griet asked, flashing the shiny ring on her finger at Minke.

Minke blushed and shook her head. Griet kept her so off balance.

"There, Pim," Griet said, smirking. "I've asked her. Now the field is yours."

"Oh, Griet, for God's sake," Pim said, and then to Minke, "I apologize for my sister. It seems that's all I do."

"But you're the one who wants to know," Griet insisted.

"Your mother told me about the gauchos," Minke said, changing the subject and sparing poor Pim.

"Did she now!" Meneer DeVries became alert. "Yes. She accompanied me once to Buenos Aires. We saw them on an outing to the countryside."

"They are such filthy creatures," Griet said.

And so was your mother's hair. Minke wished she had the nerve to say that aloud. It was a disgrace. "So you've seen them, too? The gauchos?"

"No, of course not, but how could they possibly be clean? They're outdoors all the time, and they bed down with their horses. Right, Papa?"

Meneer DeVries gave his daughter an indulgent smile. "What did Elisabeth tell you about the gauchos, Minke?"

"They thunder across the fields on horses decked with silver." Elisabeth hadn't said exactly that, but it was how Minke pictured the scene.

"The pampas," Griet said. "In Argentina they're called the pampas. And anyway, they're not fields. They're much bigger. They're pampas."

"The pampas, then," Minke said. "Even better."

"It isn't better or worse," Griet said. "It's just the correct word. That's all."

* * *

FROM THEN ON Minke took as many meals as she could in the room with Elisabeth. She'd lost her appetite because of the constant smell, her task of emptying the bedpan several times a day, and of doing for Elisabeth what she'd only ever done for herself. She grew bolder, bathing Elisabeth daily because it must be especially important to someone who spent all her days in bed. Not only that, but Elisabeth visibly relaxed into the warmth of Minke's skin moving over hers.

The first time, the process took forever to figure out, but she finally devised a workable plan. She helped Elisabeth roll to the forward edge of the bed so she could slip a length of oilcloth under her and cover it with a towel. She then very gently placed Elisabeth on the towel. While she was being moved, Elisabeth wrapped her arms around Minke's neck and hung on with surprising strength.

Minke washed one arm with warm water, then a warm rinse and a towel dry before moving on to the next, then each leg. Trying to appear confident in spite of her nervousness, she reached under the covers and washed Elisabeth's breasts, watching her face for the slightest expression of shock or distaste; finding none, she gently pulled Elisabeth's legs open to wash the area there. Elisabeth did not resist. Nor did she meet Minke's eyes. With no experience in any of this, Minke acted on a single instinct: It was what she would want were she in Elisabeth's condition. When she was finished, she removed the towel and oilcloth. She had never felt such intimacy with anyone. She knew Elisabeth's body everywhere, the bones in particular, the way they connected with tendons and sinew, ball and socket, the spine like a row of knots.

WEEKS PASSED, BLENDING into one another. Outside Minke's window, the canal sealed over with black ice, softened during a thaw, and froze solid again. People skated past the house during the deepest of the freezes, and Minke wished she could be with them, laughing and racing instead of sitting in the quiet room with its expectation of death.

Meneer began to make it a practice to come to the room at dusk after a day of work. He often seemed harried and paced the small room with his hands clasped behind his back, talking with Elisabeth or, it seemed, more at her than with her, as she said very little. He spoke of what he read in the newspapers, of rumors that abounded all over Amsterdam. A crackdown of some sort was expected. That's all Minke could glean from what he said. When he'd calmed himself, he would take a chair and draw it to Elisabeth's bed. For her part, Minke drew her own chair to the far corner of the room, near the window, to allow the DeVrieses some privacy.

If Elisabeth was fast asleep, and increasingly, this was the case, Meneer would kiss her tenderly, pull the covers up to her chin, close the cabinet door, and draw his chair close to Minke's at the window. Sometimes he spoke a little, asking her about the day. Other times he sat in silence. One evening he seemed particularly upset. He didn't even try to speak to Elisabeth but brought his chair to the window and sat, his leg quivering in agitation.

"What's the matter?" It felt like an intrusion into Meneer's private life to ask him such a thing, but it would be worse to say nothing when he was in such a terrible state.

"The damn government," he said.

"Oh."

He seemed about to say something else but shook his head sharply as though to dislodge whatever thought was there. "I have too much on my mind," he said.

"It must be so difficult," she said. "You work so hard and your wife is so ill. I can't imagine. And while I understand none of it, I hear you speak of problems having to do with your business. It's a great deal for one person to carry."

He gave her such a lovely sweet smile that she felt very drawn to him. "I don't want to worry you." He tipped her face to the light. "You're doing a splendid job, the jewel in the household, if you ask me. Elisabeth adores you." He looked long into her eyes. "And I as well." He sat back in his chair. She could barely see him in the low light. "What do you think of us?"

The only answer was one she dared not utter—that it shocked her how little attention Elisabeth received from the children. But she had to say something. "You're all quite different from one another."

He burst out laughing. "A diplomat!" he said. "Did you hear that, Elisabeth?"

THE HARD SWELLING on Elisabeth's abdomen grew. Her pain came more often, and when it did, it was severe, sudden, and caused her to scream out. Minke mixed the morphine, then raised Elisabeth up a bit so it would be easier to swallow. From the time Elisabeth asked for the morphine to the time Minke was able to pour it into a spoon and administer it—her hands steadier now that she was experienced—Elisabeth's screams, *Alstublieft, Alstublieft,* please, please, became so loud she could be heard all along the street, or so Griet said. One of these times, Griet came into the room to ask why Minke couldn't move more quickly to ease her mother's suffering. "The neighbors will think we're beating her," Griet said. "She mustn't shout so."

Minke said she was sorry, that she knew how difficult it must be for Griet to hear her mother's distress. She would try to do better in the future. She had learned to speak to Griet this way. To agree with her and mollify her, even when she was furious and knew there was nothing she could do better.

"I hope this doesn't happen to me when I'm old. I'll kill myself first," Griet said to her.

Minke busied herself with the medicines. She liked to keep the table orderly, the spoon clean, the sugar already dissolved into a syrup.

"Is she asleep?" Griet asked.

Wasn't it obvious?

Griet took up the bottle of morphine, poured some into the spoon, and swallowed it.

"Are you mad?"

"It's lovely," Griet said, her face relaxing into a far-off smile. "Have you tried it?"

"Of course not." Minke snatched the bottle from the table. "Your mother needs this."

"There's plenty more, believe me," Griet said vaguely. The effects of the morphine had been immediate. "Papa gets it from the Indies. Or the coca leaves or opium or something. I don't know exactly. All I know is it feels divine."

Minke looked Griet in the eye. "Then you must ask him for your own and not use your mother's."

Griet smiled sweetly at Minke. "Papa sails in three weeks, you know. Whether Mother is dead or alive."

That did it. She took Griet by the arm and pulled her into the hall.

"What are you doing!" Griet squirmed clumsily, still giggling. "Who do you think you are?"

"What if she *hears* you?" Minke said. "Don't say those things in her presence."

"You can't tell me how to behave, and I can say whatever I like."

"But she's your *mother!*"

"She's as good as dead. Just look at her. I wish she'd hurry up and die."

Minke hit Griet with the back of the fist that still contained the bottle of morphine, letting it smash to the floor. Griet grabbed at Minke for balance, and they both fell on the shards. Immediately, the housekeeper, Julianna, was there, dragging them both to their feet. She made them face each other and apologize. Minke crossed her fingers behind her back and did as she was told, just as she used to with Fenna. Griet got away with saying nothing.

"You, miss, come with me," Julianna said to Minke.

"You're in for it now," Griet said.

Minke followed Julianna's swaying bottom, dreading what was about to happen. She fully expected to be taken to Meneer, told on, and fired. But Julianna went down all the landings to the first floor, through the kitchen door, and once inside she wheeled around, a big smile across her face. "Slapped her, did you?" She threw back her head, laughing. "I didn't think you had it in you."

"She was saying terrible things, taking Elisabeth's medicine."

"I'm not allowed to lay a hand on either of them, not that the boy ever needed it."

"You're not angry?"

Julianna shook her head. "Quick. Come see." She led the way through a door at the front of the kitchen, down a few steps to a crowded warehouse. She pulled back a curtain of heavy canvas and shone the lamp first on her own devilishly grinning face and then onto what was inside. Shelves and shelves of textiles, brocades, silks in beautiful green and gold. She lifted the lids off trunks that held more treasures, dusty but still beautiful—bronze statues, intricately carved wooden animals and ivory fans. Julianna beamed and pointed to a dozen or more boxes neatly stacked. "Open," she said.

Inside were dozens of tiny brown bottles just like the ones for Elisabeth's morphine. Julianna's head bobbed with expectation. "You see?"

"Yes, but what is all this?"

"Your guess is as good as mine. Once I knew everything, but now Mevrouw is sick and I am no longer permitted to speak with her. What have you heard? What's to become of things when she dies?"

"I don't know," Minke said. "Griet said Meneer sails in several weeks." Immediately, she realized she should have kept her mouth shut. This was gossip of the lowest sort.

"This was one of the finest households in Amsterdam."

"I think it's quite grand," Minke said.

Julianna shook her head adamantly. "A different house when the father was alive."

"Elisabeth's?"

"Pim and Griet's."

"But Meneer—"

"He isn't their father," Julianna said, as though Minke should have known. "He came sniffing around before that poor man was cold in his grave. Him with his honey voice and his flowers." She pointed to the stacks of boxes. "And that."

"He loves Elisabeth very much."

"Elisabeth, is it?"

"I wish the children came more often to see her."

"Spoiled to the bone, that Griet is. And Pim. Poor little thing. He can't bear it. He sobs and carries on. It's not good for Elisabeth to see too much of him. It's as though he were dying and not she. She's the only decent one in the lot."

"We mustn't talk this way about them," Minke said.

"What way? It's the truth. They'll both be gone soon enough. Her to her maker, and him? Who knows?"

"He has business interests around the world. He's told me about it."

Julianna rocked with laughter. "Right," she said.

AT DINNER THAT night, Griet had a bruise on the side of her face. Minke was sure she would be fired for what she had done. And while she would be happy to be far away from Griet, who would tend to Elisabeth? She dreaded what Meneer DeVries would say, but if he fired her, she would tell him everything—what Griet had said and done.

But he said nothing. Didn't he know? He couldn't have failed to see the bruise. After dinner, Pim came to Elisabeth's room. Minke, leaning on the windowsill, got up to leave, to let him be alone with his mother, but he stopped her. "It's the way Griet is. She's been indulged. No one blames you."

"She hates me," Minke whispered. "From the beginning."

"Of course she does," Pim said. "Why do you think you haven't met the fiancé?"

"There really *is* a fiancé?"

Pim grinned. "Griet's a brat, but she's not stupid." He glanced at his sleeping mother, and tears welled in his eyes, wetting his cheeks. He wiped them away and turned from her.

Just then Meneer DeVries entered the room, looking over the tops of his spectacles. "You mustn't keep Minke from her work, Pim."

"We were only chatting."

"You'd do better to chat with your mother," Meneer DeVries said.

Pim turned, bowed stiffly, and left.

"I hope he wasn't bothering you," Meneer DeVries said.

"Not at all, Meneer DeVries."

"You must call me Sander."

It was difficult enough to call Elisabeth by her first name, but another fish altogether with a man.

"You're fatigued." He placed his large hands gently on her shoulders, warming them.

"Yes," she said. Every night, at the slightest noise from Elisabeth, Minke's eyes opened wide. If a second sound came, she bolted from bed to check. When she went back to bed, there she'd be, fully awake, her mind racing.

"How can I help you?"

"It will pass, Meneer."

"Sander."

"Sander."

He slipped his hands about her waist, smiling broadly and looking from Minke to Elisabeth in her closet bed, half sitting, her eyes slightly open. She could be awake or asleep. It was difficult to know lately. "Elisabeth's waist was as slim as yours once." Meneer DeVries squeezed his hands harder, thumb to thumb and pinkie to pinkie. Minke drew in her breath sharply, from surprise at what he was doing, and the effort made her waist even smaller. "There!" he said triumphantly. She placed her hands over his, intending to take them from her waist, but he held firm. "No need to be embarrassed, right, Elisabeth?"

Elisabeth lay quietly. "I must see to her," Minke said.

"In a moment, but first, over there in the storage." Meneer let go and pointed to the cupboard beneath the window. "Open it and remove the box, please."

Minke swung up the lid, reached in, and found a long, heavy box made of lustrous dark wood.

"Look inside," he instructed. She sat on her bed with the box on her lap and lifted the lid. Inside was a silver-handled blade in a sheath. "It's called a *facón*."

Minke lifted it, feeling a thrill pass through her. The sheath was beautiful, decorated and embossed with a tree design and a pair of clasped hands.

"Let me show you how it's worn." Meneer DeVries had her stand with her back to him. She jumped when he slid the cool knife, sheath and all, under the waistband of her skirt at the back. "You wear it in the back, this way, so if you're thrown from your horse, you won't fall upon your sword and die."

The feel was extraordinary, cold against the thin fabric of her chemise and so terribly heavy that she had to widen her stance to support it.

"Tell her about the thunderstorms, Sander," Elisabeth said, and Minke jumped again. So she *was* awake.

"You tell her, my dear."

Elisabeth pushed wider the door to her bed. Her face looked lively. "One crash after the other. Lights up the whole earth. The sound roars for hours. Terrifying." She fell back on her pillow and shut her eyes. "Magnificent."

MINKE MARKED THE level of morphine in the bottle by tying a strand of her translucent hair around it. After giving Elisabeth each dose, she could adjust the hair in minuscule amounts, the better to see if Griet had slipped in and taken any of it. She didn't care that Griet might take the morphine. But it mattered very much that there should be enough for Elisabeth. She didn't believe there was an endless supply; if they ran out, Elisabeth would suffer.

As it was, Elisabeth had entered a new phase in which she mostly slept and had little use for the bedpan. Minke fed her sips of water and soup, but solid food was out of the question. At the same time, the house became more active, as though it had already transcended her death. Meneer DeVries's trunks were packed and waiting in the hall downstairs. Griet could be heard traipsing up and down the stairs, calling out orders. She sometimes came into the room and stood beside her sleeping mother, staring down, saying nothing. Pim occasionally sat with his mother, racked with sobs. Early one morning, Meneer DeVries came to Elisabeth's room and woke Minke. "I'm taking you home today," he said. "No need to pack your things. I'll have them sent along." He was all business. All haste.

"But Elisabeth!" Minke said. She had a vision of Elisabeth abandoned in her room, dying alone.

"Griet can manage."

It was the fight. He must have found out about the fight. Griet would have said Minke attacked her. Maybe Griet had accused Minke of stealing morphine. Minke waited for him to leave the room before she dressed, throwing her hair sloppily up with pins, weeping at the suddenness of her dismissal and feeling guilt over something she hadn't done.

Elisabeth lay against the pillows, her neck stretched as if drawn to the light in the room. Minke took her carefully in her arms. "I'll be thinking of you day and night." Elisabeth made no sign of acknowledgment. Minke laid her back. "I'll know when your time comes."

MENEER DEVRIES WAS calling to her from the door. She practically flew down the half-flight of stairs leading to the first-level parlor and jumped in surprise when she saw a stranger sitting on the sofa there. He was a dark, tidy-looking man, clad in a black velvet jacket, his hands resting atop a walking stick. Meneer DeVries called again; she had time to say only a quick hello to the stranger before taking the next flight of stairs to the door, where Meneer DeVries paced anxiously. He helped Minke into the Spijker, hastened back into the house, and shut the door behind him. She waited, shivering with cold, watching people pass by the car and admire it. He was gone a long time, so long she wondered if he'd forgotten about her. Should she go back inside to call for him? Finally, the door opened and he came outside wiping his face with his handkerchief, turning back, turning again. In and out, back and forth. And then he was in the car without a word of explanation and they were on their way.

As suddenly as Minke had come to Amsterdam, she was leaving. Meneer DeVries was agitated behind the wheel. He spoke not a word, but when they were well out of Amsterdam, she finally got up the nerve to ask him, because she had to know. "Have I done something wrong?"

He seemed shaken. "My sweet girl. Of course not."

"Griet says you're going to South America."

"In three days' time," he said, making her wonder about her belongings. Would she truly get them back, or would Griet throw them out? And what of Elisabeth? It felt cruel to leave her to the care of that girl. Oh, who was she fooling? She was the outsider. She was the help. Elisabeth had made her feel important, but the truth was, she could be brought in and discharged by any one of them.

At her house in Enkhuizen, Meneer DeVries pulled his car to a stop. Mama came to the door and threw her arms around Minke. Papa had tears in his eyes.

"A word," Meneer DeVries said to them brusquely. "Alone."

Minke had no place to go but up to the attic like a scolded child. Her only solace was that Fenna wasn't there or she'd have had to face her sister's triumph over her obvious failure in Amsterdam. Meneer DeVries would be telling her parents about the fight with his daughter. She would tell her parents the truth, and they would believe her, not anyone else.

"Minke!" Her mother's voice came from downstairs, the familiar nervous laughter floating along behind it.

Meneer DeVries sat where she'd seen him the first day. He was beaming with pleasure. Her father was standing before the stove, his hands tapping up and down his thin chest as if he didn't know where to put them. He cleared his throat. "Minke," he blurted out before she had the chance to sit, "Meneer DeVries has asked for your hand in marriage."

2

APA PULLED ON his unlit pipe. Mama stared at the floor. Only Meneer DeVries looked directly at her.

"What?" Minke said. "Are you mad?"

He reached out, but she snatched her hand back. He spoke gravely to her. "How can I say this other than directly? Minke, Elisabeth died this morning."

He might as well have told her the sky was made of ice cream. "She did not. I was there."

He gave a woeful shake of the head. "We all knew it was imminent. There were so many signs." His voice was deep. "The fingernails. The discoloration. Surely you saw that. And in these past few days she has often been unconscious."

She hadn't noticed any discoloration. And although Elisabeth slept a great deal, "unconscious" was an exaggeration. "I was right there this morning. And so were you."

"Do you recall that after I brought you to the car this morning I returned to the house? It was then Griet told me. She was beside herself; she had gone to Elisabeth's room immediately and found her expired."

"And you said *nothing*?"

"I thought it best you hear the news in the company of your family."

"You were mistaken, Meneer DeVries. And now I'm the last to know." Tears filled her eyes. She wiped them away. "Who was that man in the parlor?" she demanded, apropos of nothing more than a desire to change course.

"Minke, your tone! You will apologize," Mama said.

"But Mama, she was alive when I left the room," Minke said. "How could she have died in that brief time? I was gone not two minutes."

Papa thrummed his fingers on the wooden tabletop. He lay his pipe in the dish, stood up, and pushed his chair in. He was a gaunt, formal man and carried his height in his thighs, his whole bearing like a pair of scissors. He came around the table, behind Minke, and rested his hands on her shoulders. "Minke, it's not uncommon. People often choose to die when they are alone. Death is a solitary event, and perhaps even solitary by choice."

The chaos of dismay overwhelmed her. Images of Elisabeth with her face canted toward the light of the window, the feel of her skin, the faint snore when she slept. And no one *told* her? Griet was behind it, she was sure. Griet's bow was strung with this final arrow. And a marriage proposal! She'd lost track of that part, but it came back with force. She felt like saying yes to spite Griet. She'd be Griet's stepmother. There was a thought!

"Meneer DeVries only asks that you consider his proposal," Papa said. "He must return to Amsterdam, but he will be back in two days."

"You can give me the answer then," Meneer DeVries said quickly. "If it's still no, I'll accept it. But I beg you to consider it for the time being, Minke. We would have to sail on Tuesday. My work demands that I leave for Argentina."

"What work?"

"A private word with your daughter?" Meneer DeVries said to her parents, who scrambled to get out of the room. They'd obviously known this was coming, and if Minke weren't so furious, she might have found it comical the way her round little mother leaped to her feet and fled.

"I'm afraid I've shocked you." Meneer DeVries heaved a great defeated sigh. He looked disheveled, with his fox-colored hair unkempt. His clothes, although fine—a bright white shirt and a black jacket with a large gold pin at the neck—were wrinkled. Minke fought against feeling pity, and against curiosity about Tuesday.

She leaned over the table and in a low voice said, "*Shock*, Meneer DeVries, hardly begins to describe what you've done." She rose to her feet and turned sharply with a whish of skirts. "Do you really think I'd marry a man who would behave as you have?" She felt quite terrific; she was in the right, after all.

"She meant everything to me, Minke."

"A fine way to show it. With her not even in her grave."

He stared at the floor. "Elisabeth knew of this."

"That you would deny me the news of her death?"

"My proposal. She was very fond of you. She herself said it would be a good match."

"I don't believe you."

"Will you walk outside with me, Minke? The air would do me good." His expression as he asked her this—oh, he did have the sweetest smile, and it roused her. "It's only a walk in the fresh air," he added.

She put on a heavy woolen shawl, muffler, and boots, shrugging off his efforts to help, and preceded him through the back door and down the alley to Westerstraat.

In Enkhuizen, people installed small mirrors at the edges of their windows. They claimed it was to see who was knocking on the front door, but no one used their front door, so the reason was clear: They liked to spy on one another. Minke knew all eyes were on them as she and Meneer DeVries set off. A rich outsider in his camel topcoat trimmed with black Persian lamb, his hat the same, like a Russian.

She felt claustrophobic in the maze of narrow brick streets packed tightly with small brick houses. "We'll go to the harbor," she announced, and hastened toward the gate to the Zuiderzee, and from there along the breakwater on the other side of the seawall for a distance before descending the bank to the water's edge, where they walked the frozen ground. They walked north, away from town, past fishing boats that lay beached so their catch could be unloaded; men blew clouds of steam from their mouths as they shook out the great nets, releasing thousands of silver herring that slithered down and caught in the netting. The men watched her, too, pausing in their work to stare as she passed several paces ahead of her stranger.

"Say something, Minke," Meneer DeVries said, his voice hoarse and betraying fatigue.

"You're the one who wanted to talk."

Farther along, great slabs of ice had piled on the shore, heaved up by a winter of bitter cold, and walking was difficult. He hadn't the proper shoes, but he didn't complain, and she didn't slow her pace.

"Tell me, then, when is the burial?" she asked over her shoulder.

"This evening. Small affair. Immediate family."

She glided along with perfect balance, enjoying her command of the ice and his lack of it. She knew he was laboring, knew it was wrong of her to treat him so badly, but couldn't stop. "I'm not a man to rush into things, believe me," he called. "You've made yourself clear, Minke. You don't need to keep punishing me."

She turned to see him wobble on an unstable slab of ice, a clumsy child with his arms outstretched for balance, and she felt a stab of pity. The man she had admired in Amsterdam, the man who commanded that fine house, was an imbecile on the ice.

"Circumstances are what they are!" He climbed to another slab of ice for better footing. "That's the long and the short of it. I depart very soon. I'll be gone for a year. Perhaps more. By the time I return, you'll have married someone else." He pointed back toward the fishing boats they'd seen on their way. "One of them, perhaps."

She turned and climbed quickly, farther along the ice, which was so high there it met the top of the seawall and she could see the belfry of St. Pancras. Until that moment she would have found nothing wrong in his prediction. Fishing was what all the men did in Enkhuizen. But now she saw them through the eyes of this worldly man, with the stink on their clothing and their long absences, the danger of being lost at sea, the grief of that life.

"Minke. For God's sake, stop running away. I can't keep up with you."

She stopped. He was in exactly the same spot as before.

"You run off like a child playing a game when this is a serious matter. It's a matter of the heart."

She hopped to the next slab of ice as easily as if it were nothing; when she turned again, he was leaving, making his way back down the ice. "Meneer DeVries!" she called.

She'd gone way too far. Mama would be furious if she ever found out how rude Minke had been. She scrambled down the ice and ran after him, catching his sleeve and stopping him.

"Do you consider my proposal something foolish?" Confusion had darkened his face, illuminating a thin white scar that ran from his ear to the corner of his mouth.

"You barely know me. Why marry me, of all people, and for that matter, why marry at all when your wife has just died?"

"I want you with me. I was smitten with you from the start, and you know it. And you with me, if I might be so bold. I know women, Minke. Don't play games with me. I watched you tend Elisabeth. How could I not want you for myself?"

"You could just hire me," she said, loving her own boldness.

"Your youth is a challenge," he said.

"My youth? That's what you like!" she replied, and when he didn't react, she knew she'd been exactly right. It gave her a thrill to provoke him and get away with it.

"Look out there," he said, collecting himself and gesturing to the flat gray sea. "Tell me what you see."

She studied the sea. Nothing unusual. "Ice, fishing boats."

"How many?"

She counted. "Four."

"Once you would have seen big ships out there, entering port, leaving for the Indies. For Asia."

"What has that to do with anything?"

"Bear with me," he said, and she recalled the stories of times long ago when great sea waves pounded the beaches of Enkhuizen, like those of the North Sea. Back then the water had been a dark, raging blue, capped with snow-white froth. "You know of the silting."

"Everybody knows about the silting." Little by little the Zuiderzee was filling in, becoming so shallow that a whole new kind of boat had to be developed, with a shallow keel and big paddles to port and starboard, like wings, for stability.

"Enkhuizen's position as a power will continue to diminish until it is nothing but a fishing village." He paced like an instructor, gesturing toward the sea, pivoting on his heel.

"Enkhuizen is my home whether it is a great power or not. Enkhuizen is ancient. It is beautiful, and its people are—" She tossed her head. "Kind. Definitely not like the people of Amsterdam. You're probably right, Meneer DeVries. I'll fall in love with somebody here and marry." She crossed her arms over her chest before adding, just to be cruel, "Somebody my own age."

He glanced at the mucky shore and the ice strewn with frozen fish carcasses. "Your life will be like that of the other women here."

Oh, he enraged her. "You mock me when it's you who does wrong."

"I'm not mocking you, Minke," he said. "I'm speaking the truth about your future here. That's the point."

He had struck a nerve whether she liked it or not. She looked north to the rows of small houses beyond the seawalls where lines and lines of clothing flapped in the cold wind. She thought of those wives, of Mama, even, with their chapped hands and thick bodies, and the life she had always assumed for herself—that life—looked bleak.

As if sensing the crack in her armor, he resumed in the smooth, easy voice that was more customary for him. "I understand your outrage. I see it from your point of view. Of course I do. And I wouldn't have you any other way. I like your spirit, Minke. I'm enchanted by your love for family and home, your loyalty to your town. And your loyalty to Elisabeth. I know how you came to love her. I'll say it again whether you want to believe it or not. She supported my proposal."

Minke had heard that sometimes a dying spouse picked out her husband's new wife. "Griet despises me," she said.

Meneer DeVries waved a dismissal. "Griet will marry well. She'll soon have enough on her hands to consume all her time. And Pim will take over the house and become a lawyer."

"But would we come back here after South America?"

He smiled broadly at her slip of the tongue.

"I meant you. I'm simply . . . Oh, I don't know." She threw up her hands in frustration. This was absurd. "I don't know why we're talking about it, Meneer. One minute I'm tending your wife, and the next she's dead and you're proposing. You have to admit it's too strange. I almost think you're playing a joke on me."

"I'll be very good to you." The timbre of his voice was soft, intimate.

"What does that mean?"

"A man can be good to a woman in ways you can't imagine, my dear."

She met his eyes, saw that his face was without guile, not a shred. Something thrilled deliciously inside her. She felt like touching the scar with her mittened hand, and why shouldn't she? "What happened here?"

"A man with a knife, at sea."

She was so close to him.

"We're on an arc, Minke," he whispered. "A trajectory. You can end it or see where it takes you. We have nothing but possibility lying ahead of us."

She floated free at the thought, a split second of luscious promise, to be far away, with this handsome man protecting her.

"I've gone about this badly. I should have waited and courted you properly. But I've suffered a terrible loss, and what lies in store for me is first the burial of my cherished wife and then—unless you say yes—an unbearably lonely departure for South America."

The wind had picked up considerably since they'd been out, and icy damp air blew up her cuffs and down her neck. She was chastened by the cold and by what he'd said. He went on. "I'll try to say this well and clearly. Every word of it." He faced her, his shoulders casting her into shadow. "Before you say no, I want you to have the whole picture of what would happen if you say yes. I've given it careful thought, believe me." When she didn't interrupt, he continued. "We would marry quickly here—in the old way of breaking a ring before witnesses—as there's no time for a full wedding. I would marry you properly and by clergy in Comodoro."

"What would people say?" she blurted.

He laughed.

"It would be a scandal," she said, but she enjoyed his laughter.

"Please," he said with an urgency he hadn't had before. "You must say yes. Oh, Minke, I want you so badly. I can't bear it." He pulled her tightly to him and kissed her on the lips, a kiss warm and liquid and like nothing she had ever felt.

He drew away and smiled down at her. "To answer your question, people will say whatever they will say, as they always do."

"I barely *know* you."

"This isn't a tragedy, my little Minke. It's not the end of the world. It's a proposal of marriage, a splendid thing, some would say, and the outcome is entirely up to you." He paused. "If the answer is yes, be ready to depart when I return on Monday." He put his hands on her shoulders, looked deep into her eyes. "Come with me to Comodoro Rivadavia."

"Comodoro Rivadavia," she repeated. The sound of the name went on and on like a river. She looked into his soft brown eyes, remembering the day he'd put his hands around her waist, how much she had loved the feeling, and how Elisabeth had been awake, had seen. "I don't know," she said. "I mean, I want to. Yes. It's true, I do, but I know so little about you. I know you are Elisabeth's husband. Were, rather. But before that? I don't know where you grew up or whether you have brothers and sisters, if your parents are still alive. These are things I know about every single person of my acquaintance, but not you."

"I was an only child, and my parents have died. I was born in Leeuwarden. There."

"Relatives?"

"An uncle. What else?"

The look on his face was so comical it made her laugh. "We should go back. They'll talk." She turned and headed for the gate. After several steps, he was beside her, and she felt his hand on her shoulder, where it lay until, approaching the fishing boats again, she pulled away. They walked without speaking, side by side, back through the gate into the town, where she saw and heard everything afresh—the soft clop of wooden shoes on brick, caked with mud from thawing roads, buildings crowded together like teeth, and all of them, she knew, dark inside from a lack of windows; the whole town seemed squeezed into too small a space. She couldn't help but imagine the contrast of Enkhuizen to the pampas, with its never-ending sky, its storms and gauchos.

They stopped at his car, the only one on the narrow street. Minke felt a hundred eyes on her through windows. "What's it like there in Comodoro Rivadavia?"

He clasped her hands. He was wearing a new pair of gloves just like the ones he'd ruined that day in the car. "It's an entirely new town, you see. No one there but Indians only a few years ago, and now everything will be built brand-new."

"You've seen it, then?"

"Elisabeth and I were in Buenos Aires . . ." He trailed off at the mention of her name and lowered himself to rest against the car.

"Oh, Sander."

He drew in a breath and took her hands. "We didn't see it, no. But every day there was exciting news of Comodoro Rivadavia. Opportunity, Minke! They say new houses are built every day. New stores are opening. New services being offered. And this is exactly the reason I must go now and not wait." He was so excited, like a child. Though it was a rare event when a new house was built in Enkhuizen, she'd seen it happen. The freshly hewn timbers, the smell of fresh wood and newly grouted brick and, finally, splendid wooden floors. All she had to do was multiply that image by dozens of structures all over the pampas, and there was her pristine village with the Atlantic Ocean glistening beside it.

"We're united in grief, Minke." He pulled himself up and gave the car a crank while Minke watched. She wanted so much to stay where she was and watch the grand car drive off, but she withdrew to the house instead. She didn't want to be seen mooning after him.

THE HOUSEHOLD WAS in a boil. More voices than just the family's met her ears when she came in the back door. Mevrouw Ostrander from next door was there, her shrill voice mixing with the others. Minke purposely let the door swing loudly shut, and the talking stopped. All of them, Fenna included, were crowded around the table. A half-eaten loaf of bread sat on a plate at the center. Crumbs scattered.

"What did he say?" Fenna sat astride her chair, her feet in heavy wool socks, shins showing whitely between the socks and the hem of her skirt.

"He said—" Minke began, but got no further. She needed a chance to think about it first, so she fibbed. "Many things. Too many to remember." She was particularly not going to speak about her private conversation in front of the blabbermouth Ostrander.

"Well, try!" Fenna laughed and rolled her eyes. "How difficult can it be?"

"Is it still no?" Mama asked.

"He comes back in two days. It doesn't matter what I say today."

"Oh!" Mama said. "So you've left the door open."

"I thought no was no." Mevrouw Ostrander, who was very fat, her white hair in tight curled wisps, and wearing her eternal black dress, lumbered to the hearth, took the poker, and jabbed it in the air as if sparring. "If it's no, this is what you must do when he comes back." It was a foolish old custom, this charade of running off the scorned suitor with a fireplace poker.

Minke took the poker from her and replaced it by the hearth.

"His car sped off," Mevrouw said. "He's gone without a word to your mama and papa?"

"He has a great deal to do."

Mevrouw made a disapproving face. "He should have come inside." *Lucky for him he didn't,* Minke thought, *and have to deal with you.*

"He wants you to run away with him, doesn't he?" Fenna said.

"Fenna, please," Mama said.

"Not run away. Marry," Minke said.

"By Tuesday? Impossible." Mevrouw spat out the words.

"Everybody saw, you know," Fenna said.

"She made a spectacle of herself I heard," said Mevrouw to Mama. "Out on the ice. Flirting with him, running ahead. Dancing about."

"You said yes, didn't you? You pretend it's no, but it's yes." Fenna and Mevrouw were a mean team.

"I did not make a spectacle of myself," Minke said, knowing she had, knowing what she must have looked like out there.

"And Argentina!" Mevrouw added. "It's a jungle there."

"It's a land of opportunity," Minke said.

That shut the old woman up.

"So you *are* going!" Fenna wailed.

Mevrouw sat back, shook her head, and said to Mama, "He'll take her halfway across the world, have his way with her, and then discard her. It wouldn't be the first time a man has done that to a naive young girl."

Papa cleared his throat. He sat erect, holding the bowl of his long clay pipe between thumb and forefinger. "I believe there's a bit of a storm coming," he said with a wink at Minke. "If you look to the north, you can see it's quite dark."

"The wind did pick up," Minke said. Papa had saved her. "It was blowing terribly out there." She felt on the verge of tears from utter confusion. She was unable to keep any one thought in mind for longer than a few seconds before another interrupted.

Papa continued, "As Meneer DeVries's question was put to me first, I'm the one who answers when he arrives. Therefore, I would like to be sure."

"That's only a formality, Oscar. It means nothing," Mama said.

Why did she put him down so? Minke often felt sorry for Papa. "I agree with Papa," she said.

"How will you raise a dowry in so little time?" Mevrouw wanted to know.

"He's willing to overlook the dowry," Mama said.

"You'd *better* say yes," Fenna said. "That won't happen again."

"Leave me alone with Minke a moment, all of you." Papa made a brushing motion with his pipe. "I want a word, father to daughter."

Mama put her hands on her hips and seemed ready to object, then sighed loudly and left the room, shooing Fenna and Mevrouw ahead of her.

Papa stared out the window for several moments pulling on his unlit pipe, his eyebrows low and his face gloomy. When there was no more noise to be heard from the others, he said, "We men need women. Some have a greater need than others. Marriage provides—" He searched for the word. "Equilibrium."

"I see," Minke said, not seeing at all. Sometimes Papa could be long-winded and philosophical and never get to the point. She worried he would do this now.

He pulled in his lower lip and thought longer. "Much has been made of the speed of Meneer DeVries's proposal." He gave her a look as if hoping she understood what he was trying to say.

"It was very fast."

"The speed of his proposal isn't a sign of poor character. It is a necessity in his case because of his business. I understand that you hold it against him, but try to broaden your sights a bit."

This surprised Minke. "You're in *favor* of the marriage!"

Papa thought again. "I'm only explaining something you might not be aware of. Like many men, Meneer DeVries is lost without a wife."

"You make it sound like replacing an old pair of shoes."

"Words don't come easily to me, Minke. I'm trying to speak to you in all sincerity."

"I'm sorry, Papa. Please go on."

"I can see in the way he looks at you, Minke, that you are not simply a replacement. He has had more time to observe you than you him. Until now you've thought of him only as your employer, only as your friend's husband. So it's sudden for you, a great deal to accommodate." *Not exactly true*, she thought, recalling the kiss onshore not an hour ago. Something was definitely changing. She had begun to cross over, the way one felt a shift in the wind on an autumn day. It had also happened when Sander had put his hands around her waist. She had secretly liked the feeling of it, and afterward, lying in her solitary bed, she had replayed the moment. She wanted desperately to believe Elisabeth had been in favor of their marrying.

"He said Enkhuizen is diminishing," she whispered guiltily. "He said Enkhuizen is becoming nothing."

"I'm not sure about nothing, but he's correct that we're no longer a major seaport. Not for a long time, and we never will be again."

"He's almost *your* age, Papa," Minke said.

"That's another matter, Minke. If you're put off by his age, then it's no. If you dislike him for any reason, Minke, then to say yes is out of the question. And only you know that."

"I don't dislike him." A thrill ran through her.

"I thought that was the case."

"Oh, Papa."

"What a life," Papa said. "You'll come back to Enkhuizen in a year with all your stories of the world."

Fenna burst into the room. She'd been listening in. "So you *are* going! Mama! Mevrouw! Minke's going to marry Meneer DeVries!"

3

*T*HEY ATE THEIR dinner, pea soup so thick you could stand a spoon in it, and hard-crusted bread, while the scent of peppermint steam rose from the kettle that Mama kept simmering most of the day. Fenna ate heartily, helping herself to seconds. Normally, Mama would chastise her, but not tonight. Minke had no appetite.

"It must be as proper a wedding as possible under the circumstances," Mama said.

"Meneer DeVries said there would be no time until we get to Comodoro."

"That is not up to Meneer DeVries," Mama said. "What time does he come?"

"I don't know," Minke said, and when Fenna rolled her eyes, she added, "Well, it doesn't matter if all we do is break a ring."

"There will be no breaking of rings in this house," Mama said, her color high. "It will be a proper wedding. Oscar, you must paint the door green. There must be lily of the valley and pine boughs. Fenna, you will take care of that. I will prepare the food and drink. The vicar must be notified and the church prepared."

Minke felt the cold finger of dread poke at her heart. Meneer DeVries had said the wedding would be simple. He would not expect all this. Would not want it, and what would he do if she went against his wishes? But Mama was equally formidable.

"On both occasions, Meneer DeVries has arrived in the early afternoon," Mama said firmly. "So we can assume he'll arrive at the same time. We'll arrange everything for midafternoon. If he arrives sooner, so much the better."

The sunken, hopeless feeling got worse. She was the rope, and the two of them—Mama and Meneer DeVries—were in a tug-of-war. "Mama, please don't make all these preparations."

"Nonsense," Mama said. "Fenna, you will take care of the washing up tonight. I must speak to Minke in private." She pushed herself from the table. "In the parlor, please, Minke."

Minke followed her mother and sat facing her by the window that looked out over the dark street. Mama sat erect, hands folded in her lap. She drew in a deep breath, tipped up her chin. "I will tell you what to expect from Meneer DeVries."

"You barely know him."

"In this matter, men are alike," Mama said.

Oh, no, Minke thought. "We don't need to speak of this."

Mama's fat little lip jutted out. "Certain information must come from your mother. As it came to me from mine." She settled herself, rocking on the chair to move her backside to a more comfortable position. "He will want you to be in the bed with him." She eyed Minke carefully.

"I *know*, Mama. You and Papa share the bed."

Mama nodded. "Something occurs."

"I know what occurs, Mama." Minke stared out the window. It had turned quite cold, and the brick-cobbled streets were shiny with ice.

"Tell me."

Minke could never bring herself to say to her mother the thing she had heard about what happened between a husband and wife. It was better to listen than to have to say out loud what she'd heard from other girls. "Go ahead," she said.

"It's not complicated, Minke. In the bed, the man lies on top of the woman and inserts the phallus into her in the same place through which she has her monthly courses. Very simple."

Minke nodded. "I see. It is as I thought." She felt vast relief at the quick, clinical description. She imagined lying in a bed with Meneer DeVries, but she could only picture him in his camel-hair topcoat. She rose to leave.

"Not so fast." Mama held her back by the sleeve. "You do know what I mean by the phallus?"

On the shore to the north of the town, boys swam naked, and sometimes girls did the same but much farther up the shore. The boys peeked at the girls and the girls at the boys. Certainly Minke had seen, though only at a distance. She didn't dare tell Mama this, however. "I know what it is."

Mama smiled and, with her finger, drew a tall upside-down U on the frosted windowpane. "Like this, yes?"

Minke would have had it going the other way, but she nodded anyway.

Mama rubbed at the window to erase the mark she had made. "So," she said. "What are your questions?"

Minke's main questions were still about clothing. Would she be wearing her clothes? She thought not, but if not, would *everything* be off? And if that were the case, where would she disrobe? In the bed or the parlor? What if she undressed but Meneer DeVries expected her to be clothed? What of him? Would he be clothed? "What should I wear?" she asked.

Mama frowned. "A nightgown," she said. "Like any night."

"Oh," Minke said.

"Has Meneer DeVries kissed you?"

"No!"

Again Mama frowned. "Do you feel—" She hesitated. "A warmth toward him? An affection?"

Minke nodded eagerly. Of course she liked Meneer DeVries. Mostly, she wanted this to stop. She would figure it out for herself later.

"Good. Then all will be well, I'm sure."

Again Minke rose to leave.

"One more thing." Mama had a twinkle in her eye. "Something I wish I'd known when I married Papa."

Minke didn't like to think about Papa in this way.

Mama leaned in closer and whispered, "You will think he's dying, but he's not."

"Excuse me?"

"The noise, Minke." Mama sat back. "They make such a racket."

"What kind of noise?"

Mama thought for a moment. "A howl, like a man being eaten by a bear, if you can imagine that. Or the bear himself!" She slapped a hand over her mouth to stifle a laugh.

"Is he in pain?"

"Quite the opposite!"

"How loud?"

Mama rocked back in the chair and considered the question. "As loud as a foghorn," she said, rocking with delight. "Oh, the shudders, and so red in the face. The bed makes a terrible racket, too, and the doors shake. And you on shipboard! A man of his size could rock the boat. And then!" She threw up her hands. "All at once he collapses like he's been shot through the heart." She slapped her hands against her heart, imitated a great shudder, and let her head fall to one side. She looked up, smiling her sweet smile. "Again: not dead."

"All this on top of me?" Minke asked.

"I'm afraid so," Mama said.

"It sounds terrible."

"Not so terrible," Mama said, drying her eyes. "You'll see."

THE PREPARATIONS WERE fully in place. The front door was a deep forest green, announcing the betrothal within. Pine boughs covered the floor by the stove where Minke and Meneer DeVries would sit to receive well-wishers once they were married. The vicar was first to arrive, clucking his disapproval at the speed of everything while helping himself to food and drink.

Minke greeted the guests and received their kisses, one to each cheek. There hadn't been time to get word to any of the Friesian relatives, so the wedding guests were few, just the neighbors from the street. She wore the same black Lyons silk dress Mama had been married in. In only a few hours, Minke had taken it in at the shoulders and waist, lengthened the sleeves, and dropped the hem.

Black was not an uncommon wedding color among the people of Enkhuizen or Berlikum. Such a dress could be brought out again on the occasion of funerals, although in Mama's case that would not be possible because she would never fit in the dress again. Among all the things Minke had to worry over—principally, her fear that Meneer DeVries would be angry at the elaborate preparations—the dress was just one more. The bride of a rich man should wear a white dress selected for this one occasion. Would the black dress remind him he was marrying beneath his station and cause him to change his mind? It felt like a betrayal of her own family to worry about that, but she couldn't help it.

By half past three, he had not arrived. Each time the front door opened, the guests all turned to look. Minke tried not to show her anxiety, glancing at the window mirror only when she thought no one was watching and hoping to see his beautiful car in the street. There was nothing. Just the usual bicycles, the horses, the man selling notions from his dog-drawn cart. Papa went about pouring the sweet wine abundantly, and for a time voices rose and filled the rooms, punctuated by the vicar's rowdy laughter. By half past four, however, a pall hung over the event. The few people who remained stole glances at the family.

"You wouldn't be the first," Mevrouw Ostrander said to Minke with satisfaction, attracting baleful nods from other women. "And you won't be the last."

Minke went outside in the back, where the laundry was strung out stiff and frozen on the line, but where she could be alone. In a minute or so, Fenna came outside, her head low. She had spilled something on her dress already and made an effort to brush it off. "Mama shouldn't have made such preparations," Fenna said. "This is awful. With everybody here. You're the laughingstock."

"How kind of you."

"Well, it's the truth. You should hear them in there."

"He never actually said what time."

"I'm only saying." Fenna sat down on the stoop with her back against the wall, glum. She'd had some wine to drink, and her color was high, her movements slow. "The vicar tries to reach under my skirt when no one is looking. He's so disgusting. I took his glasses." She held them up and smirked.

"The poor vicar will be blind," Minke said.

"The punishment fits the crime."

"Here I am," Minke said. "You thought I'd go away, but here I am. Still."

"He'll come."

"You believe so?" Minke never expected this from Fenna.

"Of course. You told him yes, didn't you?"

"First I told him no."

"And then you told him yes."

"Then I told him I wasn't sure."

"Ay-yai-yai."

"What?"

"You dangled him on a string. A man doesn't want to come back and hear no again."

"And you know so much about men?"

"I know that much."

Plenty of scenarios had crossed Minke's mind: that Griet had thrown a tantrum over the marriage, that he'd changed his mind, or worst of all, that he'd been toying with her in the first place. Fenna's particular scenario had not crossed her mind—that *he* had believed her when she said no, and he didn't want to hear it twice. "What should I do?"

"Nothing you can do," Fenna said. "You probably wrecked it."

"Now you're being cruel," Minke said.

"You asked me what to do, and I said."

Minke went inside and found Mama in the kitchen. "Send them all home," she said. "He's not coming." She couldn't bear all that pity.

Mama told Minke to withdraw, and if too much more time passed, she would indeed send the guests home without Minke having to be present. Withdrawal wasn't so easy in that tiny house of two rooms. The only option was to climb the ladder to the attic without being seen, and the minute she had her chance, that was what she did. From there she could hear the muted goings-on downstairs, the guests unwilling to leave until the last possible moment, the vicar's drunken laughter.

She'd been so stupid! Stupid to let the idea of marriage gather force and take over her sense of the future. She knew better. She never should have hesitated when Meneer DeVries asked. She should have said yes right away, packed, and been gone. It was what Fenna would have done. The difference between her and Fenna? Fenna always knew exactly what she wanted. She had no sense of propriety. Look where propriety had gotten Minke. Left her with egg on her face.

She lay there feeling sorry for herself, resigned to life in Enkhuizen, when the pitch of voices changed downstairs. Something had happened. Lying on her stomach, she inched forward and down the ladder, supporting her weight with her hands on the top rungs. What she saw were the backs of everyone as they crowded to get out of the front doorway. Mama must have told them to leave. It was going to be harder to get back up the ladder backward.

Her mother's voice rose. "The vicar is drunk, and the church is locked!" The little gaggle in the door loosened, and some of them were pushed back into the house. It was *him*. Meneer DeVries had pushed into the crowded space and was so close she could almost touch him. He hadn't seen her yet. He was looking in the empty parlor for her. She struggled to get herself back into the attic so she could come down properly. Then he looked up. They all did. She was by now several rungs down, practically upside down.

Face-to-face with Meneer.

He laughed loudly. "Come see this, Cassian," he said. An elegant man in a beautifully cut blue velvet coat—she could see that much, even upside down—pushed through. Minke was trying to get herself back up the ladder. This was just fatally embarrassing. "Let us help." Meneer slipped his hands under her arms, and immediately, she felt the relief of his support and let herself loosen her hold. Then, carefully, with his friend helping, he eased her down.

"I'd like you to meet my friend Dr. Cassian Tredegar," he said, barely able to stifle the laughter. He was, she saw, the same man who'd been in the parlor of the Amsterdam house that day, a fact there was no time to remark upon because everything happened quickly after that. Meneer asked Papa to step outside with him for a chat, and the doctor wanted a private word with her. Mama fluttered about like a pigeon still fretting over the drunken vicar and the locked church.

Minke led him to the kitchen, which was awash with the remains of the feast. Plates and bowls of food covered every surface. Dr. Tredegar appeared not to notice the mess. He removed his English derby; his hair shone liquid black in the lamplight. "I am to accompany Meneer DeVries to Comodoro aboard the SS *Frisia*. I am well acquainted with life on the ship. There may be hardships. I can assure you I am well trained. I studied in Wales. If there is a child once we arrive in Comodoro, I can deliver the child in the European way. I can inoculate you against certain diseases of the region. You may not have thought of any of this, a young girl like you." He looked about the kitchen. "I gather the celebration means you plan to say yes to Meneer DeVries."

"He was terribly late," Minke said.

Then everyone crowded into the kitchen. One moment Fenna was shoving her way past all of them to be closest, and the next moment Meneer DeVries was on one knee looking up at her. "Will you marry me, Minke van Aisma?"

"Yes," she said without hesitation, and the room went all quiet, as though it had been a big lark and now things were serious.

Meneer withdrew a handkerchief from his breast pocket, laid it open, and exposed a gold band. "We'll break this ring, each take a half, and we will be married."

"Nonsense," Mama said. "This is 1912, Meneer DeVries. Not the Middle Ages. You'll have to wait until the church opens tomorrow. And anyway, how do you propose to break a ring?" She was a soft white hen, flapping and clucking and affecting nothing.

The doctor produced a small mallet, a metal wedge, and a green cloth into which he carefully placed the ring.

"Please kneel with me, Minke," Meneer DeVries said, ignoring Mama's frantic chattering.

Trembling, Minke knelt. The small room was filling again with some of those who had left earlier, drawn back to the house by the arrival of the car. Meneer DeVries lay the cloth-draped ring on the wooden floor, positioned the wedge, and struck it hard with the mallet. He opened the cloth to reveal the ring broken cleanly in two. He picked up the two golden halves, kissed them, and let them fall into the palm of his other hand. He spoke to her in a whisper. "Once you have taken your half, Minke, and I mine, we are married, and it is witnessed." He glanced around at all the faces pressing in to see and said, "By all those present today. An official marriage. I, Alexander Augustus DeVries, do marry you, Minke van Aisma."

Like tiny golden eels, the two semicircles lay crossed in his large hand. She pressed her fingers deep into his outstretched palm, a sensation that weakened her with pleasure. Meneer DeVries took Minke's face gently in his hands, pulled her to him, and kissed her on the lips. She felt as though he'd opened her and looked inside.

"You must consummate the marriage for it to be legitimate!" Mevrouw Ostrander's voice burst from the back of the room, breaking the silence with raucous laughter. An enormous bowl of raisins soaked in brandy was brought in, and the celebration began in earnest. Even Mama began to enjoy herself. Minke and Meneer DeVries took their places in the chairs among the evergreens meant to symbolize the permanence of their marriage. Time had stopped. She was in a dream where she wasn't required to function any more than to smile and accept the kisses and the gifts of money people stuffed into the pockets of her black dress. She dug her index finger into the sharp edges of her half of the ring, needing something slightly painful to anchor her, to make her understand that this was indeed happening.

After a time, she was aware of a communication between Meneer DeVries and Dr. Tredegar. They didn't speak, but as the doctor circulated among the guests, chatting and smiling, he frequently met her husband's eye, nodding ever so slightly. The doctor tapped the watch in his breast pocket right before he raised his voice to quiet everyone. He produced a book with blank pages that he showed to the onlookers. "I ask all of you to sign this book as witnesses to this happy event." He moved through the guests, asking each of them to sign, then brought the book to Meneer DeVries and whispered again to him, whereupon Sander said to Minke, "It will be two hours to Amsterdam, and my presence is needed aboard ship all night."

Mama must have been watching for this moment because she was immediately at Minke's side, saying, "Upstairs with me right now."

Minke followed her up the ladder to the attic, where Papa sat against a sack of dried peas by the light of a single candle. Minke understood at once. It was customary to sit quietly before any journey, to gather one's thoughts and make the transition, something they had failed to do before Minke's first departure for Amsterdam.

Minke and Mama knelt with Papa. They joined hands and shut their eyes but said nothing. Minke clung to her father's large hand on one side, her mother's small one on the other. Anything could happen. Nothing was certain anymore. She was saying goodbye to something that had already slipped away.

The noise from downstairs grew louder as the guests called for her. She stayed where she was a few moments longer, unwilling to be the first to break from her parents. Finally, Papa's hand relaxed in hers, but Mama's tightened to the point of pain.

Downstairs, Dr. Tredegar had taken charge, opening the car doors and hurrying things along. Minke looked about for Fenna and spotted her watching from the shadow in front of the Ostranders' house. She went to her sister. They stood facing each other.

"You're so lucky," Fenna said.

"You'll have the whole attic to yourself now."

"Goodbye, Minke."

Dr. Tredegar came to pull her away. "We must leave."

She barely had time to kiss Mama and Papa goodbye before she was again on her way to Amsterdam, Dr. Tredegar at the wheel,

Meneer DeVries in the passenger seat, and Minke tucked into the small backseat. From time to time Sander—she would know him as Sander from now on—turned around and beamed at her as if needing to make sure she was there. Dr. Tredegar spoke frequently to him, but she couldn't tell what they were saying because it was noisy and bumpy in the backseat over the rear wheels. She was pleased enough with this arrangement, unable to speak, not knowing what she would say even if she could.

THE GREAT SHIP *Frisia* lay at dock, sparkling with lights and bigger than any Minke had ever seen. The pier swarmed with people, and the air was filled with the calls of men hauling cargo up the gangways and by means of spiderlike cranes attached fore and aft.

They threaded through the crowd and at the gangway, which seemed to rise straight up. Sander stepped aside so she could go first. Halfway up, he told her to stop and look behind. She had to hold on for dear life to the railing and brace her knee against the side for fear of falling, so steep was the ascent. But when she raised her eyes, she was at eye level with the roofs of Amsterdam. Sander gestured down toward the dock where they had just been and pointed to Dr. Tredegar, looking small at that distance as he removed their belongings from the yellow car.

"See over there? They've been waiting for days." Sander directed her attention to an unlit stretch of pier near the warehouses. As her eyes grew accustomed to the shadows, she saw the rounded forms. They were people, dozens of them, lying down, wrapped in blankets and forming a crude queue. "The first on get the best places. The last on must take what they can find."

"So many. Where will they all go?"

"To Argentina, like us! Comodoro is booming."

"But what are we to do there? What work will you do?"

"All that I do now and more."

"I see," she said, not seeing at all. "I pity those poor men huddling in the cold. Will they be all right?"

"They'll be quite fine. Not to worry." He laid a hand on hers, where it still clung to the rail, before giving her a gentle push, indicating it was time to resume their hike up the gangway. At the top, winded, she found herself in yet another swarm of men at work. The smell of their sweat hung in the air. Sander guided her among them, through double glass doors and down a short flight of stairs to a well-lit corridor of golden wood paneling and a highly polished wooden floor. He stopped at the last door, pushed it open, and stepped aside to allow her to pass.

The far wall was curved, with a row of small square windows. She had never seen such a place; the furniture was attached to the walls and the floor and made of the same golden wood as in the hall. The bed stood on its own four legs and had a white cover.

The bed.

She felt flustered looking at it but couldn't take her eyes away and couldn't stop thinking about what Mama had said about the noise he would make.

"What is it, Minke?"

"The bed is very large," she said, feeling her face redden.

The remark left both of them staring at the thing in a moment so awkward she could have sunk through the floor. Here she was drawing attention to the bed, the *size* of the bed, when all she wanted was to move away from the subject. It was the accumulation of sensation that had betrayed her, starting with the feel of his palm when she took the ring, the sweep of his lips across hers, his breath on her neck, his hand over hers on the rail. The whole host of sensations had each lasted only fractions of a second but had succeeded in crowding out everything to produce this very moment, rendering her stupid.

Sander's surprised look said it all. His scar showed white again against the flush of his skin. They were face-to-face, two strangers stuck in a small stifling room, she frozen with uncertainty and feeling awkward, so awkward, as if she were facing a dangerous animal—a snake or a bull in a pasture. Were you supposed to look it in the eye? Run? Stand still? The animal took in every nuance.

Sander finally broke what felt like an eternity but was no doubt only a second or two. He wiggled his tie loose. "Well," he said, and she could feel all the tension run out of her. She hadn't been breathing. "Here's the thing. Cassian has seen to putting our things away. And Minke." He cleared his throat. "I'm afraid I'm needed elsewhere again; there's always a great deal to be done at this point. So I've asked Cassian to take you to dinner. He'll be around in half an hour or so."

After he left, she took in her surroundings. She opened the door to peek down the hall. He was gone. She'd scared him off. *It's so big!* Fenna would love that. Her first time with a man and he fled.

She peered out one of the windows. Men's feet were at the level of her eyes as they worked on the deck. She pulled the curtain shut. She opened the top drawer of the dresser, where she found her things from the house in Amsterdam. Her underthings, her blouses and hairbrush. In the closet were the same two home-sewn dresses she had left behind in Amsterdam—the blue check and the maroon. But what was that she saw farther in? She pushed through to find three dresses in shades of pink and red. She burrowed among them, unable to believe the softness of the material. She pulled the skirts toward the light. They were dazzling, made of expensive fabric, two for day and one, with seed pearls sewn into the bodice, for evening. The red caught her eye immediately, and she took it from its hanger to admire the fine, tight weave and the neckline, which was deeply scooped and woven through with coral ribbon. They must be for her, but she'd better not put one on until she was sure. She'd made enough mistakes for one day.

CASSIAN ARRIVED AT nine, exactly a half hour after Sander's departure, rapping at the door and calling to her, "Mevrouw DeVries?" Mevrouw? Oh, that was *her* name now. She caught sight of herself in the mirror, a girl in a black dress, its pockets still fat with money. She opened the door, and the doctor entered, looking about. "Everything is attached to everything else," she cried. "And look!" She opened a cupboard door to show him how the shelves had little railings across them.

"In case of a storm," he said. "Everything stays put."

"Thank you for putting our things away."

"I oversaw the process; that's all."

"There are dresses in there that don't belong to me."

Still wearing his blue velvet coat, Cassian might have stepped out of an opera. "They're yours."

"I remember seeing you in the parlor before Elisabeth died. That *was* you, wasn't it?"

He checked his pocket watch. "Yes, it was. We can talk as we go to dinner."

She brought it up again in the hall. "Yes, I *thought* it was you that day." He said nothing. "What happened to Elisabeth, Cassian? You're a doctor. You must know what happened?"

"God rest her soul."

He was maddening. Once they were seated in the small dining room, flanked by two waiters in white aprons, Cassian made a show of looking over the menu, then giving his order in Spanish. "Some chocolate to begin," he said to her after the waiter left. "Cookies."

"I'm not a child."

"Everyone likes chocolate."

"I loved Elisabeth." She wasn't about to give up. She had to know.

"As did I," he said.

"I feel strange, married to Sander when so few days ago Elisabeth was alive."

Cassian raised an arched eyebrow. "You're asking if I think you've done something wrong. Sinned, perhaps?"

"That, too."

"Too?"

"What happened to Elisabeth? She was alive when I left her."

"Try to be happy, Minke."

"But—"

He swept the room with his hand. "No one knows who you are or where you come from or what's in your past. You can make of yourself whatever you want. It's the essence of travel. You can become who you tell people you are. Do you understand?"

"That's fibbing," she said. "I was taught to be truthful."

"Truth is a matter only of what you put in and what you leave out," Cassian said. "There's no one absolute truth for everyone."

"I'm a country girl. Sander paid my family so I would care for his dying wife. His children dislike me. That's the truth."

"You're a beautiful young woman who caught the eye and the heart of an adventurer. You're strong-willed, and there's fire hiding under that demure exterior. You see? Both statements are equally true. Truth is in the selection of fact."

"I have little formal schooling. I have only needle skills. I come from a house not a fraction as grand as his."

"Where you come from matters less than where you are going."

"Was she still alive when you saw her that day? The day I left? I need to know."

"No, you don't. Need suggests that grave consequences will ensue if you do not have what you say. You simply want to know."

"Was she still alive?"

Cassian made a steeple of his slim fingers and touched them to his lips. "Imagine that life is a checkerboard and every square contains a candle. So that's what? Thirty-six. At birth all shine brightly, but over time, a candle goes out here or there. Death has begun. It will be irreversible when most of the lights are out, and it will be final when all the lights are out. That can take a very long time, particularly toward the end, when a few stubborn candles refuse to give up."

"You're not answering the question." Had she ever been so bold with an adult? Something about Cassian made it possible to speak her mind freely.

"As a matter of fact, I answered it exactly."

Minke sipped her cocoa, the most delicious she had ever tasted, from the prettiest cup she had ever held. "He's giving his house to Pim, you know."

"Elisabeth's house," he said. "It's been in her family for many years. Sander could not have stayed."

"*Could* not?"

"Sander wants Pim to succeed, given that Pim is a cripple. Pim's practice will benefit from having a good address. Besides, Sander's life is no longer in Amsterdam. It's with you, Minke, and in a new world."

"And those three new dresses in the closet?"

"We sail tomorrow afternoon. You must wear one then."

He was really a delightful man, odd, too, in the way he was always clapping those exquisite hands, a surgeon's hands. He took pleasure in her. That was what she liked best.

He clapped for the waiter. "Are you hungry? Is there something else you'd like? Let's look at the menu."

She'd barely drunk half the chocolate, good as it was. And eaten none of the cookies. She had no appetite because every time she thought about the coming night, about Sander, and what could happen in that very large bed, she felt not exactly ill but certainly not hungry. Cassian read her thoughts. "My dear." His hand swept the air. "All the women in the world except perhaps for the nuns have experienced what I assume you have yet to experience. Can it be so bad?" His eyes twinkled as Mama's had. "Many women enjoy it. Perhaps you'll be one of the lucky ones."

She thought not. Girls like Fenna enjoyed it.

"Come, eat something."

"No, thank you," she said.

Cassian took her across decks to the bow of the ship. Men were still loading the cargo, and down on the pier, passengers slept in their darkened line. He pointed out the captain's bridge, the masts, and the second-class cabins that lined the main deck on both sides.

From where they stood, she could see down the North Sea Canal, which was wide and flat and black, with glimmering lights dancing across the water. The sky above was full of stars. "Let's see if we can find Sander down there," Cassian said as they made their way along the deck rail. The dock was poorly lit. "There," he said.

"How did you find him so quickly?" Even after Cassian pointed him out, Minke had to narrow her eyes to make sure it was Sander.

"I've known him a long time. I know how to find him."

"How long?"

"Very long."

Another oblique answer. Well, she was too tired to pursue it. Instead, she watched Sander examine one box after another and give the signal for them to be loaded into the cargo hold. He looked so important. She brimmed with pride.

My husband.

4

A RAP AT the door startled her out of sleep. "Yes!" she called, in a near panic over her unfamiliar surroundings and the rush with which the events of the previous day returned. Sander's side of the bed was tucked in tightly, the sheet crisply folded over the blanket. He'd never come to bed! She'd waited in a state of utter anxiety, alert to every tiny noise, and then finally she must have drifted off to sleep. Now the door opened, and she held up the bedclothes. Cassian peered in and rattled off whispered questions: Had she slept well, was she ready for breakfast, should he come back later? Yes, yes, yes, she said to all three, and before he shut the door, "Where's Sander?"

"On the dock, with the children." Cassian took a step into the room, looking stylish this morning in sky-blue velvet. "You're in my charge for now. He's asked me to see to it that you have what you want while he's busy."

"I should go." She swung her legs over the side of the bed. "I should say goodbye."

"Should?" Cassian's mischievous grin made him look quite young. "What is the meaning of 'should'?"

"What do you think? Should is should." He was nice, but his philosophical talk wasn't at all practical.

"Do you *want* to go?" He raised his dark eyebrows in delight. "Is it something you have anticipated, this farewell with Griet and Pim?" He steepled his fingers over his mouth.

"That's hardly the point," she said.

"It's exactly the point." He obviously meant no harm, but still she bristled at the suggestion that she had a choice in the matter. These were

Sander's children. Her stepchildren. It would be unspeakably rude to ignore them. "I must dress quickly," she said.

"I'll wait for you in the hall."

She opened her closet and reached for her old blue plaid dress before spotting the three new dresses, her spirits lifting to the heavens at the sight. She pulled them out and laid them on the bed, the red on the left, the mauve in the middle, and the lovely pink on the right. She bathed using water from the pitcher and bowl. She relieved herself in the tiny toilet behind the curtain. She cleaned her teeth and brushed her long hair, all the while unable to take her eyes from the dresses. She braided her hair, tied it with a black ribbon, and quickly slipped the red dress over her head. A row of cloth-covered buttons ran up the left side. She did them up, trembling with excitement. The dress fit well enough through her slim hips, but if she had time on the voyage, she would take in the midriff. She tied the sash in the back, did up the rows of buttons at each wrist, and turned sideways to the glass, unable to believe the sheen, the sumptuous drape of skirt, the way it flattered her.

When she stepped into the corridor, Cassian backed up a step to take her in. "You look magnificent."

"They must have cost a fortune." She slipped her coat over the dress.

"Just enjoy them."

"I'd better go see the children," she said, and felt odd for having called them children, since she was more of a child than they. It helped to be wearing the red dress. It helped to know she looked stunning, that she would outshine Griet.

The deck was alive with activity, crammed with the people boarding, shouting, and pushing. Three large nuns in black woolen habits and white wimples that bunched their pudgy faces into comical pies pushed belligerently past her, and she worried they'd step on the hem of her dress. Holding up the skirts with one hand and tightly to Cassian with the other, she followed him through the crowd to the rail.

"There," he said, pointing to the dock. "Do you see them?"

There they were: Sander, Griet, and Pim, three small figures among hundreds of others.

She pushed toward the gangways that surged with people and suitcases, boxes, even live chickens. In the press, people had begun using both the up and down gangways, so there was no way to descend.

A great wooden box, as big as a room and crowded with men peering over the sides, swung dangerously overhead and thudded onto a space cleared at the foredeck. One side fell open, and a dozen or so men poured out. She pushed her way toward it. At the box, the attendant was preparing to pull up the wooden side, and she jumped on quickly before he could object. The side was pushed back up and secured, and then the box, carrying only Minke, swung into the air; she had to hold on to the side to keep from falling. She tried to spot Sander, but she might as well have been trying to find him from a moving carousel. With one swing, she had a view of the full sky, and with the next a view of the crowd below, until the box skidded across pavement, the side fell open, and she had to run out before more men rushed aboard.

The *Frisia* loomed high and black. She scanned the deck rail for Cassian—she needed him to help her find Sander—and found him by his blue coat right away, still at the rail and watching her. He pointed to the base of one of the gangways.

She moved along with the crowd of men toward the gangways, her eyes lifted to Cassian as he guided her toward Sander. She couldn't see anything in the crush. Then there they were, only a few feet away. She was practically on top of them, but they hadn't seen her yet. Pim looked miserable, a little apart from Sander. Griet was red in the face. "You left us nothing!" she raged at Sander, clearly not caring who heard.

"I took what was mine, Griet. No more. No less."

"Mother was such a fool to marry you." Oh, she was vile, Minke thought. Making a scene over property only days after the death of her mother.

"Your mother bequeathed it to me, my dear. Don't interfere when your facts are on very thin ice." Sander was making a noticeable effort to keep his voice soft, but failing.

"On whose word? Yours?" Griet barked out an ugly laugh. Minke withdrew into the crowd before they saw her.

"You have a perfectly good dowry," Sander said.

"It's nothing compared to the house. Or to everything you stole. I was supposed to have what was in the lower storage."

"It was your mother's decision," Sander said.

"I don't believe anything you say." Griet was about to say something more when she spied Minke. "Oh God, and now you! Let me see your ring. It's probably Mother's, too." Griet snatched at Minke's hand. "No ring at all!"

"Behave yourself," Sander said.

Minke glanced to the deck of the *Frisia*, as though Cassian could be of any help from way up there. Griet followed her eyes. "And *that* weasel. He's going, too?"

"Let's try to part on a happy note, Griet," Sander said.

"My stepfather lets no opportunity pass untapped," Griet said to Minke. "Be warned."

She was a hostile girl, Minke thought. How sad for her to be riddled with anger at this leave-taking. "Seizing opportunity is to be commended," Minke said.

Griet threw back her head and laughed. "He does that, all right."

"I apologize once again for my sister," Pim said in Griet's full hearing. "I wish you well," he told Minke. "I sincerely do." He addressed Sander. "Sir. Safe journey. You're welcome in my house at any time, and Minke as well." With that, he and Griet disappeared into the crowd.

"I only meant to say goodbye to them," Minke said.

"Griet has never been one to allow the facts to interfere with what she thinks. Don't let her words upset you." Sander undid the top toggle of her coat and opened it a little at the neck, revealing the dress. "You found them!"

"Thank you," she said.

"Come on or we'll miss our boat."

"Is it one of yours?" she asked.

"Quickly." He guided her back to the gangway, and they ascended to the ship's deck.

A great blast sounded from the single stack on deck, and dark smoke billowed out. Then another blast. Behind them, the gangway was raised and pulled onboard. Deck sailors went about their work with new efficiency. Onshore, the heavy ropes that looped over pier stubs were raised and flung at the ship, where sailors hauled them in. Still behind her, Sander held tightly to her waist and pushed through the other passengers to the rail. All around, people waved to loved ones onshore, and those onshore waved back. When the ship emitted its final departing blast, an eerie quiet fell. The *Frisia* moved like a ghost ship as it separated from the dock and slid into the canal. Minke watched the stricken faces of the families on the pier and understood the stakes. The women might never see their men again.

The next blast broke the spell. People began moving, calling to one another, hoisting goods overhead. Sander whispered to her, but she found it difficult to focus on what he said—something about the canal, the side channels—over the warmth of his breath on her cheek, the brush of his lips against her neck, and above all, the way his body engulfed her as if she were a child, keeping her warm while Amsterdam receded.

THEY TOOK BREAKFAST at a table for two in the ship's small dining room. Two young waiters barely older than she bore pitchers of coffee and tea, fresh cream, dried and pickled fish, and hard bread, cheeses, and jams.

Sander's eyes, although heavy with fatigue from his being awake all the night before, still managed to follow the tiny silver fork as she lifted a slice of creamy white cheese from the platter, laid it on the thin hard bread, spread fig jam, then ate the confection and licked her lips with the tip of her tongue. "I like to see a woman eat," he said.

Papa sometimes said that when he saw Mama or Fenna dive into a bowl of stew and eat with gusto, but something told her Sander didn't mean the same thing. She wasn't really hungry, mostly making a show of eating, and something told her clearly that he liked watching *her* and possibly watching her doing anything at all. He was engaged with her delicate motions, the play of tasting and touching her lips with the tips of her fingers. She took a grape, rolled it between thumb and forefinger, slipped it between her lips, and saw a weakness come over him, a slight but visible slackening in the muscles of his face. He was an older man, an important man, she thought, but he was lost in watching *her*. He raised his eyes to hers. She put down the fork, nudged the plate away. His attention awakened something in her. The surroundings faded; the waiters and the muffled sounds from the ship vanished, leaving only the awareness of her husband's eyes on her lips and a slight, pleasurable tingling in her breasts.

"Let's get some air," he said. On the deck, he threw her against the rail and pressed against her so hard she felt the heat at his groin through their clothing. He kissed her neck; his lips were full and soft. She raised her arms to his neck and kissed him, allowing her lips to open under the pressure of his tongue, but he stepped back, took a deep breath, and shook like a dog coming out of the sea. He turned from her and took a few steps away, his expression unreadable.

"What's the matter?" Oh, he frightened her. It was so sudden, as though he'd been shot. *Again, not dead.* Mama's words echoed in her thoughts. Was this what Mama meant?

"There's *work*, Minke," he said in the tone people took when they expected the other person to know already.

"Work?" She had no idea what was happening.

"I must see to the cargo."

"Now?"

"Now," he said.

"Please don't go."

"I must." He adjusted his clothing, straightened his vest and tie. "I'm behind already, and you have found my Achilles heel." He breathed deeply again, as if to steady himself. "You."

In the cabin, confused and still aroused, she threw herself on the bed and rolled onto her back. She wanted his muscled body, his sensuous lips. She ran her hands along her sides, threw off the dress and left it in a heap on the floor, fell back onto the bed, and ached with desire for her husband. But he was gone and wouldn't be back for who knew how long. What had she done wrong? He couldn't wait to get her out of the dining room and onto the deck, and then he couldn't wait to get away from her.

He hadn't even brought her back here to their cabin the way he should have. He claimed work, but she'd displeased him, that was clear. She'd done something. But what? Opening her lips? That was all she could think of. It had definitely been the trigger that had sent him reeling away from her on deck. "Oh, Mama," she groaned. "What's happening?"

She could see Mama's worried frown, her pale blue eyes, and her child's face full of soft beauty. Mama would bite her lip and say it *was* peculiar that after pursuing Minke relentlessly, Sander would leave her alone this way.

But wait, not alone. He'd left her in the care of another man, although Mama wouldn't understand that either. Not at all! Cassian was more like a kind, wise grandfather. He had to be sixty, anyway; she'd noticed that morning his black hair was touched with shoe polish and the tops of his hands were a crisscross of raised blue veins. Mama was used to a man who was content with where he was. Sander was another animal altogether. The idea of Sander as an animal aroused her all over again. The thought of him, her husband now. An extraordinary man, like no one in Enkhuizen, that was certain. She wasn't entirely sure about his business. Something having to do with Elisabeth's medicine and with the beautiful things Julianna had shown her. Something that took him all over the world. Whatever it was, it made Papa's work as a shipbuilder look dull.

She sighed and lay back down, deflated. Comodoro Rivadavia. She had to admit to herself that it had been a disappointment. When Elisabeth had first uttered those syllables, they were the most exotic Minke could imagine, a whole series of lovely foreign sounds running together in a delicious river of syllables. She had thought them a single word, Comodororivadavia. But now not only had she seen the name written as two words, she also knew that in English, they meant the rank of the man who had discovered the port and ordered its settlement a few years earlier. Commodore Rivadavia.

She needed company. She'd find Cassian, that's what she'd do. She stepped back into the red dress and, without another thought, set off. She knew where his cabin would be, about opposite hers and Sander's but over on the other side, the port side. All she had to do was go forward around the wheelhouse or whatever they called it, then back down to approximately amidships. She set off down the corridor and out the glass doors to the deck, along the rail to the bow, down the other side, and through the door to his corridor.

A set of narrow metal steps led down and through another door painted a pale green, to a hallway, then another longer, downward staircase. No one was available for her to ask directions, but there was only one door, so this had to be right. Anyway, she was having fun. She raised her red skirts to her knees and skipped down the next stairs and up a few more steps, aware of the echoing clank of her heels against metal. She stopped at a place where one hallway went right and another left. She went left. After ten yards or so, a hall went off to the right; shortly after that, the chance to go left again. She really should turn back. No, she'd keep going. Just one more left turn. But the hall came to a dead end at an unmarked door. She backtracked and then wasn't sure. She found herself at the top of a spiral staircase.

Gathering her red skirts with one hand, she stepped carefully onto the staircase and, holding the center post with her other, descended round and round to the greater darkness of the lower level, where she had to crouch because the ceiling was so low. The air was rank with body smells and smoke. A snore rose from somewhere close. At a distance, closer to the ship's center, a crowd of men huddled about a light. It was difficult to count, but there had to be twenty or so of them, so caught up in what they were doing that they didn't see her. She made up her mind that if anything bad happened, she could run back upstairs the way she'd come.

She took her bearings. She was at one end of a space crowded with rows of bunks. She felt her way along slowly, stumbled, and realized the row between the bunks was a labyrinth of trunks and boxes, impossible to pass through without toppling something and drawing attention to herself. She retreated and felt her way along the low sidewall, where it was darker and she wouldn't be seen. A bark of laughter and shouts erupted. Heart thrumming, she stopped. Had they seen her? No. She wished she knew what they were doing. She crept forward down another row of bunks, feeling her way with each step, until she was close enough to see. Gambling. Not just one game but two. Numbers were called out, dice rattled, the noise subsided, and then the hoots and calls again. If only Fenna could see her now!

Her hand lighted on something soft and warm. *"Onnozelaar!"* a man's voice growled. *Stupid!* She recoiled, trying to withdraw to the darkness from which she'd come. The man sat up. She could make out his large shape, a shadow against the light in the distance. She turned to run but tripped. The man tumbled from his bed onto the floor and came toward her on all fours like a swaying bear.

She tried to back away but stumbled over something else.

Shapes moved in the darkness. Other men were stirring.

Someone gripped her arm and pulled her to her feet. She tried to yank away and run, but he had her. "All they talk about is women," he hissed at her. His voice sounded young. He was pulling hard, dragging her toward darkness. She couldn't see his face, only the bright white X of his suspenders over a dark shirt.

"Let me go!" She was terrified.

"You have to get out of here."

"I'll go the way I came."

"You can't. They'll get you." He pushed her forward in a direction she didn't want to go. The man on all fours bellowed from somewhere nearby. More light became visible beyond the raucous crowd of men. "If the others see you, run like hell for the promenade." He slipped ahead of her. "Stay low."

"I thought there would be families."

"Hush!" He was crouched ahead of her now, the X of his suspenders moving quickly but easy to follow. Another face from one of the bunks rose up so close that she could smell the man's fish breath. A silence from the group of men caused her to look back. They'd spotted her. She wasn't going to make it. Some of the men from the gambling were coming toward her. In a panic, she looked for a way out but could see nothing. She'd lost the boy in the suspenders. She backed up and felt the wall wildly for an opening. Anything. She rushed, hoping the cover of darkness at the edge of the space would protect her. There was no way to make a break for the promenade.

There! Her fingers felt an opening. A hall led down a narrow space, pitch dark. He fingers fluttered in terror everywhere. If they found her in here, she was lost. A rung? She felt with both hands. Yes. And another above it. A ladder barely wide enough for her, but she climbed and climbed. At the top was an open door only a few feet high, though large enough to squeeze through, and that gave onto cold storage. Sides of meat hung from hooks. A man appeared, wearing a bloodied apron. He looked her over. She was petrified and aware of how she looked, her red dress in this ghastly room. She found her voice. "The ship's doctor?" she said. "Dr. Tredegar." *Why not ask for Sander?* she wondered once her words were spoken.

"*Sí.*" He beckoned her inside. She only wanted to be told where to go, but she knew she wouldn't have understood him even if he'd told her. She gathered her skirts to keep from soiling them as she passed among the sides of meat. Two men at butchering tables farther into the room watched without expression.

The butcher moved heavily on, the strings of his apron swaying, through a door to the kitchen, where more men worked with knives cutting vegetables at long fixed tables. In the dining room, young boys were setting tables. The butcher opened a door for her.

"*Dankje,*" she said, passing through the door before remembering to say *gracias,* but the butcher was gone.

She leaned against the wall, still scared but becoming quite pleased with herself. She'd done something. She'd had an adventure. She wished she could tell Fenna about it.

She took her bearings. She was in a fancy corridor like the one she and Sander were on. The numbers on the doors said five, then seven. Cassian, she knew, was nine, so she'd found him after all. She listened at his door. Low voices and muted laughter came from inside. She would love to laugh right now. She wanted to tell him about her adventure. She rapped on the door. The voices inside were silenced. "Cassian?" she called. "It's me, Minke."

At first no answer. Then the door opened. Cassian was in a white shirt open at the neck. He clapped his hands in delight and ushered her in. The same two waiters who had served breakfast that morning languished inside, one on the bed and the other, his eyes half open, in a hammock slung in one corner. Ill, she thought. They made no effort to rise. She must have been mistaken about the laughter; these men appeared too weak to laugh.

Cassian said something in Spanish. She recognized her name among the words. The one in the hammock rose and joined the other on the bed, moving in a dreamlike way. Cassian gestured to the hammock, and she sat carefully on its woven edge, trying to touch the floor with her toes for balance.

One of the boys said something in Spanish. Cassian translated, "He says red becomes you."

"They are ill?" She was still trying to get purchase in the hammock.

"Tired. I let them rest here." He sat on the edge of the bed and smiled. "What brings you to me, my dear?"

"I got lost." The farther forward she shifted her weight, the more it felt like the whole hammock would swing up behind and dump her. "In steerage."

"Whatever were you doing down there?"

"Looking for you at first," she said.

"Why would you be looking down there for me?"

"I wasn't looking for you there. I mean, I was looking for you when I got lost, and I found this little staircase."

"It's nothing but men between decks on this voyage."

"Don't tell Sander," she said.

Cassian said nothing.

She had to stand or she would definitely fall off the hammock, and once she stood, she really had no choice but to leave. "Will I see you at dinner?" she asked.

"Of course." Cassian made no effort to keep her. He walked her to the door and pointed down the corridor to the right. "It's simple back to your cabin. Keep going down this corridor, through the glass door, and there you are."

WHEN SHE REACHED the cabin, she found Sander fast asleep. He lay across the bed on his back, arms and legs loose as if he'd hit the bed fast asleep, fully clothed. She watched him sleep for several long moments—the rise of his great barrel chest and the flubbing release when he exhaled. One hand twitched where it lay, as if grasping for something in his dream.

She moved closer, expecting her presence or the sound of the door closing behind her to awaken him, but he was dead to the world. He'd been working since the day before, thirty hours straight. No wonder.

Staring at him felt wrong, but she couldn't call it spying because there wasn't anything to do other than wake him or leave, and where would she go? He was her husband, and it was an opportunity to take him in, to move around the bed and look at him from different angles. His leg alone, the one closest, was a fascination. The trouser leg was pulled up over his black elastic garter, and a smooth white inch of skin showed. She leaned over him, the better to see his face and study his scar, almost invisible, a thin pink line against the white of his cheek. She touched his silky hair and admired his smooth auburn eyebrows. His eyes were not tightly shut, but open the tiniest of slits to expose a moist glint. She studied his full lips carefully. They were parted a little, and there was a small vertical pucker at the center of the lower.

His black coat lay open, its forest-green lining exposed. His wrinkled white shirt had a row of mother-of-pearl buttons running the length of his barrel chest, over his sunken abdomen, and disappearing under the loose band of his trousers.

The trousers. A man's trousers. She'd never seen such nice ones. Tan, and made of twill, she would say, but couldn't be certain without touching the fabric. They had a button fly, angled to the right, no doubt having been pulled sideways when he lay down—or fell down on the bed, as it appeared. To the left, the fabric was pulled smooth except for a small but definite rise, as if there were a large thumb under the material.

Lightly, she ran her index finger across the cloth to feel the tiny ridges. Yes, it was definitely twill. Then, her hand still poised over him, she pressed the thumb shape. It gave slightly.

She pulled her hand away. Had she wakened him? No. There was no change; his breathing continued its sonorous in and out, and his eyes were shut. Well, then. Feeling like a naughty schoolgirl, she touched it again and this time lingered, pressing gently, and was sure, yes, absolutely sure that it moved. It grew almost imperceptibly at first, then more.

The next thing happened so quickly that she didn't have time for a breath. Sander pulled her onto his chest and rolled on top of her, pressing her into the bed, cutting off her air so she could barely breathe. He pushed her legs apart with one knee and rocked against her hard, his phallus a piece of steel against her pelvic bone.

"Minke, Minke." He panted her name like a groan.

She had no air. He was too big. Too heavy. She fought to get out from under him.

"You little devil in disguise," he groaned into her ear.

"Let me go," she said.

He laughed, a great bear of a roar.

"I can't breathe," she said.

He raised himself, rolling partly off her while pulling at her dress with his free hand and tearing down her underthings. She heard the metal clank of his belt buckle on the floor, and in the next moment he lay back on her, rocking, bruising her with himself, a searing pain as he entered, the sweat rolling from his face onto hers until at last he seemed to spasm from head to foot and rolled onto his back panting, red in the face. *But not dead,* she remembered Mama had said. He got to his feet and went behind the privacy curtain around the toilet.

She lay still on the bed, her heart beating rapidly, tears welling painfully behind her eyes. This could not be what Mama had meant. She could hear him washing, humming a little.

"Are you hungry?" he called out to her.

Hungry? That was all he had to say?

He was rummaging around back there and came out from behind the curtain carrying the pink dress over one arm. "I think this one for dinner," he said, but his smile vanished as soon as he saw her. "What is it, Minke? What's the matter?"

"You don't know?"

"Don't pout like that. You can't be a woman and become a child whenever it suits you."

He was right. She undid the buttons down the right side of her dress and down the cuffs of her sleeves, each one slowly, and stepped out of it. She let him slip the new dress over her head.

"More slowly the next time, then, I promise." He fastened the buttons up the back. "You'll see."

CAPTAIN ROEMER WAS a gaunt, rigid man, with one bad eye and a gray beard trimmed to a distractingly perfect triangle. He introduced his guests; they would be dinner companions for the duration of the voyage, and he was certain, he said, that they would find one another good company. Minke had the honored seat (or so Sander explained later) to Captain Roemer's right at the large round table. To her right was Father Bahlow, an old priest from Antwerp. Then a fat, talkative woman named Tessa Dietz, her husband, Frederik, Dr. Tredegar, Sander, and finally, the Dietzes' daughter, Astrid, who sat to Captain Roemer's left. Minke judged Astrid to be about her own age.

"A thorn between two roses," Captain Roemer said with a slight bow to Astrid and then to Minke.

"You're a dog," Meneer Dietz said with a rollicking laugh.

Captain Roemer turned to Minke. "Are you enjoying your trip so far, my dear?"

"Oh yes," she said automatically. Sander had explained that it was customary for each man to devote his attention to the woman to his right. It was called protocol.

"We're expecting good weather through the channel," Captain Roemer said. "After that, nobody knows. It can be rough at this time of year."

Astrid was smiling at something Sander had said to her. She had a twinkle in her eye, and Minke liked her but was envious that Sander had made her smile. She wished the captain would say something to make *her* smile.

A bowl of clear soup was set before her. She was hungry—starving, in fact—but she knew to wait for the head of the table to eat before she began. The others were served, but no one lifted a spoon. Finally, Captain Roemer leaned over and said, "It's customary for the lady to my right to take the first spoonful."

Well, they might have told her. She felt humiliated, especially when, after lifting her spoon and carefully sipping the delicious, salty broth, the others, clearly hungry, all began to eat heartily, and the level of talk rose. Captain Roemer was going on about what was in store on the voyage. The white cliffs of Dover somewhere, and the sky, which he referred to as "God's canvas."

A platter of meats and vegetables careened over her left shoulder, held by one of the waiters she'd seen in Cassian's cabin. "Oh!" she said. "Hello again."

"Señora," the waiter said.

She reached up to take the platter from him. She thought he was offering it, but the waiter pulled the platter back.

"He'll hold it for you. Just take what you want, my dear," Captain Roemer said. She was mortified again. How would she ever learn all the rules of these fine people? She took a piece of the meat.

"What is your name?" she asked the waiter.

"Marcelo," he said.

"I'm Minke."

Tessa Dietz leaned over toward Minke and stage-whispered, "Don't ask their names, dear. And certainly don't introduce yourself so familiarly. Isn't that right, Meneer DeVries?"

Sander gave Minke an indulgent smile. "My wife does as she pleases."

"We must bring our European ways to South America," Tessa Dietz snapped. "One is always formal with the servants."

"I met him already through Dr. Tredegar, but I didn't know his name. He seems very nice."

Mevrouw Dietz gave her a sour look and called across the table to Astrid to eat her soup to keep her strength up, and she didn't want to have to say it again. Astrid directed a quick conspiratorial roll of the eyes at Minke before spooning up the soup as instructed. Minke knew for sure she would like Astrid.

"And what is your purpose in traveling to Comodoro?" Father Bahlow asked Minke. He had small gray teeth. He was the oldest of the men at the table. She turned back to the captain, not wanting to abandon him, but he was in conversation with Astrid, Sander with Cassian, and so on. You apparently began dinner by talking to the man on your left but then gave way to the man on your right. Something else Sander had left out.

She considered Father Bahlow's question. She wasn't sure, but it wouldn't do to appear stupid. Sander had said only that he had goods to sell, and since she'd seen those sumptuous things in the storeroom on the ground level of the house, she said, "My husband is to open an elegant store. And you, Father?"

He sighed. "I'm to build a church."

"Good luck to you with that," Meneer Dietz said, having overheard and, now that the discussion had shifted, having only his wife to talk to. He laughed raucously, something Minke would become only too familiar with over the course of the voyage; he expelled this laugh after almost every statement. "It's oil for me," he said to the whole table. "Rigs are in cargo. The latest. Only the very best, eh?"

"All alone?" Minke asked Father Bahlow, determined to keep up her part of the conversational bargain. "You'll build your church alone?"

"Quite."

"I saw some nuns boarding. Perhaps you know them?"

"They prefer to take meals in their cabin."

He said no more. He had the habit of crossing himself, then taking a drink of wine before each bite, with the result that he was drunk after dinner.

Conversation was impossible after that because Dietz directed his loud voice at Sander and dominated the table with his talk of oil. He said he wished the *Frisia* were a rocket that could get them to Comodoro before anyone else got there to claim it. He had all his rigs in the hold. They'd cost him a fortune. "Only the very best," he said again, with a wink at Minke. From the way he talked, it sounded as though the town might look like Enkhuizen except that crammed between the houses would be oil wells twice the height of any house. That picture changed when Dietz went on about how long he'd heard it took for things to get from one well to another. Hours, by horse-drawn pallets, so that quashed the notion of everything fitting tightly together, like at home. He said in places where the cliffs were eroded, the oil gushed into the sea. There weren't enough workers there yet to tame and divert all the oil, barrel it, and ship it. He was sweating just talking about it, wiping his brow with his napkin.

"What about the beautiful estates, the estancias?"

He gave her a blank look and opened his hands in a gesture that said *What about them?* She studied Astrid, who was moving the food about with her fork while her father talked. Astrid, she decided, would look better in one of Minke's new dresses. She shouldn't wear gray; it made her face look ashen. Astrid must have felt Minke's stare, as she looked up with an expression that said *Isn't this awful?*

After dinner, Sander guided Minke among the other tables—there were five or six of them, each seating four men. He seemed to know some of the men, but mostly he handed out cards with his name on them. The men were rougher than those she had dined with, their clothing less fine, and their manners clumsy, although they rose and stayed standing when she was introduced. Throughout, Sander held tightly to her waist. When they left the dining room, he whispered in her ear, "Did you see how envious they are?"

The corridor stretched forever before them, overly lit and overly quiet. He went on, "I saw Dietz looking at you. And you were brilliant to ask the waiter his name."

"I only wanted to know. I met him in Cassian's cabin." Which reminded her. "Cassian was very quiet at dinner."

"And the captain. That priest, even! They were smitten with you." Sander seemed so pleased with himself.

"Cassian was very quiet. Is he well?"

"He has moods."

"Astrid seems nice," she said.

"Dietz is a wealthy man. It's in your best interest to befriend them."

"Mevrouw Dietz didn't find me so charming," she said.

He pulled her to him and stopped walking. "Mevrouw Dietz is a cow," he whispered into her ear, and she laughed because it tickled and because she agreed. "It's Meneer who matters."

"But Mevrouw will buy from us."

"Repair the damage, then, if you want. I know you can."

The cabin was hazy with light entering from the portholes. She reached behind her to undo the sash to her dress. "Wait, look at yourself." He guided her to the mirror. "Little Minke van Aisma from Few Houses," he said, giving the silly translation of Enkhuizen.

She hardly recognized her dim reflection in the glass in her ankle-length dress, cut low in front to show off the white skin of her chest and shoulders and narrow waist, the seed pearls catching the twilight, her halo of white-blond hair. He kissed her neck so gently, just the lightest, most delicious of air kisses, so unexpectedly sensual. She leaned toward him. He ran his fingertips along her shoulder to her throat, barely skimming the surface of her skin, so she ached for more of his lovely, sustaining touch. He let her hair loose, another incredibly delicious feeling, and in the darkening room, he helped her out of her dress.

SANDER MADE LOVE to her again very early the next morning, before the sun had filled their cabin, and as sweetly and gently as he had the night before. Still flushed and aroused, Minke felt as if she was floating as they made their way to the dining room for breakfast.

The table was spread with dishes of cheese and sliced meats, fruit, various breads and rolls, and boiled eggs still in their brown shells. Two new waiters hovered with pots of coffee and tea. Father Bahlow and Meneer Dietz were the only ones at the table. Minke said good morning, and Father Bahlow raised a large snifter of brandy to her. "For the digestion," he explained.

She felt so drowsy and liquid from sex; it must have shown, for Dietz stared openly. The girl she'd been the night before at dinner was replaced with this new girl who couldn't stop thinking of Sander. Her appetite was gone, would be gone, completely gone, and for a long time. She ate, knowing it was necessary, but without hunger: a slice of toast with jam and some hot tea. She was glad when Tessa and Astrid arrived—Astrid in a pale yellow dress that was too big for her, and Mevrouw in orange, like a large exotic bird. Minke leaned across Father Bahlow and took Tessa's soft hand. "I'm afraid I was rude last night," she said. "Inexcusable."

"Oh!" Mevrouw beamed with pleasure. "Your apology is accepted."

"That business of asking the waiter his name. You're so right. And my mother would have told me exactly what you did."

Tessa's little mouth tightened with victory. "Good," she said. "You miss your family, then?"

"Not yet," Minke said, the God's truth. "Too much has happened for me to think."

Meneer Dietz laughed suggestively.

"There's a tug-of-war on deck this morning," Astrid said to Minke. "Let's go."

"Of course!" Minke said, and then wasn't sure she was allowed, if the tug-of-war was child's play and, now that she was no longer a child, if she was supposed to spend her time with Tessa.

"Have some fun." Sander squeezed her leg under the table. "I'll be tied up again this morning."

"Ten o'clock," Astrid said.

DOZENS OF PEOPLE milled about in heavy coats under a sky that was a uniform gray right down to the horizon. A thick rope perhaps thirty feet long lay on the deck. Here and there, men picked it up to test its weight. Minke went to the rail for a look at the sea, which was a darker gray than the sky, flecked with whitecaps. She breathed in deeply, happy to be so alive in this moment, her body still aching sweetly from the night before. Mama never said it would be like that. Mama never said that every inch of her could feel such pleasure at one time or that she would want so much of him, more and more.

She saw Astrid making her way through the others. She gave Minke a light kiss on one cheek. "At last, someone my age."

"I know," Minke said. "We're so outnumbered."

"And no real men at the table except for yours. I wish I were married. What's it like?"

"I've only been married three days."

"And what's it like?" Astrid winked.

"I never want it to stop," Minke whispered.

Astrid shrieked in delight. "I hear my parents, you know."

"Hear what?"

"*You* know!"

"Oh," Minke said, and then "Oh!" at the thought of those two large people doing what she and Sander did.

Astrid nudged her and continued, "I know. They're like rabbits."

"No!" Minke screamed laughter, drawing some glances from the people around them. They were being herded this way and that to a spot against the rail.

"That boy is waving at you," Astrid said.

Minke looked about to see what boy. Oh! She recognized his white suspenders. He stood with a group of five or six burly-looking men.

"He wants you," Astrid said.

"*Wants* me?"

"On his side, silly," Astrid said. "He's a team captain. Go, go."

Minke stepped forward and took her place in the line. The boy, who looked in daylight to be about her age, with fine blond hair much like her own, gave her a warm handshake. "Hello again. My name is Pieps," he said. "I'm happy to see you safe and sound."

"Minke," she said.

"You choose the next one," he said. She chose Astrid, who skipped forward.

"Do you know him?" Astrid whispered after she joined the line beside Minke.

"I met him in steerage."

"You're not allowed down there. You could be raped."

"Choose somebody. They're waiting," Minke said.

Astrid pointed to a man nearby and said, "You."

"Well, I wasn't," Minke said.

"Wasn't what?" Astrid said.

"Raped," Minke whispered.

"My mother would kill me if I knew a boy like him."

"How would she know?"

Astrid giggled. They were assigned places. Men took positions at the front and rear of the line and put the women in between. Pieps had the spot behind Minke. At a signal, everyone pulled at once. She completely forgot the dress she had on and gave it her all, straining back against Pieps when they inched their way to victory, then driving her heels into the deck to avoid being pulled forward. The other side let go at once, and Minke's team fell back in a heap on top of one another at the very moment the ship plunged over the downside of a swell. They rolled across the deck, helplessly laughing.

"My friend Astrid. Astrid, Pieps." Minke introduced the two as they tried to regain their footing.

Astrid had a coughing fit. She bent over, then sat up. "It's nothing, just the air. It's so damp on the sea."

"I should go," Pieps said. "They only let us up here for the manpower, then it's back to the dungeon."

Astrid coughed again.

"Can I do anything to help?" Minke asked.

"Talk to me. Keep my mind off it."

They walked arm in arm to the ship's railing.

"Will you go back to Amsterdam after Comodoro?" Minke asked.

"Daddy says there's a war coming."

"The Netherlands would be neutral in a war." It was what she'd heard Papa say a million times, and it meant they weren't to worry about any war.

"Daddy plans to get very rich, and you can't get rich in the Netherlands even if it's neutral," Astrid said, stopping her coughing long enough to imitate her father to a T. "Anyway, he plans to have a lot of land and build a house as big as a castle, with servants and a swimming pool." She laughed. "Mama can hardly wait. What about your husband?"

"I think he's to have a store."

"I'll come and buy lots of things from your store. We'll swim in the ocean. We'll have picnics."

Cassian appeared beside them. She thought he might have been observing them the whole time, and it occurred to her that Sander might have asked him to, a thought that oddly pleased her. "Look there!" he said. "Dolphins." Out to sea, dozens of dolphins leaped and wriggled in the air like piglets. "They love a rough sea," he said. The sea had definitely become rougher, the waves steeper and farther apart. "You might do well to return to your cabin soon, the both of you."

"We will," Minke said. He left them, and they watched as the sea built a great wall twenty or thirty feet high, twice as wide, and marbled with froth. From that slope, the dolphins flew from the water and arced into the air before disappearing into the foamy trough.

Astrid yelped, then coughed several times, very hard.

"Cassian's a doctor, you know," Minke said. "He can help."

"I only need dry weather."

Another swell raised and lowered the *Frisia*'s bow, slamming Minke and Astrid against the rail. They recovered their balance just as a wave came over the side and knocked them to their knees. Weak with the terror of the sea and drenched to the skin, they crawled to an inner wall where they could pull themselves to standing. Anything that hadn't been fixed sloshed around at their feet—the rope, a jacket, debris. Someone on deck vomited, making the familiar, terrible sound, and immediately, the air smelled sour as another and then another vomited. Then Astrid leaned over the rail and was sick.

They staggered and rocked with the ship's motion to Astrid's small cabin, which was only a few doors down from Minke and Sander's. Tessa was looking for her daughter in the corridor and took over from Minke in a fury of recriminations about how wet they were, how foolish to be on deck in such weather.

WHERE THE FIRST two days had been calm, the next six were a blur of hell on the *Frisia*. The waves seemed like high mountains making the ship heave. At night, waves thudded and flowed up and down the deck. Men shouted. Most passengers were afflicted with vomiting, and the stench was everywhere. The only place to be during the endless days of bad weather was in the cabin and in bed.

Miraculously, Minke and Sander weren't sick at all. They were both spared. As the ship rocked from side to side, groaning from the stress of one storm after another, and the sound of debris knocked against the outer wall of the cabin, they made love over and over. She had him all to herself for days.

Between lovemaking, lying naked in bed while the ship rolled, she stroked his skin and told him stories from her life. She'd never had anyone's rapt attention the way she had Sander's. The tiniest detail fascinated him—her skill at needlework, the suit of clothes she'd sewn for her father. She told him how she used to love pole-vaulting over the canals. "I was the champion in our town. I'm very quick," she said. "Fenna was so furious to lose to me, of all people. She accused me of cheating, as if you even could cheat. You either make it over the canal or you fall in."

"Fenna is a force to be reckoned with, it sounds."

"We're chalk and cheese. Fenna likes her coarse pleasures."

This made him laugh and stroke her breast. "What coarse pleasures might those be?"

"Fenna swam naked with the boys. She didn't think twice about it."

"Mama was scandalized, yes?"

"She didn't know, but Fenna wouldn't have cared."

"And you. Have you swum naked with the boys?"

She gave him a playful slap.

"What a lucky old bastard I am."

"It's funny, isn't it? How fast it all happened."

"Minke, I knew from the minute I saw you."

ONE DAY WHEN the seas had calmed but the wind was strong and the other passengers were still ill in their cabins, Sander brought her to the deck and showed her what fun it was to walk into the wind on the starboard side, fighting for every foot of ground against the wall of wind coming at them, and, once they rounded the bow to the port side and the wind was at their backs, being practically swept down the deck on their behinds. Over and over they did this, laughing, tumbling, and catching each other. They saw no one else; the *Frisia* was theirs alone. Afterwards they went to the mess for something to eat, just the two of them in the wrecked dining room. The crew hadn't the time to keep up, and broken dishes littered the floor. They ate alone at the table like a couple of war refugees.

During this time, Minke often brought tea to Astrid. The girl lay on her narrow bed on sweat-soaked sheets, and Minke was reminded of tending Elisabeth as she smoothed Astrid's brow and fed her sips of tea laden with cream and sugar for her strength. But poor Astrid, even a single sip was too much and came immediately up. Cassian came to see her as well and gave her morphine to relieve the nausea, a miracle drug, apparently. It seemed to cure everything.

Minke didn't know how long the storm lasted. Perhaps four days? Five? She lost track of time on the ship. But then it was over. They had crossed into the tropics under a sun that was hotter than it ever was at home, even at midsummer, and 100 degrees in the cabin, too hot for lovemaking, too hot for anything but taking the sweaty bedding to the deck and letting it air on makeshift lines. She was as tired as she had ever been, her body wrung out from the never-ending pleasure of Sander, her constant arousal, not enough food, and the harrowing agonies of other passengers. On deck, in the hot languid sun, she cut Sander's hair to pass the time and sprinkled the amber cuttings over the sea. One afternoon a sailor caught a shark. The passengers crowded around to see as the sailor hit the thing with an iron bar, cut out its heart, and dragged the carcass off. The heart was the size of a fist, a porcelain blue laced with bright red where the arteries crisscrossed it. The heart beat for an hour before it died.

That same night they crossed the equator on a flat sea under a cloudless sky. Sander took her to the deck to see the moon directly overhead, something that could be seen only at the equator. They went back to the cabin for another luscious night together, their last love-making onboard, as it turned out.

They were three-quarters of the way to Comodoro, he explained, and soon the coast of Brazil would be visible to starboard. That morning he rose early, sat on the bed to put on his socks, smoothed his hair in the glass, straightened his tie, kissed her on the forehead, and said in a businesslike way, "I'll see you at dinner, then. You should get some air, and a little sun will improve your color."

Well. She felt bruised. Get some color, indeed. She looked at herself in the glass. What was the matter with her color? She certainly didn't want her skin to darken in the sun. Worse than anything, she felt cast off, as though power had been taken from her.

Outside, the crew was washing down the decks, fixing all that had broken in the storms. The three nuns who were traveling with Father Bahlow were lying in deck chairs in their black habits, their doughy faces absorbing the sun. Farther along the row of chairs, Astrid was taking tea. Minke took the chaise beside her.

"I was turned inside out altogether," Astrid said of the seasickness. She bit into a cookie, spat it out, and made a face.

"I know. I was there," Minke said.

"We'll go riding together, you and I," Astrid said. "In Argentina. Papa will buy wonderful horses, I'm sure."

"We'll gallop across the pampas," Minke said.

"You'll come and stay with me, and we'll ride every day for weeks. We can go exploring!"

"I can't stay with you, Astrid." Minke sat up the better to see if her friend was joking. "I'm a married woman, remember?"

"You'll have to stay. It's a day's journey from Comodoro."

"What is?" Minke said.

Astrid frowned. "Our house, of course."

"Not in Comodoro?"

Astrid made a face. "Mama refuses to live in Comodoro. She insists on being out in the country, where it's quiet and where there are rivers, a better class of people, and no filthy oil wells. We'll be upland. Millions of birds. Do you like birds?"

"Birds are birds," Minke said. "What have birds to do with anything?"

"What's wrong?"

"Then you'll have to come to see me," Minke said. "There must be horses in Comodoro."

"They'd never let me do that. That's why we're so far away. You should hear Mama talk about it. Comodoro is a frontier, like in America—full of gambling and guns and whores."

"But that's a lie!"

Astrid shrugged. "Oh God, another storm." She pointed toward a bank of clouds filling the horizon. "My stomach heaves just looking at it."

But the storm never materialized, and the *Frisia* passed smoothly out of the tropics and back into cooler seas. A few days before their scheduled arrival in Comodoro, word went around that there would be a feast in the mess that night. No more pressed meat or dried beef; instead, a lamb would be slaughtered.

Minke threw her three dresses on the bed and looked at each of them with a critical eye. Which was best? Sander watched, but she didn't ask his opinion. She still smarted from his abrupt behavior of the morning. She would wear the lavender. Mauve, actually. It was not the fanciest of the three, though a dress to be taken seriously. Otherwise, with her blond hair and pale skin, she was a girl in pink. The red had taken her down between decks that time, so it held a different mood for her. No, the lavender was stately and lower-cut than the others. She knew the effect it had. She smoothed the fabric and examined it closely. There were small slubs in the fabric, as if the dress had been worn before, and it occurred to her that the dresses had once belonged to someone else, perhaps Elisabeth.

Before the looking glass, she combed out her hair until she could run her fingers down its length and not hit a single snag. She stood tall, brushing it back from her forehead, watching herself, feeling Sander's eyes on her. Then, leaning to one side so her hair hung almost to her hip on the left, she began to braid it tightly into a long silken rope. She laid the braid over the crown of her head, secured it at her right ear, looped it back left, and finished on the right side. Three times. She was transformed. Regal. And the weight of the braid over her spine gave her the perfect posture of a woman with a book on her head.

SHE WAS DISAPPOINTED to find only Captain Roemer and Father Bahlow at the table. She had so looked forward to her effect on them all, particularly Astrid. She'd show her what it meant to be a married woman!

She and Sander took their usual seats. She turned immediately to Captain Roemer, the protocol second nature to her now. "What a lovely idea to have this farewell dinner," she said.

He was the stiffest man she'd ever seen, and when he turned his face to her, his whole upper body came along, like a cardboard doll. "Astrid's unwell," he said. "Dr. Tredegar has gone to see to her."

"But she was improving."

"She's taken a turn, I'm afraid."

The soup was served. The fish. Everything delicious, although Minke kept worrying. It had to be serious for Cassian and the Dietzes to miss this special dinner. Father Bahlow told a story about an experience on some other ship, in some other part of the world, and when he burped, Minke wished for Astrid's little grin from across the table. Before the meat course, the captain excused himself, saying he thought he might go check on the Dietzes.

He was gone through the main course, the dessert, the cheese course, and coffee. Father Bahlow seemed oblivious to the situation and kept talking, making good use of the silence away from all those noisy

Dietzes. As the brandy was being served, Captain Roemer returned. "It's my great sadness to announce that young Astrid has expired."

Minke could only stare at him. Expired? Did that mean what she thought it meant? She was incredulous.

"Of what cause?" Sander asked.

"What do you mean, *expired*?" Minke demanded.

The captain closed his eyes. "Miss Dietz has died."

"No. You're mistaken. She was getting better!" Minke cried. This couldn't be happening.

"Consumption. That, combined with dehydration from her illness."

"I just saw her, and she was better. Captain, are you sure?"

Captain Roemer, eyes closed, nodded.

"Consumption! And she wasn't quarantined?" Sander shouted at the captain.

Minke watched, slack-jawed, as Sander railed at the captain about contamination, recklessness. She could think of nothing but her own role, her anger that day at Astrid for something that wasn't Astrid's fault and she knew it. She'd behaved miserably toward Astrid and all because she, Minke, had been selfish and disappointed and peevish to find out that Astrid would be living far away, and angry that Astrid had said those terrible things about Comodoro, things she didn't want to repeat to Sander or even to Cassian. And now Astrid was dead.

"Did you hear me?" Sander's face was in hers.

She shook her head.

"You'll have Cassian take a look at you right away. Can't have consumption. Can't have it."

TESSA CAME ALONE to their cabin that night. She was weeping, her hair uncombed. She begged Sander and Cassian to intervene on her behalf with Captain Roemer to keep Astrid's body onboard until it could be buried properly in Argentina. Her husband had already tried and failed. "We're only a few days away," she wailed. But Sander refused, saying he would not undermine the captain's authority on this matter. Customs at sea were inviolate.

"But she must at least be spared the desecration, Sander!"

Sander held his ground.

"Why not allow it?" Minke asked after Sander returned from escorting Tessa back to her cabin.

"The sea has its laws," he said. "Without rigid adherence, chaos is inevitable."

"What did she mean, desecrated?"

He drummed his fingers on the table. "The body must be sewn into a shroud made of sail canvas. The last stitch goes through the nose to make sure she is dead."

Minke shuddered. "But she *is* dead! Cassian said so."

"It's custom. Tomorrow the body will be laid on a table from the crew's mess and placed at the gangway opening to starboard, feet to the sea and shrouded in the Naval Jack. Scrap iron will be attached at the foot end to ensure that the body will sink." He spoke completely without feeling, just a recitation of fact. "It's the way it is."

In the morning all engines ceased, and the silenced ship lazed over the swells, its sails drawn to half-mast to signify a death onboard. Minke clung to Sander's arm as they made their way to the deck.

She found Pieps among the onlookers, his hair slicked neatly back, eyes downcast. The crew stood at attention in two perfect rows, one to either side of the table. Tessa wept and quivered in a chair, apparently without the strength to stand. Minke observed that the poor woman was unable to watch when Captain Roemer shouted out orders, and the crew removed their hats. Six men in uniform carried the body to the deck in its canvas shroud, laid it on the table, and covered it with the flag of the Netherlands.

Captain Roemer read from the Bible, but Minke barely heard the words. She couldn't believe that the small shape lying on the table covered by the flag was Astrid. That Astrid had died before ever experiencing life. "We therefore commit her body to the deep. To be turned into corruption, looking for the resurrection of the body, when the sea shall give up her dead, and the life of the world to come, through our Lord Jesus Christ; who, at His coming, shall change our vile body, that it may be like His glorious body, according to the mighty working, whereby He is able to subdue all things to Himself."

The six crew members stepped forward, slipped their hands under the table, raised it high, and tipped it toward the water. Astrid's body slid out from underneath the flag. A moment later, there came a splash.

"*Rust zacht, mijn vriend*"— rest softly, my friend—Minke whispered.

Captain Roemer then led them in the Lord's Prayer. "Our Father," Minke said, and raised her eyes. She'd never been able to keep her eyes shut during prayer. She murmured the rest of the prayer, thinking about Astrid's soul, wondering how difficult it would be for a soul to escape the weight of such deep water. Maybe Tessa was wondering the same thing. The woman clung to the rail and watched the sea, her eyes fixed on the spot where Astrid had entered.

Someone was watching Minke. She could feel the eyes. She looked about the solemn gathered crowd. Everyone else's head was bowed. But not Dietz's. He stood separate from Tessa with his feet apart, the better to hold up his great weight, his arms crossed over his chest. He was not saying the prayer with everyone else. He was looking at Minke. When she caught his eye, he smiled slyly.

Part Two

COMODORO RIVADAVIA, ARGENTINA

April 1912

6

*I*T WAS A fine morning—cool, with a good breeze. A flock of terns appeared, swooping and diving. Land was near. On deck people pushed and shoved all around her for railing space, but Minke held on tightly. She'd had that spot for an hour, and she wasn't going to let it go.

Land appeared, so distant and vague it almost could have been a cloud before turning into an uneven rope-colored strip across the horizon.

She pulled her coat around her neck against the wind. Where was the town? Nothing stood out. Even as the water became shallower and turned a milky green, there seemed to be no life ahead.

The quiet onboard said that others were as perplexed as she. "There?" someone said tentatively. Yes, she detected movement along the waterfront and beyond that, a few buildings the color of the gray surrounds. Cassian pushed through for a space beside her.

Where were the beautiful houses made of stone, the waving grasses of the pampas? Where was the town center? Sander had called Enkhuizen just a fishing village, so anyone would expect something grander, but look at Comodoro! A bunch of hovels thrown onto miserable dry land. She made out teams of horses hitched to wagons at the shore, people in dark clothing moving about. Wind devils swirled.

"Where is everything?" she asked.

"Give it time, Minke," Cassian said.

"But where will we live?"

"For the time being, in a hotel called the Nuevo Hotel de la Explotación del Petróleo."

She was interested in the prospect of staying in a hotel, something she'd never done. "What does that mean?"

"It's the hotel for the drilling of oil."

A valley of disappointment followed every small rise in her spirits. She leaned over the rail to look into the water. "At least I can swim in the sea. It looks delicious. As soon as it's warm enough, I'm going right in."

"It's almost winter."

"Oh, Cassian," she said. "It's April."

"Oh, Minke," he said.

She turned to see that forever smile on his lips, as if the world were constantly amusing. "Now what?"

"It's all opposite here. Summer is winter, winter is summer. It's hot in the north and cold in the south." He made a little circling motion with his hand. "Water swirls counterclockwise in the basin."

SHE TOOK ONE of the first tenders from the ship to the shore, along with Cassian, Father Bahlow, the Dietzes, and four men she didn't know. Sander stayed behind, seeing to his cargo. She sat beside Tessa Dietz, put an arm around her, and held the woman's coat to her face to stave off the wind. Tessa rocked miserably, her head down, moaning in grief.

At the shore, a wide plank was thrown down for them to cross. Cassian helped her with Tessa, who was barely able to stand. Men milled about in heavy woolen coats and hats. Minke felt their curious eyes on her and Tessa as they labored across the sand to a stone wall that gave some protection against the wind.

Boat after boat arrived onshore of first-class and then steerage passengers, the latter joining in the effort to pull the huge boxes and sacks of supplies up the beach on rollers made of logs, load them onto wagons, and slap the horses to get going. More wagons, more boats. Father Bahlow trudged across the sand, looking beleaguered, his three nuns following. Minke worried about Tessa, who sat in dumb silence. How would she manage in this place without Astrid? To keep from imagining Astrid deep in her black watery grave, Minke forced herself to watch the unloading.

She was surprised to see Sander's yellow car come ashore, roped to a platform tugged behind one of the boats. Somehow it was a godsend in this strange place, an antidote to Tessa's misery and a welcome memory of that first day with Sander when she drove his car out of the ditch. She jumped up to see it, to touch it.

Meneer Dietz was in conversation with Sander, who had come to shore with the car. Dietz wanted to borrow it for the journey to his estancia, and Sander took pity and gave in. Minke watched with two minds as the Spijker was pushed up the beach, the contents of its trunk removed, and then pushed the rest of the way to the top of the retaining wall. Tessa squeezed into the passenger seat, and Meneer took the wheel like cock of the walk, as if the car belonged to him. Petty, oh my, how could she be so petty when those two people had just suffered so? But she couldn't help it. Dietz was grandstanding. He wanted to be seen in the countryside with Sander's grand car so people would think it belonged to him. That was the sort of man he was.

She ran up the dusty path to watch along with some children from the town. The car left a rooster tail of dust, swerved, and stalled in a ditch, its wheels spinning in the sand. Meneer Dietz stormed back down the road on foot. He spoke in agitation to Sander, pointing down the road to where the car lay immobilized. Then he and Sander climbed into one of the waiting carriages, ordered the driver to take them to the car, and pulled Tessa out. Once Tessa was loaded onto the carriage, it continued on, leaving Sander and some of the bigger children to push the car out of its rut. Minke wanted so much to help. "Let me drive it back? Oh, please, Sander," she said. "Please, please."

He squeezed the bridge of his nose, a gesture that she understood meant he was feeling overwhelmed. "Fine." He turned and walked quickly back toward the unloading.

She had a few children around her now, and she showed the biggest boy how to crank the front while she engaged the pedals. It took several tries. Each time she moved the two pedals past each other the way she'd done in getting the car from the ditch that day, the gears ground loudly and refused to engage. Just as she was about to despair, the pedals slid smoothly past each other and the car inched forward. Ahead of her, the Dietzes' carriage was rocking its way over the barren land. There were no roads to speak of, just the marks of wooden wheels heading this way and that. Minke did not know how to turn the car around as Sander did, using the reverse gear. She could only go forward, and so she did, the children yelping and racing behind her. She lost them when she stepped on the gas, the better to make a wide arc around the Dietzes. She waved as she passed, but Tessa and Frederik did not respond. She was thrilled with herself, with how skillfully she drove the car and sailed across the dusty land back toward the *Frisia*, where she applied the brake too hard. The car shuddered to a stop, making that awful noise again because she'd forgotten about the clutch. Sander was nowhere to be seen, a relief. When he was preoccupied, a small error like that could irritate him.

SHE AND SANDER were among the last to leave the beach. Sander had to check on all his freight. He ticked off each crate on a list as it was moved from the tenders to the wagons. Minke hadn't wanted to go alone to the hotel, or even accompanied by Cassian, so she'd waited under the protection of the retaining wall. The truth was that she dreaded seeing the town close up. She had a bad feeling in the pit of her stomach that she had passed the edge of the known world and was about to drop off altogether.

Pieps was helping with the unloading, and she watched him. He was cheerful, always with a smile and a quick joke for the other men as they heaved the heavy sacks, trunks, and furniture up the beach. She wondered how he had the wherewithal to be so happy.

She wasn't aware he'd seen her until he came over and asked if he might sit beside her for a few minutes and catch his breath. Up close, she saw his pale skin was dappled from exertion, his fine blond hair pasted to his forehead with sweat. His smile was enormous. "So here we are!" he said. He gestured around. "The gem of the ocean. Comodoro Rivadavia."

"Gem indeed," she said. "I don't know. It looks a little primitive."

"It is primitive," he said. "But not for long."

He reminded her of the boys in school who talked lightning-fast and found everything funny and never waited for her to speak before barging ahead into some new topic. He pointed to a man struggling to carry a heavy bucket up the beach. "The fire department," he said. He did an imitation of Captain Roemer, tucking his chin and fixing her with crossed eyes, making her howl with laughter. "Oh, and that one." He was pointing right at Sander, who was gesturing to someone about the loading of a cart. "The gens d'armes."

She should stop him.

"He prowled through cargo day and night, checking the locks on storage, counting things. He didn't trust a one of us. Said he'd know right away if anything was tampered with and there'd be hell to pay, although he wasn't above joining in a game from time to time." He jumped to his feet and produced an exaggerated version of Sander's stride, one hand behind, palm out. It *was* Sander.

"That's my husband!" she said, wiping her eyes.

Pieps had the type of fair skin that became very red when he was embarrassed. It made her laugh a little more. The poor boy looked absolutely stricken. "I thought you were traveling with your sister and your parents," he said. "The girl who died."

"Astrid. No, she was my friend."

Neither of them spoke for a moment, then he cleared his throat and apologized. She accepted his extended hand; as she did, she noticed Sander watching them and cast her eyes down, wondering with a stab of guilt if he'd recognized himself in the imitation Pieps had done or, worse, seen the way she had laughed.

IT WAS LATE afternoon when she and Sander walked together to the Hotel de la Explotación del Petroleo, a solitary one-story structure on the mushroom-colored earth. It was flimsy-looking and made of rippled corrugated metal, even the roof. Bits of paper fluttered along its sides, shoved into the seams, apparently notices that would be of interest to the people of Comodoro.

The door opened onto a bar smelling deliciously of roasting meat. A big silver espresso machine hissed in one corner. Small square tables filled the room, each with bottles of brandy and wine already laid out. And men. Always men. Men everywhere—sitting, talking, watching.

Sander ushered her through a cramped foyer, where birds in cages made a racket, drowned out only by the rattling of wind against metal outside. Their room was no bigger than her kitchen at home, filled with a sagging bed and a single bureau.

Sander took off his boots, put them outside the door, and fell heavily onto the bed. "Come, my little minx," he said, pulling her on top of him, causing the bed to groan and sag. "My bum just touched the floor," he said, and they laughed. He bounced until they were giddy. "We will begin our life properly in Comodoro Rivadavia, by fucking!"

"Sander!"

A smile played at his lips. "What?" he whispered.

The forbidden word rinsed through her like liquid fire. It exhilarated her. She threw her head back and laughed; there was no one to scold her for hearing such a word, no one even to know. The word belonged to them, here in the privacy of this peculiar hotel on this barren strip of land. She slipped out of her clothes and onto the bed, loving the protective, healing warmth of his skin. They made love, rocking, hitting the floor in their fury while the wind picked up strength and black night fell.

COMODORO RIVADAVIA—VAST, colorless, and like nothing Minke had imagined. Instead of the lush green of Holland, it was a brown mono-tone. A single hill called the Cerro Chenque rose to the east, smooth as an upside-down funnel.

Although Sander hadn't been to Comodoro, only to Buenos Aires, a thousand miles away, he seemed to take the primitive conditions in stride, and Minke knew better than to complain. He immediately set about building a house for them. For the time being, it would be like all the other houses—corrugated metal sides nailed to a wooden skeleton, a hard-packed dirt floor, and the roof weighed down with slabs of concrete and lengths of lumber to keep it from blowing away in a high wind—but once his business was established, he would build them a fine house of wood and stone.

He hired some local men and chose a spot near the center of town, and while he worked, she walked the dusty surrounds in her black wedding dress. Everyone was dressed in dark colors, and she didn't want to stand out. Nor did she want to dirty her lovely new dresses. She clopped along in wooden shoes because of the mud and dirt, seeing rabbits and mice, an armadillo and sparrows. In the distance far to the west, the hills, or maybe they were mountains—she had no experience with either—were gray in some light and the softest brown in others. A few worn paths led here and there, but mostly the wagons and the animals crisscrossed the land every which way, since nothing was there to stop them. No trees, no rivers or rocks. What grew in Comodoro was a thorny plant that broke off and tumbled across the plains.

On a day when the air was fine and crisp, the sky cloudless, she found her way up Cerro Chenque by means of a well-worn path. From that vantage point, she could look down on all of Comodoro, with its little cluster of buildings at the center. The Explotación, and a store called the Almacén, which smelled of polish and whose owner, Señor Bertinat, followed her about like a pet dog, suggesting she buy this or that. She worried that the Almacén was competition for the store they would build. It provided for all needs—soap and food and clothing, tools and equipment. What else could Sander provide? But she pushed those thoughts down. Sander, after all, was a man of experience, and she knew nothing of the world. Better to trust him.

Beyond those few buildings, everything was placed so randomly the town might have been a score of jacks thrown across a floor. Sprinkled about for miles were the little metal sheds where people lived, and oil wells that sprouted here and there, some covered entirely in metal sheeting to protect them from the ever-present wind.

One fine day—the house was nearly finished by then—she was on the Cerro when a tiny dark shape appeared on the northern horizon. She narrowed her eyes, concentrating, trying to decide if it was a mirage; people talked about mirages here, how not to trust what you saw until you could touch it. The speck grew larger. It took the shape of several wooden wagons that rocked and swayed from side to side, loaded dangerously high. As they came closer, she saw teams of skeletal horses, eight for each wagon. They stopped at the Almacén.

A few children came running to see. The children of Comodoro were peculiar. They didn't play outside but stayed inside the little metal houses and came bursting out when something happened in the town. Soon the adults came out of their houses and made lines to unload the wagons of their huge bulging burlap sacks and lumber. That seemed to be the way of the town. When anything arrived, men formed lines.

The horses stood motionless, their heads lowered while the unloading took place. Then something happened. There was agitation, a disengagement of the line. One of the horses had dropped to its knees. Its companions in the team were skittish, jostling and sidestepping. Men shouted and slapped the downed horse, trying to make it stand. They stood back, looking at the animal. One of the men finally released the horse's harness. The horse fell over and lay still in the dust while the rest of the team was pulled clear of it. Now more men came from the hotel and looked the horse over, walking around it, gesticulating, arguing with the driver of the rig. A horse was unhitched from the team and used to drag the downed horse across the expanse that was San Martin Street to the rear of the hotel, where it was hoisted, hind feet first, by a pulley. The cook, in his white apron, came jauntily out from the hotel. He slit the horse from chest to groin, stepped back, and let the entrails spill onto the ground. People applauded.

Minke's stomach heaved. She leaned forward just in time to keep from throwing up on her dress. The heaves came in waves, over and over until she was vomiting bile. She shut her eyes, holding her stomach, rolled over, curled up on her side, and sobbed without bothering to wipe her mouth. She cried for the horse at first, for that poor pathetic broken animal who had pulled its load and done its work, then died before anyone even thought to give it a drink of water. She cried for the other horses, for the loss of their companion. And then she hauled in a long breath and cried out loud for Elisabeth and for Astrid, snatched from her so quickly. She cried for Elisabeth's miserable, lonely last moments, for the murk that shrouded the events of her death, and for her own guilt at having let Sander persuade her to leave that day. She cried because if Astrid had lived, the two of them might be up here together right now, giving each other comfort. She cried for Mama and Papa, imagining them huddled together in their closet bed, devastated by her absence, and then she cried for the deep featherbed itself, all dark, cozy, and safe, and much as she hadn't enjoyed bedding down with Fenna every night, she still cried for her sister and wished she could see her again. Finally, she cried for herself. She lay flat out on her back and sobbed loudly to the heavens for everything she had lost, her home, her family, everything she knew. Why had she ever said yes to Sander? It was true, she loved their times alone. She had thought she could endure anything as long as she had the safety of his arms at night, the lovely arousal, reaching such heights that her own intense feeling swallowed the world. She sobbed into her hands. She thought of those entrails again and produced another stream of vomit and bile.

She dragged herself to a sitting position and looked down the Cerro for Sander. There he was, dragging a sheet of the ridged metal across the dirt, upending it, and hammering it into place. It was only the middle of the day, too early to go back. She rose and walked to the western slope of the Cerro, where she could see to its base and the house Cassian was building, a house that stood all by itself, far from any others. Smoke puffed from his chimney; he was there.

She made her way down the path to flat land, backtracked to the right, and knocked at Cassian's door. The metal door rattled, and she waited, cold seeping through her clothing, the wind an out-of-key violin that wouldn't quit.

No answer. She knew he was there. She entered and found herself in his consultation room. "Cassian?" He'd made it so cozy. Persian rugs covered the whole dirt floor, a cushioned examining table stood at the center, and glass cabinets stood against the wall in which his medical tools were lined neatly in rows. Dangerous-looking scissors and knives with sharp points. Ten or so bottles of morphine.

She passed through the room and knocked at the door to the back room before cracking it. Four young men lay about like a litter of nursing puppies who'd fallen asleep on top of one another at the teat. They reminded her of the waiters on the ship, only these men were deeply asleep, absolutely still.

She pulled the door closed. "Well," Cassian said, and she jumped. He stood in the doorway.

"I didn't see you," she said.

"I know."

"Who are they?" She pointed to the young men.

"They work here," he said with a shrug. "In the laboratory, as guards in the night."

"Why the need for guards? What's going on?"

"You look distressed."

"I was sick. I saw a horse hung up and skinned. But why do you have guards? They're not very good guards."

He indicated she should take the leather chair and stood behind her, running his fingertips over her neck and throat. His touch was soothing. She could be drawn easily into the sleepy world Cassian created here.

He moved to the chair facing hers and held her hands. His smile reassured her. It took in every bit of his face, crinkling the skin at his eyes and mouth. "You're safe here."

"And yet you have guards," she said.

"That's different." He made a dismissive motion of the hand, thought a moment, and then said, "At home the dangers are known, but there are still many of them. Falling through the ice, drowning in the sea, catching a fever." He shrugged again. "Here everything is new, and you don't know what can kill you and what cannot."

"I'm not afraid of dying," she said.

"All fear is ultimately about death. A great change like this requires a great deal of time to accommodate." He smiled. "But you will. You'll see."

"And in the meantime?"

"There is no meantime, Minke, that's the point. There is only now." He rested two fingers on the inside of her wrist and shut his eyes to count. "You seem to be fine. Do you feel better?"

She did. The nausea was gone, and her calm was restored. "I want to see what they're guarding."

He thought a moment, smiled. "But of course."

He led the way across the dirt yard to another building, mostly finished, with a low flat roof and three big metal chimneys puffing out steam. She had to duck. Inside, she found herself in a large darkened space that smelled as loamy as a mushroom cellar. Three large metal pots hung over loud gas burners tended by a young man with a long wooden paddle, stirring. Overhead, cloth bags hung from the ceiling, each holding something about the size of a small cannonball. Large tables in the center of the room held square trays of powder the color of honey. "What *is* all this?" she asked.

"Medicine," he said.

"You make your own?" She recalled the boxes of small bottles in the storeroom of the house in Amsterdam. "Is Sander involved as well?"

"We've been partners in manufacture for many, many years."

"And are you also partners in the store?"

Cassian shook his head. "The store is only a plaything."

She didn't understand the world of men, or at least not these men. She walked back to Cassian's house with him. It was still too early to return home, and she fell into the big comfortable chair. "At home there was a great deal for me to do. Here, very little," she said. "I sew in our hotel, but I wish there was more to do."

Cassian disappeared into his bedroom and emerged with several books. "You might spend time learning the language."

"Spanish?"

"Of course. You'll need Spanish and, while we're at it, English as well. I find it's easier to learn two languages at once rather than one at a time. Besides, English is surprisingly close to Dutch. Come." He sat opposite her and began with English. "Repeat after me. 'I am. You are. He, she, it is. We are. You are. They are.'"

THAT NIGHT THE hotel smelled of roasting horsemeat. She had no appetite, unlike Sander, who had worked all day. She waited in their room under the covers and listened for Sander to return. When she heard his steps in the corridor, she jumped out of bed. The moon was full, and she wanted to walk outside with him for a while. She wanted to see the moonlight on the ocean.

He'd been drinking and was in a sweet, mellow mood, hugging and kissing her as they walked outside and toward the sea.

"I thought seeing the sea would remind me of home," she said. "But this sea is empty, whereas at home, there are the lights of fishing boats, the sound of the bells, the buoys knocking about." She stared at the black vastness feeling small and lost. "Hold me, Sander."

He put his arms around her from behind, and they both looked out to sea. "You miss home," he said.

The wind had stopped its constant blowing, and the air was quiet. "Not that, exactly, Sander, but I do wonder sometimes."

"Wonder what?"

"From what Elisabeth said, I imagined waving grass and lovely ranches and streams." She could feel him loosen his hold on her. "Not that I'm complaining. I suppose there's a beauty to it that grows on a person." His arms slipped from her waist and rested at the sides of her hips. Had she gone and offended him? "It's just that there isn't much color here, you know? And I haven't seen any girls my own age, and when will I ever wear my beautiful dresses?" She was chattering away like a schoolgirl, but she couldn't stop, and tried to undo the damage. "But I'm sure in summer it's beautiful. And Holland isn't so different, when you think about it. It's just as bleak in the winter."

"You think Elisabeth exaggerated."

"I'm not blaming her." She drew in a deep breath. "I shouldn't have said anything at all. I don't know what got into me."

"Speak your mind, Minke."

She mulled this over a moment. What did she want to say? She tried to organize the thoughts that had been tumbling about for weeks. "Why here, Sander? Why Comodoro? It's a peculiar choice for a man like you."

"And what sort of man is that?"

"A wealthy man such as yourself. And starting over with so little?" She wished he'd put his arms around her again, as he had at the start, and make everything good again.

"It's not enough for you?"

"For me, it's enough. But you had that grand house in Amsterdam."

"You're disappointed," he said.

"I'm trying to make sense of things." She spread open her arms to take in the whole town. "It's just a surprise." His calmness was maddening. "*Say* something, Sander. You asked me to speak my mind, and I did."

"Let's have a look at the house," he said.

She felt baffled. He could be such an enigma, which, she reasoned, was a function of the difference in their ages but had to be resolved, even so. She didn't know how to think things through the way he did. She would have to learn how to be more clear and not to be taken the wrong way. Blaming it on Elisabeth! That was the furthest thing from her mind, and yet she could see how it might have sounded that way to Sander. She walked beside him, zigzagging around the wires that marked property lines. It was impossible to walk a straight line in some places. Once at the house, Sander put a key into the lock, swung the door open, and lit the torch in a large room with a low ceiling and stacked with crates and sacks. A clean smell of wet plaster reminded her of home. Here was the house. He was giving her answers after all.

"What do the boxes contain?"

"The things we're to sell. We'll use this space for a store." He opened another door. "Come."

The door gave onto another space about the size of the front room but divided down the center by a shoulder-level partition, so that from the door you could go either way. The space to the right was divided down the middle by another partition into two smaller spaces. Sander, pointing to the right, said, "Our parlor," and then to the left, "Our bedroom." She hastened into it and looked about, seeing immediately a window that looked toward the sea. This would be home.

Just then came whooping sounds at a distance, and they rushed outside to see what was happening. They were met with an otherworldly sight that she would remember clearly for the rest of her days. A bright orange halo lay to the west with a more brilliant orange center. Fires. Five or six small ones and one very large—all sending out arcs and pinwheels of blazing sparks into the black sky. In all her life, she'd never seen so much fire or heard such sounds. She didn't know if the sounds were animal or human.

People materialized from all over Comodoro, dark shapes, singly and in pairs and threesomes, coming out of their homes to see. It was beautiful to watch but even more beautiful to hear. The cries were jubilant. It was like looking at hell and hearing heaven, she thought.

Sander wrapped his arms around her. "The gauchos have come."

7

THE VIBRATING BASSO profundo of hooves awakened her, and she jumped out of bed to the window. There was dust everywhere, along with massive horses and glints of silver. She dressed hurriedly— her red dress for the occasion. Sander had already left, saying as he went that he wanted to ready his goods for trade with the gauchos. This was the day he'd been waiting for.

She had no appetite, but it was necessary to eat. Sander had insisted on it. She was becoming too thin on the diet of meat that was so prevalent in Comodoro. She could be ravenous, but one look at a plate heaped with beef kidneys and she lost her appetite. Only at breakfast could she count on the small portions of bread and cheese she loved, the dark roasted coffee loaded with sugar.

The Explotación bar was transformed. Liquid smoke hung in the air, and it bustled with men from the town and with gauchos and smelled of yerba maté. The men standing parted for her to pass through to her small table at the back. The gauchos wore heavy silver spurs and red *bombachas* oily with use. The glinting everywhere of red and silver was all she registered as she passed among them, nervous, excited to be at her table, where she could watch unnoticed.

Her coffee was brought immediately, and she sipped the sweet dark liquid. They were stealing glances at her, and she lowered her eyes to the cup, pleased with herself for wearing red in their honor. She couldn't keep herself from smiling and tucked her head so the smile wouldn't be noticed.

"Mevrouw, may I join you?" a voice said, and when she looked up, she saw it was Pieps, but without his familiar white suspenders. His blond hair was longer and dusty. He'd grown a beard that had come in a startling red. "Do you mind?"

"Of course not." She was desperate to speak to someone her own age, in her own language.

"They've been touching my hair," he said with a laugh. "They'll want to touch yours as well. They've never seen hair like ours. They'll think we're brother and sister."

The owner, Meduño, brought her a piece of coarse dark bread and a thick slice of hard cheese, the closest she could come to an echo of the breakfast of her childhood.

"How do you like Comodoro now?" she asked Pieps.

"I love it. I belong here." He opened his hands, thick with calluses and scars. "I have a future here. I'm a seal skinner. It's what I did at home, but here I can advance."

"Where are there seals?"

"Up and down the coast."

A gaucho was headed their way through the crowd of men. His sheer size was spectacular, not so much his height—he wasn't nearly as tall as Sander—but his chest was enormous with power, so he looked as big across the shoulders as he was tall. At the table, he extended a big-boned hand covered in skin so thick it could be the hide of a reptile. His black bangs were cut straight over his eyebrows, and he had a black scarf knotted at his throat, the ends spread jauntily to the tips of his shoulders. "Señora." He flashed white teeth in a face that was as weathered as his hands, the skin carved in troughs across his cheeks from squinting. His hand squeezed hers like a vise.

"Señor?"

"His name is Goyo," Pieps said, and at the sound of his name, the gaucho grinned and bowed his head. "They were in the north when they had news of the arrival of the *Frisia*. May he sit with us?"

"Of course," she said, and sat down gingerly.

"They are prepared to trade," Pieps said. He talked about the horse-drawn pallets that had come in carrying more things the gauchos might want, the same wagon train that had stopped at the Almacén that time, how it always happened this way. News of any arrivals by ship or shore in Comodoro were always known somehow by the gauchos, who would travel hundreds of miles to trade. While Pieps spoke, Goyo stared at Minke, his face a grinning mask.

"Is he dangerous?" she whispered. Pieps poked Goyo and must have asked that exact question because Goyo made a fierce face at her, baring his teeth, and the two men laughed.

"You're making fun of me," she said.

"A little," Pieps said.

"You can tell him my husband is a merchant."

Pieps translated, and Goyo's eyes narrowed with interest. "*¿Qué?*"

"What does he have?" Pieps asked.

"I don't know exactly, but we can go there together." She would bring Sander a gaucho, and he would be proud of her. They left the hotel and headed to the store, and she wished the people of Enkhuizen could see her now in her red dress, side by side with a gaucho.

Outside, the town had a holiday feel. Everything was transformed, amplified. The gauchos rode wonderful horses, all of them the same gray with silvery rumps, their reins, bridles, and saddles sparkling with silver and turquoise. They raced one another down the main street, putting on a show. The ones on foot moved elegantly, in the same slow gait as Goyo, graceful for all their bulk and bowed legs.

She spotted Sander's yellow car, crowded about with people. "There he is. Sander!" she called, aware of the spectacle she made in her red dress walking with Pieps and Goyo. "I've brought you Señor Goyo. He wants to trade with you," she said.

"Goyo Mendez," Goyo said.

Sander slipped an arm around Minke's waist and pulled her to him tightly. He looked Goyo over and took in Pieps with an expression that told Minke he didn't recognize the boy as the one he'd seen talking to her that first day.

"I can translate if you like," Pieps said.

Goyo ran his hand over the shiny metal of the car.

"He wants to buy merchandise from you," Minke said.

Sander squeezed her waist again. "Come in," he said to the men.

Inside, he had opened the sacks and crates and arranged things artfully about. Minke ran from item to item. It was all so exciting. "I remember this!" she said, picking up an ornate silver vase. "It was in the dining room in Amsterdam. And this!" She held out a brass lamp. "It's all from the house, isn't it?"

Sander pinched the bridge of his nose, a signal that she was doing something wrong, that right now she should keep quiet and behave like a lady. But it *was* from the house. "I was only making an observation," she said, feeling unjustly scolded.

Goyo ran his hands along the items without a change in expression, stopping at a case filled with textiles. The bargaining began immediately, with Pieps translating. When the numbers started to fly, Pieps couldn't keep up, so Sander and Goyo bartered by making numbers on the dirt floor with a stick, scuffing them out with their shoes and ultimately coming to some sort of agreement, whereupon they shook hands. It had all happened quickly. Minke flushed with the pleasure of having brought them together, of having been useful to her husband after all.

"I need to see what he has in trade before this is concluded," Sander said to Minke. "So it's best you return to the hotel."

"Oh, no, I'll come, too."

Sander frowned. "A word in private, Minke," he said. They went outside. "Don't contradict me in front of others."

"I didn't contradict you."

"You're doing it now. The trading station is no place for a woman."

"Neither is the hotel," she said.

"You're going back to the hotel." He called inside the store. "You, Pieps, is it? Escort my wife safely to the hotel."

"I don't need an escort." She threw off Sander's hand.

"See her back," he said to Pieps.

With her head down, arms tight across her chest, and fighting back tears, she headed toward the hotel. She never knew from one minute to the next how Sander would behave. She stopped and stamped her foot at the injustice of it.

"What is it?" Pieps asked.

She'd forgotten about him. "Nothing," she said. The thought of staying in the room all day took the air out of her. And that was something else. Their room. It was her haven, her sanctuary with Sander. No matter what else happened during the day, she could always count on feeling safe and free in the room with him. But the night before, something peculiar had happened. After they got back from their walk, Sander had told her to move around the room naked. Not such a strange thing—she often walked naked in the room and thought nothing of it—but he was taking swallows from a bottle of whiskey, smoking his cigar, and signaling to her to walk this way and that, to turn around, to pick something up off the floor. She'd refused. She hadn't liked the game at all and had told him so, had told him it made her feel like a whore. He'd said, "Whore or Madonna?" something she hadn't understood at all. She put an end to the whole charade by slipping on her dressing gown and tying the sash tightly. "I guess you've chosen," he'd said, and she'd let it go, combing out her hair in front of the mirror.

"Do you know who Dr. Tredegar is?" she asked Pieps.

"I know who everybody is."

"I want to go to his house and not the hotel."

"Your husband gave instructions."

She made a face. "I'll go alone, then."

"I promised to escort you to the hotel."

"Then you can drop me at the hotel and fulfill your duty to my husband, and I'll go alone to Cassian's, and nobody can stop me."

"You shouldn't run about alone, Mevrouw. It's not safe."

"Call me Minke. And I run about alone all the time."

He sighed deeply and shook his head. "You have to be careful."

"I'm going to see Cassian. What you do is up to you."

They set off around the Cerro toward Cassian's, neither of them speaking. When they rounded the bend, she saw two horses tied to Cassian's rail. Closer, she saw they were better horses than the sorry old things that had hauled all those goods across the pampas, although not nearly so fine as the gauchos' horses she'd seen that morning in the street. She ran her hand over their soft, warm noses.

Cassian pulled open the door, and who was with him but Meneer Dietz! It had been months since she'd seen him. The man's face was brightly sunburned, and that plus his scowl made him more repulsive.

"Come in, come in," Cassian said to Minke.

She expected to see Tessa inside. She actually *hoped* to see Tessa in spite of the fact that she hadn't liked the woman much. But the very prospect of talking to a woman, any woman, *and* in her own language brought sweet relief. She fumbled through the introduction of Pieps to the two men, looking around for Tessa. "Is Mevrouw Dietz here?"

Dietz shook his head. "She won't travel. She's hoping you might see fit to visit her."

"Yes!" Minke said without a second thought. "Of course I will."

"I brought her horse for you to ride. It has a lady's saddle."

"You mean now?"

Dietz threw open his hands. "Now, tomorrow. I don't care. I'll be in town for some time. You go at your convenience."

"Then today," Minke said.

Cassian laughed. "Not so quickly, Minke. It's a long ride, eh, Dietz?"

"Several hours."

Cassian turned to Minke. "If night falls before you arrive, you won't have an easy time finding the estancia in the dark." He paused. "Do you know how to ride, Minke?"

"No."

"I do," Pieps said.

"Go along, then, the two of you. Teach her to ride," Dietz said, making a flicking motion with his fingers. "If she learns quickly, you can go tomorrow."

"You'll need to ask Sander," Cassian said.

"I can learn to ride without asking Sander." Minke clearly needed to learn to ride in Comodoro. "Besides, Sander is busy." She ran outside to see the horses again. They snuffled in the dirt, looking for something to eat. "Which is mine?"

Dietz and Pieps saddled the horses. Dietz gave her a leg up, and she found herself suddenly up high on this large animal and having to slip her right knee over the pommel on the side, arrange the folds of her red dress, and clutch the reins, all while the horse danced backward.

"Relax the reins," Pieps said, and as if by magic, the horse stopped. "Gentle," he went on. "The animal should be under your control. Not a step taken that you don't wish him to take. But command with kindness."

They set off at a walk. Back around the Cerro and then, instead of going into the town, they headed away, out to the plains toward the gaucho camp. The saddle, although comfortable once she was aloft, was unlike any she had ever seen. Instead of sitting astride, as people did in the Netherlands, she sat with both her legs to the left, as if climbing sideways up a ladder. Once or twice the horse broke into a trot, and she bounced along, hanging on to the pommel for dear life. If she moved in opposition to the horse's gait, the ride became smooth. It took a long time to get it right, but she was determined, and Pieps told her she was a natural. Up down, up down.

"Can we see the gaucho camp?" she asked Pieps.

He took off at a canter, and she followed to the camp. Several fires still burned, and animal bones littered the area around them. At home such fires would never be allowed to go unattended, but here there was only dirt and gravel, nothing to catch fire. Most of the gauchos had gone to town, but a few remained, sitting around one of the fires, eating meat from a spit. One spoke with Pieps in Spanish, and then a broad smile swept across his face. He lifted his hat to Minke. They wore odd hats, she thought, with the brim sharply up in front and down in back. The shoes were even more bizarre, made from the hide of a horse's back legs, with the bends serving as heels and leaving the toes bare where the hoof had been removed. She said, "*Buenos días.*"

A figure approached fast on horseback—Goyo in a blur of dust, grinning widely with those big white teeth. He spoke to Pieps, and she recognized the words "señor" and "señora." "Your husband would like us to come back," Pieps said.

Minke said adios, and the three rode back to the Explotación, where Goyo hobbled their horses. Inside, the bar was even fuller than it had been in the morning, smokier, more animated. The men were drinking liquor and playing cards. Sander was at the same table in back where

Minke had eaten breakfast. She slipped in beside him and grasped his hand under the table, excited to tell him of her adventure.

"I looked for you in the room. You weren't there. That gaucho saw you out running a horse." Sander withdrew his hand.

She indicated the bar, the noise. "I feel too strange in this hotel, with so many new people. I went to Cassian's instead. You've always told me to seek Cassian out when I needed something."

"But you were not at Cassian's. You were out running horses. What's gotten into you?"

Then she remembered. But of course! Sander didn't know about Dietz being there with the horses or that Cassian had given his blessing for the riding lesson. "Dietz is at Cassian's with two horses, Sander. He wants me to visit Tessa, who is ill and unhappy, and I want to go. I wasn't running horses, I was learning to ride, and I'm quite good at it. I'd like to go so much."

"Dietz is in town?"

"You'll be so busy, and what can I do here in Comodoro? If I go to visit Tessa, I'll be safe, and you won't need to worry about me."

Sander turned to Pieps. "You, boy, go to Dr. Tredegar's and invite the doctor and Meneer Dietz to come join us."

Minke whispered, "Sander, please! He's not a servant."

"He's a skinner, Minke." Sander ran a hand over his face.

"I brought you Goyo," she said with a petulance she knew he wasn't going to appreciate. "I thought you'd be happy."

"Look at yourself," he said. "Like a child with your hair all wild like that. You're my wife, Minke. Behave like it." He took a sip of brandy and blotted his lips with a napkin. "I need to know I can trust you."

"Trust me! How can you say that? It's not fair." She poked him in the arm to get a rise out of him. "Astrid would have taught me to ride if she'd lived, remember? But Astrid is dead, and there are no women who will teach me anything, in case you haven't noticed. The women here ignore me. They speak no Dutch. They don't even meet my eyes when I pass. It's as if I don't exist, so what am I supposed to do? Maybe if I had a child, they would treat me better, but I don't. I'm either alone or with men, and not by choice!"

He finished off his glass in a single swallow and waved for another. She had to control her voice. She was afraid of making a scene, aware of being watched wherever she went, whatever she did. He didn't trust her! How was that possible? She knew nothing of men, nothing at all, apparently. And even less of Sander. Perhaps he needed reassurance. Perhaps that was it. She slipped her hand over his under the table and was encouraged when he didn't remove it. "Our nights, my love," she whispered, leaning in to him to breathe her words into his neck, desperate for him to understand. "I *live* for our nights." She looked into his eyes. "You have to believe me." He smiled, but she wasn't convinced. "When you're angry with me, I have no one, Sander. I'm alone."

"They're here." He withdrew his hand and gestured to Dietz and Cassian. When Pieps made a move to join them as well, Sander stopped him. "This is a business meeting, young man. I'm afraid there isn't room."

She nudged him but was not about to press things any further, and Pieps had the grace to bow and withdraw.

They crowded around the little table, a haze of smoke resting overhead, a loud game of faro in a corner. Glasses and bottles were crammed on the table; a big bowl in the middle was filling with the ash from the men's cigars. Cassian raised his glass. "Dietz has struck oil, Sander. Imagine that." Those two had an understanding. She'd seen it often enough, as though they shared a secret language, so Cassian's remark wasn't so much praise of Dietz but something quite the opposite.

"Here, here," Sander said, clinking glasses with Dietz and Cassian. "Where, may I ask?"

"To the west." Dietz motioned vaguely with his free hand. "It's just as they said. We float on a sea of oil here in Comodoro."

Minke knew that only too well. Here and there canals of oil flowed in the open air. From the Cerro, those same streams resembled black ribbons glistening in the sun.

Dietz folded his hands over his belly. "And you, Sander? How is your business coming along?"

"Magnificent, eh, Cassian?"

Cassian nodded.

"Good for you, my friend," Dietz said. "Good for you."

"I understand Tessa wishes Minke to visit," Sander said.

"Where's that boy?" Dietz stood up and looked about the bar. "You!" he shouted. "Over here!" Pieps was instantly at the table. "I saw you ride today. You can accompany Mevrouw DeVries to my estancia."

"Wait a minute, now," Sander said. "I'll decide who's to accompany my wife. This boy is a skinner."

"Goyo is your man, then," Pieps said. "He knows every inch of Patagonia." Pieps signaled the gaucho, who rose and approached. Dietz addressed Goyo in rapid Spanish, and the conversation became a spirited three-way among Dietz, Goyo, and Cassian. When it was over, Cassian said to Sander, "It's done. He knows the estancia. You will pay them both, the money to be given to them on Minke's safe return in several days' time."

"Both?" Sander said. "No, no. Only the gaucho."

"Sander," Cassian said, "he's a good sort, but if something should happen, one man needs to stay while the other goes for help. It's the way these things are done."

"Splendid," Dietz said. "Then it's settled. Oh, and Minke, bring medicine to Tessa. She's run out already."

Minke eyed Sander warily. He'd been all in favor until Pieps got in the mix, and now he was unhappy, the lines of his mouth drawn down at the corners. "We must move our things to the house now that it's ready."

"All the more reason for her to be gone," Dietz roared, grinding out his cigar. "A lady shouldn't be asked to do that, Sander. Look around you. A dozen strong backs in this room are for hire."

"He's right, my friend," Cassian said.

"Go ahead, then," Sander said, without even looking at her.

SHE WAS TOO excited to sleep, and when at last she began to nod off, she was awakened by the sound of breaking glass. She sat up and checked her watch. Two A.M. This was their last night together, and Sander was spending it drinking and probably gambling in the hotel bar. She went to the window. Outside, a skim of light snow blew across the sand. She'd just go get him.

She covered herself with his robe, a striped woolen thing, heavy as a horse blanket, and tiptoed down the hall toward the chaos of the bar, where another glass or bottle of something smashed. A pair of glass doors separated the hall from the foyer of the hotel. She peered through to the table and spittoon, the shabby Persian rug and gas lamp. She drew back when two men stumbled from the bar into the foyer, bumping into each other, laughing, ready to go out into the cold night, bulky in their heavy coats and hats. They stopped at the door outside and, as if something had suddenly sobered them, cast a quick glance back toward the bar and kissed the way a man and woman kissed. In that same moment she recognized one of them as Cassian and almost called out to him but didn't. He obviously didn't want to be seen. She felt both shock and calm, as though this, whatever it was, was something she'd known all along. He swung open the door, and the two vanished into the night. She stood rooted in place. Now she understood the boys on the *Frisia*, the sense she often had when visiting him that someone else was present in the house.

She slipped into the foyer and peered into the Explotación bar. The smoke made it difficult to find Sander, but she made out the back of his head—tawny in this crowd of black-haired men—at the table in the corner. He was playing cards with Dietz and several other men. A stranger staggered toward her, blinded by drink, and she scurried back to her room, locked the door, and lay on the bed, listening.

Sander didn't come back. At daybreak, a loud knocking woke her. She'd barely undone the latch when Sander charged into the room and fell facedown on the bed.

"I leave soon for Tessa's," she said to the back of his head.

He made a growl of assent.

"You were gone all night."

He rolled onto his back. "Little Minke is angry at her Sander." He pulled the pockets out of his pants so they stuck out like a pair of big white ears.

"You lost all our money?"

He seemed to think it was very funny. "Not all."

"How *could* you?"

"Come on. Come to Papa."

"You're not my papa."

"Come here."

Reluctantly, she sat beside him on the bed.

"Give poor Sander a smile."

He was being so silly she couldn't help herself.

"Do something for me?"

She sighed. "What?"

"Find out about Dietz."

"Find out what?" she asked.

"Anything at all." He rolled onto his back and shut his eyes.

8

THE HORSES WERE tied to the rail in front of the hotel, prancing and snorting warm breath in the frigid air. Pieps, Goyo, and Cassian were waiting, and as soon as she came through the door, Pieps and Goyo mounted. Cassian wove his fingers together for a leg up into the saddle. She felt bulky in her coat, wool mittens, a hat, and heavy scarf, which she pulled up over her nose against the wind. Underneath, she was wearing her wedding dress again, the only dark one she owned, tattered at the hem from walking through the muck and ice.

"Sander worked late into the night," she said over the wind and the anxious sidestepping of the horses, hoping to explain away his absence.

Cassian said something in Spanish to Goyo, blew her a kiss with the fingers of both hands, and the three were off into the bright, cold day. They moved along at a canter out of town toward the rolling hills. It was amazing how quickly her spirits lifted in the presence of the majesty spread before her. The pampas, she thought with a thrill. An eternity ago she had sat at Sander's dinner table while Griet spoke with disdain of the pampas and the filth of the gauchos. Now she watched Goyo's back. The man was nothing short of magnificent. He sat his horse as if one with it, he and the beast moving in unison. Every so often he would take off at a gallop, come back smiling broadly, and they would continue on. None of them spoke, but there was comfort in the silence, and she felt bound to them and small in the midst of such splendor.

Over low swells of land, they traveled to terrain that was flat as a table and where shallow pools as big as lakes had formed from the rains and now were covered in the thinnest veneer of ice. Goyo galloped through them, sending up arcs of water. She dug her heels into the sides of the horse and galloped as well, to her own great clattering of hooves and sprays of water. Occasionally, a herd of cattle was to be seen and, once in a while, a distant horseman, but otherwise they saw no one on their journey. Twice Pieps pointed out clusters of trees marking estancias in the distance. Trees, he explained, had to be cultivated here. They didn't grow on their own.

In the early afternoon, cold and stiff from the journey, they came to a wide river. Goyo pointed across it to a hill rising sharply on the opposite bank and spoke to Pieps, who translated. Apparently, Dietz's estancia was at the top of that hill, and they would have to ford the river. The horses circled, snorted, and stamped their hooves in their reluctance to cross. Goyo made a hissing sound that calmed them for a while, but it was clear the water made them nervous. Minke had never seen such a river, so swift and frothing over rocks, almost placid at the center where it was deepest.

Without a word, Goyo plunged his horse into the river. "Watch him," Pieps said to Minke. "So you'll know what to do." Her heart pounded as she took in every detail. Goyo let the reins go slack, lay forward on the horse's neck, and held the mane in both hands. The horse took cautious, unwilling steps into the rushing water, its hooves sounding on underwater stones. When the water was up to its chest, Pieps said, "The horse will swim now." He cocked his head. "Scared?"

"Of course not." She was terrified, but if they could do this, so could she.

"Good girl."

Goyo's horse sank low until only its head showed above the water, straining high to keep its nostrils clear. Goyo slid off the left side. She stifled a scream, afraid he had fallen and would be washed away, but Pieps laughed. "He did that for you. You may need to do as he does."

Goyo held on to long leather strings that trailed from the saddle, his body pressed against his horse by the current. He slipped well behind his horse, where he had the animal by the tail. He was pulled along until the horse regained her footing on the opposite bank. Goyo swung back into the saddle. The horse gave a violent shake and water pinwheeled, glistening in the sun. Minke's mare danced, sidestepped, threw her head.

Pieps drew up alongside. "Stay in the saddle if you can. If you go in, grab anything. Best is the tail. Don't get in front of your horse by any means. Do you understand? It's opposite in water from on land. Behind the horse is safe. In front is not." He gave her horse a slap on the rump, and she was on her way. The horse moved reluctantly forward.

"I wasn't ready!" she screamed at him over the rush of water.

"You are now," he shouted back. "Give her your heels!"

She kicked hard, leaned down on the mare's steaming neck, pressed her cheek to the warm fur and gripped the mane in her mittened hands. Icy water filled her boots and flooded over her coat and skirts. She hung on, water up to her waist now, everything soaked through, and in only moments the horse was swimming with a lurching grace that made it easy to keep her seat. Then the whole ordeal was over, the horse clattered over stones and out of the water, and she'd stayed on. Pieps was right behind her, coming up on the bank. "Hang on hard," he shouted, and at that moment her horse shook like a dog from the head all the way back, the great barrel of a midsection throwing her this way and that. Pieps was laughing and pointing up the hill, where Goyo had already begun the climb.

At the crest of the hill, the land flattened again onto a vast steppe, on the other side of which, way in the distance, higher mountains began in earnest. The estancia came into view, a long, low building made of dark brick, its roof thatched with rushes, and standing in a grove of naked willow trees. The three galloped toward it, clattered over the brick terrace, and dismounted quickly. Pieps and Goyo hurried the horses toward the barn, which was separate from the house by about a hundred feet, leaving Minke alone to rap at the door, shaking all over, teeth chattering. When no one answered, she entered, stooping under the low door and into a white-plastered room with a brick floor. "Hello?" she called. No answer. The furniture was made of black and white cattle skins stretched over frames. Little figurines crowded every table surface, and paintings of saints hung on the walls. "Tessa?"

From deeper in the house came the squawk of birds. Shivering, she crept from room to room, stooping at each low door and calling Tessa's name until she found her. Tessa was sitting up in bed, her pink face puffy and bulging over the stiff collar of her gown. A blue parrot sat on one shoulder, and several smaller yellow birds flew about the room in alarm.

"Tessa." Minke managed the word through chattering teeth.

Tessa rolled from the bed. Although it was midafternoon, she still had on her nightclothes and smelled a little ripe. "Well, well. I didn't know if you'd come." She hugged Minke to her large bosom and recoiled. "Ach! You're soaking wet!"

"We c-c-c-crossed the river."

Tessa pouted, considering, then led the way down a dark hallway. Minke followed along unsteadily until they reached a small room in which some clothing lay folded on a long bench. "Put those on," Tessa said, winded, and lowered herself into a chair.

Minke removed her clothing, too cold for modesty. It took a long time with her stiff fingers. Her coat and dress dropped to the floor, and when she accidentally stepped on the pile, water squished from it. Her skin was blue.

"So," Tessa said with a frown when Minke had finished. "Look at you in my Astrid's clothing."

She should have recognized Astrid's gray skirt and black blouse. "Oh, Tessa, there must be something else I can wear until my clothing dries. I don't want to bring you pain."

Tessa shouted for someone, and an Indian girl appeared, scooped up the wet clothing from the floor, and fled.

"Who was that?"

"Just one of the servants."

"You have a lovely home."

"You should have seen my house in Amsterdam. Does my husband send news?"

"No news, only medicine."

Tessa lit up. "You brought it?"

"In my bag."

"Let's go get it before we forget." She lumbered from the room, the parrot rooted to her shoulder. The house was a chain of rooms connected by a narrow hallway. "Don't go in there," Tessa cautioned at one of the doors. "It's Frederik's study. He knows when things have been touched."

The room Minke was to sleep in was at the back, with a narrow bed under the window, a table, and a door to the outside. The estancia walls were so thick that the windowsill was as deep as a table. The brick floor was covered in carpets that overlapped here and there. Minke's case had already been brought to the room. She rummaged among her things and found the package Dietz had given her for Tessa, who slipped it into the pocket of her dressing gown.

"How did you get here?" Tessa asked.

"I rode one of your mares. I was accompanied by the gaucho Goyo and Pieps from the ship."

Tessa's face soured. "Are they in the house?"

"They took the horses to the barn."

"Don't let them in the house. They'll steal."

"They won't!" Minke said. "They're fine men, both of them. You have nothing to fear."

"Elisabeth would have seen things my way."

"You *knew* her?" That came as a surprise.

"Of course. And the children." Tessa's chubby hand batted the air.

"You knew Sander before we sailed?" She hated to belie her ignorance all the time, but here it was again. She thought they'd all met for the first time on the *Frisia*.

"In Amsterdam everybody knows everybody. Come, I'll show you the estancia, such as it is."

Minke's room gave onto a courtyard where the dirt floor was hardened to a shine. Opposite was the kitchen, where two women were at work. Neither one raised her eyes, but Minke recognized the younger as the one who'd taken away the wet clothing. Beyond the kitchen and across another courtyard was an enormous heap, as high as the house, of dried stalks. "Wild artichoke," Tessa said, anticipating the question. "The stuff burns like tissue and throws off no heat. Ach! This country!"

Pieps and Goyo were tending the horses outside the barn. Pieps straightened, but Goyo kept working. They were a sight, Minke thought. Both men filthy and foul-smelling, still wet, the horses steaming in the cold air. Goyo's hair lay in tangles across his shoulders. He was seeing to his horse, carefully combing out its tail.

"How long will these men be here?" Tessa asked.

"As long as I am," Minke said. "They'll see me home again."

Goyo kept on combing his horse.

"Perhaps you remember Pieps from the *Frisia*," Minke said. Tessa shook her head. "He taught me to ride your mare." Minke ventured, "Astrid said she would teach me. She must have been a fine rider. I miss her terribly."

"We'll have tea," Tessa said, turning to leave. "And I mean real tea, not that dreadful maté they drink. You," she said, turning back to address Pieps. "You can sleep in the barn, if you like, and him"—she motioned to Goyo, who was still ignoring her in favor of his horse—"those people sleep outside even when there's a roof available." She shook her head and headed back toward the house. Minke whispered quickly to Pieps, "Please excuse her. She grieves for her daughter."

They settled into the parlor at the front of the house on the rawhide chairs before the fire. Minke had stopped shivering but was exhausted and now deliciously drowsy from the heat and fighting off a powerful desire to sleep. The blue parrot flew hugely into the room and found its way back to Tessa's shoulder. "It's a backward country, don't you agree?" Tessa asked.

"But it's also beautiful," Minke said. "The sea, the mountains."

Tessa smiled. "You're blinded by love."

"He treats me like a princess."

Tessa jutted her lip. "It was like that for me once."

The serving girl came in with tea just then, and Minke thanked her.

"Don't thank them. They're only doing their jobs," Tessa said once the girl was gone. She fumbled in her pocket and removed the package of medicine, poured a few drops into her tea, and sipped.

"And Meneer? He does well with his oil drilling?"

"Who wants to know?" Tessa eyed her shrewdly, stuffing the package back into her pocket.

"That was his purpose in coming to Argentina, yes?"

"Are you hungry?" Tessa passed a platter of bread to Minke. "I look at you and mistake you for my Astrid. Then I remember."

Minke had the urge to put her arms around the woman and soothe her. It must be the worst thing in the world to lose a child. "I'll change into my other clothes as soon as they dry."

"I need to accept the fact that I have no child," Tessa said.

Minke bit into the bread. "We're both in the same situation, in many ways," she offered. "European women alone in a country where there are no other women to talk to. It can be lonely. We can be allies."

"If she hadn't been up on deck with you that day and caught a chill, she mightn't have died."

Minke looked blankly at Tessa. "The wave just rolled over us."

"You knew she was frail."

"You blame me?"

"They never should have thrown her into the sea. It was barbaric."

"I thought so, too, at the time." If Tessa needed to lash out in her grief, Minke could withstand the assault.

"Your husband was behind that."

"No, he wasn't. Sander deferred to Captain Roemer. The owner defers to the captain in such matters."

"Owner?" Tessa came to life. "Owner? Sander DeVries?"

"I thought so." The whole business of ship ownership was murky. Minke tried to recall where she'd gotten the idea in the first place. Mama? Before Sander ever came to the house that day, people had said he owned ships.

"Sander is scarcely the owner of the *Frisia*."

This was going all awry. Minke was supposed to be learning about Dietz, and here she was being interrogated. She sat up straight, smoothed her skirt. "Your husband was telling us about his many oil discoveries."

Tessa shut her eyes for several moments. Her whole face seemed to melt. "There," she said with a sigh. "That's better now, once the medicine takes hold."

"You're not well?"

"How could I be well after what I've suffered? The loss of my Astrid has been a knife plunged into my heart."

"I understand."

"No, you don't. How could you? A child yourself."

"You have your husband."

"I can still have a child, you know. The doctors have said."

"Of course you can."

"Tell me what's become of that car?" Tessa asked in an almost lilting voice.

"I saw it yesterday," Minke said, relieved for the change in subject. "It's in storage most of the time, I suppose, along with Sander's other goods."

"What goods might those be, dear?"

"For our store," Minke said. "All kinds of things. Splendid fabrics and art objects."

Tessa fed her parrot bits of bread. "That car is his pride and joy, isn't it? His only real possession."

"Tessa, you do say such odd things."

"Mmmm," Tessa said, her eyes at half-mast. "And Dr. Tredegar. He's well?"

"Very."

"A fairy," Tessa said dreamily. "Did you know that about him? He moves from place to place because of it, just a few steps ahead of the law."

"It pains me to hear you speak of him unkindly."

"Not unkind, just factual. What he does with other men is illegal, of course. But ach, those people can't help themselves." Tessa sniffed. "Whether they're kind to you or not."

"He would never hurt us."

"Elisabeth never liked him, you know."

"How well did you know Elisabeth?" Minke asked, and then added before Tessa could respond, "She wanted us to marry."

Tessa shook with laughter, and the bird flapped its ratty wings. "Says who?"

"Sander."

"And you believe him."

"I was very close to her," Minke said. "Of course I believe him."

Tessa poured another bit of medicine into her cool tea and drank it down. "This place can make a person go mad. Perhaps you're right about Elisabeth. I don't know. I don't know anything. You should excuse me." She closed her eyes and rocked back and forth while the lines of her face loosened. "No matter. We will leave here soon. Frederik has promised."

"Oh?" At last she was finding out something that would interest Sander.

"The Germans will pay us very well. Very, *very* well." Tessa's eyes opened a slit. "And then we can go."

"Perhaps Sander will have oil wells," Minke said. "There's so much of it to be had."

Tessa gave her a frown that said *Are you crazy?* "The land is all spoken for. That happened two years ago." She sneezed, causing the parrot to lose its balance again. "I must sleep now."

AT BREAKFAST, TESSA fussed about Pieps and Goyo again, wanting to know where they were at every minute. Minke said she'd go look for them and found them in the barn, tending to one of the Dietzes' mares. She was happy to see their open smiles and cheerful greetings. Goyo said something, and Pieps translated. "He asks if you're enjoying yourself in the company of Mevrouw Dietz."

"She's my hostess," Minke said.

Pieps translated again, and Goyo shook his head. "For Goyo, they commit the worst of crimes. Take a look here." Pieps ran his hand down the mare's flank. "Saddle sores. The coat is dull. They're not well fed, and look at Mevrouw. She's very well fed!"

"She's mad with grief over her daughter," Minke said.

Pieps translated for Goyo, who spat in the dirt.

"I can't stay," Minke said. "She just wants to know where you are."

"I'll bet she does!" Pieps said.

When Minke arrived back, Tessa was allowing the parrot to walk on the table and eat from the food that was laid out. "And?" Tessa asked.

"They're tending the horses," Minke said. "They're quite fine."

"You look—" Tessa said, studying her. "Are you pregnant?"

Minke had no answer. What a thing to ask!

"Oh, come on. You're a married woman. Don't be so modest. Do you get sick? Are you tired?"

She was tired, that was true, and it was a peculiar kind of fatigue that overtook her from time to time, so that she might fall into leaden sleep anywhere. Indeed, she'd almost fallen asleep on the horse the day before, when they were crossing mile after mile at a walk. "A little tired," she said, taking in the enormity of the new possibility.

"Ach! Poor girl, a baby in this place. I pity you." Tessa piled a slice of bread with jam, took a bite, and said, crumbs flying, "Make them boil everything. Everything! When your time comes, I'll come to Comodoro to help you. It's June." She counted on her fingers. "I predict the baby will come at the end of the year, summer here. At least that's a good thing."

"It can't be June already." Tessa had to be mistaken. True, Minke had no sense of passing time. There were no calendars in the hotel. But June?

Tessa's eyelids lowered, and Minke realized she must have taken more medicine while Minke was out seeing to Pieps and Goyo. "Your husband will be pleased?" Tessa said.

Pregnant.

"I understand Pim inherited Elisabeth's house." Tessa's voice was thick and dreamy.

Minke was utterly shaken by the idea of a baby but loath to show it. "Sander thought it best for him." The bird pecked at her plate, lurching its neck to swallow. "We won't be in Comodoro long, either. Like you. We'll no doubt go back to Amsterdam."

"I don't think so," Tessa whispered.

The woman really was quite impossible. "We plan to return to Enkhuizen for a visit." There was, of course, no such plan, but Minke felt the need to put up armor against Tessa.

Tessa shook her head.

"What now, Tessa?"

"It was the talk of the ship. You didn't know, because you were off with my Astrid." The heavy lids lifted. She still wore her beige nightdress with its matching woolen robe. Her hair hung down her back in a long unkempt red braid. "The conference at The Hague?"

"I don't know what you're talking about and you know it, so just tell me."

"Sander imports opium for the manufacture of morphine. You didn't know this. I can tell from the look on your face. You married a man without knowing what he did."

"I know about the morphine. Of course I do. Cassian produces it."

"They both do, but no longer in the Netherlands." Tessa snapped her fingers dully. "Just like that. Suddenly, it's illegal to import opium, and anyone connected to it is criminal and their property seized. Sander is no longer welcome in the Netherlands." She sighed. "I'm personally grateful, of course. Without my morphine, the pain I feel over Astrid would be excruciating." Tessa slumped back in her chair. "I must become pregnant. I just must or I will lose my mind. It's so easy for you but not for me." She pushed herself from the table and stood. "I need to lie down for a bit."

"Wait, Tessa." Minke caught the sleeve of her robe.

"That's all there is," Tessa said with a disinterested shrug. "I've told you everything." With that, she took her parrot and was gone.

Her mind on fire with this information, Minke walked outside. The sky was ice blue, not a single cloud. She wrapped her arms around herself to ward off the cold. Frozen shallow lakes sparkled in the morning sun. The hills were painted in layers of purple.

So Sander did not own the *Frisia*. He had not owned the house. It was Elisabeth's to pass along to Pim, not Sander's. Sander's business was *all* to do with opium. That day in Amsterdam when Minke slapped her face, Griet had said there was plenty more, and now Minke understood. But still, it was medicine. What was wrong with that?

It was the talk of the ship.

She walked farther out onto the plains.

Pregnant.

Could Tessa be correct? How would she know for sure? Where was Mama when she needed her more than anyone? She racked her brain for what she knew about birth. Women at home had children, but the children just seemed to come. And it wasn't ever discussed. Ever! The women who had babies spent time indoors for months before the baby was born. The confinement, it was called. And they grew very fat. What went on? How did it happen? Worst of all, how did the baby come out? Was it cut from the mother? Whom could she ask? Not Tessa. Minke would be too humiliated to have the woman explain one more thing. How did it all connect, though? The courses, the nausea, the confinement?

She walked farther along, hands protectively over her belly. She was very cold. She stopped walking. She would ask Cassian. Of course! He would explain. He would help her. Oh yes. She clapped her hands and headed back.

A baby.

The idea finally sent a thrill through her. She fairly danced her way to the barn in search of Pieps and Goyo.

"You're looking very happy," Pieps said.

"I am many, many things right now," she said.

They'd built a small fire, and Goyo turned a spit with some meat that still had the skin and hair attached, causing her to look away. Pieps offered her his seat, an upside-down wooden bucket. The fire felt lovely on her hands and feet.

"We leave tomorrow, I think," she said. "Will that do for you?"

"We can leave now if you want," Pieps said.

"Tomorrow," Minke said. "One day early, not two. As it is, I'll have to make an excuse." She wanted to see Sander as soon as she could. And she needed to speak to Cassian before she talked to Sander. She'd go directly to his house when they got back and find out what was what.

"Goyo has been speaking to Juana in the kitchen." Pieps bounced on his heels, warming his hands over the fire. "All Mevrouw does is eat, sleep, and teach the bird to speak. But the bird is deaf."

Minke smiled. It explained the quiet parrot.

"Have you been into Meneer's study?" Pieps asked, looking up at her with a devilish grin.

"No one is allowed," Minke said.

"He keeps shrunken heads."

"Oh, Pieps, please. Don't make up stories."

"It's done in the Amazon, Goyo told me. They remove the bone and sew the eyes and mouth shut." Pieps held up his fist. "A head shrinks to this size. Meneer has a collection."

"That's grotesque. Why would you want to see such a thing?"

Pieps considered the question. "Because I may never have the chance again, that's why. Because I'm interested in the customs of the Indians, and because Mevrouw Dietz treats us so badly. It would be fun to disobey her."

"She'd kill us if she caught us. I can't."

"I see," Pieps said.

"What's that supposed to mean?"

"This from the girl who wanted to see steerage. You came below all by yourself in spite of the danger, just for a look, and now you stand in my way when I want to see? One rule for you and another for me."

"This is different," she said. "I didn't know of the danger. I didn't know I wasn't allowed."

Pieps translated everything for Goyo. She could tell by his tone that he was making her sound unreasonable. Goyo tore at a piece of meat with his teeth and jutted his chin like someone considering both sides of an argument.

"If you'd been caught belowdecks, Minke, it would have been far worse. A pretty woman like you. Any woman, actually."

Pretty? Well, now. He thought she was pretty. Goyo stared, daring her to go, she assumed. He said something. "He agrees with me," Pieps said. She sighed and gave in. She and Pieps would swap one danger for another. If they were going to do it, though, it would have to be right that minute, while Tessa slept her morphine sleep.

"We take nothing," Minke said.

Pieps jumped up and offered his hand.

"What of Goyo?" she asked.

"He won't enter the house of people for whom he has no respect."

THEY ENTERED BY the door farthest from Tessa's bedroom and tip-toed to the study door. The lock was large but primitive, and Pieps was able to gain access by jiggling it with a bent horseshoe nail. The room was small as a closet, shuttered and dark, the only light coming from the open door. Pieps swung it wider.

"She'll see us!" Minke said.

"We need the light."

"Quickly," she said.

The desk was barely visible at first. Pieps took up a paper spike on which bits of paper were impaled. He took them to the door to see. "IOUs," he said. "People seem to owe Dietz a great deal of money." He paused. "There!"

She barely made them out, small brown misshapen objects in a row on a shelf. Pieps took one, held it for a moment, passed it to her, and before she knew it, she had her hand around a thick mass of hair. She took it to the door, the better to see. The skin was dark and as hard as leather. Long strings hung from the corners of the eyes and mouth where they had been sewn shut, a thought that reminded her, with a shiver, of Astrid sewn into her shroud. How had it happened to this man, a life snuffed out and then kept on a shelf for the pleasure of that boor Dietz?

How could she help but think of her own baby, tiny and delicately forming, its bones still soft, its hair not yet begun? She practically threw the thing back to Pieps. "It's bad luck." She should not have exposed herself, exposed the baby, to this. "Let's go. This is a terrible place."

"Wait." Pieps had a box and opened it with the same horseshoe nail he'd used on the door. "Oh, Jesus," he said. "Take a look at this." He held up a bundle of thousand-guilder notes. "There are boxes more in here. Lots more."

"We have to leave. Right now." The longer she stayed in that evil room, the more harm would befall her baby, she was sure of it.

She peered up and down the hall. Nothing. Pieps locked the door behind them, and they hurried through the parlor and into the courtyard. He was grinning and dancing around. "We've seen shrunken heads, Minke. Aren't you glad you did that?"

She might be sick. "No."

"What is it?"

"I feel awful."

"You're green."

"I'm going to faint."

Pieps caught her in his arms before she could fall. She came to immediately and took a deep reviving breath.

"Well, well, well." Tessa waddled from the house toward them, her face pink with rage, shaking a finger. "I take you in. I feed you and your men. I confide in you, and *this* is how you repay me? You enter my husband's study when I specifically told you not to. I *heard* you. I *saw* you. And with *him,* no less! And now kissing him!" She shook with anger. "You're nothing but a little Dutch whore."

Minke pulled herself away from Pieps. "I was not kissing him!"

"Leave. And take off my Astrid's clothing. You'll wear your own, whether they've dried or not."

Back in her room, Minke struggled with her clothing, her whole body burning with the shame of entering the study and then being accused of kissing Pieps. When she was dressed, she knocked on Tessa's door. "Mevrouw," she said, cracking the door. Tessa lay in bed stroking the parrot. "I apologize very deeply, Mevrouw. It was wrong of me to betray your hospitality." She stared down at the floor. "But I was not kissing Pieps. I would never do such a thing. I was holding on to him. I felt unwell." Still, shame made her bones ache.

Without even looking at her, Tessa held out a sealed envelope. "Deliver this to my husband in Comodoro."

TO FORD THE river, they rode an extra half hour upstream, where the water was only as high as the horses' knees, so they wouldn't be soaked for the long ride home. Minke sat folded over, head down against the wind and hands under her arms for warmth. Pieps cantered forward to ride beside her. "I'm to blame," he said.

"We both acted badly."

In her pocket, the letter for Meneer burned. No doubt it would tell him of her infamy, and he would take great pleasure in telling Sander. With stiff fingers, she removed the letter, limp from being pressed against her damp clothes. The words had leached through the envelope. The flap had come loose. She could find out exactly what Tessa had said. She could throw it away.

But she would do neither. As Mama would say, the truth was always best. And if Sander didn't believe her? Then she would just throw herself into the sea and drown.

They'd ridden two hours when dark clouds rolled down from the west, blackening the air. Goyo's horse swung its silver rump this way and that, anticipating the first crack of lightning, which, when it came, illuminated the whole landscape ahead, just as Elisabeth had said. The rain pelted down. Crash after crash of lightning electrified the sky, with no shelter to be seen. Without a word, Goyo galloped into the storm. Pieps circled around her. "Give your horse her head! She'll follow him." Minke let the reins go slack, and the horse set off at a canter after Goyo. She hung on tightly to the pommel, head down, eyes raised only enough to watch the streaming ground directly ahead.

After a time, lights appeared in the distance, and the horses broke into a gallop after Goyo, rain beating at their faces, until they reached a small, low building. It was made of mud and held together by rushes. Goyo signaled to them to stay on their horses while he went inside. He came out again, gestured toward the door, and spoke to Pieps.

"He says we are welcome to enter while he takes the horses to shelter," Pieps said.

The doorway was even lower than the one at Tessa's, and Minke had to stoop to enter. Inside was a single room with eight or nine people warming themselves by a fire. A girl of about Minke's age regarded her with solemn interest. The girl had skin as white as Minke's and hair as black as Goyo's. An old woman, leather-skinned and smoking a spit-slick cigar, stood over a pot on the fire. Boiling meat; Minke knew the smell by now. A man with an immense black beard that spread across the width of his chest was the center of attention. He paused when they entered, nodded, and resumed telling a story in a voice so loud it was almost a shout.

Minke and Pieps settled down against the wall and listened. Pieps said it seemed to be about an armadillo outwitting a fox, and they both laughed. Goyo came in after seeing to the horses and sat beside them, and Minke had the delicious feeling of being safe between her friends while thrilling to her own situation—that she was pregnant—and her baby, still in the very early days of his life, was actually here, in this estancia, with such surprising people. She had never felt such joy and such contentment at once.

They slept where they were, and in the morning Goyo awakened them for a hasty breakfast of boiled meat and rice boiled in milk. There was a great commotion outside; a dozen or so horses were fully saddled, splendid in their silver tack, including heavy bell-shaped silver stirrups. The bearded man—his name was El Moreno, the dark one—took the lead.

"They're showing off for you," Pieps said with a wink.

The showing-off became dangerous. The men rode much too fast and shouted at one another. At first the shouts seemed only spirited, but then a hint of anger crept in. El Moreno spotted a guanaco—a beast that resembled a llama—at a distance and took off after it, swinging his *boleadoro*, three leather-bound stones on a long tether. He swung it round and round over his head, then let it fly, and the thing sailed through the air, wrapped like a whip around the legs of the animal, and brought it down. One of the other gauchos dropped from his horse, cut the animal's tendons with a half-moon-shaped knife, and the fight began in earnest.

"What's happening?" she asked Pieps. Even her horse had laid its ears flat back.

"El Moreno should have been the one to cut its leg." Everything happened quickly in a language she didn't know. A circle formed. El Moreno dismounted, wrapped his filthy poncho around his left arm, and held it up as a shield against the man who'd cut the guanaco.

"Come on," Pieps said. "We're leaving."

"Can't we watch?" She was beyond fascinated.

Pieps had her horse by the reins and was leading her quickly away. She kept looking back. "What about Goyo?"

"He's the one who said we must go."

"We don't know the way."

"In this country it's not so difficult." He pointed. "We go that way. Toward the sea."

"Will someone be killed?"

"Yes."

"Over a guanaco?"

"Over an insult."

They rode on. The weather was fine and clear after the storm. She thought about the gauchos, that at that very moment one of the men she'd seen had had his throat slit. "Is that where they are when they're not in Comodoro?"

"Some of them," Pieps said. "There are thousands more. They move about with their horses and cattle."

"But those people live in that estancia."

"They'll move on. Others will live there. There's little sense of ownership among the gauchos. Property ownership, I mean. Plenty of other ownership, as you just saw."

"How do you know all this?"

"Goyo. I'm as interested as you are. It is said that once a man has proved his prowess by killing his enemy, he is left in peace."

AT COMODORO, PIEPS offered to come with her to Cassian's, but she said no, she'd face Dietz alone. She tied up her horse next to Dietz's. Cassian appeared from one of the outbuildings, wearing black rubber gloves up to his elbows. He beamed when he saw her. "You're back early!"

Dietz appeared behind Cassian.

"Tessa sends you a letter," Minke said.

Dietz made a face at its damp, crumpled condition and put on his glasses.

She watched him read, her heart racing, willing herself strong.

"I see." He folded the letter and put it into his vest pocket.

"Come inside where it's warm, Minke." Cassian preceded her into the morphine works, where the boiling opium had made the air warm and humid.

"Tessa believes I'm pregnant."

It always amazed her how, up close, Cassian's skin wrinkled delicately when he smiled, how his eyelids were almost translucent, and how he found something amusing in whatever she said. "She does, eh?"

"She says December."

"She's the doctor." He took her heartbeat and asked her to lie back so he could feel her abdomen. "Indeed," he said. "Tessa is correct."

"How will the baby come out?" She hadn't meant to blurt that out, but she'd worked herself into a state over it.

"The same way it got in. Your mother surely told you, eh?"

"Not possible." Did Cassian have any idea how small that was?

"Trust me."

"Will it hurt?"

"I'll give you something."

When she left, she hoped to find Dietz gone, but he was waiting to escort her to the Explotación. "Did you like my wife's parrot?" he asked as they walked.

"It's deaf."

"So they say, so they say." As usual, he punctuated what he said with a laugh. They walked a few moments without speaking. "But how does anyone really know?" Dietz laughed loudly, a man bursting with his own amusement. "It's clear the parrot doesn't speak, but that only indicates it is mute. I think it understands everything that's said and simply plays dumb. Smart parrot, don't you think?"

Minke kept walking. The path was narrowing, and she ducked ahead so she could put distance between herself and him.

"An all-knowing parrot. It hears all and sees all, and then it whispers its secrets into my Tessa's ear," Dietz said.

She wished he would just shut up. Or, if he was going to say something to her about the letter, get it over with.

"The parrot must have seen you enter my study," Dietz said.

She loathed him. She stopped dead in her tracks and turned to face him. "What would possess anyone to own such things?"

"One day they'll fetch a good price," he said. "She's going mad. Do you agree?"

"Anyone would, way out there. She's alone too much. What do you expect?"

"I can't be doing for her what she should be doing for herself," he snapped.

Minke started walking again. "She shouldn't live so far from other people. She should be here."

"Look what it's done to you."

"What is that supposed to mean?"

They were the same height, eye to reptilian eye. He smiled at her. "Fucking that blond boy." His voice came out a thick whisper.

She raised her hand to slap him, but he caught it midair. "My wife is like her parrot. Nothing escapes her."

Minke wrenched away from him. "She's a liar."

"A shame if Sander were to find out."

"Sticks and stones, Meneer Dietz."

"Did you and the boy rob me, too?"

Oh, to hell with him, with his oil wells and foul breath. She ran toward town, toward the hotel, until she stopped cold in her tracks. How could she have forgotten that while she was away, Sander would have moved them to the new house? She backtracked, down toward the Almacén, left on Pellegrini. The house stood solitary, faint light leaching out through the seams. She ran to the back. "Sander!" she called. Her own house!

He held her at arm's length. Her coat was a dusty streaked mess, her hair disheveled. "What happened to you?"

"Let me see!" She broke away and ran from tiny room to tiny room, touching the bed, the little table, and more things she remembered from the house in Amsterdam that he must have brought for them. It was a palace! She was its mistress. She spun, arms out. "Oh, Sander!"

They sat side by side near the gas lamp in the new parlor, and she excitedly poured out the tale of her visit to Tessa Dietz. How her horse swam across a river, and then the parrot, and the terrible shrunken heads tied up with string. IOUs and money. She opened her hands wide. "This much." She told him of Dietz's plan to sell to the Germans. "Tessa was furious when she found us in his study!"

"Us?"

"Goyo found out about the heads from the servant, and Pieps found out from Goyo," she said without thinking. "But then Goyo refused to enter the house."

"So just you and the boy?"

"Yes."

"I see."

She flung herself against the back of her chair and kicked at the table leg. "Tessa told me you don't even own the *Frisia*," she said. "And that you had to flee the Netherlands because of your opium imports."

Sander gave her a quizzical look. "The *Elisabeth*," he said. "I own the *Elisabeth*, not the *Frisia*. Of course I don't own the *Frisia*. I was protecting the *Elisabeth*."

"From what?"

"The government."

"How can you protect a ship from the government?" He was making no sense to her.

"By sailing it far away, where it will not be seized."

She sighed. "Anyway, I'm pregnant."

He raised his eyes slowly to hers.

"Well?"

He took in a breath and sighed.

"Are you pleased?"

He nodded. "Of course."

How was it possible to fit so much happiness and so much dread into one heart? She was ecstatic to be pregnant and terrified that something would happen to undo her joy. She should tell him about Tessa's accusation and get it out in the open. But what if Sander didn't believe her? She'd been a fool not to have thrown away the letter when she had the chance.

$\mathcal{G}$

THE SS *ELISABETH* arrived in Comodoro harbor on June 21 at ten o'clock in the morning. The sun had not yet risen. Sky, sea, and land lay shrouded in darkness, and the ship twinkled with lights like the approach of a small village. People on shore moved about like shadows, waiting. Children darted, their small shapes leaping, running, using the cloak of darkness to throw pebbles at one another.

The ship moored offshore, and soon the tenders began to arrive, four oarsmen each, something Minke wouldn't have seen but for the lanterns at their bows. It was so cold, with blowing snow and the grunts of the men on the oars over the howling of the wind. She pulled in her coat, tucked in her face. It was darkest winter, and there would be no light for another hour; even then it would be nothing more than an hour's worth of milky gray, incapable of casting shadows.

The first tenders brought in a few dozen passengers, reminding Minke of the conundrum of Comodoro. The town should have eclipsed itself over and over; new people arrived every month, but they evaporated. They were taken by horse-drawn wagons inland to live in barracks and work in the oil wells. Only a few stayed in the town itself. The area's population must have doubled, and yet Comodoro itself remained much as it was when she arrived.

From her perch, huddled in her coat on the seawall, she saw how the beach was divided between Sander and Dietz. To the left was Sander, animated as he oversaw the loading of damp bales of raw opium onto waiting carts and sent them up the path and around the Cerro to Cassian's. Even at the distance at which she stood, she could breathe in its flowery smell. Morphine production ran many hours a

day now. Cassian had culled out a larger staff of young men from the
town, hardworking and good-natured, who ate and slept at *la morfina
obras*, the morphine factory. They were well paid, better paid than the
men who worked in Frederik Dietz's oil fields, where the work drew
desperate men. Knife fights sometimes broke out among them, and
everyone in Comodoro had heard the explosions when one of the
wells caught fire. Lives were lost, although the town showed no
evidence of it.

Dietz inhabited the other realm of the shore, strutting about, his
great bulk supported on little chicken legs, lining up the men who'd
come to work for him and assigning them to wagons that took them
away.

The last tenders carried merchandise for Sander's store, where the
white sign in front of the house now said EMPORIO DEVRIES. If you asked
Minke, the store was more of a museum. Most of the goods were still in
their boxes. Women of the village peeked in the door and stepped inside
for a look around, smiling shyly at Minke, talking among themselves in
rapid Spanish, picking things up, marveling at them, then slipping back
out the door without buying a single thing. The bolts of rich textiles and
elegant bits of furniture were too expensive, too out of place. It was like
buying a chandelier for a barn.

But the *obras* was doing well, and Minke felt sanguine as she watched
Sander raising tarpaulins and laughing with people. Everything was
falling into place. The baby had quickened inside her the week before.
The house was not only finished but had become a home to her, with its
cozy rooms and European furniture.

As the last wagon was loaded with the goods for the Emporio
DeVries, the first wagon returned full of crates rattling with brown
bottles of finished morphine, destined for shipment to buyers north up
the coast to a dozen ports, including Bahia Bustamente, Puerto Madryn,
and Buenos Aires. After the Antilles, the SS *Elisabeth* would turn around
and head south, arriving again in Comodoro on her way around the
Horn and back to the East Indies for more raw materials.

All around, men shouted in Spanish. Minke knew what they were saying from her time spent with Cassian's primer. She liked to translate into Spanish what she saw. "*El amanacer,*" she whispered to herself, and in English, "the rising sun." She practiced often with Cassian. "*Estoy feliz.*" She loved the rhythm of her new languages and, most of all, the absence of that sound so common in Dutch, like a man preparing to spit. "*Tu madre es una puta,*" one of the men shouted, and even that sounded lovely in spite of its meaning: Your mother is a whore. She had discovered that to hear such things aloud in a language not her own was very much more benign.

The sun had set by the time the work was done, and it was only four in the afternoon. Sander swung a torch up the ramp to her. He was wonderfully full of himself these days. He stood straighter, laughed easily. "Come on," he said, taking her hand. "We're going to the hotel. All of us. My treat." He fumbled in his coat pocket. "But first I have something for you."

She felt him clasp a necklace about her neck. Her fingers found its large links, the largest in the center, with a stone embedded. "Let me see!"

"In the mirror at the hotel," he said, and gave her a light tap on her bottom.

She twirled around, walked backward, facing him, and laughed. She was so happy. "Who will be there tonight?"

"Cassian, of course. Dietz, our Bertinat."

"The important men of Comodoro," she said.

"Indeed."

"Bertinat is very nice, but I think I scare him to death. He's so shy."

"A man afraid of his own shadow is always terrified by a beautiful woman. Did you hear what Bertinat calls you?"

She shook her head.

"*La princesa de* Comodoro."

Once when she was at the Almacén, Bertinat had invited her to climb the ladder that was attached to the shelves and could slide down the length of the store. He'd given her a ride on it, sending it down a row of shelves while she hung on for dear life, skirts flying. "Are you jealous?" she asked.

"Stark raving mad with it," he said, and they both laughed.

THE BAR AT the Explotación was crammed full, densely smoky, and loud tonight. Before going in, Minke removed her coat and ran to the mirror to see what Sander had put around her neck. A cameo, an ivory profile of a woman, but the greater surprise was her own reflection, something she hadn't seen in months. Her face was fuller than she remembered, from the pregnancy, no doubt. Her color was high from the cold. She smiled, turned this way and that, and strode into the bar with new confidence.

A large table, covered in a perfectly ironed white cloth, had been set for them in the center of the room. It seemed elevated somehow, but that was an illusion, a function of her excellent mood. The chair between Dietz and the amiable Bertinat had been saved for her. The men rose partly to their feet as she sat down. She'd learned her lesson well on the *Frisia*, turned to Bertinat to her left, and flashed princess eyes at him. She spoke in a voice for the whole table to hear and let her hand rest on his for a moment. She was heady with the arrival of Sander's ship. Everyone was. "A pleasure to sit beside you." *Un placer sentarme a tu lado.*

He was such a sweet man, so kind, and always willing to help with her Spanish when she bought at the store. He blushed and said no, it was his pleasure.

"A toast!" Sander raised his glass. "To Comodoro Rivadavia!"

Dietz refilled all the glasses. Minke took a small sip of cognac and said to Bertinat, "Tell me what has arrived on the *Elisabeth* today that I will find in your store tomorrow."

Bertinat straightened in his chair. Cassian translated, but Bertinat knew well enough what she'd asked. "I am honored to show you *mañana*."

"For *los niños*, eh?" Dietz tipped back in his chair and blew out a long trumpet of cigar smoke. "Eh, Sander?" He smacked his stomach with both hands and laughed his hoarse laugh. "Nice going, there."

Now it was Minke's turn to blush. Bertinat sighed beside her. "*Azúcar,*" he said. "*Leche enlatada.*"

"Sugar." She clapped her hands. She was ravenous for sweets. "And some sort of milk. What's *enlatada?*"

"Tinned," Cassian said.

She patted Bertinat's hand. "*Puedo comprar,*" she said. "I can buy!"

"And what arrived for *your* store today, Meneer Dietz?" Bertinat asked, with Cassian again translating.

Dietz laced his thick fingers across his stomach. "What store might that be, señor?"

Bertinat said something quickly, and Cassian translated. "He says you're playing with him, Dietz. You know what he's talking about."

Dietz signaled to Meduño for another round.

"What's this about a store, Dietz?" Sander ran a white napkin over his lips. "All joking aside."

Dietz shrugged, a man wrongly accused. "For the men. Nothing more. For the things they need."

"No profit, then, eh?"

Dietz wove his clubbed fingers. "I'm a businessman like you, Sander. Of course I profit. I'm not stupid."

"May I shop in your store, Meneer?" Minke asked with a wink at Sander. She was enjoying their little game of cat and mouse. They were all friends, but competitors, too, Sander had explained.

"My dear, there's nothing there for you unless you would like to bathe with lye soap or shave that pretty face of yours with a straight blade. That sort of thing," Dietz said.

"Your men have no opportunity to buy their soap from Bertinat, or so I understand," Minke said. "I heard they aren't allowed to come into town, that they must buy from you at very high prices."

"Who told you that?" Dietz asked.

It had been Pieps, of course. "People talk," she said.

"Watch out for her, Sander. People are filling her head with nonsense."

"So it's not true? Your men can buy from anyone?" she asked.

"Well, my dear, your husband and the good doctor understand all about monopolies. I suggest you ask them," Dietz said testily.

"Oh, settle down, Frederik," Sander said. "We're only having some fun with you."

Dietz took a spoonful of stew. "We came to celebrate the arrival of the *Elisabeth*," he said. He held out his glass. "To the *Elisabeth*."

"Hear, hear," Cassian said.

The talk shifted to the *Elisabeth*'s schedule. Dietz pressed for information about who was buying what up and down the coast, what other merchants were involved. Thousands of those little brown bottles of processed medicine were reaching people in ports big and small all over South America. Minke was half listening, though, because her attention was drawn to something blue at the door. It took a few moments to recognize Tessa's parrot. The bird took a look about, then bobbed along toward their table. A brief hush fell over the room as the men in the bar watched Tessa, a grand vision of opulence, thread her way among the tables. Her hair was parted down the center and swept up at the crown into a pouf of orange curls. She wore a dress of orange and yellow brocade laced with gold.

A chair was quickly pulled up between Minke and Bertinat and another place laid at the table. Tessa crowded in and whispered, "I as well. Can you believe it? A miracle." She smelled of a delicious flowery cologne.

"As well what?" Minke was still flustered at seeing Tessa for the first time since that awful moment at the estancia, confused by the woman's warmth.

"Expecting, you goose! I'm almost certain of it."

Dietz nudged her, and when she turned, he cocked his head. "See? You're not the only one."

She returned to Tessa. It was like a game of tennis. "You came to see Dr. Tredegar?"

"Why would I see him?" Tessa sniffed. The parrot spread its wings, wobbled from foot to foot, and opened its mouth as if it wanted to speak.

"To help with the baby."

"That so-called doctor let my Astrid die." Across the table, Cassian watched Tessa without expression. He must have heard. "Frederik has arranged for a real doctor." Tessa paused, looked from face to face. "What is everyone staring at?"

"We're delighted for you," Cassian said. "This is very happy news."

What a gentleman he was.

"Sander!" Tessa laid a bejeweled hand on Sander's. "I must say it's a pleasure to see the *Elisabeth* in harbor." She addressed the table at large. "The ship was named for our dear departed Elisabeth when she was only a child, you know." And then to Bertinat only, she said, "Sander's late wife, a lovely woman. Minke cared for her when she was ill. Isn't that right, Minke?"

The ship had belonged to Elisabeth? Minke had assumed that Sander had bought the ship and named it for her.

Tessa nudged Minke in the side. "It's the smart man who smuggles his wife's ship out from under the nose of the government." The bird flapped and lit on her other shoulder.

"When is your baby due?" Minke wanted to change the subject.

"Another month is needed to be sure. But I'm certain. I remember exactly how I felt with my Astrid." She dabbed at the corners of her eyes. "Astrid would have been thrilled with a baby brother or sister."

Dietz interrupted and called for Meduño to bring another chair. "For the young skinner."

Minke looked through the haze of smoke to see Pieps pushing his way through the crowded tables.

"Come on, come on." Dietz, impatient, made space for the chair to be drawn in between himself and Sander. "Any friend of Minke's is a friend of ours, eh, Sander? What'll it be, young man? Sky's the limit tonight. Meneer DeVries is paying, eh, Sander?" He belted out another big coarse laugh.

"I came over to say hello," Pieps said. "I won't stay."

"We won't hear of it," Dietz said. "Tessa, you remember this boy. This is the boy who accompanied Minke to our home."

Tessa barely glanced at Pieps.

"He doesn't want to sit down with us," Minke said. "Can't you see? He's happy with his own friends."

"But you're his friend," Dietz said. "His very *good* friend, if I recall." He gave a bark of insinuating laughter.

"Hold on, there Dietz," Sander said.

Dietz said, "All in good fun."

"Sander," Minke said. "Let it go."

"Yes," Tessa said. "Let it be. I'm sure it was all perfectly innocent." She wrinkled her nose at Sander.

"What was perfectly innocent?" Sander got to his feet.

Tessa said, "You married a young wife."

Pieps addressed Sander. "Mevrouw Dietz misunderstood an event that occurred at the estancia. Minke was feeling unwell, and I was trying to help."

Tessa flapped her hand. "It's all in the past now. Of course you were trying to help. No matter."

"Sander." Cassian tugged slightly at his sleeve to make him sit.

"Tell us what's new in the skinning business," Dietz said.

Pieps raised his hands as if in surrender. "My friends." He pointed to the bar. "I must get back." He bowed slightly and backed away.

"Handsome boy there, eh, Cassian?" Dietz said with another guffaw.

Sander took bills from his wallet and laid them on the table. "My wife has informed me she is feeling light-headed and must be going home."

Minke pulled her wrap around her and said good evening quickly. Sander took her by the wrist, and they made their way among the tables, through the foyer, and outside. She could barely keep up with him. "What was that about?" he raged as he spun her around to face him. "What went on out there?"

She snapped her hand from his and jumped back, rubbing where he'd held her. "I told you what happened out there. I spied for you."

"What did Tessa mean, 'all perfectly innocent'?"

"I fainted and Pieps caught me. Tessa made up a story. That's it."

He came close, his face deeply lined in the light from the hotel. "That boy isn't to be trusted. I knew it from the start. I want you to keep your distance."

"He's my friend."

"I've been in the world longer than you, Minke. I know. One day you'll regret it. Keep your distance, I command you."

He led the way home, walking a few paces ahead. When they reached the house, he saw her in. "I have to go back," he said. "I'm the host."

"Please, Sander. I can't stand it when you're angry with me."

"Then you'll mind how you behave."

10

*T*HE BIRTH BEGAN early in the morning with a rush of water and the onslaught of pain. Jozef Alexanders DeVries, Zef for short, was born on December 14, 1912. Sander sent someone to fetch Cassian, who arrived immediately with Marta, an old woman whom he had selected as his assistant. Cassian administered morphine so that, although the pain persisted, Minke floated at the top of the room, looking down on herself and the people who came and went and spoke as if through gauze. When she emerged from the fog, Sander was at her bedside, presenting her with Zef swaddled in white flannel.

Large and healthy, with fine white hair, a tiny cherub mouth, and pink cheeks, he was a miracle. She felt intense love, more than she had imagined possible. She opened the blanket to touch his little fingers and toes, the toes like tiny pink grapes, then wrapped him again and stared at his sleeping face.

In the ensuing weeks, her bedroom was always crowded. Women of the village emerged from their houses and came to see him; they stood in line at the door, chattering away and bearing gifts: the foot of a white rabbit, a rattle made from a small gourd. By now—she'd been in Comodoro for nine months—Minke had enough Spanish to say good morning, and to speak of the weather, and to say "nine pounds" and receive their gales of laughter at such a big baby on such a narrow girl, and to laugh with them and their mock grimaces of pain. She told them he took right away to the breast; he was a good baby who awakened only twice during the night to be fed. He cried little. The women cooed over him, made little noises to draw a smile, and touched his silken white hair. Two of the women, Rosa Corcoy and

Maria Mansilla, held infants only weeks older than Zef and came often, treating Minke with the warmth of old friends, as if the birth of her baby had made her legitimate.

One hot afternoon, she spotted Pieps waiting to see her. His skin was a ruddy brown, hair bleached to ash and slicked back, and he was clean-shaven. When it was his turn, he gingerly reached for Zef's tiny fingers, but Sander clapped his outstretched hand. "Don't touch him. You've been skinning sheep. You carry disease." Minke tried to apologize to Pieps with her eyes.

"Seals, not sheep, and I no longer do the skinning myself, Meneer. I hire the people who do." Pieps gave a tight bow and opened the bundle he was carrying. The women gathered closer to see. It was a snow-white sealskin wrapped around a polished silver maté cup and *bombilla*. "The cup is from Goyo, and the skin is my gift."

"They're back?" Sander asked. "The gauchos have come back?"

"No," Pieps said.

"How does Goyo know about the baby?"

"So many questions, Sander," Minke said. "Pieps has only come to welcome Zef. Be reasonable!"

"Goyo left it the last time with instructions to present it to the baby. He'd have given it himself in July, but it's bad luck to give a gift to an unborn child."

"Our baby would have been born whether he received a maté cup or not." Sander made a point of examining the fur's underside as if it might still bear remnants of the animal. Minke took it from him and made an equal point of laying Zef on the soft fur.

Rosa giggled, pointed to Zef, Minke, and Pieps, then to her own hair and said to Maria, "*Todos las misma,*" which Minke knew meant "all the same." She shot a look at Sander to see if he would react badly to the comparison. Fortunately, he never paid attention to what the village women said and had made no effort to learn Spanish. He was looking instead toward the door, where a new commotion had his attention.

Tessa. She filled the door in a pink and blue dress swishing about her, advancing and pushing her way through the women, eyes brimming with tears. "Oh, oh, oh." She crossed her hands over her breast as if to still her beating heart. "Let me," she said, sweeping Zef up in her arms, twirling once around, a kaleidoscope of pastels. "I came as soon as I heard." Then she gave Zef back. "Well?"

"Well what?" Minke never knew what Tessa meant, where she was headed, in any conversation.

Tessa clamped her hands over her stomach.

"Oh!" Minke said. Tessa was indeed pregnant. "Congratulations. When, may I ask?"

"Summer, I think."

"Meneer is well?" Sander asked.

"He sends his best."

To crowd things further, in came Cassian with Marta, who immediately picked up the baby.

"I'll help you, Minke," Tessa said. "Have you quite forgotten?" She began to rattle on, saying there was no need for any woman from the village when Tessa herself knew all there was to know and was European to boot. Hadn't she offered to help all those months ago? Minke should have called for her immediately. Minke shot a look at Pieps and shook her head. Pieps rolled his eyes at Minke to show he was sympathetic, a fact that didn't escape Sander's notice. The whole crisscross of animosities in the tiny room made the air crackle.

"The baby is heavy," Cassian said to Tessa. "It's not a good idea for you to exert yourself, helping with the care, in your condition."

"You're not my doctor," Tessa said.

"Cassian's right, Tessa." Minke didn't take the offer seriously for a minute. It was all show. "I can't allow you to take that on."

"You're a strange one," Tessa said to Minke, and left.

TO GIVE TESSA her due, she'd been correct all those months ago about having to boil everything. Cassian insisted on it, too. Not just the diapers but the clothing and the utensils and, of course, as Zef grew older, any water that passed his lips. He slept in one of the small rooms with Marta because Sander wouldn't hear of the baby sharing their room. He wanted his wife to himself, he said. Marta was to wake and tend to Zef's needs, but Minke found that at the smallest sound from her son, she was awake and out of bed, on her feet, and tending to him, telling Marta to go back to sleep.

February brought the arrival of full summer; the wind relaxed, and finally, there was green—not a great deal, but the brown landscape turned an olive color on the plains, and the dry brush that had tumbled through town all winter was gone. The water along the sea was calm and shallow, the beach covered in sand that was the consistency of talcum and the color of rust.

Every afternoon Minke bathed Zef behind their house in water that had been boiled for purity, then cooled to the proper warmth. Oh, he was such a fat little thing by now, firm and slippery in her hands. He kicked his bare feet and squealed. He was a child who laughed at everything. On the day he turned over for the first time, from his stomach to his back, he lay gurgling with pleasure.

After the bath, she rinsed him and wrapped him in one of the towels that Marta washed daily. She walked about singing to him while he made his own sounds back. Then she lay him in his little bed in the room he shared with Marta and read aloud, until finally, he slept.

One very warm night, Zef woke as usual, demanding to be fed. Instead of sitting in her rocking chair, as she usually did, she carried him from the house and went barefoot along the trail that ran around the retaining wall to the beach, where she stood up to her ankles in the lapping surf. The moon was bright enough that sea and sky were bluely visible. She stood swaying with her baby, feeding him first on the right side, then on the left. He ate hungrily and was gaining well, according to Cassian, although the same was not true for her. Her clothing fell loose on her body. She was supposed to drink a pint of heavy cream each day, but try as she would, she could barely eat enough to keep up with Zef's demands, let alone her own.

A great deal had changed in her. Not that long ago, she had stood in the same spot with Sander and her heart had ached for home with its buoys and boats and noises, for its busy, narrow streets. Now she was glad for the raw expanse of sea. Every inch of the Netherlands was groomed, tilled, built, and rebuilt over many centuries. Not a speck remained untouched. Until Comodoro, she hadn't considered there could be anything different in the world. But here! This country was virgin. She felt her blood rush at the thought of its vast wildness.

She hugged Zef to her. He would see it all. When he was old enough, she would teach him to ride, and they would spend their days exploring. What would be old enough? Nine? Ten? They would begin by riding the few miles along the coast south to Punta Piedra. They'd see a forest she'd heard about where the trees had actually turned to stone. When he was older, they'd go farther. They'd see the Andes.

"You're a child of Argentina," she said, and swung him around in a circle, then paused. Born in Argentina, yes. So he was Argentine. But he was Dutch, too. She would take him there as well. Alone, of course, because Sander couldn't return. Just as she had marveled over the rawness of Argentina, Zef would be in awe of the well-tended Netherlands. He would be the child of two magnificent countries.

"We're joined to your ancestors by this ocean," she told him. "Your other home is across that water. Right now it's deep in winter, with snow and ice piling up along the shoreline and people slipping and sliding all over the cobbled streets. But in summer the Netherlands are so green it would hurt your eyes.

"Your father is from Amsterdam, and one day you will meet your brother and sister, whose names are Griet and Pim. You'll like Pim."

She thought a moment. "We are from Enkhuizen." Images flooded in. The tiny houses, the narrow streets. What she told him surprised her. "We are the poor van Aismas. The other van Aismas live to the north, in Friesland. They have large farms and many acres of land." She thought a moment of Papa. "This bothers your opa terribly." Minke laughed, thinking how Papa loved to say they were the descendants of royalty, although the royalty was Johan Klazes van Aisma, who had been mayor of the tiny town of Beetgum a hundred years earlier. "And you have an aunt Fenna. One day you'll meet them all. Fenna will tell lies about the family. She gets that from Papa. They are not content to be only who they are." She wrapped him tightly in his blanket. "But we have something better, Zef. We are adventurers."

Back at the house, she lay Zef in his bed. Marta woke and curled herself around the baby so he wouldn't fall. Minke tiptoed into her bedroom, closed the door, and slipped back into bed beside Sander, who waited for her to come back so he could make love to her. Her nights, once the province of Sander only, now had to be shared with Zef, and she was becoming exhausted. Sander wanted her to leave the night feedings to Marta, but she worried about the water. Marta, as good as she was, boiled everything she was supposed to but clearly didn't agree that it was necessary, given that water wasn't boiled for the other babies in the village. If Minke allowed Marta to feed the baby at night, well, one slip and Zef could become very sick.

ON RAINY OR windy nights, she was unable to take Zef down to the water and sat outside with him, protected by the overhang of the house, while lightning flashed over the sea. Otherwise, she would gather him up and go down the path to the water. Zef expected it. He held on to her neck as they went, facing the sea. And she'd taken to swimming on warm nights. She would lay Zef on a blanket on the sand after feeding him, strip off her nightdress, and enter the water. She'd never seen a soul there at night, and it wasn't possible to swim in the daytime. Women in Comodoro didn't do it. She'd have felt foolish. So this was her chance, and she never swam far.

One particularly bright night, she lay for a long time on the blanket with Zef while he slept, his stomach full. She was on her back, looking up at the stars, trying to sort them out. She'd been taught the stars when she was a girl, but here, the sky was all new.

She was interrupted by a sound from a long distance away. She gathered up Zef and stood. It was a horse in the distance. The tiny shape grew larger as it approached. Who could it be at this hour? she wondered. Someone with an important message, perhaps? She would be as visible to him as he was to her in this half-light. She felt apprehensive, but not for her safety, exactly. Something else.

The horse stopped a quarter mile or so up the beach and circled before the rider turned it up the bank toward the town. It was exciting for her to see the horse in the moonlight, yet another surprise in this land of surprises. She laughed with Zef over it. "I frightened him off!" She bounced him on her way back to the house. She paused at the door, listening for the rider, but all was quiet, not even noise from the Explotación tonight.

ONE HOT, BLUSTERY day, news raced around town like wildfire that the *Elisabeth* had returned to the harbor after its voyage to the north. Sander insisted on taking the car with the top down to meet the ship. He wanted to be seen, and the family was a sensation in their yellow car, she luscious in red, little Zef in her lap, wearing the bright green sweater Marta had knitted, the wind whipping their fair hair. Sander parked at the top of the retaining wall, which was already crowded with people jostling for position to watch as the tenders arrived. He helped Minke from the car, then strode down to the beach, where Cassian waited with his pallet of boxes containing the small brown bottles of processed morphine. Once again, these boxes would be loaded onto the *Elisabeth* and shipped to ports along the route to the West Indies.

On the beach, Sander met the crew of the *Elisabeth*, with his lists and notes, gliding among them, shaking hands, embracing them, while Frederik Dietz strutted, cock of the walk, up and down the sand, calling attention to himself. He'd set up a small table and two chairs and kept motioning to men disembarking the tenders to come on, get a move on, and those poor men, with all their luggage and bundles, ran tripping across the sand, where they formed a line at the small table. Minke recognized the man sitting at the table as Dr. Pirie, a Boer who'd come down from the north to treat all the men who worked for Dietz. Since she'd first heard of the new doctor from Tessa, she'd learned that Dietz forbade his workers to visit Dr. Tredegar because he provided morphine, which made them lackluster at their work. Dr. Pirie, so it was said, believed that hard work cured illness.

At the very end, four stragglers descended the gangway—three men and a woman. The woman was clearly European; Minke knew that by her cabbage-colored coat. No woman in South America would own

such a thing, or walk so aggressively. They milled about, checking on
their luggage, but the men seemed to keep away from the woman, so
Minke deduced they were traveling separately.

Dietz distracted Minke from the new people. He had assembled
forty or fifty men who waited in a line for Dr. Pirie. One by one they sat
opposite the doctor so he could look over each man's papers and then
examine his hands, eyes, and tongue before sending him to join another
line. Eventually, they would all go to the barracks out near the oil wells.
Dietz had struck oil many more times, and some of the wells were inside
Comodoro itself.

The woman who had gotten off the tender was speaking to Dietz
about something. She was bundled up, a hat with a scarf wound around
her face against the wind. Dietz pointed down the beach, and the woman
strode off with a definite sense of purpose.

She was looking for Sander! Sander, of all people. She ran to him,
threw open her arms, and gave him a long hug. Who on earth? Could it
be Griet? Sander and the woman spoke a bit longer, and she made Sander
laugh. Sander turned to Minke and pointed to where she was sitting on
the retaining wall with the other mothers. The woman raised a hand to
shield her eyes from the sun; she waved frantically. Minke waved back,
still not knowing. The woman was running up the beach toward her,
holding her skirts high. She stopped at the bottom of the seawall, out of
breath. "Minke," she screamed up at her. "It's me. Fenna!"

11

$\mathcal{F}$ENNA RUSHED UP the ramp and took both Minke and Zef in a great crunching hug, then held them at arm's length for a good look. "I'm really here!" she gasped, out of breath, her face flushed. "I can't believe it. I've been throwing up for two weeks, but here I am at last." She spotted the car. "Even Sander's car, Minke. I remember the car!" She threw herself down on its hood, arms out, with one side of her face pressed against the warm yellow metal. She seemed to notice Zef for the first time, even though she'd practically suffocated him in her hug.

"Zef" was all Minke could manage.

Fenna plucked the child from Minke's arms and held him out. Zef studied her back, this new person, then laughed and flapped his small hands in pleasure.

"He likes me," Fenna said, returning him to Minke.

Minke could not stop staring. Could not take in the fact of her sister in this place. Fenna's coat was askew, and she fixed on that detail, which seemed to prove it was in fact Fenna because one of her shoulders had always ridden slightly higher than the other. Jackets and coats gapped on the low side of her neck and rode up on the high side, giving her a look of perpetual untidiness.

"What's the matter?" Fenna asked with a big grin. "Cat got your tongue?"

"It's strange, seeing you here," Minke said.

"Well, here I am," Fenna barked, hands on her hips.

"I had no idea."

"Not my fault, Minke."

"I'm not talking about fault, Fenna, but you asked what was the matter, and I'm trying to explain. Can't I simply be surprised?" Already they had entered into their old ways of bickering.

They piled into the car and drove the thousand or so yards up the hill to the house; Minke saw the whole town through her sister's eyes. She had come to take for granted the open oil channels and no longer noticed the odor. But it didn't escape Fenna. "This place smells worse than home." Nor did she fail to notice the rusty metal siding on their house and the concrete slabs on the roof. "Why is all that crap on the roof?"

"To weigh it down," Minke said.

"Why not just attach the roof to the house?" She barged inside without waiting for an answer. "Where am I to sleep?" she asked, looking around the small space. "Mama said you would live in a big house with plenty of room for me. But this is all very cramped. This is nothing like I expected. I thought we'd be rich. I can hardly believe this. And dirt floors, like peasants."

"Boor." It was the worst of insults, and Fenna was being exactly that, with her coarse mouth.

"You'll take Marta's place," Sander announced.

"Sander!" Minke said. "I need Marta." He couldn't do this to her. Minke had come to depend on Marta, with her soft voice, gentle ways, and vast knowledge. "You can't replace Marta just because Fenna shows up without warning. This is an outrage," she hissed.

"Without warning," Fenna said. "Hardly. Your husband sent for me."

Minke must have heard wrong. "Without consulting me?"

"You need help with the child. She can take the place of Marta. And she speaks Dutch. You always complain that no one speaks Dutch. I'm under no obligation to consult you," he said. "The matter is settled."

"She won't care for Zef, Sander. I won't allow it."

"She'll do as I say."

"I cook," Fenna said. "I don't need to take care of the baby. Show me the kitchen."

Minke pointed to the table with its collection of gas burners.

"That's your kitchen?" Fenna went to investigate.

Sander slipped his arms around Minke. "Don't be cross with your Sander," he said. "All will be well, I promise. And now we must come together and welcome Fenna into our home."

They sat in the crowded little parlor, sipping celebratory brandy from tiny glasses. Fenna dug about in her bag and drew out an object wrapped in tattered white tissue and tied with a red ribbon. "Mama sent this." Minke knew by the feel of it that it was Mama's little silver keepsake box. Mama's mother had given it to her, and as a child, Minke had loved to run her finger over the engravings on each of its six sides while Mama had explained what each one meant. There was love, harmony, trust, truth, fidelity, and tenderness. She was overcome with memories of home.

"Everything is going to hell," Fenna said. "Papa lost his job, and now we take in boarders. I sleep with Mama and Papa in the closet bed again. They snore. They stink. Worse than here." She'd taken off her coat and had on the plaid dress she'd worn the day Sander came to the house, too low in the front for a big girl.

"What's the talk of war?" Sander asked.

Fenna shrugged. "The Germans took a Dutch ship and raised German colors. It's all very boring, if you ask me." She resembled Mama, particularly the way she rocked forward and back in her chair when making a point. "Mama said you would be sad and lonely."

"I am *not* sad and lonely," Minke said. "I'm very happy."

"So you *like* it." Fenna winked at Sander.

"Like what?" She wasn't going for her sister's bait. She was the married one; she was the one in charge of the household.

"Sander, is she still the ice princess, or have you thawed her?"

"You'll mind your tongue in this house, Fenna," Minke said.

"I'm only asking a question!" Fenna said indignantly. "And of Sander, not of you."

Sander eyed them with indulgence, as if they were his two squabbling children.

"Your sister is a force to be reckoned with," he said later that night, as they were preparing for bed.

"In what way?" Minke knew exactly what way but wanted to hear him say it, what everybody said at home, how inconceivable it was that the two of them were sisters. Chalk and cheese. Oil and water. She could tell him all sorts of things about Fenna, how hard it had been growing up always to be extra-good, extra-sweet, no trouble to Mama and Papa because of Fenna. And now Fenna was here. Now she was their problem.

"She doesn't hold much back."

"That's putting it too mildly," she snapped. "She holds nothing back."

He was sitting on the edge of the bed in his underclothes, pulling off his stockings. He stopped what he was doing. "Are we arguing?"

"No. Yes."

"Why? What have I said?"

"It's what you did, Sander, inviting Fenna without a word to me. I'm in shock."

"You need help. I thought you'd be happy. You mystify me, Minke."

"Mama has washed her hands of her."

"How do you know that?"

"Because I know Mama."

Sander threw himself back on the bed, laughing. "Come here," he said.

She lay down beside him.

"Take her around tomorrow. Introduce her to that boy Pieps at the skinners. Maybe he'll have a job for her. And if he's looking for a woman," Sander said with a laugh, "which he no doubt is, she'll be off our hands in no time."

Minke tensed at the thought. She didn't want to see that at all. Pieps was *her* friend.

Sander must have sensed her reaction. "What's wrong?"

"It's obvious. He's a thoughtful person, and Fenna is all action."

"Many men like a woman who is all action." He lay a hand on her breast. She pulled away. "Now what?" he asked her.

"I can't make love. I'm pregnant again."

"Another?" He slumped onto his back. "Isn't one enough for you?"

She had been so excited to tell him. Now she was miserable. "Well, I didn't do this alone." He said nothing. "We're both responsible," she added weakly.

"Elisabeth took care of these things." He dragged his hands over his face.

"If you didn't want children, Sander, then why did you marry me?"

"Just give me time to adjust to the news," he said.

"I thought it would make you happy."

"All the better your sister has come."

IN THE MORNING Minke was nauseated, so it was Sander who took Fenna to meet Pieps. Afterward he reported that Fenna was not in the least impressed, that after the fishermen of Enkhuizen, she had known enough of men who smelled of animal guts. The good news was that they had continued on to the hotel, where Meduño had taken one look at Fenna in that low-cut plaid dress and hired her on the spot. So in the space of a single morning, everything was resolved. Better than resolved, because Marta could continue to help with Zef but sleep at her own house. Fenna would work at the Explotación in the afternoons, into the night. Sander would be free to work at the *obras*, where he was needed to keep the records and manage the money and inventory while Cassian saw to the actual production.

The following week, Minke and Fenna walked to the *obras*, pushing Zef in his rickety little pram across the rutted path. Minke wanted her sister to see its scale and importance. Tucked behind the Cerro, it had grown to consist of Cassian's house and some larger structures, one large metal-sided building with stacks on top to emit the fragrant opium steam around the clock, another for the bottling, and between them a large courtyard where the paste was dried on metal sheets in the sun, protected from the wind.

Two young men stood guard at the entrance, the butts of their guns visible in the waists of their trousers; both bowed slightly to Minke, a gesture of respect that was sure to impress Fenna. Minke stopped and introduced her sister to them.

"*Hola, señorita,*" the boys said.

Pam Lewis

"*Hola* yourself," Fenna said, and shimmied her bosom at them.

"Oh, Fenna," Minke said, laughing, once they'd continued. "You're incorrigible."

At one end of the courtyard, eight or nine people with various ailments stood in line waiting to see Cassian, waiting for medicine. Again Minke greeted each of them. "They're our customers," Minke said. "They pay the bills."

"*Hola!*" Fenna called out loudly to them, her accent making the word unintelligible. "*Hola, hola!* There. How was that?"

After the courtyard, they came to the small room Sander used as his office. It was just a corner of a larger space cordoned off by a hanging blanket and barely large enough to hold his desk and chair. The desk was piled with papers, all in disarray, unusual for Sander, who was generally tidy.

"The lovely van Aisma sisters," he said, rising. He wore a dark vest over a crisp white shirt and looked so handsome with his amber hair, grown long now. He brought in chairs for them, took Zef in his lap, and spun to make the baby laugh.

Fenna began to regale Sander with gossip from the village, the same stories she'd already told Minke, of the vicar, the very same lecherous vicar who'd been at the wedding, and how he was found dead, frozen in an ice bank at the edge of the Zuiderzee. "And surely you remember Mevrouw Ostrander," she said to Sander.

"The next-door neighbor." Minke was bored with Fenna's stories and annoyed to see Sander finding them amusing. "Her husband fell into the canal."

"I'll tell it," Fenna said.

"Drowned?" Sander asked.

"Drunk," Fenna said with delight. "They say it's what saved him. He relaxed and floated to the surface." She thought a moment. "An American was seen, too. A tall man in a brown suit walked through the streets. People said he was connected to the war. A spy."

"Nonsense. The Americans have nothing to do with the war," Minke said, tired of all this.

"The Americans have everything to do with everything," Sander said.

"See?" Fenna said. "I told you."

At that moment two gauchos in red *bombachas* and their funny porkpie hats came to stand in the line for morphine. "Those are gauchos!" Minke pointed to them. "See how they dress? They all dress like that. And see how bowlegged they are? They're all bowlegged from living on horseback."

"They steal little girls," Sander said, and that got Fenna's attention.

"That's a rumor," Minke said. "People say terrible things about them, but none of it's proven."

"What else do they say?" Fenna asked Sander.

"They ride only stallions, never mares."

"They hunt on horseback," Minke said. "They eat on horseback, probably sleep on horseback. They do everything on horseback."

"Everything?" Fenna winked at Sander.

"Don't be coarse." Minke was furious that Fenna turned everything around like that.

"I'll tell *you* who's coarse. Your friend Dietz sticks money down the front of my dress every chance he gets. You've seen that plenty, I'll bet. I take the money but don't give him anything." Fenna addressed Sander as if he was the only one present.

"Guess what he collects?" Minke said. "At the estancia in the country?"

"How should I know?" Fenna retorted.

"Shrunken heads," Minke said. "Dozens of them."

"One for you, Minke. Now it's my turn. Guess who people hate most in this town? I'll tell you who. Your friend out there." She indicated the boiling room with a shake of her head. "That Tredegar."

"What do you know about that?" Sander asked.

"All those boys!" Fenna said.

"The employees?" Minke asked. "What about them?"

Fenna rolled her eyes.

"They *work* here," Minke said. "He takes care of them."

"I'll say he does," Fenna said. "And you've got your head in the sand, as usual."

"What is it they say, Fenna?" Sander pressed. "About Dr. Tredegar."

"Men at the bar talk. They taunt the men whose sons live and work out here." Fenna pointed out the window. "The fathers are ashamed."

"What do you tell them?" Minke poked her sister's arm harder than she'd intended. "People say such things, and what do you say back to them?"

"I earn my tips by keeping my mouth shut about such things."

"What else, Fenna? Is there anything else we should know?" Sander asked.

"They say he has a tail under those fancy clothes, and cloven feet. People have seen it. And horns if you look closely enough under that cap of hair. You'll be tarred with the same brush if you're not careful."

12

AS THOUGH FENNA'S words had opened the floodgates of hell, a week later a gang of men attacked Cassian on the path behind the Cerro. His clothing was ripped from his body, and they left him for dead, naked on the gravel path. Fortunato, one of the guards from the *obras*, found him several hours later. The boy's first thought was to get Sander. It was four in the morning, dawn already breaking, when Minke and Sander, leaving Zef behind with Fenna, drove at lightning speed over the rocky trail to the scene of the attack. Fortunato had covered Cassian with a blanket and lifted it to reveal his bare thigh, grossly shortened.

Cassian rasped that his femur was broken; the bone ends had been snapped past each other by the strength of his muscles. "Traction," he groaned. "Now." Through the pain, he instructed them. Fortunato pulled Cassian's foot while Sander secured his upper body beneath the arms to keep the bone ends apart and the jagged edges from ripping open the artery.

"Get more help," Sander called back to Minke.

Without a second thought, she cranked the car, got in, miraculously put it into gear, and sped back across the plain to the oil barracks, a long, windowless one-story building, where she hammered on the door with her fist and was met by shouting and swearing from inside. "Dr. Pirie!" she shouted. "It's an emergency!"

The door opened, and there was Dietz, eyes at half-mast.

"Cassian has been hurt."

"Hurt how?"

"Where is Dr. Pirie?" She was frantic.

"Get a grip on yourself," Dietz said. "For God's sake."

"They can't hold him forever."

"You're making no sense. Hold whom?"

"Dr. Pirie!" she screamed, hoping the doctor was within earshot.

Dietz took her by the shoulders. "Look here, girl. Stop this screaming at once. You're waking my men. Pirie's not here. What happened?"

"Dr. Pirie!" she screamed again.

Dietz turned back into the darkness of the barracks and let the door shut behind him.

She could think of only one other person. She drove north across the plain to the brick huts that housed the skinners. Inside, half a dozen men stood at skinning boards in the rank-smelling place. Pieps took one look, followed her to the car, and held on as they sped around the Cerro. People everywhere must have known something was happening because of all the dust kicked up by the car crisscrossing the plain. She explained over the noise of the engine what had happened.

Sander and Fortunato were just as she'd left them and exhausted by now. Pieps took over from Sander, and Cassian instructed them on what to do. Find a stick longer than the leg. Without letting the leg slip, jam one end of the stick into the shoe on the foot of the broken leg, put the other shoe at his crotch, and jam the other end of the stick into it, then bind the whole thing with strips of their own cut-up shirts, and carry him home this way.

Once he was in his bed, Minke sponged away the dried blood. His skin was purple, and welts swelled along the side of his body.

"Who did this?" she asked.

Cassian was trembling, as though the terror and trauma had just caught up to him. "*Schwul.*" His voice broke achingly. "They said *schwul.*"

"*Schwul?*" Fortunato asked.

"*Maricón,*" Cassian whispered to the boy. And to Minke, "*Flikker.*"

Fortunato crossed himself. Minke reeled at the very sound of that word. In the Netherlands, a person was stoned for being *flikker.* She felt weak in the knees. Cassian *flikker?* True, she'd seen him kiss a man that time, and on the *Frisia* with those bleary boys, even here at the *obras*. But she never would have put this word to him. *Flikker* was something else. Dangerous, wicked, a threat. Like the bogeyman. Cassian was none of those things. He was unusual, but he was kind. He wouldn't hurt anyone.

She heard horse hooves and went outside to see who had come. It was Dietz, galloping into the courtyard on horseback with Fenna clinging to him. He circled a few times. "Where did you go? My God, woman, I came out and you were gone. What's the matter with you? I went to your house and found Fenna instead."

"What about Zef?" Minke shouted at Fenna. "Who's with Zef?" Was the whole world crazy?

"Sound asleep. He's fine." Fenna was pressed against Dietz, not so appalled by his advances after all.

"Go back to the house and stay there!" Minke commanded.

"I'm not your slave." Fenna slid down from the horse. "You're his mother, you go."

"Sander, make her go back right this minute! Zef is alone. My baby is all alone!"

Dietz kept circling on his horse. "Who did it? Did Cassian see?"

"Take Fenna back to the house this minute!" Minke shouted at him.

Dietz ignored her. "So he doesn't know who it was."

"Meduño may have gotten wind of it," Sander said. "I'll go to the hotel and ask around."

"Don't stay to play faro." Minke glared at him. Since Zef was born, Sander had been spending more and more time throwing their money away.

"Meduño hates *flikkers*," Fenna said.

"I'll take Fenna back," Dietz said. "Come on. Up, up, Fenna." He extended a hand, but Fenna got into the car.

"I'll ride with my brother-in-law," she said.

After the car left, Minke and Pieps went inside, and Dietz went looking for someone to take his horse. They drew two chairs close to Cassian's bed. Cassian had taken a heavy dose of morphine and was breathing evenly.

"Get out of here," Pieps whispered to Minke with a startling urgency.

"No, I need to stay with him."

"I mean Comodoro. You and your husband, your baby, your sister." He gestured to Cassian. "All of you."

"Are you serious? This is our home, our business."

"First him and next Sander."

She studied his solemn face. "But Sander isn't—"

"That doesn't matter. They see you all as one. You arrived with Cassian. You're in business together."

"What do you mean, *they*? Who did this?"

"I've heard talk at work."

"Who?" It was terrifying to discover that people were talking about them.

"There are many Catholics. In their eyes—" Pieps glanced at Cassian. "In their eyes, he sins against the laws of nature, the worst possible thing. In their eyes, you and Sander condone it. Some of their sons work here. It brings shame to the families."

"But Cassian is good to them. He treats them well, pays them well."

"Minke, wake up. They hate him and, by extension, you. He's your friend, and he's corrupting their sons." The words were all the more frightening because they came from Pieps, who was always so carefree, so pleased with the world. She was forced to see herself, her family, in a new light—as corrupt, even evil—and protection was something that could vanish in the wink of an eye.

She got to her feet, so agitated by Pieps's words that she needed to pace, to breathe in deeply and settle herself. "I was taught it's important to stay when you're innocent, not to run away."

"That's fine, but it's naive. We're not in Europe, Minke."

"There should be no difference."

"But there is a difference." He stood and came toward her, grasped her hands tightly to underscore his point. "We came here to Argentina. We act as though the laws of the place we are from protect us, but they don't exist here. There are no real laws yet. No shared laws. Don't you understand? In order to have law, everyone must agree on the rules. Here there is no such thing."

She looked into his eyes and then at the sleeping Cassian. "Germans did this to Cassian, not Argentines. They called him a name in German."

"They're no longer German. The way we're no longer Dutch."

"Cassian did nothing! It's not fair."

"Look at me, Minke. Try to understand. Not what he's done. Who he is."

"Am I interrupting something?" Dietz's oily voice filled the room and although Minke had the impulse to withdraw her hands from Pieps's, she left them as they were. Dietz would not bully her. Pieps made to let go, but she clasped his hands.

"What is it?" she asked.

"Is the good doctor awake?"

"You can see for yourself that he is not," she whispered, still holding on to Pieps. "Keep your voice down."

"I want to be told when he wakes," Dietz said.

After Dietz left, Minke withdrew her hands.

"He's a snake," Pieps said.

Fortunato and several other *obras* workers appeared at the door.

"Cassian," she said softly. One eye opened; the other was swollen shut. "Tell us what to do about your leg."

It took all of them, seven in all, including Fortunato and the four *obras* workers. Step after painful step, with Cassian twice fainting from the pain and biting down on a wooden stick whenever they had to move the leg and often breaking into desperate sobs, even through the morphine. The goal was to fix the leg with the bone ends just close enough to mend. They measured his good leg against his bad for length, covered it in plaster, and raised it to a forty-five-degree angle counterweighted with bags of sand to keep it taut. By the time they finished, Minke was so tired she could have slept on the floor. She asked Fortunato and the others to stay with Cassian.

Cassian grabbed her hand. He was wide awake, terrified. "Don't leave me."

She smoothed his brow. His skin was cold to the touch. "Oh, Cassian," she said. "You poor, poor thing."

Pieps drew up his chair to Cassian's bedside. "I'll stay with you, Dr. Tredegar. Minke needs to see to her baby."

"I'll be back first thing tomorrow," she promised.

Tears formed in Cassian's eyes. "I didn't mean to keep you from Zef."

"He'll come, too, tomorrow."

Cassian managed a bleak smile.

JUST BEFORE SHE reached the house, she saw curls of smoke rising to the west; the gauchos had come back, the only good thing to happen all day. She would see Goyo again, show him Zef, and thank him for the maté cup.

Inside, she found Fenna and Sander at the kitchen table, a half bottle of brandy between them. Fenna sat with her knees apart, leaning on her elbows, like a man.

"Where is Zef?" Minke asked.

Fenna indicated the baby's room. "Sleeping."

Minke tiptoed in to see him. He lay curled, sucking his thumb in sleep. She kissed his forehead and gently pulled the thumb out without waking him, then drew the blanket up.

"What happened at the hotel?" Minke asked Sander when she joined them.

"I was just telling Fenna," he said.

"Well, tell me."

Sander sat back saying nothing, letting her know he didn't like her tone. She was too tired, too distressed, for this. "Please," she added.

"I've offered a reward, put up notices at the hotel and at the Almacén."

"The reward was my idea," Fenna said. "People talk if there's money to be had."

"But what did Meduño say?"

Sander squeezed the bridge of his nose. "That these things happen."

"Cassian might have been killed."

"His leg was broken," Fenna said. "He'll live."

"Meduño suggested that one of the workers at the *obras* did it," Sander said.

"They all get along well out there. Do you believe it, Sander? That it could have been one of the employees?"

"It's time I went to work," Fenna said.

"Pay attention to what people say, will you? Someone is bound to let it slip," Minke said.

Fenna saluted.

MINKE WAS FRIGHTENED all the time after the attack on Cassian, as in those early days, except this time she didn't have him for solace because now he depended on her. She went daily to tend to him, to bathe him and empty his bedpan.

His day bed was in the front room, covered in tapestries and pillows that she could adjust for his comfort. The entire floor was covered in Persian rugs, giving the room a warm and slightly exotic feel. The leather chair was beside the bed. Sometimes they spoke, sometimes not. She practiced her English, which had improved over time. Sometimes he trembled and spasmed like a person freezing to death. Other times he lay limp and breathing such shallow breaths that she worried he would die. *You can handle this*, she kept telling herself. *Just concentrate on taking care—of Cassian, of Zef, and of the baby growing inside you.*

"Forgive me," Cassian said one day.

It was early morning, and she was tucked into her leather chair, sipping black coffee. "For what?"

"Just say you forgive me."

"There's nothing to forgive."

"You know what I mean." He was curled like a child on his side, his eyes imploring her.

"They're the ones who need to ask forgiveness, not you." She ran a hand over his damp forehead.

"For being—"

She leaned forward to give him a kiss on the cheek. "Shh. That requires no forgiveness."

"Just say it, please."

"I forgive you."

He shut his eyes and sighed. "Have they been found?"

"No," she said.

The reward money had generated a rash of accusations. People pointed a finger at their neighbors, their in-laws, and the gauchos. In the end, the reward had caused nothing but trouble. People were angry with Minke and Sander for not giving them the reward money, but how could they? Nobody had proof, just grudges, and now they were more unpopular than ever.

Sander came in then. He was working at the *obras* full-time, doing his own work plus the work Cassian had done. The sweet smell of opium clung to him these days, and he looked haggard, his clothing limp from working in so much steam. He rubbed his hands together, as if warming them, with a gusto she knew was false.

"Cassian was asking if anyone came forward with information," Minke said.

Sander pulled up a chair to join them. "Sure they did. All of it nonsense."

"According to the people of this town, it's a miracle the gauchos haven't murdered all of us in our sleep," Minke said. "People here will use any excuse to accuse them."

"The gauchos *do* kill, Minke," Sander said. "It's well known they enjoy it. And they are known to kidnap."

"I know that, Sander," she said. It was true the gauchos killed their enemies. Everyone had heard that. "People who steal their horses and cattle or offend their honor. It's ridiculous to think they're involved in this."

"Well, well." Sander tipped back in his chair. "You hear that, Cassian? She knows a great deal about these people. I wonder how."

She went on. "If the gauchos had wanted you dead, Cassian, you would be dead of a slit throat, and dead in broad daylight; gauchos don't attack like cowards under the cover of night. But the gauchos like you."

"And just how do you know all this?" Sander asked.

"Pieps told me," she said.

"That boy is German, isn't he?"

"He's Dutch, and you know it."

"Pieps would know a word like *schwul* whether he's Dutch or German."

Cassian pulled himself to a sitting position. Gray showed at his temples where he'd been unable to darken his hair. He adjusted his pillows and settled back, pulling the covers up around him. "Don't cast aspersions, Sander. It certainly wasn't our friend Pieps."

"What about those Germans who are here looking at Petróleo Sarmiento?" That was the new name for Dietz's oil works. "Maybe one of them attacked Cassian." Even as Minke said it, she knew how unlikely it was. She rocked back in her chair. "Pieps *likes* Cassian."

"Somebody might have put him up to it. Where money is concerned, a man like that will do anything."

"A man like what? Why do you hate him so? He'd never lift a finger against Cassian!"

"You seem to know him very well."

"Well enough to know that much."

"Please," Cassian said. "You two are giving me a headache. Go fight somewhere else. But, Sander, she's right. Pieps has been good to me."

"Did you bed him, too?"

"Sander!" Minke said. "What's gotten into you?"

Cassian touched her hand. "I'm used to this from him," he said with a wan smile. "He's merciless, aren't you, Sander?"

"I asked you to be careful, Cassian. Was it too much to ask?"

"I *was* careful." Tears filled Cassian's eyes. "I swear to God. We never—"

"Who was it this time?"

"Fortunato," Cassian said.

"He's long gone," Sander said. "First one to get out of here."

Cassian was visibly shaken. "Where did he go?"

"Working for Dietz. Fenna heard it at the bar."

Cassian turned his face to the wall.

"That's where they've all gone. Their families won't allow their sons to work here. We're lucky there are still two. Otherwise we'd have to shut down."

"You make it sound like it's Cassian's fault, Sander. Did it occur to you that morphine production is the problem for the families? There's a stigma attached. People want their sons involved in oil."

"It puts the clothing on *your* back, my dear."

"Pieps thinks we should all leave," Minke said.

"Him again, eh?" Sander said. "She listens to him now and not to me. What do you think of that?"

"Fortunato must have been terrified," Cassian said. "He didn't even say goodbye."

"None of them say goodbye," Sander said.

"We need to talk about money," Cassian said.

Minke had seen Sander counting money once when he hadn't known she was there. He'd laid it out on his desk, counted once and then a second time. *Lovingly,* she'd thought at the time.

"What about money?" Sander asked.

"What do you think? No one comes anymore to buy morphine. Dietz's men apparently are well supplied by that new man, Pirie, and the people of Comodoro will do without rather than come here. That's what about the money," Cassian said.

Sander shut his eyes. "The *Elisabeth* will come back with raw materials. Things will change."

"I can't process raw material without help, and we lack that," Cassian said. "You and I cannot manage on our own for much longer."

"If there's not enough money, why do you continue to gamble?" Minke asked.

"I've told you why I spend time at the hotel."

"Tell me," Cassian said.

"The worst would be to disappear from sight, hanging my head. I must be seen about town. Business as usual."

"How much have you lost?" The weariness in Cassian's eyes told Minke this news came as no surprise to him. She remembered that Pieps had mentioned Sander's gambling on the *Frisia* with men belowdecks. She began to wonder how much of the time he was away from her was actually spent at cards.

"I win all the time," Sander said, his voice level, challenging Cassian to disagree.

"No one does that," Minke said.

"What's left, Sander?" Cassian wasn't about to back down.

"Plenty." Sander got to his feet. "Don't worry. Get well. I come in to see how you are, and all I get is trouble."

This was her chance to speak up, with Cassian right there to support her. "Sander, Tessa and Frederik will go to America when they sell to the Germans. We should go to America, too. We could have a new start. For the baby, Sander. For Zef. I feel so frightened since Cassian was hurt. I sense hostility everywhere."

"Except from that boy Pieps."

Chilling, the way he looked at her, as if she were a stranger.

A FEW DAYS later, Minke heard the clatter of hooves in the *obras* courtyard and ran outside, carrying Zef on her hip, to find Pieps and Goyo circling on a pair of fantastic piebald horses. Goyo jumped down, took the baby in his arms, and shouted, "*¡Es un muchacho magnífico!*" Zef's eyes were wide as an owl's.

"We came to help," Pieps said. "We heard your men were leaving."

Sander appeared at the door of the boiling room to see about the commotion. Goyo strode over, still holding Zef, took Sander's hand, and congratulated him on such a fine son.

Whether Sander liked these two or not, he couldn't say no to the offer of help, and he put them to work right away. All that afternoon and into the weeks ahead, Minke and Cassian could hear their jokes and laughter carrying through the courtyard. Cassian's leg was healing. Although still in its cast, it lay flat on the bed and not strung up by wires. His bruises were gone, and his mood had improved in spite of the returning winter with its constant howling of wind. Zef had found that he could pull himself up and hold on to things with his fat little fists and then make his way about the room to Cassian, where he would bounce in delight.

In July Cassian's cast was chipped off with a pick and hammer; afterward, bits of plaster lay on the floor like drifted snow. The leg was so white it seemed blue, but the worst surprise was the way the bone had set. Mended, yes, but bent so that when Cassian stood, his left thigh bowed, and he had no feeling in the foot.

He was, as usual, more concerned with Minke than with himself. The baby was due in only ten weeks, and she was still too thin. He could hear the baby's heartbeat through his stethoscope, but still, he said, she must have rest, and when she insisted on staying to look after him, he insisted back. Doctor's orders, no two ways about it.

IT WAS IN fact lovely to be in the house during the day again. She was so tired and slept side by side with Zef during his naps. She kept the fire in the stove going, and the little house was warm enough that she could sit at the window and watch the snow swirl outside. She drank the cream. It made her gag, but she thought of the baby growing inside her and swallowed.

Every afternoon, just before their nap, she bundled Zef and took him down to the water, as she had on summer nights. In winter the sun shone only during the few hours at midday. By the time they went, the sky was darkening and the sea was violent, with great black waves breaking along the shore, boiling with white foam. It was splendid. The wind swirled snow along the sand.

Men on horseback often raced up and down the beach, the hooves churning up rooster tails of ice and sand. Zef looked for them each time, his small head swiveling to find them. He always saw them before Minke did. She didn't know who they were. She told Sander about them, and he said gauchos. But she knew differently. The horses weren't fine enough, the bridles were too plain, and the riders allowed the horses to work up a white sweat on cold days, something a gaucho would not do.

*T*HE DAY WAS abnormal. A thaw had left the air irresistibly warm after weeks of cold; the sky was a milky blue at high noon, and the light lingered past two o'clock. When Zef woke from his nap, Minke put a fresh diaper on him and took him outdoors. It was much too nice to stay inside. She held out her hands, found she could comfortably be without gloves, and walked with him down the path to the beach. They didn't bother with coats. "You can smell it, can't you, Zef?" she asked him. "Doesn't the air smell different? The warmth is unlocking the smell of things today."

At the beach, she lowered him to the sand. He held on to her leg at first, then let go, took some steps on his own, and plopped down on his bottom. He laughed, tipped forward, righted himself, and tried again, this time supporting himself, with one hand against the seawall.

She wasn't paying attention. She was wrapped up in the day, and while Zef amused himself with trying to walk, she held her arms out and spun, her face tipped to the sun. She reveled in the feeling, ran down to the water's edge, and stood looking out to sea. If she concentrated, she could pretend to be on the prow of a boat and not on land at all. She laid her hands on her belly and spoke to the baby inside her about the sun and the sea—the place she would be born into. Minke was sure the new baby would be a girl.

She felt the vibration of approaching horses through her feet and squinted into the dimming light to see. "Zef! Sweetheart!" She pointed north into the direction from which the horses always came. He'd been pounding his fists against the sand, rolling it about in his chubby fingers, but stopped what he was doing. The horsemen were just boys, she thought, racing along the beach for the fun of it, free and fast. One day that would be Zef. They often came at lightning speed but veered to the left, up the bank, before reaching her and Zef. Recently, they had kept coming, and the excitement was awesome. They would thunder toward her and Zef, then swerve right, galloping through the surf and sending up sand, ice, and water. They had never once uttered a sound.

Today they did not veer off. Zef sat like a little statue, transfixed. They approached thunderously, three of them, all with scarves over their faces. The one in front brought his horse up short. The horse reared and whinnied. The other two caught up and stopped.

"I worried you hadn't seen us," Minke shouted with relief, breathing again. She'd been afraid that if she tried to run to Zef, she would be trampled.

The horses circled, snorting. The riders said nothing.

"Hello!" she said.

But she was invisible to them, inaudible. She made a move to go around them, to get to Zef, who was all alone on their other side, but it was all confusion, with the horses jockeying, their hindquarters swinging dangerously around, and it was difficult to separate the men from the moving horses; she had to jump back or be kicked. The men slid down from their horses. "Hello," she said again, the slick of fear rising like bile in her throat. "I need to get to my baby."

One of the riders held his horse deliberately in her way.

"Zef?" she screamed. She couldn't see him. "*Cuidado con el bebé,*" she cried. Don't hurt the baby. She made a dash for him around the horses, but they blocked her again. "*Cuidado con el bebé,*" she screamed. She couldn't see him. She charged forward again, flailing with her fists, and there was the uproar of horses rearing, hooves pawing at the air, and then they all raced off down the beach. She was left in total silence.

"Zef?" she whispered. No sound returned. He wasn't where he'd been. "Zef?" Had he scrambled out of their way, frightened by all the commotion? She ran up and back, looking for him.

"Zef!" she screamed, giving herself a moment to listen. She screamed again.

He was gone.

Part Three

NEW YORK, NEW YORK

April 1914

14

THE DECK WAS jammed with people as the steamship *Maceió* entered New York harbor on a bitterly cold Sunday. Ice blocks lined the shore, and the railings held a cold slick. Several hundred people, all quiet as mice, stood in awe. It was the same reverent pall that had fallen over the *Frisia* the day Minke had left Amsterdam harbor for Comodoro.

"Looks just like its pictures," Minke whispered to Cassian. Tall concrete buildings rose hundreds of feet high. Other buildings were as wide as ten buildings in Amsterdam. The skyline was impossibly jagged, as if a draftsman had gone berserk with his pen, drawing in thousands of tiny windows and doors.

"*¡Estatua de la Libertad!*" someone shouted, and she turned to see Liberty swathed in her metal gown and holding a torch over her head. Minke clutched Elly's little hand. Elly took in the scene with her usual baleful expression, as if, after all she'd seen in her little life, this was nothing.

Beyond Liberty, an exotic structure rose from the water, like a European castle with four turrets, bright red brickwork, windows lined in white, and soaring arches in the front over three doors. One look made Minke's heart flutter with excitement and fear. Ellis Island. *Sander.* She could barely contain herself at the thought of seeing him again after so much time, of lying in his arms that very night, introducing his new baby daughter. For the first time since Zef's disappearance, she felt the luxury of hope.

But between this moment and the moment when she was in Sander's arms would come the ordeal. A woman onboard the *Maceió* had told terrifying stories of what happened on Ellis Island. Madame Gil reminded Minke of Tessa Dietz in the way she spoke with a great flourish of the hand, only without the parrot and with a somewhat more compassionate disposition. She sat at the head of the long wooden table where they took their meals. People listened to her as though she were the messiah because she'd gone through Ellis Island once before. Rumors were rampant about what went on there—painful medical tests and trick questions. Madame said, "They do what they can to turn people away. They want only the strong, the healthy, and the rich in America. And you." She pointed a finger at Cassian. "With that limp, you'll be back on the high seas before you've taken a single American breath! You must not limp inside Ellis Island. You must start practicing immediately, because there are spies. They watch us all."

With Minke and Madame's help, Cassian practiced ascending the ship's stairs without limping. He had to keep his good leg slightly bent to match the length of his bad leg. The process exhausted him, and he barely made it up a few stairs the first time he tried. But Minke was a taskmaster. She made him do it over and over until both legs grew stronger. Finally, he was able to ascend the full twenty stairs as though he was almost normal.

"Be vigilant, Dr. Tredegar. You must not let them see that limp." Madame Gil lowered her voice and addressed the whole table. "You see, the real test begins at the stairs that lead up to the grand hall. Immigration police are everywhere, but you won't know which ones they are because they look like everybody else; their job is to watch from above and below every single person who climbs the stairs. Sometimes thousands go through in a single day. Believe me, they know what they're looking for. Don't pause to catch a breath even if you need to. One little show of weakness and they'll put a big L on your shoulder in white chalk." Madame made a big L in the air with her finger. "It means your lungs are bad, and you'll be turned away. Don't cough. Swallow it. If they see that limp, you're done for. You'll get an LL on your coat, meaning 'left leg.'"

"Worst is an X," she announced. She tapped her head with a finger. "It means you're cuckoo." Everyone at the table had to be feeling as hopeless as Minke. It seemed you had to be perfect to be allowed into

America. She thought of Fenna with her strapping build, of Sander with his good looks and charm. The two must have breezed through easily. She and Cassian were pitiful compared to them.

"Eye infections are the worst," Madame intoned. "You can't hide those; the doctor examines every single person's eyes through a magnifying glass." Everyone sneaked a look at everyone else, checking for signs of disease.

"And just answer their questions. Don't volunteer anything. Like this." Madame turned to Minke. "What is your name?" she asked in a quick businesslike voice.

Minke was startled at the abrupt change. "Um," she said.

"Not quick enough!"

"Minke Johanna van Aisma DeVries," Minke shouted.

"Where are you going?"

Minke swallowed. "America," she said, as if to say, *Of course*.

"Everybody on this ship is going to America," Madame said. "*Where* in America?"

"I don't know. My husband meets me at the ship, and then I will know."

"Say New York, then," Madame said.

"I'm going to New York."

"Just answer the question. All you say is 'New York.' Not 'I'm going to New York.'"

"New York."

Madame leaned over so she was nose to nose with Minke. "Are you an anarchist?"

"Of course not! What a terrible thing to ask."

"Just answer the question."

"No," Minke said.

"They always ask that," Madame said with great satisfaction. "If you answer oddly, they'll think you're lying and send you away. They don't want anarchists in America."

A few people at the table laughed.

"Don't laugh!" Madame scolded. "It's a real question. Say no. Don't make any jokes. Don't smile. Any questions?"

"When do we see our loved ones?" Minke asked.

"At the very end. You will go down the stairs of separation. Freedom is to the left and right. May God be with you that you will not be sent down the middle. Those people are detained or sent home. Your loved ones will meet you at the bottom of the stairs."

"My husband will be at the bottom of the stairs, then?" Minke asked.

"What did I just say?"

"But can I see him from the top?"

Madame threw up her hands. "If he's there, of course."

ON THE DAY she arrived in America, Minke was wearing a black wool dress that she had fashioned in Comodoro to wear during her pregnancy. It was much too large and hung like a great tent on her, but she had been grateful for it on the voyage for the warmth it provided.

All Madame's information swam in her head. Do this, do that. The ship settled at the dock in front of the beautiful building. She clung to Elly in the lovely sling she had made from fabrics Bertinat had provided as a parting gift. "The colors of Comodoro," he had said, and indeed they were—the blue-green of the ocean, the brilliant cerulean sky, and shades of gray and brown for the landscape, all dressed up with bright ocher ribbons woven through.

With her other hand, she clung to Cassian. They descended the gangway. All around them, people were weighed down by their earthly belongings. They carried enormous bundles wrapped in hopsacking, as well as suitcases and trunks. The rule, she knew, was that you could bring into the country only what you could carry yourself. She carried nothing but Elly. Cassian carried their small valise of things they would need for the journey. Sander and Fenna, who'd gone before, had brought the bulk of their belongings.

The line inched slowly but steadily forward toward the three towering doors. It was so cold, with the wind blowing off the water. Minke worried Elly would get frostbite. She worried they would be turned away. She worried Sander hadn't had word of the ship's arrival date. She worried about everything.

"We'll be fine," Cassian assured her.

"Cross your fingers." People said if you were turned away for any reason, the steamship company had to take you back where you came from.

Once inside the center door, she was overcome by the racket of dozens of languages spoken at once, the heat, and the terrible smell of fear from thousands of people all crammed into one large space. They were instructed in multiple languages to leave their belongings on the pile and walk to the staircase to their right. Minke nudged Cassian. "Those are the stairs where the medical exams are done," she said. "Are you ready?"

"Yes," Cassian said. "You?"

She shifted Elly to her other arm. "Let's go, Uncle Cassian."

She'd discovered that Cassian was in fact Sander's uncle one night in their tiny cabin aboard ship. She'd been curled around the sleeping Elly, as usual, and dared to ask Cassian what she had long wanted to know. How did Elisabeth die? Cassian had been still for a long time. Finally, he said, "I ended her suffering." In the moonlight that came through the porthole, she saw his hand drop over the side of his bunk, and she took it. The news came as a shock but not a surprise. She'd known it in her deepest self. "Sander called upon you to do it?" she said.

"Yes," he said.

"Do you always do as he says?"

Cassian squeezed her hand. "It was best for her."

"Did Elisabeth know what was happening?"

"Perhaps."

"Is it murder, then?"

"Of course," Cassian said. "The taking of life is always murder."

"How do you know Sander?"

"He's my sister's son. I was Elisabeth's family's physician. I introduced them."

She withdrew her hand from his. Uncle and nephew! "Why did neither of you tell me?"

"It's not so important."

But it was. It cast a new light over everything. That Cassian had known Sander since birth, that he had ministered to Elisabeth since she was a child. Minke had known Sander only two years. Her time with him felt like her whole life, but it was insignificant compared to all that had gone before. She was but a bud on the tree of Sander and Cassian's family. "If you're related to Sander, you're related by marriage to me and by blood to Elly." She drew in a breath. "And Zef."

IF THE WATCHERS were stationed here and there along the stairs at Ellis Island, Minke could not tell who they were. People hung over the rails, looking down from the second level. Others milled about the bottom of the stairs, looking up, but it was impossible to tell the immigrants from the staff. She glanced sidelong at Cassian as they began climbing. He was doing well enough, but the effort showed in his bloodless face.

"Don't grip the rail so hard," she said. "It looks like you're hanging on for dear life." She took strength from knowing the ordeal was only a matter of a minute or two. She made a show of smiling, of holding Elly up so the baby could look around. She was trying to divert attention from Cassian. She turned to him. "Smile," she said. "Look pleased." Cassian smiled. He had cut the remaining black from his hair, and it was now all white. He was seventy years old, he'd told her. Old enough to be her grandfather.

At the landing, the stairs took a turn. A woman had stopped and was catching her breath. Without a thought, Minke slid her free hand through the woman's arm. "Keep moving. Don't stop." She didn't know if the woman understood the words, but she ascended arm in arm with Minke. At the top of the stairs, the man who was marking people with white chalk paid no attention to Cassian, Minke, or the strange woman. They'd all passed the test.

The grand hall was a cathedral with a vaulted ceiling that seemed a hundred feet high, tiled in exquisite patterns and colors. At eye level, however, things were very different. It was a swarm of people shoulder to shoulder with crying children and smelling even fouler than on the first level. A maze of wooden fences had been set up, and they entered behind a Russian family—parents and grandparents and four small boys. The line wound up and back across the grand hall. The mother of the family smiled often at Minke and at Elly as if to say they shared something, no matter how different they were.

Minke had been in America for two hours.

At the end of the line, uniformed doctors in smart khaki uniforms with bright red epaulets and caps with shiny black visors stood waiting for them, holding evil-looking instruments. The eye exam. "Let me see your eyes," Minke said to Cassian. Her heart was beating so fast. His black eyes looked healthy to her. Any trace of an eye disease, and you were gone. She'd already seen people pulled from the line, taken up to the balcony that ran around the entire grand hall, and shown through a door that shut behind them.

When it was her turn, the doctor smiled kindly, and she took a deep breath of relief. Madame Gil had prepared her for hostility from the Americans, but that wasn't the case at all. So far everyone was being kind. The doctor took Elly from her arms, laid her carefully on his examining table, and peered into the child's eyes. He dipped his buttonhook into a beaker of blue liquid and used it to peel back the eyelid for a closer look. Minke made to snatch her baby back, but a nurse restrained her.

She watched, horrified, as the doctor proceeded to roll down Elly's lower lids and upper lids. Elly made not so much as a whimper. The doctor turned to Minke. "Not Argentine, with those blue eyes of yours," he said. His hands were gentle, and in spite of the terrifying instrument, she barely felt the exam. Before she knew it, she, Elly, and Cassian were moving on to the next station.

What Madame Gil had said turned out to be excellent advice. Minke felt each hurdle as a victory. They'd passed every test so far: the dreaded stairs, the long lines, and the eye exam. All that was left was the final check of their documentation.

They sat on long wooden benches. Ahead of them, the Russian family huddled together, taking up barely any room. As people's names were called, others moved down to fill the empty spaces. Elly was fussing by now, squirming in Minke's arms, throwing her head back so Minke would put her down. The Russian woman held out her arms to Minke, nodding quickly and indicating she could hold Elly for a time.

Panic swept over Minke at the thought of handing over her baby to a stranger.

"I think it's all right," Cassian said. "She's not going anywhere. You'll need to learn to trust people again."

She helped the woman take Elly into her lap, and Elly's expression was comical, her chubby little face and her eyes unblinking at this strange woman. The woman and all of her children stared back at Elly the same way. The children broke out in giggles, drawing a tentative but unmistakably pleased smile from Elly. They touched her silky auburn hair. Elly turned and reached for Minke. She'd had enough. The family slid down the bench a few more feet as room was made. The closer Minke was to the document stations, the better she saw what went on there.

At each station, an official checked the papers. People she'd seen with white chalk letters on their clothing or eye infections were gone, sucked through doors that led to hospitals and infirmaries or sent back to their homelands. Those who remained were people like them, people on the cusp of reaching America.

"Remember to answer plainly," Cassian said.

It was the Russian family's turn. Minke, Cassian, and Elly slid to the end of the bench. An interpreter was called over to assist the Russian family. The father did all the talking; the official made notes.

It took a long time, but finally they were cleared. The mother waved goodbye to Minke before gathering up her children and setting off down the stairs. Then it was their turn. Minke rose, trying to keep from trembling, which could upset Elly, who was sleeping in her arms. They were called to the last station in the line, the one closest to a wide staircase leading down. Two brass banisters divided the staircase into three parts. Her heart leaped with recognition. This was the staircase of separation. Madame had said she could see Sander from there. She bent over, the better to see the area beyond the stairs. There had to be a hundred people down there, faces upturned, waiting. She trembled with excitement. Somewhere in that milling of humanity were her husband and perhaps Fenna. It was so difficult to tell. People flooded down the stairs, obstructing her view. Too much was happening.

"Miss!" a man shouted.

She flinched and turned. The official to whom Cassian was speaking was glaring at her. "He's down there," Minke said excitedly, pointing down the stairs.

The official indicated a white line across the floor. "No one is permitted to cross," he said.

Cassian was smoothing out their papers on the official's desk. He was speaking in English. She would do the same when it was her turn. Cassian said it showed their bona fides to have learned the language of the country they were trying to enter.

She still could not take her eyes from the crowd of people on the lower level. She thought she found Sander's face. Her heart skipped a beat, but the man took off his hat, and it was not Sander.

"Your paper," Cassian said, nudging her. "Pay attention!"

While the man read, she bent deeply, looking again for Sander. There he was! Yes! Her knees almost buckled at the sight of him, and the familiar luscious fever spread through her. She waved frantically with her whole arm. He saw her. Their eyes met. "Elly, see your papa?" She held the baby up for Sander to see.

A commotion erupted behind her. Four officials crowded about the desk, one of them an interpreter. The men conferred. Minke's heart quickened. What was wrong? "Come here, madam," the official snapped at her.

"He disputes our passports," Cassian said.

She searched again for Sander.

"Madam, *look* at me."

She raised her eyes to his. He was so impatient.

"Come with me." The official led the way down one of the dreaded corridors. This couldn't be happening. "Sander!" she screamed into the crowd and caught a fleeting glimpse of him. "My husband is right there," she said. "He can fix anything."

They were taken to a room with wooden chairs and families scattered about, children crying, women crying. The door shut behind them. They were told to sit. Another official was moving among the miserable inhabitants of the room, taking names, checking a heavy book for something. "What's going on? What's the matter?" she hissed to Cassian.

"They think we're Argentine, but we sail on Dutch passports. It will be cleared."

"That's ridiculous." She made to get up.

"Sit down. They are bureaucrats. They have all the power. Be respectful, for God's sake." Cassian had never spoken so sternly to her.

"*Maceió*, correct?" a new officer asked.

Minke nodded. Every time the door opened and more people came into the room, Minke's head swiveled, sure it was Sander, sure they would be delivered. But only more people came in, shock registering on their faces.

"Mrs. DeVries. Dr. Tredegar." The voice was different. "I beg your pardon. You are free to go."

She didn't wait but threw open the door and ran back down the corridor, Cassian limping along behind her. Once back at the passport desk, she waited impatiently for Cassian to catch up, desperate to find Sander and let him know all was well. The official stamped passports, stamped the ship's manifest in several places. Thump, thump, thump. He pushed the passports back to her. "Welcome to America," he said, but he was looking beyond her to the next people in line.

The noise, the smell, the people all came to life again. She clutched Elly and pushed her way down the stairs of separation, taking the ones on the right, where she'd seen Sander. Frantic with excitement, she jostled the people around her, Elly bumping against her hip. All over, people ran for freedom, and in the plaza outside, people hugged and kissed and children were swept into the arms of parents and aunts and uncles. She stopped, looked about, jumped to see over people's heads. "Sander DeVries," she shouted. Where was he?

A ferryboat was pulling up to the dock, and the crowd began moving toward it. She pushed her way through. If Sander thought she and Cassian had been denied entrance to America, he could be in that crowd. She didn't dare take the chance. If he left now, how would they ever find him? She shouted his name at the top of her lungs and pushed through the people, who swore at her in all languages. Clinging tightly to Cassian's hand, she forced her way through the crowd, not caring whose toes she stepped on. She had to see if Sander was on the ferry. Onboard, she searched faces, and there he was, standing near the rear. "Sander!" Oh, she was so unbearably happy to see him, but he was white as a sheet. "What a fright we had," she said when she reached him. "You saw it. We were almost sent back." He looked like a person in shock. "Sander!" She covered his face in kisses, though his kiss in return was leaden, nothing but the coolest brush of his lips across hers. She appealed to Cassian and saw a glance pass between the two men. Something was very wrong. For the briefest moment, she understood. The plain fact. Sander hadn't been afraid they would all be sent back.

He'd been hoping for it.

15

THE HUDSON RIVER glittered. Ice chunks banged against the gunwales. Her nose would be bright red. It always happened in this weather. Sander was all business, peeling off the tickets for the ferryman, shoving through the people to get seats together on a bench, and only then did he reach for Elly and hold her up in both his large hands. The two regarded each other like a pair of wary dogs.

"Sander?" she said.

He returned Elly to Minke's lap, leaned back, and threw an arm on the top of the bench behind her. Around her shoulders but not quite touching.

"Cat got your tongue, Sander DeVries?"

"It's been an extremely difficult period for me" was all he said. She didn't need to be told that. Who'd had the worst of it since they had parted? Zef's kidnapping had been much harder on her, and then childbirth by herself.

"What of Fenna?" she asked, studying him in profile.

He reddened. "What of her?"

"Where is she?"

"Not feeling well," he said.

She sat back and held Elly tighter. She glanced at Cassian, who turned his hands over, finding something interesting to observe on his shiny fingernails.

The ferry pulled up to a wide wooden dock, and people pushed past, clogging the passageways with luggage. She, Cassian, Sander, and Elly were the last to debark.

She'd expected the yellow car, imagined them driving home, Cassian and Sander in front and she in the back, very much like the night she'd left Enkhuizen for Amsterdam and the *Frisia*. Instead of the car, though, they walked block after block. Great piles of slush met them at every curb, and she had to hop over them, sometimes landing ankle-deep in the wet filth. She practically froze in her black dress, which let drafts of frigid air in through the cuffs and sagging neckline. She must have looked so ugly to Sander. She kept Elly tucked tightly to her to keep her warm. In spite of the fumes and sounds, the hundreds of people, she was awed at the sheer height of the city, the way the buildings soared into the air.

Sander forged ahead without ever stopping to take his bearings. She hung on to his sleeve when the crush of people threatened to separate them, looking over her shoulder and asking him to slow down for poor Cassian.

They reached a place where trains thundered overhead and cars drove like racers underneath. A long set of stairs went to a platform, all enclosed, as big as a ballroom, with worn wooden floors and train tracks cutting down the middle. A train came and went, but Sander made no move to board it. Not theirs. He knew that somehow, and again she felt the old familiar pull toward him and appreciated his knowledge of things. She reached for him and squeezed his arm, pressed her fingers down the inside of his palm.

"The money is gone," he said before the rattling of another train prevented further words. The doors opened with a screech. She stepped aboard. The train had rows of shiny butterscotch-colored wicker benches.

"How?"

He shook his head. *Don't ask.*

She'd never been on a train, never gone this fast. It took her breath away. They careered over streets dozens of feet beneath them. She was dazzled and couldn't think about the money. Sander would figure something out. Doors hissed open and then hissed shut. People got on and off, no one meeting anyone else's eye. The crowd on the train thinned, doors opened again, Sander shepherded her and Cassian through the door against the press of people getting on. They were in another enormous station. Sander led the way down a set of covered stairs to the street level, where children ran in the streets shouting to one another in German and Dutch. Their mothers sat huddled on stone stairs, warming their hands over small fires. They watched suspiciously as Minke passed. A row of stores stretched up West 121st Street. The smell was of fish cooking. The whole was more like Enkhuizen than the New York she'd seen a half hour earlier. Sander was still the Pied Piper, several strides ahead of her and Cassian. The slush along this street was dirtier and deeper than in the streets around the ferry.

Sander finally stopped beside a grog shop with beer barrels in its windows, men on chairs looking dully out to the street and drinking from steins. One of them raised a stein to Sander. He opened a door on the left side of the bar, and she was reminded again of arriving with him in Amsterdam. But how different this was. How much more bleak.

The stairs were narrow and stank of garbage. They went up one story, then another and a third, until they reached a small landing with two doors, one marked 3A and the other 3B. Sander inserted a key into the lock of 3B and swung open the door to a darkened foyer. Ahead was a long hall with a filthy window at the end and doors leading off it.

They went through the apartment, Sander in the lead, then Minke and Cassian. There was a front parlor with only a couch and a chair in it, a small kitchen, and then two rooms, neither bigger than a cell. In one of the rooms, Fenna's clothes lay in a heap on the floor.

"Where is Fenna?" she asked just as Sander swung open the door to the slightly larger room with a double bed. Their room. The bedclothes were pulled mostly off the bed onto the floor, as if the bed hadn't been made in days.

"Right here," a voice behind her said.

Fenna stood in the doorway in her nightdress, lank blond hair falling over her shoulders, her eyes and nose red. "Fenna?" Minke took a step forward, then stopped. She felt as though she'd walked into something very personal, something that didn't include her. Fenna clutched at her stomach, moaned, and fled. Minke followed and found her sister slumped over the toilet. She thrust one hip to take Elly's weight while she found a cloth, wet it with water standing in the sink, and held it to Fenna's forehead. "Cassian," Minke called. "Can you come?"

"Something I ate," Fenna said. "You have to be careful in this stinking country."

Together, Minke and Cassian helped Fenna to the room where they'd seen her clothing. Since there was no bedding, they spread her old green coat over the mattress, bunched up her other clothes for a pillow, and lay a blanket on top of her.

"Go to Sander," Cassian said. "I'll see to Fenna."

Minke had been carrying Elly for a long time by now, and when she went back to the bedroom, where she'd left Sander, she needed to sit. *Let him speak*, Minke told herself. *Don't rush headlong into this.*

Sander made a show of righting the bedclothes, to no avail. He stood arms akimbo at the window that looked onto the side of an adjacent building, and cleared his throat. She kept her determination to stay silent. At last he turned to face her. "You look tired," he said. Elly swung her head around to see where the voice had come from.

Don't speak, Minke told herself. If she said a word, the whole flood of her anger would come roaring out—his cold reception, this awful place, and above all, Fenna.

He sat on the bed, his body touching hers, and hung his head. She recoiled. He said, "We have had a very difficult time in this country."

Minke kept her silence.

"Everything is up to me. Breadwinner for everybody now. You, the baby, Cassian, that sister of yours. I do my best."

"The baby's name is Elly," she said.

"Don't look at me with those accusing eyes, Minke."

"Where did our money go?" He'd spoken in glowing terms of America. The streets were paved in gold. He would find work easily. Fenna would find a magnificent house for all of them. "You were to have begun your business, found a decent place to live."

"That's all you care about. Money. I know you. I know what you're thinking."

"What am I thinking, Sander?" She waited, but he did not reply. "You don't dare say aloud what I'm thinking, do you?"

"Mind your place, Minke."

"I'm thinking—" She had to stop and take a deep breath. "I'm thinking that for this I gave up the chance of ever finding Zef." Her lip trembled at the mention of Zef and brought back vividly the terrible night he was taken.

Her hysterical screams had drawn people to the beach. She'd been frantic, clawing at them. "My baby," she kept calling. "Zef." In her panic, all she could think was that the entire world had to stop, to freeze, until Zef could be found.

They led her from the beach, but she fought them all the way. What if Zef came back and couldn't find her? She couldn't leave him. Their small house was crowded. Everyone talked at once. Sander gave her a small amount of morphine because she was hysterical. She'd tried to fight him off. She must go back. She must find Zef. But hands held her down and slipped the spoon between her lips. The morphine clouded her thoughts but didn't take away the jagged pain. She clutched herself as if pressing Zef to her. She thrashed until Fenna held her tight and told her to think of the baby inside her, to be calm or she would damage it.

Sander had become the grand inquisitor. Whom had she told about going to the beach with Zef? She had told no one. "What about that boy?" he had asked. "That German boy." She'd slurred because of the drug, saying no, never, she hadn't seen Pieps in months, but Sander pressed on, explosive in his conviction that Pieps had had something to do with it, and she had bolted from her bed and made for the door because no one was *doing* anything. They were only shouting and talking. She'd run to the path that led to the shore. "Zef!" she had screamed over and over, her voice just a hoarse cry.

Sander had brought her back to the house and to bed. Before she knew it, she was being held down again. She'd struggled, flailed her head from side to side, but on Sander's orders, Fenna had forced more liquid between her lips.

She had awakened the next morning to find the small house eerily quiet, Sander on the bed beside her and Fenna slumped in a chair nearby. "What happened?" she'd asked, dreading the worst, that Zef had been found dead. Sander had leaned his weight against her in case she tried to bolt again. He had told her in detail the events of the night. He'd gone to the skinners and demanded Pieps come outside and face him, but the boy had taken off at a run. For all his youth, he was no match for Sander, who had caught up and wrestled him in the dirt. Only the guilty need to run, he had said, and Pieps had admitted to everything, had broken down sobbing and begging forgiveness, "like the blubbering coward he was."

"Pieps has him, then?" she had said, hope swelling enormously. The question had only angered Sander, who said Pieps had sold the boy to the gauchos, who were a hundred miles away, no doubt, and then he had railed at her that it was her own fault. How many times had he warned her and she hadn't listened? He said Pieps had bragged like a rutting schoolboy, had said a child like Zef—fair, blond, European—had brought a huge price. And so what? Minke was capable of having plenty more, and one day she'd forget all about Zef.

Her only thought at the time, not the rage at Pieps—that came later—but that they must go to him, must demand information. Which gauchos? Where might they be? Her words had infuriated Sander further. Didn't she understand? Pieps was dead. Sander had shot him through the heart and left him to die in that godforsaken rubble. And now they would have to leave Comodoro because there would be repercussions. "God justifies what I did. A man takes my child, I'm justified," Sander said. Nevertheless, they could expect the gauchos to take their revenge. Pieps had been their friend. Minke had fought the plan tooth and nail. To leave was to abandon any hope of ever finding Zef. Sander had said it would do them no good to stay and be murdered in their sleep.

Guilt overwhelmed her, weighed her down with the force of a thousand stones. What she could not tolerate was that Pieps would have done this thing to her. How was it possible for a friend to turn so hatefully against a friend? And yet he had confessed. She ached with a pain so intense, as though the skin had been ripped from her body, and at her center, a feeling that Zef was connected to her by a strand of her own flesh that pulled at the core of her, that unraveled the farther he was taken away.

Sander had instructed Marta and Fenna to be sure Minke stayed deep in her morphine fog. She lived shrouded, as though through a curtain of wool. The morphine did nothing to ease the agony; it only made her unable to act. She had been powerless to stop the plan from moving forward, a plan in which Sander would go to America immediately, for his own safety.

He'd hidden away money and would take it to America, where he would set about establishing himself in business. Fenna would accompany him and find a grand home. Minke begged to go with them, but that was impossible because of her advanced pregnancy; the ship would refuse to take her, and even if she were able to board with the pregnancy undetected, Cassian was adamant that she must not travel. A ship's journey was far too dangerous for a woman in her condition— both the baby and mother would be in grave danger, and they dared not risk losing another child.

Now Minke gathered Elly to her again and rocked, turning her back to Sander. She hadn't wanted to break down, didn't want a scene in front of the baby, but she felt it coming. To keep herself steady, she sang the little song that calmed them both.

Sleep, baby, sleep
Today I saw a sheep.
Its feet were white
Its milk so sweet
Sleep, baby, sleep.

But she couldn't bear to be with her husband at that moment. She rose and took the baby to the parlor, where she could have solitude. She rocked and thought with a bitterness she hadn't known was in her about the way she always fell for Sander's fantasies. She didn't need a big house or money. She didn't care. She could live in anything, hadn't she shown that? But the reversal of expectations each time was exhausting.

She thought back over their years together, almost three now. Why hadn't she seen his character before? The signs had been there. Now

they swung up and practically slapped her across the face. He'd married
Minke because she was present in his house. He hadn't had to miss a beat
from one wife to the next. Nor from Minke to Fenna. He had Cassian
give Elisabeth an overdose—not for Elisabeth's sake but for his own.
What was it Griet had said on the day the *Frisia* sailed? Be warned; he
was a man who never passed up an opportunity. That was Sander,
indeed. And his business. Why had he never been forthcoming and
simply told her he traded in morphine? Instead, he had muddied the
waters whenever she asked. And the store. What had been the point of
it? The store had made sense at first, but the Almacén sold what people
needed. The so-called store at the front of their home was a shambles of
boxes and knickknacks from the Amsterdam house that Sander traded
with Goyo for God knew what.

He'd barely done anything at the store. The whole thing had been a
pipe dream, given that the Almacén was already well established. What
did they sell, anyway? Scraps of fabric to local women, the occasional
piece of furniture or gewgaw traded with the gauchos. That store was
never intended to support them. It was the *obras*, but there Cassian
produced the morphine, not Sander. Come to think of it, the *Elisabeth*
had belonged not to him but to his first wife. The more Minke thought,
the plainer it all became; she'd been blind not to see it until this moment.
While Cassian was healing, she hadn't seen Sander do a lick of work.
Mostly, he'd counted his money. The *obras* might have been saved if
Sander had rolled up his shirtsleeves and pitched in. Finally, she thought
bitterly, hadn't it been easier to leave her behind to clean up the details
of their lives in Comodoro, leave Minke to have the baby without him,
and set sail with Fenna and money in his pockets? Money that was
apparently gone after three months.

She shuddered. This dismal flat with its filthy windows. He was a
weak man. He'd left his children behind to start a new life. He was
capable of that. He'd left her behind to start a new life. And look at the
mess he'd made this time.

For richer or for poorer, the wedding vows said. But she had never
actually taken those vows. Sander had promised a real marriage in
Argentina and never followed up. She had half a ring.

Sounds came of Fenna retching in the bathroom. She gathered up Elly, returned to the bedroom, and pulled the door closed behind her. "Is Fenna pregnant?" she asked him, rocking Elly gently as she spoke.

He was slumped on the unmade bed.

"Answer me."

He met her eyes. "A man has needs, Minke. Not that you'd know. You made yourself unavailable with babies, with pregnancy. What was I to do?"

She almost laughed at the brazenness of it, that he was laying the blame for it on her shoulders. "So I'm responsible?"

"I didn't say that."

She stepped closer, looking down at him. "You're my husband, not hers. You already have a wife and a child to care for."

The door opened behind her. "A word, Sander?" Cassian asked.

"How far along is she, Cassian?" Minke asked. "I want to hear one of you say it."

Cassian glanced at Sander. "She says it's a few months. Maybe three."

Minke handed Elly to Cassian and asked him to take the child from the room. She shut the door behind him, crossed the floor, stood over Sander, and slapped him with all the force she had. His head snapped to one side from the blow. "How will we live now?"

The door swung open. Fenna, big, with muscular arms, broad shoulders, and full breasts, said, "So now you know."

"*Lichtekooi,*" Minke said. "You always were. *Stom rund.* Stupid."

Fenna shrugged, unfazed.

"How could you?" Minke said.

"Ask Sander," Fenna said with a laugh. "He likes a certain thing that you know nothing about. You're the stupid one. While you slept, we did it. While you tended Cassian, we did it. Wake up, Minke!"

Minke turned back to Sander. "Say something!"

Sander lifted his eyes to her. "Don't take that tone, either one of you," he said, but his voice was dull. "We will all need to look for work."

"Not me," Fenna said. "I can't work when I throw up all the time."

"Swallow it," Minke said. "You'll work, all right."

"Sander already said I won't have to. You're the one who'll work. And Sander and Cassian. I stay here and take care of Elly, right, Sander?"

"When hell freezes over."

"You'll do as I say," Sander said.

Unable to bear being in their presence for another minute, Minke addressed Sander. "Ask Cassian to bring Elly to me. I want privacy." She turned to Fenna. "You get out of here. This is my room. I'm the mistress of this household, whether I like it or not."

Fenna crossed her arms and seemed about to start another war, but Sander intervened and guided her out. A few moments later, Cassian came in with Elly drowsing in his arms.

They sat on the bed, Cassian with his arm around Minke's shoulders, which helped to quiet the trembling that had begun. "Did you know about them?" she asked.

He hung his head.

She sighed when he remained mute. "Why didn't you say? Never mind. I know. He's blood. You either betray him or you betray me. It's the devil's bargain for you. I forgive you."

"I thought it would end. I didn't understand it. How he could stray with your own sister?"

"She goes after what she wants." They sat in silence a moment. Then Minke said, "They must have spent all the money."

Cassian's black eyes fixed on her. "Sander is a gambler, Minke."

"I know that. He gambled at the Explotación with Dietz and the others."

"Sander has the compulsion."

"Don't they all?"

"No. Only some will gamble until nothing is left."

"Then we're doomed."

"You need to be careful. I as well. And not let them have the money we earn. It won't be easy."

"I don't know how I'll earn money. I have no skills. And Elly."

"You're stronger than you know, Minke."

"Five mouths to feed, and Fenna is pregnant. How will we survive this?"

"People never see how it will happen, Minke. That's not the gift. Strength is the gift. You have it."

After Cassian left the room, she opened the black dress to feed Elly. The baby's eyes stayed on Minke's the whole time. Then she lay Elly carefully on the floor while she made up the bed, taking care to tuck in tight corners so the bed had a crisp, unyielding look. She lay down, curled her body around Elly's. At first she could only suffer over the terrible thing that had been done to her, Sander's atrocious behavior, Fenna's betrayal, and a well of worry so deep she thought she might die of it. She longed for her mother's comforting arms, but that was impossible now. The shame of it would kill her mama—Minke's failed marriage, a lost child, destitution.

But then, as if waking from a bad dream, her despair gave way to clarity. Why hadn't it come to her sooner? For the first time—not just today but in a very long time—the curtains of worry parted, and she knew exactly what she would do. She would go back to Comodoro with Elly. Just the two of them. She would figure out a way. Somehow she would find work, save her money, and go.

She would find Zef if it took her a lifetime.

16

MINKE MADE A plan. She would start at the corner of Broadway and 121st Street and enter each store no matter what it sold. Cassian had instructed her to speak only to store owners, no one else. He had buoyed her up when she despaired over finding a job. "You sew like a professional," he told her. "You speak English."

"But who will pay me for any of that?" she asked. "I'm seventeen."

"Be patient," he said.

Her first store, tiny and fetid, sold typewriters and ribbons. "I can sew," she explained shyly. The owner just shook his head. When she left, she felt like a fool. What would a typewriter store need with sewing? In the next store, the merchandise was more varied. Canned goods, bolts of cotton. Again she told the owner she could sew. He laughed. "Everybody can sew," he said. "Get out of here."

"I speak English," she told the next shopkeeper.

"We don't need English," he said. "English don't come in here. Only the Dutch, the Germans, the Poles."

"I speak Dutch, of course."

"The whole city is Dutch." In case she didn't understand, he slapped the map hanging over his desk and said in a thick voice, "Konijnen Eiland, Bouwerij, Breukelen, Haarlem, Greenwijck, Vlissingen, Staaten Eylandt."*

"I do figures, too."

He sighed. "We'll try you, but leave that baby at home." When she refused, he threw her out.

---

* Coney Island, the Bowery, Brooklyn, Harlem, Greenwich, Flushing, Staten Island

And so it went. There was nothing to be had. Everywhere the same: Either they had no need of her or they were willing to hire her but without Elly. She was one of thousands looking for work.

One night Fenna told her about someone in the neighborhood who needed a girl to model clothing in a small department store. Minke knew Fenna spent her days on the stoop gossiping with other women and that the lead had come from one of them, but she followed up. Things were becoming desperate. She went to the address. The store was called Murphy's, and it was in a neighborhood much farther north. She was told to wait behind a curtain for Mr. Murphy. The store was nicer than the places she'd been, she had to admit that much.

A man of about Sander's age pulled back the curtain. He was heavyset and florid. He told her to stand. "Put that baby somewhere else. What do you think this is?"

She took Elly, sling and all, from her shoulder and carefully laid her in a corner. The man stepped back, told her to turn this way and that. He handed her a blue silk slip to put on. Her heart beat at the prospect of a job. She let the black dress fall to the floor and had the slip over her head, ready to slide it down, when the curtain was pulled. The man stood watching, eyebrows raised in expectation. She yanked the curtain shut, threw the slip to the floor, put on her black dress again, grabbed Elly, and brushed past him in her haste to escape.

The next morning before dawn, there came an ear-splitting sound from the hall, a banging on the door and Fenna's voice demanding to be let in. The door flew open and bounced against the wall. "He's mine!" Fenna said. "He belongs in my bed!" And then to Sander, "Now. Right this minute. You will come now or pay the piper, Sander, I swear it. I'm carrying your baby, you son of a bitch."

Minke was on her feet in a heartbeat. This was the last straw.

Sander swung his bare legs over the side of the bed. Cassian limped in from the hall, wrapping a dressing gown around himself.

"Now!" Fenna shouted louder. She grabbed for Sander's hand to pull him from the room. "I won't stand for this arrangement one more minute."

Fenna had obviously been awake for hours, building a vicious head of steam, her rage and self-justification exploding in this fury. She could be terrifying, but Minke felt something let go inside her as she swung at Fenna with her fist and cracked her sister hard on the shoulder. Fenna wailed, doubled over, but was upright in only a second, lunging for Minke, who dodged the clumsy girl. Cassian—frail as a spider—inserted himself between them, his arms out, like a referee at a boxing competition. Minke drew back, although it took Fenna a moment longer, and for a second Minke was afraid Fenna would harm Cassian. Silence fell except for their heavy breathing. Minke had had enough. She trembled in the aftermath of her own rage. She felt sick.

It had all taken only a few seconds. Elly's screams pierced the silence. Minke scooped up her baby and made her way shakily down the hall to the parlor, collapsed onto the couch, and tried to calm Elly. The baby's cries subsided as Minke rocked gently back and forth.

Outside, snow was falling, covering the grimy streets in white, lighting on winter trees. And so quiet under the streetlights. She rocked and tried to think. Fenna had won this one for sure. Sander hadn't the backbone, and Minke was tired of fighting for a man she didn't want.

When dawn finally broke, she made her way to the small kitchen. Normally Cassian left the apartment early to look for work, but not today. She sat opposite him, and he poured her some coffee. "I have an idea," he said.

He'd spoken about the new public library. He'd been reading about its construction in the newspapers. It was on Forty-second Street and Fifth Avenue, he told her, and they could walk to it if they took their time. They put on their heavy coats and set out. Down Broadway they went, block after block through the snow and slush. Cassian had to sit on benches often to rest. "Aren't we a pair. What must we look like to others? You with that big sling and your terrible dress, me with a limp, my white hair."

When they reached the library, the sight took her breath away. It took up two city blocks. Two enormous fierce lions carved in stone and covered in snow flanked the grand stairs leading up to it. Cassian said the library contained seventy-five miles of shelves, which had to be a mistake. There weren't enough books in the world for that.

Inside, Cassian asked an attendant where to go. The man led the way to an area where newspapers hung like laundry on wooden dowels. He showed Minke how to remove the newspaper still on its dowel and spread it on a reading desk. He turned to the section called POSITIONS AVAILABLE. Minke hadn't known such information existed, and she read greedily. There were offers of employment for cooks and drivers and ironworkers. And then she found it. The ad said:

Dressmaker/laundress wanted.
Room and board included.
Call at 131 Riverside Drive, Apartment 2,
between three and four o'clock P.M.

17

$\mathcal{T}$HE ONLY SPACE large enough was the parlor floor. Minke moved the couch and chair out of the way to make room for what she was about to do, took off her dress, and, wearing only her petticoat, laid out the dress. It was like a giant tent made of black wool and smelling of sweat, smoke, and grease.

Elly lay on a blanket at her side, examining her fingers in the shaft of sunlight that filled the room.

"What do you think you're doing?" Fenna sank onto the couch, her pale eyes dull.

Minke didn't answer.

"Cassian has found a patient," Fenna said. "There will be money."

Minke took a razor and carefully sliced each stitch along the side seam of the dress.

"What are you doing?"

"Making a better-fitting dress."

"But I'm going to need it for later. When I'm big." Fenna stuck out her lower lip, the same little pout she'd had since she was a child.

"It's my dress," Minke said. "I made it." She opened the dress and spread out the two halves. Then she began cutting the stitches that joined the top to the skirt. It was coarsely made and came apart easily—the arms from the top, the cuffs, the pockets, the plackets, everything carefully laid flat. She soon had all the pieces of black wool spread before her like a puzzle.

"I'll tell Sander."

"Go ahead," Minke said.

It took all of the afternoon to cut down each piece, pin the pieces together, hold it up to herself for fit, unpin, and repin, until it was right. That evening she washed each piece of the dress in cold water in a basin. The water got filthy as the wool let go of all the smoke and dirt and grime it had sucked in through the months. She hung the pieces over the radiator to dry. All night the wet wool gave off a lovely clean odor that reminded her of home.

By the light of dawn, she began sewing the pieces together. It took hours. And when she finished her dress, she took Elly's sling apart and turned the fabric so the bright parts, those not faded by sun and dirt, would show on the outside. Fenna crabbed to Sander about what Minke was doing. When he didn't intervene, a screaming fight broke out between them. The door slammed at one point. Sander was off to the tavern or to wherever he gambled. Minke no longer cared. But when Cassian came back, she stopped her work. "I understand you have a patient," she said.

His color was better. He'd spent days on the streets looking for work, too. He'd found the new patient, he explained, at a bar that sold drinks to men like him. "You know what I mean," he said in English. Cassian spoke to her only in English so Fenna and Sander would not know what they said. "They treat me like the second coming of Christ. I'm a miracle." He laughed. "And what is all this, may I ask?"

She slid the dress on, buttoned up the front. "*Mooi*," he said, slipping into the Dutch for "beautiful." The new dress fit her slim waist and came down to her ankles. She combed out her blond curls, braided them into the familiar coronet, and slung Elly onto her hip. "I plan to come home with a job," she said.

SHE WALKED TO Riverside Drive, the posh part of the city. Women passed in pairs pushing large, expensive prams, and Minke held tightly to Elly in her beribboned sling. The contents were what mattered, not the vehicle.

The building was gray stone with a canopy over the door and a man in uniform who took her name, pressed a buzzer, and saw her up in an elevator.

She'd been practicing assiduously with Cassian, putting special care into certain words. She must say *the*, not *se*, and *was*, not *vas*. "I come about the position advertised in the newspaper," she would say. "I am a seamstress. I have made this dress myself since only yesterday."

Which was exactly what she said to the woman who opened the door to her.

The woman wore a gray dress with a high collar. She was petite and old. Perhaps Mama's age, which meant at least forty. The woman smiled at her. She had a whitely powdered face, a circle of rouge high on each cheek, and red lipstick. She asked if she might peek into the sling, and Minke opened it slightly so she could see Elly, who lay peering up with her wide brown eyes. The woman raised her eyes to Minke's for a long moment. "I'd like to have my sister here," she said at last, and rang a little bell that stood on a nearby table.

A second woman appeared, like the first but stouter. She wore half-glasses and peered at Minke over the tops.

"Do come in," the first one said.

The room Minke was shown to was large, with heavy velvet drapes over the windows and shining wooden floors. The sisters sat side by side on a divan. The larger of the two indicated a chair for Minke.

"We're the Misses Wiley," the small one said. "I'm Miss Anne Wiley, and my sister is Miss Amanda Wiley. You will call us Miss Anne and Miss Amanda. It's much simpler, don't you agree?"

Minke nodded. Miss Anne spoke as if they had already hired her, although that was impossible.

"Tell us about yourself," Miss Anne said sweetly.

Minke hadn't expected this. Cassian had prepared her to show off her skills. He'd expected them to test her with a small sewing project. She didn't know what to say to such fine women with their lovely apartment and good manners. How could she ever admit that her husband had become a drunk and a gambler, that he'd impregnated her own sister, that the family, once sound, was desperate?

"I believe I heard you say you made the dress you're wearing." Miss Anne said, helping her. "Tell us about it."

That was all she needed. She explained in the best English she could muster, standing and showing the sisters, the way she'd sewn up the sides, how she'd had to cut it down. Her fingers trembled from nerves. She explained the placket, which was complicated and difficult to describe in English. "And all since yesterday," she said. "Because I could not have arrived in the dress the way it was. Oh, it looked terrible," she said before realizing she'd perhaps made a mistake in admitting that and, out of nerves, launched into a description of the ship from Argentina, the cramped quarters and cold nights.

Miss Anne interrupted. "But I thought you were a Dutch girl."

The whole fiery story came flowing out of her in broken English; then she lapsed into Dutch, then corrected herself. She might as well tell it all and take her chances. She spoke of Elisabeth's death in Amsterdam, her marriage, the excitement of being onboard the ship to Comodoro and Comodoro itself. And the *obras* and the gauchos and crossing rivers on horseback, even the shrunken heads of Frederik Dietz! She couldn't stop the words from coming, egged on by Miss Anne's small noises of encouragement. The two sisters sometimes glanced at each other, but Minke couldn't read what was passing between them. She sensed approval from Miss Anne, at least.

She explained about the beating Cassian, Dr. Tredegar, had had because he was a homosexual. The sisters didn't bat an eye. "He was terribly injured. His leg will never be the same again. But he's a doctor. He delivered both my babies!"

As if on cue, Elly awakened, squirming and making small chirping sounds. The sisters both laughed, and the spell was broken. "And what of your husband?" Miss Amanda inquired.

Minke drew a small, quick breath. She'd already said everything else; there was no turning back now. "He betrayed me, and now I've left him."

The sisters were a pair of dolls, composed if slightly startled. Finally Miss Anne spoke. "May I hold her, please?"

Minke drew the child from the warmth of her sling. It was safe in there, like the pouch of a kangaroo. "My only regret at never marrying," Miss Anne said, taking the child and swaying back and forth with her.

"Amanda?" Miss Anne cocked an eyebrow at her sister. Miss Amanda frowned. "It sounds like the truth to me. But we don't like surprises. You've told us everything, yes?"

Minke swallowed. "Yes."

"Well, then," Miss Anne said. "Here are the job responsibilities we are seeking."

She lay out the guidelines for perhaps the easiest job Minke could imagine. It involved living in rooms off the kitchen. On the ground floor of the building were several rooms, one of which belonged to the sisters and their brother, Louis, but more about him in a minute. The downstairs room would be hers for the mending and sewing. She was free to take in other work so long as she got theirs done on time. There was a mountain of mending to be done, as well as some dressmaking. In addition, Minke was to do the Wileys' personal laundry in the kitchen. The sheets and clothing were taken elsewhere. A housekeeper named Mrs. Bowen came in to do the cleaning and prepare the meals. So there was no need of those services. "We don't see the baby as being an immediate problem," Miss Anne said in conclusion, "but you must understand that if you are unable to manage your work and the tending of the child, we must let you go."

"Does this mean you'll hire me?" Minke said, astonished.

"It does," said Miss Amanda.

"I never expected—"

"That's what I like in you," said Miss Anne.

"I suppose you'll need to go and pack your things," Miss Amanda said.

"I have little."

"And inform your friend, that doctor, of your whereabouts."

* * *

HOW COULD SHE be so lucky? She practically danced home. The apartment was its gloomy self. Sander was asleep on the couch in the parlor. She crept down the hall to where Cassian had carved out a space for himself in the area by the back door. He, too, was asleep on his mattress there. She didn't bother looking for Fenna. Cassian was the one she wanted. She shook him awake.

"I have the job!" she whispered so as not to wake the others. He had been sleeping in his clothing, a worn velvet jacket. Once she was established in her little sewing room, she would do to his clothes what she'd done to her dress. She told him everything. "I'm leaving," she said. "I won't stay and be shamed. I need to think of Elly."

He sat up. "Didn't I say you were strong?"

She wrote down the address on a slip of paper and pressed it into Cassian's hand. "Don't let Sander or Fenna know where I am."

In the morning she rose, bathed, fed and changed Elly. When she was ready to leave, she threw open the door to Fenna's room. Sander and Fenna looked like an enormous mound under the blanket, a great hulking moving thing. "Sander." He started like a frightened child who'd been caught stealing. She remained calm. "We won't be back," she said. "We're leaving."

"Who?"

"Elly and I."

"Where?"

Fenna lumbered from the bed. "You can't," she said. "You need to work. We have to stay together. Everybody says that. As soon as the family breaks apart, there's no hope."

"I'm not the one breaking apart the family, Fenna. Anyway, I have work," Minke said. She hadn't meant to say anything, but she'd slipped.

"Where? How much?"

"Goodbye, Fenna."

"I'll find out," Fenna shouted after her. "We're a family."

"I wish Mama could hear you say that," Minke called back over her shoulder. "We're not a family at all."

"You can't take Elly. She's Sander's."

Minke couldn't resist. She came back to the room. "Sander?"

He threw the blanket back, exposing his naked chest.

"Is that true? You want to keep Elly?"

Sander shut his eyes wearily.

"See? He has no interest in Elly. He'll have no interest in your baby, Fenna. I pity you."

"You can't just leave and not tell us where you're going," Fenna shouted after her, and for a moment Minke felt sorry for her sister, for her desperation. But only for the briefest moment. She closed the door behind her.

18

MISS AMANDA LET Minke in by the service door off the kitchen. Because it was a Saturday, two things would be different from normal. First, the weekend was the housekeeper's time off, so Minke would not meet Mrs. Bowen until Monday. That meant Minke would cook for herself. Once the tour of the apartment and small sewing room downstairs was complete, she could make a good breakfast. She'd eaten so little for so long and was depleted enough by Elly's needs that the idea of food made her salivate. Miss Amanda showed her the kitchen with its icebox full of eggs, milk, and vegetables. The coal cookstove, the soapstone laundry sink and mangle. A larder, filled to the brim with canned goods and boxes of delicious-looking biscuits. Her quarters off the kitchen consisted of two rooms bigger than those in Sander's apartment, each with a window that overlooked the alley and a stable next door. In one of the rooms was a single bed and a bureau. In the other room were a couch and two chairs. Dividing the two rooms was a narrow tiled space that held the toilet, small sink, and tub. Incredibly, it was all hers.

Miss Amanda was all business as she led the way down the service stairs to the ground floor and a darkened hallway with doors on either side. The third door on the right was to the sewing room. It was flooded with light from two high windows. A treadle sewing machine stood in the center, and beside it was a large basket of notions, scissors, thread, and needles. Minke touched everything with her slender fingers. Lovely equipment. Miss Amanda showed her the pile of mending to be done. Most of it, she explained, was clothing that had to be taken in for their brother, Louis. And that was the other oddity. Louis was in residence, as it was a Saturday, his day off from work. He looked forward to meeting her and having a fitting right away. There had been many hapless seamstresses, and he had high hopes for Minke. "My brother is a very important man," she said. "You will be very respectful of him. And I'll have you know I'm not so won over as is my sister. I expect you to prove yourself here."

Minke's heart sank like a stone. If others before her had failed, who was she to succeed? She had the skills of the self-taught. She had made the best sampler in her class at school. Mama had taught her everything else she knew. But this was New York, not Enkhuizen. The sewing in a place like this, for people like this, must be far more sophisticated.

She was given a key to the sewing room, but for the time being, Miss Amanda said she would enter through the service door to the building and come up the service stairs. It was premature to give her a key to the apartment.

"I understand," Minke said. She would have done it that way herself.

"Come, then," Miss Amanda said, "and meet Louis."

Minke followed Miss Amanda's long black skirts back up the stairs, through the kitchen, the dining room, and the foyer, which she now saw was hung with tapestries and decorated with things that must have come from all over the world and reminded her of the exotic items in Sander and Elisabeth's house in Amsterdam. Just before the living room, they passed a large mirror, and Minke startled to a stop. The girl she saw there was such a shock. She went in close, the better to see herself. Her face was so much thinner! She had fine high cheekbones, and her skin was brown from the sun and wind of the ship. Her blue eyes seemed to shine brighter than she remembered. Her eyelashes were bleached from the sun to a white-blond, and her hair, too. She almost fainted when it came to her, when she understood why the resemblance had practically taken the wind out of her.

She was Zef.

"What do you think you're doing?" Miss Amanda stood waiting for her with an expression of incredulity that Minke would stop to stare at herself in the mirror.

There was no explaining. "I'm so sorry," Minke said.

The next door gave onto a hallway and more rooms—an apartment in itself, much like the public library with its bookshelves and shiny wooden furniture. At the last door, Miss Amanda knocked. A man appeared. He was short and plump, with a massive head and an engaging smile. He held out a hand to Minke. "My sisters have told me about you. Come in, come in." In the room was a large desk of carved wood and several leather chairs. He indicated one of the chairs. Miss Amanda parked herself at the door. He spread his arms out wide. "I'm a difficult man to fit. I'm vain as well. Don't laugh. I like my clothing to fit perfectly."

She was trying to evaluate the fit of his trousers and vest. The sleeves of his shirt were a bit too long and the cuffs too loose. She felt encouraged; it was something she could fix. And the trouser seams were wavy. Oh yes. She was better than the last seamstress. "I believe I can do that."

He nodded, indicated her sling. "What's that you have there?"

The sisters must not have told him about Elly. "My baby," she said, opening it slightly so he could see the sleeping child.

He reared back a little. "My sisters surprise me every day." He addressed Miss Amanda. "I wouldn't have thought you'd take a woman with a baby. Anne, of course, but not you."

"She'll be no trouble," Minke said quickly. "I promise you. She's a good baby."

"We know nothing of babies in this household," Mr. Wiley said.

"And we don't wish to learn," Miss Amanda added.

"I understand you'd like me to begin making some alterations today," Minke said. She was so afraid the Wileys would find a reason to change their minds. She was on very thin ice, and everything she said seemed to make Miss Amanda even more skeptical.

"Indeed," he said. "We'll see how you do. I'll come fetch you in an hour. How is that?"

Miss Anne hovered in the kitchen. She'd found a stack of clean rags Minke could use for Elly's diapers. She showed Minke where she would find things for her lunch. Mrs. Bowen would be in on Monday, she said.

The kitchen was Mrs. Bowen's domain, and it was best to keep it orderly.

Minke was so hungry she felt she might almost faint. The moment Miss Anne retreated, she buttered two slices of bread and wolfed them down. She drank a large glass of cold milk. Everything was strange and new, like being in Elisabeth's house, except her own parents had sent her there, which had made it all seem safe at the time. *Oh, and look how well that turned out,* she thought. The sisters kept coming into the kitchen for one reason or another. To fetch this or that, to see if she was finding what she needed. To check that she wasn't stealing, no doubt, which made sense. She was as strange to them as they were to her. She had to be careful to keep this job. To do everything right. While she did her dishes, Elly began to fuss. She finished quickly, before Elly's cries grew loud, and took the baby to her room to change and feed her.

"Shall we?" Mr. Wiley's voice came from the kitchen. "Where did that girl go?" he asked the sisters. Miss Anne rapped lightly at her door. "Louis is ready for his fitting." Minke rose immediately, slipping Elly back into her sling as she hastened back to the kitchen. Elly squirmed and fussed at this hasty treatment.

"Leave the baby with Anne," Mr. Wiley said.

"I always keep her with me." Minke panicked at the thought of leaving Elly.

"Come, come." He made an impatient gesture that meant she should give Anne the baby.

"I can't."

Mr. Wiley frowned. "Can't what?"

This would be her ruin. "I can't leave her."

"Nonsense," Mr. Wiley said. "That's nonsense. The child is perfectly safe."

"It's too far," she said, realizing the absurdity of what she had said. They would think she was crazy.

Mr. Wiley gave Miss Amanda a look, and Minke knew she was in trouble.

"I lost a child in Comodoro. I've been afraid to let Elly out of my sight."

Mr. Wiley frowned.

"His name was Jozef. In all Elly's life, I've never been more than a few feet from her."

"Well, that's a terrible thing," Mr. Wiley said. "But you can't be with her forever."

"Louis," Miss Anne said. "Show some compassion!"

"I don't understand the problem. My brother would like to be fitted," Miss Amanda said.

Miss Anne said, "I'll tell you what. I'll hold Elly, and we'll *all* go to the sewing room."

Mr. Wiley frowned at them. He clearly was a man used to giving the orders in the household. "That won't do. We've hired you for a particular job, and we expect you to perform it." He wasn't exactly angry. That was the disarming part. He was just stating the facts as he saw them. Either she did the job the way he wanted her to do it or she would have to leave. Without the job, she and Elly would have to return to the apartment with Sander and Fenna. Unthinkable. She took Elly from her sling, handed her to Miss Anne, and followed Mr. Wiley down the back stairs.

It took everything in her to keep the panic at bay, the terror that at that very moment Miss Anne was running out of the building with Elly in her arms, passing the baby to a stranger, and taking money. *Stop it!* she told herself. That was ridiculous! Yet she had trusted Pieps, and he had done the unthinkable. Once in the room, Mr. Wiley went behind a screen in the sewing room and emerged in a seersucker suit. It seemed to fit him well enough. What did he want from her? The length was good, the sleeves right.

"I've given up at J. Press. They never do it right."

She pretended to study the suit while she talked herself down. Mr. Wiley was waiting, hands on hips.

"Can you take a few steps," she said, stalling for time. For the life of her, she couldn't see anything wrong with that stupid suit and only wanted to bolt for the stairs to see Elly.

He walked across the floor, spun on his heel, and walked back. That was it. When he moved, the suit seemed to move independently of his body. The jacket buckled, the pants bunched. No wonder he didn't like it.

"Hold still," she told him. She pinned darts up the front of the jacket and in the pants along the sides, "Walk," she commanded. She studied the movement of the fabric, pinned a few more places. Now she saw that the crotch was too long. The jacket was too wide under the arms but fitted well around his waist. The point was to make him appear longer and leaner. It wasn't such a difficult task. "There," she said when she'd finished marking the suit with chalk and sticking pins in the fabric.

"I feel like a voodoo doll," he said. "Do the gauchos have voodoo dolls?" He shook his head with a laugh. "No, of course not. What am I saying? Wrong part of the world altogether."

"Mr. Wiley?"

"What is it?"

"May I ask what happens to the newspapers I saw in your study after you are finished with them?"

"Incinerated."

"My friend Dr. Tredegar says the best way to improve my English is to read the newspapers."

"A wise man," he said. "I'll arrange for you to see them."

THAT WEEKEND, THE telephone in Mr. Wiley's office rang frequently. The Misses Wiley were constantly answering the doorbell as people came to see their brother. This seemed normal for the household. Minke caught glimpses of well-dressed men in bowlers and fur-trimmed coats, even a woman, as they passed through the foyer and into Mr. Wiley's apartment. He barely had the time to try on the seersucker suit, but he finally managed on Sunday afternoon. The alterations slimmed him to the fullest extent possible, and he was pleased. She was elated: Her first challenge was met, and well met at that.

On Monday morning, however, the mood changed. Before dawn, she heard people in the kitchen whom she identified as Mr. Wiley and a woman, but not one of the sisters. She assumed it was the voice of Mrs. Bowen.

She lay in bed wondering what to do. Should she go into the kitchen or wait until she was called? Elly stirred, awakened by the voices; she would need attention. Minke got out of bed in hopes of reaching Elly before she began to cry from hunger, but she was too late. Elly drew in a deep breath and wailed. The door to Minke's apartment opened, and a woman stood there. She wore a long black dress with a white collar and white cuffs. "Where in 'ell did you come from?" She looked at Elly and crossed herself.

"That's the new seamstress," Mr. Wiley called from the kitchen. "Let her be."

Mrs. Bowen narrowed her eyes at Minke, a warning of some sort, and then pulled the door closed. Minke hastily fed Elly, changed her diaper, rinsed out the dirty one, washed her face, put Elly back on the bed, then picked her up again, not knowing what to do. She longed to take the child with her, but with Mr. Wiley there, was it best to keep her out of sight? She decided to go alone to the kitchen.

Mr. Wiley sat at the kitchen table with a newspaper spread out, reading assiduously. Mrs. Bowen stood over him with the pot of coffee, glaring at Minke as though daring her to get between herself and Mr. Wiley. He seemed oblivious. He scanned the paper and then turned the page, lifting it at one edge between thumb and index finger delicately, as though it were the finest lace, and raising it high, then carefully settling the page flat and starting to read something in the upper left hand.

Minke didn't know what to do with herself.

Mr. Wiley glanced up. "Well, give the girl some coffee, Bowen," he said. "Don't just stand there."

Mrs. Bowen indicated the cabinet where the cups were kept, and Minke drew one from the shelf. Mrs. Bowen pointedly put the coffee over the pilot light on the stove and returned to stand behind Mr. Wiley while Minke poured her own. She sipped the fine coffee and watched. As Mr. Wiley finished a section of the paper, he laid it to the side, and Mrs. Bowen snatched it up for her stack on the counter.

"Might I?" Minke asked, reaching for the paper.

"Might ye what?" Mrs. Bowen said.

"Mr. Wiley?" Minke asked.

Mrs. Bowen gave her a cross look and put a finger to her mouth.

"Mr. Wiley," Minke said again. She wasn't about to be bullied by this woman. He looked around, a man startled into the present. "Might I take your papers when you're finished?"

"Of course, of course. We settled all that yesterday. Bowen will tell you where they go when you finish with them."

Minke felt an urge to stick out her tongue at Mrs. Bowen. Just then the kitchen door swung open, and a young man came into the kitchen. He reminded her of Pieps with his youthful grace and blondness. He colored when he saw Minke.

Mr. Wiley wiped his mouth with a napkin, put down his cup, and got to his feet. "Off we go, then," he said, and was swiftly out the door.

"Seamstress, are you?" Mrs. Bowen said.

Minke nodded. Instinct told her the less she said to this woman, the better.

"His secretary, that was," Mrs. Bowen said. "Name of Bill."

"I see."

"The boy follows him to work, taking notes the whole way. Comical to see, that Bill behind Mr. Wiley, scribbling like the devil all the way down Riverside Drive. People talk about it."

"I'll be going down to see to the sewing," Minke said. "There's a lot to be done."

Mrs. Bowen grunted. She filled a bowl with oatmeal, lay it before Minke, and drew up a chair. "Who are you?" she asked.

"The seamstress," Minke said. "I answered an ad in the newspaper."

"You and ten others. I mean, who are you? Don't banter around. I like to know who is working with me."

Minke met the woman's eyes. "I'm decent, clean, and hardworking, Mrs. Bowen. Just like you."

"What are you going to do with that baby? Don't think I'll care for it."

"I will not leave my baby with you," Minke said.

"You'll be just like the others."

"I've done nothing to deserve your anger."

Mrs. Bowen smiled. "What is he paying you?"

"I'm lucky to have the rooms."

"That's what I thought."

"Seventy cents a week."

Mrs. Bowen pouted.

"What do they pay you?"

"None of your little business, miss," Mrs. Bowen said. "You'll see that boy Bill get his walking papers soon. Mr. Wiley goes through secretaries faster than seamstresses."

"What about housekeepers?"

Mrs. Bowen made to clear the remaining newspapers from the table. "The man works too much."

"What of the sisters?"

Mrs. Bowen swept a dark curl from her forehead. "You want gossip, is that it? You people are all the same."

"Not gossip," Minke said. "I wondered if they work, too."

"The Misses Wiley have their charities and so on. This is a decent household, so don't go getting designs on that man."

"You have no business saying such a thing."

Mrs. Bowen made a face. "Well, Miss High-and-Mighty, you'll serve at dinner tonight, and no two ways about it."

"Oh?" Minke was surprised but not displeased. The job duties hadn't included that.

"Didn't know about that, did you?" Mrs. Bowen grinned. "You'll do as I say."

"I'll be happy to serve. And I'll take the rest of the newspapers with me now." She winked at Mrs. Bowen to irritate her a little.

Mrs. Bowen reached into a bag and drew out a dark dress. "Mend this," she said. "Under the arm is a rip."

"I will not mend your clothes."

"I would hate to have to complain about that child disrupting my kitchen," Mrs. Bowen said.

Minke snatched the dress up. "It had better be clean."

A heap of mending sat waiting in the sewing room. She set Elly down, threw back the curtains to let in the light, and decided to start at the top, a woolen coat with a triangular rip, the most difficult thing to mend because it had to be invisibly rewoven. She slid an extra-fine needle in and out of the cloth, her moment alone, and yes, after having said his name aloud, she was finally unafraid. "Zef," she said in the small room, and the sound of it brought back to her his sweet laugh, his times playing peekaboo with Cassian at the *obras*.

"We'll find him," she said to the sleeping Elly. "I know it in my heart. I'm certain of it." She paused to hold the cloth up to the better light. "But where do you suppose he is?" She'd given this so much thought, made herself mad with it sometimes. "If we assume for a minute that it really was a conspiracy between Pieps and Goyo, something I still cannot bring myself to believe, then Zef is being raised as a gaucho." A smile spread over her face at the prospect of her little Zef on horseback or in an estancia before the fire, crowded in with other children and listening to a storyteller like El Moreno. "Gauchos take very good care of children. He'll learn their ways." A new thought stopped her. "Perhaps he won't want to leave. If that's the case, we'll simply wait until he's ready. That's what we'll do. Bide our time so he comes willingly. But if we find him right away, he'll be only two years old, and the task won't be so difficult."

She sighed. It was all so much. "If he's not with the gauchos, and I have always thought this more likely, he is with a family who paid a high price for him, and in that case, we'll steal him back as he was stolen from us. It will take us a long time to find him. He could be in Santiago, Buenos Aires. He could be anywhere, but here's our advantage, my little love: Zef is as blond as a Viking, a rarity. Oh, we'll find him."

Elly slept on.

Minke sat back and considered what was left to mend in the basket.

She'd made good progress and decided she would take a look through the newspaper. The articles were difficult, so she concentrated on the photographs and the captions underneath. Mostly, they were people's names, but often the caption described what was happening in the photograph, and it became a game to look carefully at the picture and use it to help understand the words. When she didn't know a word, she wrote it down. She would ask Cassian when he came. She hoped he would come soon.

When the pile of mending was finally smaller and the finished items were on hangers on the rack in the corner, she quickly stitched up Mrs. Bowen's dress, gathered up Elly, and went back up the stairs. The apartment was in an uproar. In addition to Mrs. Bowen, three robust women were in the steaming kitchen: one chopping vegetables at the table, another stirring a large pot of something that smelled delicious, and a third at the sink. Minke hurried through on the way to her rooms.

"Get back in here," Mrs. Bowen commanded. "I'll be needing you."

Minke turned to face the woman and spoke before she could stop herself. "Don't order me about. I won't stand for it." Mrs. Bowen seemed taken aback and was about to speak when Minke cut her off. "I'll help you after I take care of my child," she said, and shut the door behind her.

She changed Elly's diaper, trembling at what she'd done. But she wanted to make her point by taking the time she needed, so she washed and hung the diaper to dry in the bathroom, nursed the baby, and tried to remain calm. She wondered if Mrs. Bowen had the power to fire her. She thought not, since it was the Wileys themselves who had hired her and never said a word about serving. She set Elly down on a blanket in the corner of the kitchen where she could keep an eye on her and where Elly might have something entertaining to watch.

Mrs. Bowen, red-faced, shouted out commands. Minke was to lay the table for ten; she'd better know place settings, by God. Forks on the left, butter knife across the top. In Comodoro, Meduño had made a point of his skill at table setting, so at least she'd seen it done correctly. Well enough that Mrs. Bowen found nothing to complain about when she came to check.

When the guests arrived, Minke took their coats and put them in one of the bedrooms in Mr. Wiley's apartment, where she heaped them on a bed. Then she and two of the other women were sent from the kitchen to the dining room to serve the fish course and fill the water glasses. The talk around the table distracted her terribly, but she concentrated on her work as topics changed in midair, leapfrogging from the war to a crime in New Jersey to outrageous gossip about people they apparently knew—adulteries, embezzlements. The air rang with laughter and raised voices, people happily talking over one another.

"Our new seamstress," Mr. Wiley exclaimed, grasping her hand as she reached to clear a plate. "She comes to us from the Netherlands via Argentina. Comodoro Rivadavia."

"Pull up a chair, young woman," the man at the head of the table instructed her. "How long did you live there?"

Minke sat tentatively, not knowing if she should. "Almost two years."

"See some growth, eh?"

"People came on every ship. Hundreds every year."

"Tell me about the oil."

She was surprised these people knew about a tiny place so far away. "It is a sea of oil under the town. It gushes from cliffs and runs in the streets."

The man whistled. "How many wells?"

"Dozens."

"Twenty-four? Thirty-six?"

"More. Maybe a hundred."

"How is it transported?"

"Eh?"

"How do they ship it?"

"In barrels."

"Is there a railroad?"

"Talk of one, I think."

The kitchen door swung open, and Mrs. Bowen stopped in her

tracks, seeing Minke at the table. "I must be getting back to my work," Minke said.

In the kitchen Mrs. Bowen shook her head in disgust. "What do you think you're doing?"

"They had questions about Comodoro."

"You must never sit with them," she said.

"They asked me to."

"Even so." Mrs. Bowen sniffed. "Especially when it's Mr. Ochs."

"Who?"

"The swarthy one and his dark wife. He owns *The New York Times*. A very important man."

A FEW WEEKS later, Minke was in her sewing room when there came a knock at her door, and there stood Cassian. She threw her arms around his neck and hugged him hard. She'd never in her life been so happy to see anyone. Elly clapped her fat little hands, recognizing him even though he'd dyed his hair black again and had on a new velvet jacket in a lovely shade of rust.

Minke regaled him with her stories about the Wileys, Mrs. Bowen, the dinner parties—of which there had been several by that time—and the guests and their astonishing conversation about meteors and art exhibits and a riot in Paris over a ballet. Oh, and Elly was eating solid food, a little bit of porridge, which was a relief, and Minke was gaining some weight. The sisters sometimes asked her to play canasta with them—well, Miss Anne asked, and Miss Amanda went along with it. Best of all, she was reading the newspaper every day, getting better and better at it, and both sisters were happy to tell her the meaning of the words she didn't know. She excitedly showed him the stack of newspapers that was growing taller every day. Cassian laughed as she spoke. "And you?" she asked at the end of her spiel. "Tell me!"

He drew in a breath. "Where to begin," he said. Chiefly, he had a number of patients. All of them were homosexual men who did not dare visit regular doctors who might report them to the police. There was quite a large population of such men in lower Manhattan, Cassian explained, and he planned to move to an address in a place called Washington Square quite soon.

"And Sander?" Minke asked warily.

"The baby is due in October," Cassian said, shaking his head. "Pregnancy does not suit Fenna. She's in a sour mood most of the time. Sander has a job as a driver for someone. It pays him a little. I try to help out when I can."

Minke shuddered, the reality of Fenna's pregnancy sinking in all over again.

"When we're out of Fenna's hearing, Sander asks after you. He wants to know if you're well."

"Let him wonder," she said.

"I tell him I don't know. He rages at me."

"I regret putting you in such a situation."

"He knows I'm lying."

"You were careful when you came here, weren't you? That he didn't follow?" The thought of Sander showing up at the apartment sent a chill down her spine.

"One day he'll find out, Minke."

"How? He'll never know if neither you nor I tell him. Besides, I'll be gone one day." She told him her plan. She'd worked it out to the penny and to the day. If she managed carefully, she would have saved enough money to debark for Comodoro on March 15 of the following year. The cost was thirty-three dollars, steerage to Comodoro for her and Elly. Once she arrived, she would immediately go to the Almacén to talk to Bertinat. He had always liked her. She would offer to make alterations. She would be aggressive about her skills as a seamstress. After all, she'd been the tailor to one of the most important men in New York City. She would put up advertisements in all the public places. "I shall make sure everyone knows I'm looking for Zef. Maybe when I arrive there will be news. In a country like that, a towheaded boy is noticed. I can do it. I know

I can. Already, after only a few months, I'm managing well and saving my money. Elly is thriving here."

Cassian gave her a shrewd look. "Then you have a difficult choice."

"What do you mean?"

"The chance of finding Zef is small, Minke. And here in New York, you have the certainty of a good life for yourself and for Elly."

19

*E*VERY EVENING AFTER Elly was asleep, Minke pored over Mr. Wiley's newspapers in the kitchen. Mrs. Bowen had gone home to her husband by that time, and the Wileys were in their rooms. She read everything. The range of subjects covered in the newspaper was astonishing. There were stories of murders and politics and the threat of war and, on Fridays, the society news. A woman named Iris Singer went into people's homes and took photographs of rich families posed formally with children and dogs surrounded by opulence to match royalty. Minke had never seen such lavish interiors, thousands of square feet. Iris Singer described what she saw the way a starving person might describe food—full of longing. Minke liked to try out the words she learned on the Wileys. "Quite luscious," she might say about a piece of fabric one of the sisters had brought home, or "the epitome of rococo-esque design," she attempted once with Mr. Wiley, who glanced at her oddly and said, "Precisely right, but I think you mean eh-pih-to-me, not eh´-pi-tome."

She was always on the alert for news of Argentina, a country *The New York Times* said was like America in its rapid expansion and ability to attract immigrants from all over the world. People were flocking to Argentina to make their fortunes. Occasionally, there was even mention of Comodoro, always related to oil production. Minke read these reports over and over, as if she might find news of Zef between the lines. In August two photographs of Comodoro appeared in the paper. She borrowed Miss Anne's magnifier and hunched over them. One showed a Comodoro oil well, "sheathed in corrugated metal to protect it from the blowing sand and dirt," the article said. Outside, a dozen workers posed stiffly in their woolen hats and heavy coats. She looked closely at each face, hoping to see one she remembered. She thought perhaps she'd seen some of the men, but there was no one she really knew. Still, her heart fluttered with nostalgia at the sight of the familiar rubbled landscape, the smooth rolling hills in the distance.

The other photograph was looking down from the Cerro. It took her a moment to recognize the barracks at Dietz's camp, the same buildings she'd ridden to on the day Cassian was attacked. The operation was so much larger now, like a town unto itself. The article called Comodoro "primitive by any standard but experiencing rapid growth." It went on to say that the most valuable land had been bought up by speculators who were agents for major European oil companies working under cover until agreements with Argentina would allow for foreign investment. It mentioned Dietz's oil works by name: Petróleo Sarmiento.

This explained everything! He'd been certain from the start he would sell to Germans. Oh, this world. You thought a thing was true, and then it wasn't. Dietz wasn't an independent but a pawn in a much larger game of chess.

On her next day off, a splendid September afternoon, she set out for Cassian's apartment. Eight months old now, Elly was too restless to stay long in the sling, but Minke kept her there until they were settled in seats on the Ninth Avenue Elevated train. Then Elly sat on her lap and watched alertly everything that happened as the train swayed and screeched over the city.

As she did every week, Minke carried the week's newspapers for Cassian to read, but this week she was breathless to show him the photographs of Comodoro. When she reached the Thirteenth Street station, she zigzagged around the blocks to Cassian's building, a tall narrow structure made of brick and, like all the others on his street, with a metal fire escape down its front. She rapped at the door to his small office on the ground floor and, getting no answer, climbed the stairs to his apartment, where she rapped again and didn't wait for an answer before swinging open the door.

His flat was decorated with colorful wall hangings and big pillows like something Turkish or Moroccan, crowded with furniture and bookcases, so much like his house in Comodoro. She set Elly down, and the child crawled to a couch, covered in tapestries. Cassian opened his arms to her. He was much stronger now. His face had filled out, his dark eyes shone with their old spirit, and his hair was longer and oily black. Two of his neighbors were present, a couple who lounged on the couch, drowsy as Indian summer. Royal was a painter, and many of his paintings were stored on Cassian's walls. His wife, the frail, dark Ivy, watched her husband with doting eyes. They were often at the apartment on Sunday afternoons, Royal raging against this or that government, spouting opinions about whether there would be a war, about the corruption of public officials.

Minke nodded a quick hello, drew the papers from the bottom of Elly's sling, kept out the article about Comodoro, and dropped the rest with a thud on the stack in the corner. "Look at this one."

Cassian put on his glasses and sat down to read. Placed a hand over his breast. "Dietz was working for an oil company?"

"It looks that way," Minke said.

"He pretends to have everything at stake, like the rest of us, but he was on a payroll," Cassian said. "No wonder."

Cassian brought out the tea things, and Minke burrowed into the sofa, sipping her tea. She felt so utterly peaceful at Cassian's, watching Elly move from one set of knees to the next, fall on her behind, then pull herself up again.

A great racket sounded on the stairs to the apartment. Minke recognized the voices immediately and froze. The door was flung open to reveal Sander and Fenna, Fenna in her green coat, wide open in front to expose her nightdress. Sander's face was shiny with sweat from running up the stairs. Minke shrank into the sofa as if to keep Sander from seeing her. She stared at the two of them the way she might observe actors on the stage. Fenna was doubled over in pain and hanging on to Sander. Fenna made a terrible sound, a combination of a wail and a retching sound, clutched at her abdomen, and fell into one of the armchairs.

"Help her," Sander said, giving Cassian a shake. "For God's sake, man. The baby is coming."

"It's too early," Cassian said.

"It's coming anyway," Sander said.

Cassian helped Fenna to her feet. She didn't seem to have noticed that Minke was even there. Ivy and Royal must have fled. Only Sander and Minke remained in the living room. She was sharply aware of a change in him, a bleariness in his eyes, the result of drink, she assumed. His clothing—once his great pride—was limp and soiled, and while she might have felt vindicated, she felt only sadness at what had become of him. At last he took notice of her and was visibly shaken at the sight. Her painstaking efforts to hide her whereabouts had come to naught unless she could flee immediately. He ventured a weak smile. "Minke," he said.

Fenna screamed again from the bedroom. Minke drew herself up to standing. "Go to her," she said. "I'll put on water to boil."

Fenna screamed again. The baby was eight weeks early. Way too early. Minke put a hand to her forehead, and Fenna opened her eyes. She clutched at Minke's arm. "Help me, Minke. Help me," she sobbed. "The pain is too much."

The kettle shrilled in the kitchen. Cassian returned and dispensed some morphine to Fenna, and it calmed her a little. "More," she said. "Please, more."

But the baby wasn't waiting. Fenna screamed out and then was quiet.

It was a boy not much bigger than Cassian's hand, with thin, sharp features. Cassian ordered Minke to warm a blanket in the oven. In the kitchen, Sander held the kettle, clearly not knowing what to do with it. She went back to the bedroom as Cassian laid the child on Fenna's abdomen and covered it with another blanket. Such a mess, the bedding soaked in fluid and Fenna's clothing wet and bloodstained. She had to be cleaned and kept warm where she lay, cradling the child. "We mean to call him Woodrow, after the newly elected president," she whispered.

If he lives, Minke thought. He weighed only four pounds on Cassian's scale. "The baby," Cassian said to Sander in the living room, "must be kept at a uniform temperature."

"Impossible," Sander said. "It's growing cold now."

You would give up without even trying, Minke thought.

Cassian cleared his throat. "Difficult, Sander, yes, but not impossible. It has been done with success. The child must be kept in the oven with only the pilot light burning. The temperature can be kept close to the mother's temperature that way."

Minke was frightened for the child, whose parents could be incapable of this care. She fought the urge to go with them, to give up her life and take care of the child, who might otherwise die.

Cassian must have sensed Minke's dilemma. "Fenna will stay here with me for the time being, and I'll help with the infant." He indicated the stove, a massive cast-iron thing with an oven and a warming compartment. "Like so." He opened the doors to both oven and warming compartment, removed the blanket from the oven, raised it to his face to test the warmth, flapped it open to cool it, and folded it again. He brought it to Minke. "Feel." She reached out a hand. The blanket was perfect to the touch, exactly the temperature of her hand.

She gathered up Elly. "Go see your son, Sander."

He seemed about to speak, but she put a finger to her lips. After he left the room, she used the chance to slip out the front door with Elly and ran as quickly as she could to the Ninth Avenue Elevated, looking behind her in case Sander had followed. She wondered, perhaps even half wished, she'd catch a glimpse of him behind her. No such thing, of course. He wasn't a man to try hard.

20

AGAINST ALL ODDS, and facing a life with Fenna and Sander as his parents, Woodrow hung on, struggled for breath every day, and finally began to put on weight. This Minke learned from Cassian in November, when he came to see her. His mission was to tell her the coast was clear. Fenna and Woodrow had gone back to the apartment on 121st Street, and it was safe to visit again.

She had news of her own. The money was piling up in her stocking. On March 8 she would set sail for Comodoro. Steerage, but what did that matter? She was strong. Elly was strong.

"You'll be going into winter again," Cassian said. "Just your luck."

It didn't matter. She would be closer to finding Zef. That was what mattered. He would be twice the age he'd been, almost two. "I see children Zef's age in the park when I take Elly, and my heart breaks with missing him. I picture him all the time, Cassian. Has someone cut his hair? He must be walking, running, exploring by now. Will he know me when I find him?"

"Have you communicated any of this to your mama and papa?" Cassian asked.

Minke shrugged. She'd written them about Elly, about New York. But how could she break their hearts and tell them the rest?

"What's the news there?" Cassian asked.

"If they knew my address, they would give it to Fenna even if I told them not to. I don't dare. I write to them. I hear nothing back."

She returned to her work, smocking a dress for Miss Anne. Cassian settled onto the daybed to play with Elly and then began to look through the stack of newspapers Minke kept in her sewing room.

"Read to me while I sew, will you, Cassian?" she asked. He obliged, going from story to story. He often read only the first few paragraphs, the most interesting part, then skipped to another story, and when he'd finished with one day's paper, he would rummage around in the pile and find the paper from another day. It didn't matter to either of them that the news was old.

She was just finishing off a buttonhole when Cassian stopped reading. He'd been regaling her with stories of the rich. "God in heaven!"

"What is it?" She lay down her sewing.

Cassian held out the paper, shaking his head. "They're here in New York!"

"Who's here in New York?"

"Dietz and his wife."

She grabbed the paper from him and read the story.

A WARM WELCOME

No clearer proof is required that the center of New York's fashionable society is set firmly at Fifth Avenue and Sixty-second Street than the arrival of Mr. and Mrs. Frederik Dietz and their baby son, Hendrik.

Eight-ten Fifth Avenue, for decades home to Astors, DuPonts, and Fricks, is now also home to the Dietz family, newly arrived from Argentina. Mr. Dietz is the recently named president of Pan American Petroleum & Transport, with offices in the Woolworth Building.

The triplex boasts a ballroom on its main floor, two fireplaces, a grand center staircase, and a penthouse apartment with gardens overlooking Fifth Avenue.

Through her interpreter, Mrs. Dietz, who is of Dutch descent, thrilled over the view of Central Park and proximity to fine restaurants. Mrs. Dietz was stunning in a richly embroidered day dress by Callot Soeurs and black turban made especially memorable by its fan of striking blue feathers—tail feathers, she explained, of a rare Patagonian parrot.

Minke started to laugh. "She made that parrot into a hat!" She fell on the daybed beside Cassian.

"Look at the photograph," he said.

She hadn't noticed it, but at the top of the page, separate from the story, was a photograph. She held it close to her eyes, the better to make it out. In it, Tessa looked like a swami in her turban, the feathers fanned over the top of it like a peacock tail. Dietz stood behind her, hands firmly planted on each end of her chair back. And in her lap, the child. Minke drew in her breath. It was sharply painful to see Tessa with a son.

"That's a very big baby!" She studied the child in the grainy photograph. She tried to remember when he would have been born. Tessa was newly pregnant, not even sure of it, when Minke gave birth to Zef. The boy wore a ridiculous beret and a sailor suit of crisp white cotton. He was very large, but then the Dietzes were very large.

Minke kept going back to the photograph. Something about it. "Please hand me my magnifier."

The child's beret rode low on his forehead, and Tessa's large hand rested on his little shoulder, obscuring one side of his face. Still, the resemblance was there. It was in his smile. Her heart skipped a beat. "Cassian?"

"I wondered the same. Come."

As they packed up Elly and slipped out into the street by the rear service door, she kept telling herself to be calm, but it was no use. She was trembling, finding it difficult to breathe.

Cassian hailed a taxi. "Sixty-second Street and Fifth Avenue," he said. "Do as I say, Minke. We need to proceed in steps. We'll wait until one of them comes outside with the child. Perhaps not today, but someone has to come sometime. We must first lay eyes on the child to see if he's indeed Zef. But that's all. We won't take him. Promise me."

"How can I possibly promise that?"

"I've never done wrong by you, Minke. You must promise."

At 810 Fifth Avenue, they crossed over to the Central Park side of the street and looked up at the building. It was a fortress, a great block of stone with hundreds of windows. Her eyes traveled to the top floor, where the article had said the Dietzes were in residence.

"We wait," Cassian said. "We stay here and wait."

Fifth Avenue was lined with park benches, plenty of room for them to sit and let Elly move about while they kept their eyes on the front door of 810 Fifth Avenue. People came and went, ushered in and out by a man in a black uniform with gold braid on the shoulders. Minke was in heaven and hell at once. Cassian said they must not under any circumstances go to the door, for fear of being turned away and the news of their arrival given to the Dietzes.

They waited for an eternity, it seemed. The lights dimmed along the avenue, and then, not from the door but from down the street, Cassian spotted a woman pushing a carriage. "Look. There," he said. "She's going toward the building."

Minke strained to see through the gloaming. The woman was slight, not Tessa. "It's not her," she said.

"Let's get closer," Cassian said. "But do as I tell you!" She hoisted Elly onto her hip and crossed Fifth Avenue behind him. "We're only going to look," he said. "Don't do anything rash."

The woman was perhaps thirty feet away—governesses, they were called in New York, according to what Minke had read in the paper. She was pushing the carriage, unrushed. Minke's heart raced so fast that she thought she might faint. Cassian took her hand and held it much too tightly, a reminder that she must behave. Her sights were set only on the child in the carriage. It was a large expensive thing, shiny black with a hood, and it allowed the child to sit upright, facing forward. His face was a white moon against the dark blanket that bound him tightly in place. Not even his arms were free.

She let out a strangled cry and lunged, unable to stop herself. "Just a minute," Minke said to the startled woman. "I just want to see him."

The governess hesitated before swerving out of the way and hastening past them. But Minke had seen enough to know.

Cassian spun her away, clapped a hand over her mouth, and pulled her back across the street while she tried to escape his grip. He held her tightly as the woman practically ran through the glass doors into the lobby of 810 Fifth Avenue, pushing Zef in his carriage.

Minke was out of breath. Elly whimpered from fright. "Why did you do that? Why? I was this close!" Minke said, gasping.

"You almost gave us away."

"It was Zef!"

"We'll get him," Cassian said. "But we have to use our brains. You almost ruined everything."

She rocked against the bench, staring up at the top floor of the building, where lights were on in the windows. "I could have had him!" She shook Cassian's hands off her. "Them! Those dreadful people have my Zef."

"If it's Zef, Minke."

She groaned. "What do you mean, if? It was Zef. You saw him."

"No, I didn't. I might have seen better if I hadn't had to pull you away."

She felt sick. *Her* baby boy had been snatched away all over again.

"They're very powerful people now," Cassian said.

"It's my child! What has power to do with anything?"

Cassian held her back with force and didn't let go until she gave in to his grasp. "Look, Minke, maybe we could get Zef by barging into the building, but the risk is enormous. You know how those buildings work. You live in one. The doorman will stop us. He'll call the Dietzes, and they'll refuse to allow you upstairs. They might well call the police after that ruckus outside. We don't stand a chance against them. We'll be the ones taken for wrongdoers."

"But he's *mine*."

"He's safe for now, Minke. He's warm and fed. It won't be long before we have him, if it is indeed he. Come on now. We need to leave before we're arrested for loitering."

She took a last look up to the penthouse apartment. There. Right there. "We could go to the police."

Cassian sighed. "We must do nothing. We must think this through to the end before we act, and for now Zef—if it is Zef—is safe."

"He's with Tessa Dietz! That's hardly safe."

"In the critical ways, he's safe. We have to assume the worst, that the governess will have told them about a woman on the street."

"All the more reason to act now."

"No," Cassian said. "All the more reason to allow time to pass before we do anything else."

ONCE BACK AT Riverside Drive, Minke left Cassian in the sewing room while she rushed upstairs. She'd been gone a very long time. Mrs. Bowen was leaving, having done the supper dishes. "And where might you have been?" she asked.

"I might have been outside with Elly."

"Don't be fresh with me, miss."

"Did something happen?"

"You tell me next time you decide to go out. What if one of them wanted you?"

"Did they?"

"You just ask before you go gallivanting."

Minke waited until she was sure Mrs. Bowen was out of the building before returning to the sewing room. She sat carefully on the divan and began to nurse Elly.

"We sort it all out before we make a move," Cassian said. "Understood?"

"Tessa was pregnant. What happened to that child?"

"Understood?"

"Understood."

"It must have died or Tessa had a miscarriage. She was not in good health for a pregnancy." Cassian shrugged. "Or she was never pregnant at all."

Minke drew in a quick breath. "You think they planned it from the beginning? If there never was a pregnancy, it explains why she refused to see you."

"A possibility."

"All that time they were planning to take Zef?" She had to let go of one set of beliefs and make room for another, like a fog lifting, a world come newly into focus. "If Dietz was behind the taking of Zef, then it wasn't Pieps who took him."

"Unless Pieps was acting for Dietz. It's a possibility. Dietz hired him to take the child. He confessed, after all."

"He confessed to Sander, Cassian. To no one else." Her next thought blew through like a cold wind—that Pieps might never have confessed, that Sander had shot him because of his hatred and suspicion, that there might have been no confession. "Pieps never would have colluded with him."

"We must keep our expectations in check. I hope desperately that it's Zef, but I dare not believe."

"You're too cautious, Cassian."

"Let's address some possibilities. For example, could the Dietzes have somehow found Zef and brought him to America with the intent of returning him to you?"

"They told that reporter and all of New York the child was theirs. They even named him Hendrik. Everybody said it was gauchos. They ignored me when I said no, those were not gaucho horses. The horses that night weren't fine at all but common. The type of horse used to pull the oil rigs. Dietz had arranged for Zef to be taken and given to his wife. It's the only explanation. Their baby died, and they took mine."

"If it's Zef."

She put her fingers into her ears.

SHE LAY IN her narrow bed, getting no sleep whatsoever, hope searing her dreams, waking her with its silken pleasure and then darkening her mood with guilt and loss. Hatred for Pieps had filled every corner of the house after Zef was taken. And as if their lives hadn't been ugly enough, Sander wouldn't stop spewing his rage, saying he wished he'd castrated the boy before he shot him. He had railed against Minke for befriending someone of the lower classes. Such alliances always ended up the same, he shouted. He accused her of sleeping with the boy. Dietz had told him as much and more than once. Tessa had seen them together during that trip to the estancia, and don't think he didn't know! She wasn't to be trusted, just a trollop from a poor Dutch village. She had pleaded, denied, sobbed that she had been faithful to him every day and would be for the rest of her life, but through it all, she'd been racked not only by the unbearable loss of Zef but also by her own guilt and shame for having befriended Pieps. Now her mind was on fire with a new possibility. Pieps had had nothing to do with Zef's disappearance. He'd died for nothing.

21

*E*ACH DAY CASSIAN came to her small sewing room, and they talked as she worked. In the evenings she did laundry or helped with dinner parties, and all the while she felt a new peace settle over her, knowing exactly where Zef was.

"We need help," she said to Cassian during one of his visits. "We can't do this ourselves. Look at us. I an immigrant seamstress with a baby and no husband, no family to claim, you a physician who works with people this city regards with distaste, hatred, even."

"Exactly," Cassian said. "If we try to take him, Dietz can easily pay the police to take care of us, and we'll never find Zef again."

"We need the help of someone with influence." She met his eyes. "We need Mr. Wiley."

"I've had the same thought. We must approach him without asking for anything," Cassian said. "We will tell him what has occurred, under the guise of your commitment to letting him know everything about you. You are, after all, an employee in his household, and it behooves you to inform him. He will either have it in his mind to help us or not. It's all we can do for now."

"We'll go to his office on my next day off. It won't do to approach him when I am supposed to be at work. And it won't do to approach him here. He's a businessman."

Two days later, they stood before the most remarkable structure she had ever seen. The New York Times Building was dozens of stories high and thin as a rail, as if it could be blown down in a high wind. "How does it stay up?" Minke asked.

"Magic," Cassian said.

No one else seemed the slightest bit worried. They hustled along the street or slowed to read the latest news reports posted behind a plate-glass window. Inside, in a large marble-lined space, a man sat at a desk watching them. "We're here to see Mr. Louis Wiley," Minke said.

"You and everybody else." The man looked them over. Even having made their best efforts to look respectable, they must have looked like the immigrants they were, even down to the baby draped in her gay sling across Minke's front.

"Please tell him Minke DeVries is here. I work for Mr. Wiley at his home. It's not an emergency, but it is very important."

The man wasn't sure, but she guessed he wouldn't dare to deny her access. He called for one of the boys sitting on a bench nearby and said something. The boy disappeared through a hallway, reappeared several minutes later, and whispered something to the man. "Just follow him," the man said.

It was a warren of narrow halls, loud machinery, voices, and rooms and staircases, not unlike the *Frisia*, she thought, that time she'd become lost and Pieps had come to her rescue. She had to tell the boy to slow down twice because Cassian, even though vastly improved, still could not keep up. Finally, they arrived in a hall with floors so shiny she could see herself in them. The smell was of fresh shellac. And much quieter than the places they'd been. At the end of the hall a door with a glass panel stood ajar. On the door was written MR. WILEY. Minke poked her head inside.

He sat at a desk in the center of his office, his feet on a hassock, just as he did at home. Five or six men sat erect in chairs against the wall, apparently awaiting their turn to speak to him. He nodded to Minke and Cassian, indicated that they should sit down, and went back to his papers. A few moments later, he raised his large head and looked about the room as if startled to see so many people. With a swish of his hand, he asked the waiting men to leave. Once they'd left, a cautious smile spread across his face. "So, Minke, what brings you here? Has something happened at home?"

They had rehearsed, of course. The point was to give him the necessary information without taking up too much of his time. Minke began. "Everything at home is fine, Mr. Wiley. But something has happened."

He tipped back in his chair. "Tell me."

"I believe I told you that I lost a child whose name was Jozef when I lived in Comodoro?"

"I believe you did." He was looking at her like a grandfather indulging a child.

"In truth, my baby was kidnapped from me."

Mr. Wiley leaned forward, frowning. "I understood you to mean the child had died, my dear."

"At the time I preferred not to explain." She drew in a breath. "In Argentina it was my custom to take Zef to the beach. One day a group of men on horseback surrounded us and stole him from me. There was a search. People were questioned, of course. My husband suspected a particular young man. He went to see him. The young man confessed to the kidnapping, and my husband shot him dead."

Mr. Wiley was a man accustomed to appearing unsurprised.

"There was talk of retaliation against my husband. It was why we had to leave."

Cassian smiled his encouragement, and she drew out the newspaper clipping. "I found this item in the newspaper." She handed the clipping to Mr. Wiley and studied his face as he read. His face showed nothing.

"Frederik and Tessa Dietz, the people in that picture, were acquaintances of ours in Comodoro. In fact, we all arrived together on the *Frisia* three years ago. Dr. Tredegar also knew them in Amsterdam." She had to choke back her tears. "Mr. Wiley, the baby is my baby Zef." Her voice broke. She had done very well so far, but this was too much. Elly was waking, beginning to squirm in her sling.

Cassian stepped in. "This couple was childless in Comodoro less than a year ago. The child in this picture is approximately two years old. I'm aware that that information alone does not prove anything."

"It's my Zef, I know it is," Minke said.

"You think *these* people were behind the kidnapping?" Mr. Wiley flicked the clipping.

"Yes," Minke said.

Mr. Wiley produced a soft whistle.

"We went to the address given in the paper and waited, and I saw Zef. He was in a carriage being wheeled by a nursemaid. Cassian said it wouldn't work to simply snatch him. The Dietzes could do us harm. They're ruthless people."

"I know nothing of children, Minke," Mr. Wiley said. "But a year has passed since you saw your child. How can you be sure this is he?"

"A mother knows, Mr. Wiley."

"Dr. Tredegar, are you of the same opinion? Do you also believe this child to be Zef?"

"I err on the side of caution as a rule, but I'm inclined to think it's possible."

She wanted to hug him. It was the closest he'd come.

"This Frederik Dietz." Mr. Wiley rubbed his temple. He seemed to debate with himself for a moment. "It's a very serious accusation you're making."

Cassian said, "It has not yet come to an accusation, sir. At this point we merely seek to affirm the child's identity. If it's Zef, the other questions will follow. The Dietzes must be given an opportunity to explain."

Mr. Wiley squeezed the bridge of his nose. He checked his pocket watch and got to his feet. Minke laced Elly back into her sling and rose as well. Their meeting was over.

"But will you help me?" Minke blurted.

Mr. Wiley stiffened and checked his watch again.

"Thank you for your time," Cassian said, taking Minke by the arm. Once outside, he hustled her along the corridor and back down to the lobby, where she wrenched free of him.

"He offered nothing. He doesn't believe us!" she said.

"You don't know that."

"He offered no assistance at all."

"Think of the risk to him," Cassian said.

"He's not like that."

"Everybody is like that."

"I'm going back to the Dietzes' building and watch. They'll take him to the park. If Mr. Wiley won't do anything, I'll just have to do it myself."

"Who said he won't do anything?"

"He was so abrupt with us!"

"He's a busy man."

"I want my Zef." She bolted through the door to the street. "I'm going to get him. I'll wait all day and all night if I have to."

Cassian struggled to keep up with her. It was cruel of her to outrun him, but today she didn't care. "If the Dietzes see you, Minke, I don't need to tell you," he called to her. "You'll never see Zef again. And if you're arrested, you'll lose Elly as well!"

She stopped and he caught up to her. She hadn't even considered this. He was out of breath. "How about this. If nothing happens by the end of the week, you go ahead and do it your way. But we can't do it your way and then do it mine, because once it's done your way, the cat is out of the bag. We have no more leverage. It has to be my way and then yours."

"What's your way? No way?"

"We've told Mr. Wiley the facts. Give him the time he needs to consider them."

"Sometimes I want to kill you, Cassian Tredegar."

He laughed. "I know," he said, "but then I'd be dead."

22

THE NEXT DAYS were harrowing. Mr. Wiley said nothing about her visit. He gave not the slightest indication they had even spoken but treated her as before, with polite respect. If she came upon him in the kitchen with Mrs. Bowen, he gave her his usual smiling nod and said good morning. He brought a shirt to her sewing room to have the collar turned, and even then he said nothing of their meeting, and neither did she. She had promised Cassian not to pester him.

Cassian arrived to see her on a Friday. Had Mr. Wiley said anything? he wanted to know.

Nothing, she said, feeling surly about having to wait, sure nothing would happen. By now she was looking forward to carrying out her own plan. She had three more days to go before the week was up and she could walk into the lobby of 810 Fifth Avenue and demand to be taken to the Dietzes' apartment. Zef would see her, throw his head back, and laugh. They would have a tearful reunion. She would bring him to the apartment and show Mr. Wiley she had been correct. *So there,* she would say. He might not keep her on with two children, and with egg on his face, but no matter. She would figure it out.

The days had dragged terribly. Her work suffered. A collar, ordinarily such a simple matter, came out crooked. Mrs. Bowen complained that she was slacking off. It didn't matter. Everything was about to change. She couldn't wait to face Tessa Dietz. To see her expression. To bring her low.

But on Saturday afternoon while Cassian happened to be there, Mrs. Bowen pounded on the door. "Upstairs now, miss," she called.

"Mr. Wiley wants to see you. And if you have that doctor in there, him, too."

Minke gathered up Elly, who had been playing with scraps of fabric on the floor, and the three of them emerged to find Mrs. Bowen, arms crossed over her chest and with a frown on her face. "Aren't you just the happy little family," she said. It wasn't the first time she had made an insinuating remark about Cassian's presence. Minke was not going to stoop to that level and explain. Let her fret. She followed Mrs. Bowen upstairs.

Mr. Wiley sat in the kitchen flanked by Mrs. Bowen, Miss Anne, and Miss Amanda. "I've told them everything," he said.

Miss Amanda eyed her warily. She had never quite accepted Minke. Only Miss Anne smiled conspiratorially at her.

"Might we ask further questions, Louis?" Miss Amanda asked.

"Please," Mr. Wiley said.

"How well do you know these Dietzes? If you'll excuse the comparison, there's a significant difference in your places in life."

"We were equals in Comodoro. They were in business there, as were we."

"And yet *you* arrived here penniless," Miss Amanda continued.

Cassian explained. "After I was attacked, we were unable to maintain our business, which was morphine production and export. Frederik Dietz took all our workers into his oil fields. No one was left to produce the morphine."

"How was it possible for these people to have your baby without everybody knowing?" Miss Anne asked. "It sounds like a very small place, where word would travel fast."

"Tessa lived at an estancia many miles away," Minke said. "She must have kept him with her there."

Mrs. Bowen looked unconvinced. "Did you call the police?"

"There were no police to call."

"What kind of a place has no police?"

Minke looked at Cassian for help. How did one describe Comodoro?

"It's a place much like your Wild West here in America," he said. "We had a constable, but he had little authority and little power."

"What did you think happened to Zef?" Miss Amanda asked. "You must have had theories."

"People thought he had been sold to wealthy people, perhaps in another country." Minke paused. "A lot of people blamed the gauchos for being behind it. No one would listen to me when I said that was not true."

"And of course there was a confession," Mr. Wiley said.

"I have never found it in my heart to believe the boy my husband shot had anything to do with it," Minke said.

"And you, Doctor?" Miss Amanda asked.

"The boy was a decent fellow, and yet, as you say, Mr. Wiley, he confessed."

"And then sold the child to these people," Miss Amanda said.

"How can you be so sure it's your child? The picture is small." Miss Anne looked as though she hated to ask the question.

"I saw him in his carriage."

Mr. Wiley cleared his throat to draw attention. "You must admit, this whole affair is far-fetched, to say the least." He smiled. He really did have a lively and wonderful face. "But I'm intrigued, and I do love to be intrigued. What's more, I have my own reasons for wanting to know these people."

Minke was dumbfounded. "You do?"

Mr. Wiley shrugged. "Oil is to be the most important commodity of the twentieth century. You'll see. These Dietzes could shed light on the subject."

"Then you'll do something?"

Mr. Wiley withdrew a folded letter from his vest pocket. "There's more. The name Dietz was familiar to me when you came to my office. You see, at the paper, we had a letter from him. It's not at all uncommon. We receive the most letters about matters that appear in the society news. Corrections and so on. People hate to see themselves under-represented to their peers." He slid the letter across the table to her. "Mr. Ochs turned the matter over to me."

Adolph Ochs
Publisher
The New York Times

Dear Mr. Ochs:
    My wife wishes you to turn your attention to inaccuracies in
an article that appeared in your newspaper of late. If you would
be so kind as to publish the corrections in the society columns, a
good measure of peace will be restored to our household. Please
note that:
    Our triplex boasts three *fireplaces, not two.*
    The blue feathers were not those of a Patagonian parrot
but belonged to my wife's beloved Brazilian hyacinth
macaw.
    Cordially,
    Frederik August Dietz
    Trans: Miniver Rustrup

"He complained!" Minke said.

Mr. Wiley grinned. "He did indeed."

"We'll have them to luncheon," Miss Anne burst out.

"Oh, Anne," Miss Amanda said. "Let *Louis* do the talking."

"We'll have them to luncheon," Mr. Wiley said.

Miss Anne giggled.

Minke wanted to kiss him. Wanted to leap across the table and smother him in kisses of the purest joy she had ever felt. He pushed another sheet of paper toward her. "The invitation has already been sent. I made it clear that we wish for all three of them to come. I expressed special interest in the child. This"—he tapped the letter—"is the reply. We'll see if the boy is indeed yours, and if not, I shall have made inroads with a knowledgeable fellow."

Dear Mr. Wiley,

Despite our regret that Mr. Ochs himself is not available and did not respond to our letter of complaint personally, we accept your invitation to luncheon this coming Sunday. My wife wishes me to inform you that she is unable to eat the following:

Onion

Fish of any type

Unsalted food

In addition, our son requires a chair that allows him to sit at a level with the adults present. He is two years old and becomes restless. I trust a member of your household will be available to amuse him if this is the case.

Yours sincerely,

Frederik August Dietz, President

Pan American Petroleum & Transport

"Tomorrow!" Minke felt very glad she had listened to Cassian. The smile on her face would never go away.

"Onions," Mrs. Bowen intoned. "Fish of any kind." Her eyes sparkled devilishly.

Miss Anne clapped her hands. "Let's cook fish."

"Will a member of the household be available to amuse Zef?" Minke was trembling at the prospect. "Oh, I do believe the seamstress will step in."

"Best for all of us to call him Hendrik for now," Cassian said. "I continue to worry that our hopes are being raised too high."

"Oh, Cassian! I despise the name Hendrik. Anyway, I know it's my Zef."

Miss Amanda tapped the letter and said with distaste, "We may have invited a kidnapper to luncheon."

"Exactly," Mr. Wiley said. Sometimes it seemed as though it took great strength for him to hold that head upright; it was so big. "But tell me, does the child have identifying marks? Something that will make us absolutely certain?"

"I delivered Zef," Cassian said. "He has a small mark on his lower back. We refer to such marks as Mongolian blue spots. Harmless but unmistakable."

"Excellent," Mr. Wiley said.

An almost unbearable joy erupted inside her that Zef was found. That she would see him tomorrow. The joy softened her every edge. She loved them all. Minke threw her arms around Mr. Wiley. "Thank you." The man stiffened but allowed the hug. He was apparently not accustomed to being touched.

"I think it will have to be a feast," Mrs. Bowen said.

Minke threw her arms around her as well.

23

*M*R. WILEY WAS in his element. At work he managed a large team of people employed at something called public relations. It meant reaching out to hundreds, even thousands, of people mentioned in the newspaper, people from every possible walk of life from the grandest to the most humble, and soliciting their views and their favor. He had, Miss Anne explained, almost single-handedly elevated the reputation of *The New York Times*. Such was his great skill, and he would apply it to Tessa and Frederik Dietz.

The household was electric with the excitement of preparation. Turtle soup, oysters, roast beef with Yorkshire pudding. Even the sisters helped with laying the table and polishing the wineglasses. Minke herself set the place for Zef. She drew a chair from the parlor and stacked onto it the most colorful pillows she could find to raise him to the height of the table, like a colorful little throne. She set his place with a small bud vase and a rose and placed in a semicircle around his plate little yellow and red balls she had made from scraps of fabric.

A Japanese screen of lacquered black decorated with red and gold flowers was set up in front of the swinging door to the kitchen. The screen consisted of three panels, allowing an inch of visibility in the spaces where the panels joined. In this way, the kitchen door could remain open, but the kitchen would not be visible from the dining room. Minke and Cassian would sit in chairs hidden behind the screen and watch the luncheon from the slits in the screen.

They were in their places by a quarter to one. While they waited, Cassian offered Minke a sip of morphine to calm her nerves, but she declined. She wanted to be fully aware of every moment. True, she was agitated. But it was the agitation of having what she wanted most in the world almost within her grasp.

At one-fifteen the buzzer in the foyer sounded, and Mr. Wiley picked up the receiver to the house phone. "Yes?" he said crisply. "Yes, good. Please send them up."

She waited, heart pounding, peeking around the edge of the screen to see a slice of the foyer. There came the sound of the brass gates opening on the elevator and then a knock at the door. Mr. Wiley passed before her vision. Disappeared. There came the sound of the door opening, of Mr. Wiley greeting his guests. She hadn't expected the revulsion that the voices of Tessa and Frederik Dietz would produce in her. She strained to see or hear Zef.

"And this must be little Hendrik," Mr. Wiley said in a loud voice meant for Minke and Cassian to hear, so they would know for certain the Dietzes had brought the child.

Minke leaped to her feet, her response automatic, but Cassian gripped her arm so hard he might have bruised it. "Just one look," she hissed at him. "I'll be careful."

Cassian gripped her arm harder. It was a promise not to be broken under any circumstance. If, for any reason, Minke was mistaken and it was not Zef, Mr. Wiley and his sisters' reputations could be irreparably damaged. She recovered her wits in time and sat again.

Mrs. Bowen passed on her way from the kitchen to take the coats. She motioned to them to push their chairs back a little so she would have room to navigate. The sounds of Mr. Wiley's and the Dietzes' voices faded as they made their way to the parlor, where the Misses Wiley awaited. Mrs. Bowen returned from hanging the coats in the closet.

"Well?" Minke asked.

"How should I know?" Mrs. Bowen whispered.

Twenty minutes passed with nothing but the occasional sound of Frederik Dietz's laughter at the far end of the apartment. Minke listened intently. She rose and tiptoed into the kitchen. "How much longer?" she asked.

Mrs. Bowen sat at the table doing nothing. She opened her hands as if to say, *Who knows?*

"Can't you announce luncheon?"

Mrs. Bowen made a tippling motion with her thumb to her mouth. "Mr. Wiley thinks it's best to serve them a few glasses of sherry before lunch."

Minke smiled at her. "Brilliant!"

"Go sit down, miss. Or you'll ruin everything."

Why did everyone keep telling her that?

After another ten minutes, Mrs. Bowen finally got to her feet, passed them outside the kitchen, and went to the parlor to announce that luncheon was served. Back and forth she went, laying out platters of this and that, and all the while the gaggle of voices grew closer, with Tessa's annoying giggle and Dietz's eruptions of mirthless laughter.

It was agony.

The voices were close. They were entering the dining room. Minke was able to stand and not be seen over the top of the screen. She peered through the slit, but her view was limited to the tunnel of what was directly in front of her.

"Yes, of course," Dietz was saying. "The future of the world lies in the discovery of greater deposits of oil."

"Unregulated, I understand, in Comodoro."

"Acch," Dietz said. "Of course."

"Won't you sit here, Mrs. Dietz?" Mr. Wiley said, pulling out the chair farther. "And Frederik, if you would kindly take the seat beside your wife." It had been decided that the Dietzes' backs should be to the kitchen, an extra precaution. "And little Hendrik, I see that someone—a good elf, perhaps—has made a fine high place for you to sit and put out these little colored balls."

"You might need one of those high chairs yourself, eh, Wiley?" Dietz boomed out.

"Of course," Mr. Wiley said. "That is very amusing."

"What a dear little boy," Miss Anne said. "I am honored to have the place beside him."

"And I the other, if I may?" Miss Amanda said.

The Dietzes had broad backs, both of them, and try as she would, Minke could not see past them to Zef. She mouthed the words to

Cassian, "Is it him?" Cassian shook his head and mouthed back, "I don't know!"

Mrs. Bowen went in and out past Minke and Cassian, carrying the hotter dishes.

"Oysters?" Tessa said in her clotted Dutch, apparently to her husband. "I thought you told them no fish."

Dietz translated this loosely.

"Mrs. Bowen," Miss Anne called out to the kitchen with a mock sternness that would escape Tessa. Mrs. Bowen rushed into the dining room. Miss Anne scolded, "What*ever* were you thinking? You've served fish against our instructions!"

"Where I come from, a fish has a pair of eyes and a big mouth. An oyster, as you can plainly see, has neither of these, miss."

Dietz translated this as "She says an oyster isn't a fish."

"Tell them to take it away immediately," Tessa said.

Minke could see enough to observe that the child swung his head with keen interest when the conversation shifted from one person to another, but he still was not fully visible. Mrs. Bowen passed into the kitchen, carrying Tessa's plate.

"Servants," Tessa said in English, then made a guttural sound of disgust.

"She's such a trial," Miss Anne admitted.

"Not half so bad as our seamstress," Miss Amanda added.

"What's she saying?" Tessa asked her husband.

"They have a seamstress."

"All to themselves?" Tessa asked.

"Louis won't have it any other way. Tailoring is so important, don't you agree?"

"Frederik, we must hire a seamstress," Tessa said in Dutch.

"Hendrik," Mr. Wiley said. "Look what I have for you." Minke didn't see what it was. It didn't matter, because the child laughed, and in that one moment she knew beyond any doubt. His laugh. Cassian turned to her with a smile so big it brought tears to her eyes. They clasped hands. But the plan was to wait. Difficult as it would be, she was to wait.

"Splendid, splendid," Dietz was saying.

"Say thank you to the nice man," Tessa barked at Zef in Dutch.

There was a sound.

"Hendrik!" Tessa shouted. Mrs. Bowen rushed past them again. "You're a very bad boy!" Tessa scolded. Mrs. Bowen swept past with a roll of her eyes and carrying a cloth.

"He's such a clumsy child," Tessa said. "My Astrid was so much more delicate than this boy." Dietz translated this exactly.

Minke could barely stand it. How *dare* they insult him? She was proud of him for spilling whatever it was.

"Boys are different," Mr. Wiley said. "It's what makes the world go round. Don't you agree?"

"No manners at all," Tessa said.

"If the child needs manners, Mrs. Dietz," Miss Anne said in her quiet way, "then isn't it up to you to teach him?"

Dietz translated this as "She says it's our job to teach him manners, and if he has none, his behavior reflects very badly on our servants."

Minke could see Tessa's bowed back as she dove into her lunch. Mr. Wiley took the opportunity to ask if she had seen the correction in the newspaper. Dietz translated, and Tessa responded with her mouth full that she had indeed, but that it was run in a place where none of the important people of New York would see it, and she would prefer if they ran it again prominently on the social pages and perhaps with another interview, which she would be willing to grant, given the circumstances.

Dietz translated this as "She said everything was fine."

"I'll just be a moment," Mr. Wiley said. "We've arranged a special dessert for little Hendrik. I want to check with Mrs. Bowen." With that, he rose and came behind the screen. Cassian and Minke followed him into the kitchen and let the swinging door close behind them. "Well?" he asked.

"Absolutely," Minke said. "It's my baby."

"And you concur?" Mr. Wiley asked Cassian.

"I want so much to say yes, but I remain not sure. It's been a very long time since I saw him."

"We must take no chances."

Mr. Wiley returned to the dining room. "I say," he said to the Dietzes, "before dessert, Mrs. Bowen wants the boy to go in the kitchen to clean his hands. Eh? What do you say? Mrs. Bowen rules the roost around here. We all do as she says."

Mrs. Bowen, hearing herself summoned, sailed back to the dining room. Minke took up her station behind the screen, watching anxiously through the slit as Mrs. Bowen lifted Zef from his chair. Minke was wild with excitement and almost knocked down the screen in her haste to follow Mrs. Bowen to the kitchen.

Minke took Zef in her arms and held him so tightly, feeling his small heart beating against hers. She was sobbing, trying not to make too much noise. Cassian ushered her into her room and shut the door. They sat on the bed. "Do you believe it now?" she asked Cassian. She couldn't take her eyes from Zef's face, couldn't stop kissing him. How he had changed, lost the chubby cheeks, his hair grown somewhat darker, his blue eyes clear, alternately wary and delighted by so much attention.

Cassian lifted Zef's shirt.

Mrs. Bowen crowded into the room. "Well?" she said.

"No question," Cassian said.

"Let's go," Mrs. Bowen said.

Tessa and Frederik didn't see them enter, as they were still both engaged in their lunch. Zef shouted, causing Tessa to look up. "What is it now?" She turned to look and barked a little cry. "What the devil?" Dietz said.

"It seems this child is not your son, madam," Mr. Wiley said.

"*Jij, pompoen kop,*" Tessa said in disgust.

"Tessa." Cassian clicked his heels together to get their attention. "Frederik. The game is up. We all know this is Jozef DeVries. We all know he's not your child."

"*Flikker!*" Tessa muttered.

"Let's all remain calm," Mr. Wiley said.

Mrs. Bowen was standing in front of the screen, her arms having been crossed over her breast for some time, her mouth ajar.

"You know there's a mark on his back, Tessa," Cassian said.

"He's mine," Tessa said flatly.

"Zef?" Cassian said. The child's head spun around. He remembered.

Cassian knelt. "Let's have a look," he said, and made to lift Zef from Minke's arm.

"Bring us our wraps this minute," Dietz said to the Misses Wiley. Neither of the sisters made a move.

"You know the spot is there, Tessa," Minke said. "And he has a small scar on his wrist. Just there." With the index finger of her left hand, she indicated the inside of her right wrist. "Perhaps you haven't even noticed it." She reached for Zef's hand. "Zef, sweetheart?"

"Dr. Tredegar doesn't need to look for the marks, does he?" Mr. Wiley asked.

"I lost my baby, Minke," Tessa said, weeping alligator tears. "Take pity on me. First my Astrid and then—" She broke off. "You have another child already. You'll have more."

"If you won't bring our wraps, I'll get them myself." Dietz stood up.

Minke's nose touched the top of Zef's blond head, and she breathed in the sweet scent of her son, a smell both fresh and distinctive.

Tessa stood unsteadily. "I must take my Hendrik now," she said to Minke, reaching out. "It's time for us to leave."

"Sit down, both of you," Mr. Wiley said. "If a crime has been committed, this is far from over."

"How could you do such a thing to us?" Minke asked Dietz, lapsing into Dutch. "Cause such suffering."

Dietz remained standing. "Ask your husband."

Tessa used a napkin to blot the perspiration from her throat. "He's our boy now. We paid. We brought him to America. He has our name on his passport. We have raised him, and there's really no more to be said."

"What do you mean, ask my husband?" Minke shot back.

"I'll say no more," Dietz said.

"Paid whom, Tessa?"

"Sander, of course," Tessa said.

"Money burns a hole in your husband's pocket," Dietz said. "It's been known for years. He married Elisabeth for her money, and she carefully guarded her belongings. You should have done the same, you foolish girl. You should have protected your boy." He stepped behind Tessa's chair and pulled it out for her.

"For God's sake, all of you speak English!" Mr. Wiley broke in.

"Mrs. Dietz has said they bought the child. She believes the transaction to be binding," Cassian explained.

"Not *buy*," Dietz snapped in Dutch. "There was no money involved."

"But you just said."

"He owed me the money."

Mr. Wiley threw up his hands. "Stop all this speaking Dutch. Just show me the mark."

Minke raised Zef's shirt, feeling numb. The spot was small and smooth but distinct. A bluish patch of skin just above his waist.

"Mr. and Mrs. Dietz," Mr. Wiley said. "Frederik and Tessa. I'm afraid an arrangement of the type you describe is illegal if it was made without the mother's consent. It will need to be decided in a court of law, with all parties testifying to what occurred. Mrs. DeVries clearly contests the appropriation of her son. I believe her when she says the boy was kidnapped on the beach. Hardly a legal adoption, wouldn't you say?"

"They stole him!" Minke held on to Zef with one arm and pointed fiercely with her free hand.

Dietz shot back in Dutch, "Take him, then, for Christ's sake. He's been nothing but trouble."

"Nee, nee!" Tessa shouted.

"It was never Pieps, was it?" Minke asked.

"Of course not." Dietz turned away as if to leave.

"Then who?"

"Some boys."

"Funny how it's always boys, so anonymous. Like the ones who attacked Cassian." It dawned on her then. "The same, perhaps. The very same. I wouldn't be surprised if you were behind that as well."

"Do you want me to explain here in front of Mr. Wiley?" Dietz said.

"Please," Cassian said.

"*Dokter homoseksuele,*" Dietz began.

"English!" Mrs. Bowen demanded.

"I don't know the word—"

"We have the same word in English, Mr. Dietz," Mr. Wiley said coolly.

"Dr. Tredegar was beaten for it," Dietz said. "Such things happen everywhere to people like him. These people are the devil's spawn."

Mr. Wiley raised a thick eyebrow. "Is that so?"

"Kidnapping is a grave offense in this country," Cassian said.

"Who said anything about kidnapping?" Dietz said in English. "She's having delusions."

Minke was past her anger. Squeezing Zef to herself made her want to shout with joy. Tessa had put far too many clothes on him. She unbuttoned his vest, his sweater, and removed them. He laughed when his arms were free. He seemed to have forgotten Tessa altogether, never looking for her once.

"Minke will bring charges," Cassian said. "You can expect that."

"Dr. Tredegar." In a condescending tone, Dietz spoke in Dutch. "I don't think that will be wise. Mr. and Mrs. DeVries gave their boy to Tessa for safekeeping because they were destitute, and then she changed her mind. There are any number of possibilities. And we're well set to handle the cost of attorneys. I might add that her story of the kidnapping on the beach was peculiar. Only she was witness to it. What's more, our witnesses, these Wileys, have understood nothing of what's been said."

"Mr. Dietz, are you familiar with the custom of extradition?" Mr. Wiley scowled thoughtfully. "I'm not an attorney, but I know this much: A crime that occurs in another country must be resolved in that country. When Mrs. DeVries brings charges, you will likely be returned to Argentina. It will be up to Argentine authorities to prosecute. From what I understand, people accused of a crime wait in prison for many years for the trial. Theirs is not as efficient a system as our own."

"What did he just say?" Tessa asked.

Minke was only too happy to translate.

"Oh, no," Tessa said. "I'll never go back. I did nothing wrong."

"Shut up," Dietz said.

"Mrs. Bowen, will you please summon the police?" Mr. Wiley said, then turned to Dietz.

"You don't know who you're dealing with," Dietz huffed. "Come, Tessa." The two of them swept from the dining room and could be heard arguing in the vestibule. There came the rattling of the elevator door and then silence.

"What did she call me?" Mr. Wiley asked. "That Dietz woman. She called me a name in Dutch. I want to know what it was."

Minke stole a guilty glance at Cassian. "She called you a pumpkin head."

Mr. Wiley laughed. "How very original."

"What will happen?" Cassian asked.

"He'll be visited by police tomorrow."

"Is it true about extradition?" Cassian asked.

Mr. Wiley shrugged. "Wasn't it wonderful the way that scared them?"

24

MISS ANNE, EVER expecting things to come out well, had already found a child's bed for Zef, as well as toys for both the children, which she revealed once the Dietzes were gone. Everyone crowded into Minke's little apartment off the kitchen to observe the children meeting each other for the first time. Elly, newly awake from her nap, looked from face to face with her usual solemnity. Minke sat on her bed holding Zef in her lap, and the two children stared at each other for what seemed like an eternity. It occurred to Minke that Elly could be the first child Zef had been in contact with, and he studied her carefully. For her part, Elly's big brown eyes were wide, her little cherub mouth slightly open. Neither child seemed to know what to make of the other. Finally Elly drew herself unsteadily to her feet and reached a chubby hand out for Zef, who wriggled off Minke's lap and approached his little sister, leaning down so they were face-to-face. Again the two spent some long moments taking each other in, a spell Elly broke when she reached out and grabbed for her brother's nose, causing him to burst into fits of giggles and she to do the same.

For Minke, there was more to be done, and it had to be done immediately. She wouldn't rest until it was behind her, and although she found it nearly impossible to leave Zef and Elly behind with Cassian, she comforted herself knowing how many happy years they had ahead. Before she left, she asked Cassian to notify the police after an hour had elapsed.

She took the same route back to Sander's apartment that she'd taken to the Wileys' on the day she'd left, a lifetime earlier. She sat on the same bench in Central Park where she'd sat that day. She needed her ducks in a row, as they said here in America.

She walked north along Broadway and then west on 121st Street. Nothing had changed in Sander and Fenna's neighborhood. Women still sat on their stoops, watching the children play and warming themselves over small firepots. Men from inside the tavern observed the goings-on in the street with the same dull expressions. Minke pulled open the door to the building and climbed the stairs. When she knocked, a baby cried. Woodrow.

She heard Fenna say something angrily to the baby. It took a minute or so for her to open the door. She was haggard, heavy-breasted from nursing. Seeing Minke, she hesitated, then stepped aside. The apartment was exactly as it had been, but now it smelled of rank milk and dirty diapers.

"Is Sander here?"

"What do you want?"

"To speak to Sander."

Woodrow went from crying to screaming, and it was clear Fenna intended to do nothing about it. Minke picked the child up from his makeshift bed. He was a beautiful baby, with honey-colored hair and blue eyes. "His diaper needs to be changed. Get me something." Fenna left the room and returned with a folded cloth. She was clearly too tired to argue. No doubt relieved to have someone, anyone, even Minke, help with the child.

"Why did you come?" Fenna asked.

Minke had already told her. She wasn't about to say it again.

"Where do you live, anyway? Mama wrote to me. You haven't told her where you live. They think you're ashamed of something."

"I'm ashamed of this." Minke indicated the baby, the apartment.

"If you wanted to hang on to Sander, you should have fought for him. Everybody says so. You gave up without a whimper."

Minke felt like a tennis ball, bouncing back and forth across the net separating her rage at Sander for what he had done and her bliss at having found Zef. It was like switching from fields of ash to the Garden of Eden. She found Fenna's words very funny. "I'll bet you wish I had fought for him and won. You'd be better off now, wouldn't you?"

Fenna sagged onto the chair. "There's no money. He barely works. He drinks all the time."

"Poor you. Poor innocent Fenna." She finished changing the baby and hoisted him onto her shoulder. "Mama and Papa must be so proud," Minke said, the sarcasm dripping.

"They don't know."

"So you're the one who's ashamed."

"Everybody is the same in this country," Fenna snapped. "You ask any of those women out there." She indicated the street. "It goes one way or the other. People either bring their families over or never see them again. I'll never see ours again. They sent both of us away, you know. No more mouths to feed."

"I'll see them again," Minke said.

"There's a war coming. They're stuck." Fenna frowned, remembering. "Where is *your* baby?"

"With Cassian. When does Sander come back?"

"He comes and goes."

They were watchful with each other, circling, keeping their distance. Minke looked at Fenna's chapped lips and reddened face, her sorry life here. *You reap what you sow,* she thought.

Fenna drew a handkerchief from her cleavage and blew her nose. Minke would never see her sister after this day, and although it gave her pause, realizing that her children would not know Woodrow, who was both brother and cousin to them, it was a price she would accept. She didn't despise Fenna. That would have required passion. No, Fenna had shown her true colors, and Minke was no longer interested. How strange that the decision was easy to make, as if it had announced itself to her.

"Something has happened, hasn't it?" Fenna said.

The joy erupted inside Minke like fireworks.

"You're smiling."

She looked away, asked again, "When will Sander be back?"

"I told you, I don't know."

"Cassian says he works as a chauffeur."

"He drives somebody's car. Somebody knocks on the door any time day or night, and he has to leave. He goes away and comes back after some hours."

"I can wait."

"I don't want you here."

Minke shrugged.

Fenna cocked her head. "I hear him."

Heavy steps approached in the hallway. The door burst open. He wore an untidy black suit, the sleeves too short, the shirt open at the neck, revealing pasty skin. Pitiable on anyone else. Upon seeing her, a slight smile crossed his face. "Lonely, are we?" He took off his coat and threw it over a hook.

He was thinner, his hair and eyebrows going gray. He lowered himself to a chair at the table, drew off his shoes, and kicked them to the corner. "Get me something to eat," he said to Fenna, who rose automatically. After she was gone, he made a circle in the air with his forefinger at Minke. "Turn around. I want to see you."

She didn't move.

"Suit yourself." He ran the back of his hand over his mouth. How could she ever have loved him?

Fenna returned with a bowl of something and laid it on the table before Sander. She fetched Woodrow, who had begun to fuss, took the chair opposite Sander, and began to nurse the child. The room had become tense in only these few minutes, with an air of expectation even while Sander and Fenna went about their dinner. Minke felt the power that came from the seconds passing, of gaining the upper hand while not saying a word.

Sander must have felt it, too. He smacked the table. Fenna jumped. "What the hell?" he said to Minke. "Why did you come here?"

She had promised herself to be calm. All the way to the apartment, she had told herself not to scream and rage. "How could you?"

He broke into a laugh. "How could I what?"

"Zef." That changed things. All motion stopped. She paused for a few more seconds before saying, "I found him."

Sander lurched as though an invisible hand had pushed him. Fenna sagged and seemed to forget about Woodrow. *She knew.* The child lost his hold on the nipple and began to squirm, desperate for food.

But Sander recovered, like the fox he was. "Prove it. If you found him, where is he, eh?" He shoved his bowl of soup away. "You come in here and say such a thing after the tragedy we suffered. You should be ashamed."

"He's at my home this very minute. In good health."

Woodrow's cries became louder. The baby's face was red from frustration. "But I thought—" Fenna said to Sander.

"You thought what, Fenna?" Minke asked.

"Keep your mouth shut," Sander said to Fenna. "Your sister needs to leave our house."

"I thought you'd be happy," Minke said. "Your son is found."

"If it were true, I would."

"Don't you want to know *how* I found him, Sander?"

"What is she saying?" Fenna asked over the baby's cries.

"Feed your baby," Minke said. "Look at him." The child was fumbling for Fenna's nipple, red in the face from frustration and anger. Fenna hoisted him, and the crying stopped.

"Well?" Minke fixed on Sander's hazel eyes, daring him to look away first. His only claim—that she was lying—was pathetic. They glared at each other. "I know everything, Sander."

"Then what do you want?"

"What do I want?" she asked, then again, louder. "What do I want?"

He stared at the table, opened his hands. "You think I have something for you?"

She sat down in the third chair at the table, leaned in close to him. "I want to see you in prison, is what I want. I want to pull out your eyes with my bare hands. I want to castrate you. I want to hang your sorry head on a spike. What do I want? That's all you have to say? You sold our child. My baby. There's a great deal I want, Sander."

He grunted, shrugged. As if that was the end of it.

"You murdered Pieps, you bastard. You knew he was innocent. You must have enjoyed killing my only friend. You were so stupid, so jealous of him. What you didn't know was that you had all my love, all my faithfulness. Not for one second did I give you a reason to be jealous. You killed him because you wanted to."

Sander stonewalled her.

"I'll tell all of it to the police. Kidnapping, murder. You'll never see the light of day again, if I have anything to do with it. You'll rot in prison along with Tessa and Frederik Dietz. In all Zef's life, I will never tell your son about you. You'll be lost to him. You're already just a ghost."

"What will become of me?" Fenna shrieked. "What about Woodrow?"

"You knew," Minke said flatly. "What do I care about you?"

Fenna looked down at the baby. "We needed the money. Without the money, we'd have starved."

"Don't look at me for this. It was Dietz," Sander said.

"He didn't take Zef, Sander. You gave him Zef in exchange for your gambling debts."

"I did what I had to do. For us."

She belted out a peal of vicious laughter. "For us. You bully, you outlaw. For us. Money, money." She reached into her pocket, found some money—coins and paper bills—and threw them at him, hitting him hard enough in the face to make him jump to his feet and raise a hand at her. The baby was screaming at the raised voices. Fenna gathered up the money and stuffed it into her pocket.

"Don't let him go to jail, Minke," Fenna sobbed. "Please. Please." She rocked and cried. "Think of Woodrow. If not for me, for the baby."

"You think of Woodrow. Protect him yourself. From the world. From Sander. My God, from yourself. I pity this child more than you know. What a life he has in store with you two as parents."

"You have no proof," Sander said. "No proof at all."

"The whole village knew of the kidnapping. They'll tell."

"Grow up, Minke. It's thousands of miles away."

She realized something new, fresh. A new side that darkened it more. "You knew exactly where he was all along. You knew he'd be well fed, have a roof over his head. Dreadful people, the Dietzes, but you knew Zef was safe while I didn't. You watched me suffer and let me suffer. No wonder you were so cold, so sanguine. I, on the other hand, was left to the terrors of my imagination." She pushed him. "Look at me, you bastard."

Outside there came the sounds of a siren, car doors slamming, and raised voices. That got to him all right. He sat up, whipped his head around. Glared at her. "You didn't."

"I did."

She fingered the half wedding ring in her pocket. Since the beginning, it had been the same contrast of smooth curved metal to jagged edge. She withdrew it and laid it on the table.

ᴘᴀʀᴛ Fᴏᴜʀ

COMODORO RIVADAVIA,
CHUBUT PROVINCE,
ARGENTINA

December 30, 1920

*T*HE *MACEIÓ* STEAMS into Comodoro Rivadavia harbor on a hot
December day across a calm cerulean sea. At its bow, Minke, Zef,
and Elly stand at the forefront of the press of passengers against the rail.

The town opens wide before them. It has spread to double, no, triple
in size. Some of the buildings are three stories tall. New houses have
sprouted to the north, the south, and up the base of the Cerro Chenque.

Minke has to pull Zef back from leaning too far over the rail. At
eight, the boy is fearless. Elly, the cautious one, draws back into her
mother's protection, but her brown eyes are keen with excitement.

"On the new year, we'll swim in the sea," Minke promises, and they
all look down into water so clear they can see to the bottom. In only ten
days at sea, the sun has colored their winter-city faces, whitened Zef's
hair, and streaked Elly's with honey gold.

They are among the last to board the tender and the last brought to
shore, where wagons are being loaded with goods, logs, boxes, and
barrels—a familiar scene but on a larger scale than before. Some
children are playing games on the beach. They stop to watch Zef and
Elly with interest. Elly and Zef watch them back.

Minke recognizes that she is at exactly the place on the beach where
Zef was kidnapped. She stops. Zef and Elly gladly stop too and drop her
hands so they can take in their new surroundings. She has relived the
moment of Zef's capture so often she expects to remember every inch,
every grain of sand. But it has changed. The sand, packed solid from
activity over the years, has become as hard as the surface of any street in
New York City. Heavy chains for the hauling up of goods are

permanently fixed in the seawall and extend across the sand to the water. She is reentering a world that is at once familiar and lost to her.

She takes the children's hands again, up the ramp to the top of the seawall toward San Martin Street. Toward the Almacén. Everything depends on what happens next. She must accomplish this before she does anything else. Without it, they are doomed.

She barely finds it, crowded among the other buildings. The sign has changed from the rough black sticks spelling out the name to a blue-and-yellow-painted sign that hangs over the street and says simply ALMACÉN.

Inside is familiar, but only just. Now there is a quantity of goods to rival that of the stores in New York. The shelves reach to the ceiling. A balcony runs all around, reminding Minke of the great hall at Ellis Island, replacing the ladders that Bertinat used to reach merchandise on the high shelves. There are Goodyear tires for sale, Singer sewing machines, packs of cigarettes, and cameras. The place bustles with customers. She scans faces; some are familiar, but she sees no one she knows. To the left are fabrics, exactly where they were before but now so many more bolts, with more variety, more colors, more textures. Spools of ribbon take up an entire shelf.

She spots Bertinat on the balcony, where he is pulling out a bolt of cloth; he sees her and stops. He blushes. His hair is gray at the temples now. "Señora?" he asks, looking down on her and the children. It's been seven years.

"Señor," she says. "*Es bueno volver a verte.*" The children are startled to hear their mother speak an unfamiliar language. "It is good to see you again."

Bertinat pushes back the bolt of fabric, disappears from the balcony, and in a moment is crossing the floor with a smile. He speaks to her in rapid Spanish. So happy to see her. What a surprise. Is she well? On and on. He has certainly taken note of the children, of Zef in particular, and she knows he remembers the kidnapping. He must be wondering, but he is far too polite to ask, for fear of causing her distress. Elly presses against Minke and takes in every detail of the meeting. Zef examines a pair of shiny binoculars for sale on a counter nearby.

"May we speak privately?" she asks.

"Sí, sí." Bertinat directs them to a small back room, crowded with boxes and containers of merchandise. She has dressed herself and the children for this exact moment, wearing clothing she has made by hand with the greatest of care to show off her considerable skill. "Señor. Allow me to show you what I have learned in America." She holds out her wrist and indicates the cuff. "See how the stitches are so fine as to be almost invisible." Bertinat examines the sewing and nods approval. Zef removes his summer jacket and she shows Bertinat the work, inside and out, the finishing of the seams, the difficult tailoring. Bertinat knows his fabrics, and he knows sewing. He says nothing but looks with great interest. He smiles when she shows him the buttonholes, not just stitched but bound in fabric, and for the finale, the curved seams on her own and Elly's dress and the skillful matching of patterns.

"It's excellent work," he says.

"I propose a partnership, señor. A collaboration." If he will allow her a small space to use in the store, she will be the finest seamstress in Chubut Province. She will pay him 10 percent of what she earns in return.

Mr. Wiley has told her that such arrangements are commonplace in the grand department stores of New York City. He insisted that she join as an independent businesswoman, not an employee. He made her promise not to bury herself away in a room alone, taking in other people's mending, but to put her gifts on display.

Bertinat smiles broadly. He can see nothing wrong with the plan. Mr. Wiley assured her the man would be a fool to turn down such an offer in which he had virtually nothing to lose.

"Then I shall begin on Monday," she says.

LIKE THE ALMACÉN, the Nueva Hotel de la Explotación del Petróleo has competition. Two newer hotels made of brick and mortar stand nearby and look more prosperous, with motorcars drawn up in front. Minke swings open the door to the hotel and is almost overcome by its familiar smell—of men and smoke and roasting meat. She has expected this feeling of being in two worlds at once, of having two warring emotions at every turn: the bliss she associates with her year in Comodoro and the heartbreak of what came afterward.

Their bags, their only possessions, have been brought to the hotel and lie in a corner of the lobby. She feels electric with certainty and the power of her own courage.

After finding Zef, she had made a comfortable life for herself and the children in New York. The Wileys were good to them. But Zef was restless and needed so much more to keep his interest. And Elly was content to stay quietly in the sewing room. Too content. They were becoming children of New York, their lives spent too much in the kitchen and small quarters of their mother. New York was not a place to raise her children. She had tasted better, far better. Comodoro was her gift to them.

WAITERS AT THE Explotación bar wear crisp white aprons and black waist-length jackets. Minke enters, her head held high. Chin up. People look at her, then go back to what they were saying. Guiding the children ahead of her, she threads her way to Meduño, who has become stout, his face a cinnamon balloon. He sits by the cash register, hands thrust into his pockets, directing his staff with a tip of the head, a dart of the eyes.

"Señor Meduño, do you remember me? I am Minke DeVries."

"Sí," he says. His face is utterly placid, but the eyes are alive with interest. They dart across her face to the children. Meduño was always shrewd. He has not forgotten her. At an invisible sign, two waiters leap to set up the table that once was Minke's. Perhaps also the same table where Sander had gambled away his son and their life in Comodoro. Meduño himself pulls out the three chairs and settles his great bulk in the fourth. He opens his hands, rolls his eyes heavenward. She had forgotten the man has a streak for the dramatic. "You've come back to us for a visit," he says.

"To live," she says.

"*Magnífico.*" He squints at the children, his eyes resting on Zef. He counts on his fingers and makes a face that says, *Can this be the child?*

"Sí," she says quickly, before more questions can be asked. Meduño will not be so polite as Bertinat. Mr. Wiley warned her that to speak of Sander's infamy is to brand the children as offspring of a heartless criminal. Cassian reminded her of what he had said all those years ago on board the *Frisia*—truth is what you put in and what you leave out. There's no one absolute truth for everyone. "Tell what is public," Cassian said, "but not what is private."

"My son was found in the care of Frederik and Tessa Dietz," she says, and gives him a warning look that means *Let's put the matter to rest.* "Safe and sound," she adds. She draws the money from her purse. "We would like a room."

Meduño takes the money, but he is distracted. He can't take his eyes from Zef. She puts a finger to her lips when Meduño is about to speak, to ask more questions. As it is, the news will spread like wildfire.

THE NEXT DAY there is everything to be done. She enrolls the children in Escuela No. 24, which is in the solid brick building that once housed the bakery. Forty students are enrolled, covering grades one through ten. Zef and Elly stand holding hands before a nun who asks them questions in Spanish. Minke replies for them. They are eight and seven years old, she says. They have attended school in New York City. They speak English and Dutch flawlessly, and for that reason they will learn Spanish in no time. The nun is new to Comodoro. Perhaps she belongs to the order of Father Bahlow and the nuns from the *Frisia*.

Minke takes them to the house where both were born. They stand together on the street, observing. The roof no longer is weighed down with debris to keep it from blowing away. The new owners have secured it with nails. There are flowers planted in front. Minke takes the children's hands again, and they walk to the Cerro Chenque. Zef and Elly run ahead, and by the time Minke reaches the top, they have been there for some time.

"It was different then," she says. They are children, not interested in the way things were but in the way things are. They are excited by seeing their school from the Cerro, the hotel where they slept, the

Maceió still in the harbor. They are excited by seeing how what they have already seen is joined together. She points out anyway what's left of the *obras*. "Uncle Cassian built every bit of it," she says, and they take notice but only at the mention of their beloved uncle. There's nothing to see. The *obras* is a shambles of blowing weeds. The house and the factory have collapsed. "And that—" She points to the now booming oil production, with its four sets of barracks and an impressive stone building, the office, she supposes, covered in green creepers. "That once belonged to Meneer Dietz."

They know the name and peer down at it with interest. They know that Zef was kidnapped by Meneer Dietz and lived with him and his wife for a year before Minke found him again. They do not know that Tessa subsequently suffered a breakdown and was sent away. Nor do they know about the case against their father and the Dietzes or that it failed. Dietz hired the best attorneys to fight extradition and defend himself. His claim? Incredibly, that the Dietzes took Zef in with the full consent of both Sander and Minke, and no money changed hands. His attorney stated that Minke and Sander were only too happy to give away their son because calamity had befallen them when the *obras* collapsed after the attack on Dr. Tredegar. Kidnapping? Ludicrous!

In the end, the case never went to trial.

And what of Sander? Minke knows only that Fenna and Sander found employment as cook and driver for a large household on Fifth Avenue. Woodrow, age six, is enrolled in the Lillie Devereaux Blake School, Public School 6, which is reputed to be excellent.

Something catches Elly's eye in the distance. "Mama!" she cries. A cloud of dust rises in the distance, kicked up by the hooves of approaching horses. As Minke had hoped, but had not told the children for fear of disappointing them, the gauchos often come to Comodoro when a ship arrives.

By the time they have descended the Cerro and walked back to the center of town, the races have begun up and down San Martin Street. The streets are lined with people—hundreds, it seems, and most of them foreign. Like them. The gauchos race on their splendid ponies. The ground vibrates with hoofbeats, and the air is alive with red and silver and the shiny flanks of the beautiful ponies. From the Almacén to the outskirts of town, the men race one another, thundering past. They are exactly the spectacle Minke wanted, the glue that will cement her children to this place. Zef must be restrained; he is completely enthralled and twice gets dangerously close to the races. Nothing in New York City can match this. The crowd stays to watch until long after the dinner hour because the sun remains long in the sky. Minke, Zef, and Elly fall into their beds at the Explotación, exhausted.

In the morning Zef and Elly are up with the sun, tugging at their mother's arm. "We want to go for a swim in the ocean," Zef says. "You promised."

And so she has. They pass through the center of town on their way to the water. All is quiet this morning.

Minke spreads a blanket at a spot where they will have solitude. The children play, and she stands with them, skirts raised up to her calves, in the lovely green water. The children have swum at Coney Island in New York and cannot believe that this is the same ocean. The waves are gentler, the temperature so much warmer.

She feels the vibration of approaching horses, and her heart skips a beat. She calls the children to her. She wants to hold their hands until any danger is past. But the horses slow and approach at a walk. The rider is a gaucho, practically square, he's so strongly built, with wide shoulders and chest, his porkpie hat riding low on his forehead, leading his string of seven or eight ponies.

The gaucho comes to a stop and studies her. "*¿Te acuerdas de mí?*" Do you remember me?

She cannot believe her good fortune. "Goyo."

He smiles, showing large white teeth. Zef's mouth is agape, seeing that his mother knows someone like this. Minke is beyond excited.

"I saw you yesterday. I saw today when you came to the water. I followed."

"I hoped I would see you again," she says.

"I see you found him," Goyo says with a tip of his hat toward Zef. It is a statement of fact, no more.

"You were blamed," she says. "My heart breaks over the terrible injustice to you."

Goyo smiles and shrugs. "Long ago. No matter," he says.

"I bleed for our friend Pieps," she says, coming up with the Spanish words, to her own surprise. "He lost his life for a lie."

"Eh?" Goyo frowns, and Minke tries again, thinking she hasn't stated it correctly, but he cuts her off. "I know what you said." He throws his head back and laughs.

She wonders if laughter is the gaucho way of honoring the dead.

"He didn't die," Goyo says, as if it is obvious, and he laughs again.

"Mi esposo le disparó." My husband shot him.

"Es verdad." It's true. Goyo opens his massive hands in a show of agreement. "But Pieps didn't die."

She makes him repeat it several times.

He sits beside her on her blanket, holding the reins of the lead pony. Elly falls to her knees in the sand beside Minke and stares as Goyo tells Minke what happened. Zef can't take his eyes from Goyo's horses. He reaches out a hand for the lead horse.

Pieps, Goyo says, was wounded and left for dead, left for the ravens to eat. He lay bleeding for a time before one of the skinners came looking for him and carried him home. Word spread among the gauchos, who brought a *curandero*, a healer, to minister to Pieps. Over time, Pieps recovered from his wounds. Goyo, with a quick look to the children, said, "I came to Comodoro to kill your husband, señora, but he was gone."

"He's not my husband," she said.

"Come," he says. "We'll go."

He gives her a leg up onto one of the ponies and lifts Elly to ride with her. She expects Goyo to take Zef with him, but instead he tells Zef to choose a horse of his own. Zef glances quickly at Minke, grins, and points to a piebald.

"Bueno," Goyo says, and gives Zef a leg up. The child sits bareback on the horse, holding on to its mane, and they set off at a walk to the skinners. As they approach, Minke breathes in the long-forgotten, slightly sweet smell of the place, and with it a rush of memories so rich and full they bring tears to her eyes.

"*Hola!* Pieps!" Goyo shouts as they approach.

A man appears at the door of the skinners, fair-haired, clean-shaven. He frowns in confusion at the sight of them. Goyo speaks to him in rapid Spanish, and Pieps answers. The two men laugh. She hears her name. Catches a few words. Pieps is quiet for several moments as he looks from her to her children and back to her. He comes forward, the better to see her, holding up a hand to shield his eyes from the sun. His face is brown; he wears a white shirt open at the neck. He sweeps back his hair with one hand. He says in Dutch that he is overwhelmed to see her again.

Zef and Elly swivel their heads at the first Dutch they have heard spoken in this place.

Minke is speechless. There is everything to say and no way to say it. Pieps throws back his head and laughs.

"So you're going to live in this place," he says in Dutch to Zef and Elly.

"Yes, sir," Zef says.

Pieps undoes a pony from Goyo's string. He leads the horse to a mounting block and hops on. "Come on, then," he says to Zef, with a wink at Minke. He rides alongside Zef. "I will teach you to ride, as I once taught your mother."

Acknowledgments

A YOUNG WIFE IS very loosely based on events in my maternal grandmother's life. Born in the Netherlands, she moved as a very young bride to Comodoro Rivadavia, Argentina, and subsequently to New York. My thanks go out to the people who were able to fill in so many geographical and domestic details of those times, as told to them by my grandmother and great-grandparents. My thanks especially to my aunts Winifred Schortman and Tia Baldwin, and to my second cousin Ada Castro.

For the many nuanced translations to and from the Dutch, I depended on Jan van der Leij of Beetgumermolen, Friesland, the Netherlands. Jan was also an enormous help in sorting through the genealogy of the family and in locating the many houses in which the family once lived. His assistance greatly enriched the Dutch section of the story.

At the center of my writing universe are Bruce Cohen, Leslie Johnson, Terese Karmel, Wally Lamb, and Ellen Zahl. These excellent writers and critics helped to steer the development of *A Young Wife* over two years with intelligence, humor, and fine wine. Jane Christensen provided careful readings and observations, as did Doug Anderson and Sari Rosenblatt.

As she did with both *Speak Softly, She Can Hear* and *Perfect Family*, the lovely Jennifer Walsh gave her usual deft advice that helped shape the story. Amanda Murray was kind enough to buy the manuscript and start the editorial process. Kerri Kolen, my remarkable new editor, guided the manuscript to its current and much improved form. Thank you all.

And finally, I want to thank my dear husband, Robert Haskins Funk, whose love, support, and wisdom are my rock.

A Young Wife

This reading group guide for A Young Wife *includes an introduction, discussion questions, ideas for enhancing your book club, and a Q&A with author Pam Lewis. The suggested questions are intended to help your reading group find new and interesting angles and topics for your discussion. We hope that these ideas will enrich your conversation and increase your enjoyment of the book.*

Introduction

Amsterdam, 1912. When fifteen-year-old Minke Van Aisma travels to Amsterdam to care for the dying wife of a wealthy man, she has no idea what journey lies ahead. Only hours after his wife's death, her employer, Sander DeVries, proposes marriage. Within days the couple has set sail for the oil fields of Argentina. They settle in the rough coastal town of Comodoro Rivadavia, where Minke eventually learns that her husband is not a successful trader, but a morphine producer. The future that seemed so bright takes an even darker turn the morning their toddler son, Zef, is kidnapped. Sander seeks murderous revenge for the kidnapping, and he must flee Comodoro and start over in another country. Already pregnant with their second child, Minke has little choice but to wait for the new baby's arrival, then follow Sander to America, leaving their firstborn behind forever. But when she arrives in New York and discovers that Sander has betrayed her, she leaves him, finds works as a seamstress, and vows to find her son, no matter how long it takes.

Topics and Questions for Discussion

1. When we first meet Minke, she is a fifteen-year-old girl from a tiny Dutch town. How does Minke change over the course of the novel? What risks has she taken by the end of *A Young Wife* that she might not have seemed capable of at the beginning?

2. Consider Minke's relationship with Elisabeth DeVries, Sander's dying wife. How do Minke and Elisabeth bond? Why does Elisabeth's death haunt Minke? What lessons does Minke fail to learn from Sander and Elisabeth's marriage?

3. On the way to Comodoro, Cassian tells Minke, "Truth is a matter only of what you put in and what you leave out. . . . Truth is in the selection of fact." How does Minke learn about the flexibility of truth and lies? How does Cassian use selective truths to his own advantage?

4. Discuss Minke and Sander's relationship to the Dietzes, their fellow travelers to Argentina. What are Minke's first impressions of the Dietz family? How do the Dietzes react to the death of their daughter, Astrid? Do you think they hold Minke and Sander responsible for Astrid's death? Why or why not?

5. What are Minke's first impressions of Comodoro as she arrives by ship? What dangers and thrills await her in this "vast, colorless" land?

6. Consider the gauchos of Argentina and their relationship to the settlers of Comodoro. Why is Minke fascinated with the gauchos' traditions and lifestyle? How are the gauchos' values different from the settlers' values, and what tensions exist between these two groups?

7. After Cassian is attacked in Comodoro, Minke is "forced to see herself, her family, in a new light as corrupt, even evil, and protection

as something that could vanish in the wink of an eye." How does Cassian's attack serve as a turning point in the novel? What other acts of violence and betrayal follow soon after? What does Minke realize about her role in Comodoro's community?

8. Compare the two scenes of immigration in the novel: Minke's arrival in Comodoro with Sander, and her passage through Ellis Island with Cassian. What are Minke's expectations during each scene of arrival? How are her expectations met or thwarted as she settles into a new life?

9. After Sander's infidelity, Minke "thought back over their years together, almost three now. Why hadn't she seen his character before? The signs had been there." What signs of Sander's true nature did Minke miss, and why did she ignore them? How did Sander deceive Minke? What motivates this complicated character?

10. Trace Minke's relationship with Pieps, from their first meeting on the *Frisia* to their unexpected reunion in Comodoro at the end of the novel. How does Pieps help Minke feel at home in a foreign land? What does Minke learn from Pieps? Do you think their friendship will evolve into something more?

11. Discuss the relationship between Minke and Fenna. How are the sisters similar, and how are they different? Facing Fenna after her betrayal, Minke realizes, "She didn't despise Fenna. That would have required passion. No, Fenna had shown her true colors and Minke was no longer interested." What are Fenna's "true colors," and what price does Fenna pay for her deceptions?

12. Minke's mind clears when she realizes the conspiracy behind Zef's kidnapping: "Like a fog lifting, a world comes newly into focus, she had to let go of one set of beliefs and make room for another." Name another occasion when Minke learns to let go of her beliefs. What does she learn from others' deceptions?

13. Revisit the luncheon scene between the Wileys and the Dietzes. How is this scene funny as well as suspenseful? How do the Wiley siblings outsmart the Dietzes, and how does Minke prove that their little boy is Zef?

14. *A Young Wife* ends with Minke's return to Comodoro with Zef and Elly. "New York was not a place to raise her children. She has tasted better, far better. Comodoro is her gift to them." What is it about Comodoro that draws Minke back, even when her children's future seems more secure in New York? What opportunities await this small family in Comodoro?

Enhance Your Book Club

1. Arriving at Ellis Island, Minke and other immigrants could bring into the country only what they could carry. Brainstorm a list of what you would take if you had to start your life over in a new country. What would you pack in your suitcase, and what would you leave behind?

2. Minke speaks three languages: Dutch, Spanish, and English. Teach your book club how to greet each other in Spanish and Dutch. Start with some Dutch phrases here: http://www.omniglot.com/lan guage/phrases/dutch.php.

3. What is the history of morphine, the drug that Sander and Cassian produce? View a timeline of opium's history, from 3300 B.C. to the present day: http://www.pbs.org/wgbh/pages/frontline/shows/heroin/etc/history.html.

4. *A Young Wife* is based on a true story from Pam Lewis's family. If you could write a novel based on any story from your family's history, what would it be? Write a paragraph or two about the most interesting story from your family—past or present, real or imagined—and share it with your book group!

A Conversation with Pam Lewis

A Young Wife is based on your grandmother's secret past. How did you come to learn this extraordinary family story?

We moved often when I was growing up, and my grandmother's rare visits were highlights of my childhood. She told stories of a disaster at sea, a burning ship, circling sharks, and a husband's heroism. She spoke of her life as a new bride in a place called Comodoro Rivadavia, Argentina, of handsome gauchos who rode into town on fabulous horses decked in turquoise and silver and their thunderous races down the dusty main street.

There the story stopped. It picked up again with my grandmother's serene life in California, her four daughters fully grown and a smattering of grandchildren.

After my mother died in 1984, information began to flow. I learned from relatives that at age fifteen, my grandmother had been hired to tend a dying relative in the home of my then thirty-five-year-old grandfather. They fell in love, and, causing a scandal in the small town where they lived, sailed to Comodoro Rivadavia to start a sort of trading post there. He ultimately abandoned her in New York with four young daughters to begin another family with her own sister. Astonishingly, my grandmother continued to love him until the day she died.

This scant but rich information was a rare gift for a fiction writer. The exotic settings, the passion, and the devastating betrayal became the bones on which to build my story. I was glad not to know everything—virtually nothing of my grandfather to this day—so that my imagination was free to make up the rest.

A Young Wife is a new direction for you as a writer, after two books of suspense fiction. Was your writing process different this time? What elements of suspense were you able to incorporate into this turn-of-the-century saga?

My writing process didn't vary much with this book. In all three, the suspense was added relatively late in the writing process. For *A Young*

Wife, I knew the general shape of the story but surprised myself with the suspense. My grandmother lost a child in Comodoro when a nurse mixed water that hadn't been boiled into his food. I loosely intended for this to happen in the novel, but when the time came to write it, I couldn't bear to see the child die and decided he should be kidnapped instead, which raised the far more interesting questions of who did it, why, where was the child taken and would he ever be seen again?

From gauchos' traditions to Ellis Island medical exams to New York fashions, *A Young Wife* must have required a lot of research. How did you learn what Amsterdam, Comodoro, and New York looked and felt like a hundred years ago?

I was reading W. H. Hudson's *The Purple Land* on the elliptical machine at the gym when I realized he was writing about the same part of the world where my grandmother had lived. This started a fury of reading. Hudson's *Far Away and Long Ago* and *Idle Days in Patagonia*, the novellas of Eduardo Mallea. Bruce Chatwin's *In Patagonia*. Incredibly, I was able to find a book of photographs of Comodoro from 1910 to 1915. There was the Almacén, the Explotación, and the Cerro Chenque. I was shocked at what a hardscrabble life my grandmother must have had there compared to what I had pictured, and I could conclude only that her memory of that time was so lustrous not because of the place but because of her intense love for her husband.

My sister, Gail Tobin, my aunt Winnie Schortman, and I went to Enkhuizen, which had barely changed since my grandmother's time. I also Googled furiously to learn about everything from life on board ship, life in New York City, right down to the name of the school that little Woodrow DeVries would have attended.

A Young Wife features several morally questionable characters, including Sander, Fenna, and the Dietzes. Which of them was the most fun to create, and why?

I often write with my eyes closed. That way, I can picture the scene unfolding in front of me and write what I see. I can't do that so well with dialogue, but I love to do it when several people are in a scene, and I want to know what they look like, what they're wearing, how they move, and so on. Tessa Dietz really came to life when I saw her at the estancia with that big ratty blue parrot on her shoulder. She was hands-down my favorite morally challenged character. I loved her outrageous sense of entitlement, so awful to the people who worked for her, and so completely narcissistic.

Minke proves to be a talented seamstress and dressmaker. Which fashions do you find more interesting, those of the 1910s or the 2010s?

In terms of construction, the fashions of the 1910s are more interesting because of the hand sewing. I live near Willimantic, aka "thread city." Interestingly, when those mills started mass-producing thread, people started owning more than two sets of clothing. So the clothing of today is more interesting to me; there's so much more of it and so much more variation than in Minke's day.

In *A Young Wife,* morphine is a common drug, and its characters treat everything from broken legs to childbirth with a dose. How did you learn about morphine's past uses, while keeping today's knowledge of its dangers out of the plot?

The early twentieth century was a murky, semi-legal period for cocaine and its derivatives. For example, until 1903 Coca-Cola contained significant amounts of cocaine. At the same time, morphine required a prescription and a bright red label with the word "poison" spelled out clearly in white letters, and it was used for everything from lesions to childbirth. In Europe, morphine production was not a crime until the Hague Conference of 1912, which meant that entrepreneurs like Sander and Cassian could no longer freely mix up batches. They would have had no choice but to leave the Netherlands and set up shop in a more tolerant place. The dangers of the drug were there, of course. We see Griet helping herself to her mother's medicine just for the rush, and we see the young men who always lounge around Cassian. But morphine was still easy to get, and I had the sense that although there were laws, they weren't yet rigidly enforced.

This novel is refreshingly frank in its sexual attitudes—Minke's passion for Sander, as well as Cassian's sexuality, are important to the plot. Did you ever find it difficult to write these scenes? Was it ever challenging for you on a personal level, given that Minke's character is based on your own grandmother?

I come from a long line of dishy women on my mother's side, so these scenes were not at all difficult to write. I'm pretty sure my grandmother's great love for her husband couldn't have been prim Victorian admiration. She was an absolute lady when I knew her, always in stockings, heels, and a dress, but photos of her as a young woman show a great spirit. And as far as Cassian was concerned, his homosexuality was secondary to his character but turned out to be essential to the plot. I hadn't known it would be a problem until there was an entourage of young men who gravitated to him at the morphine works. In a small, predominantly Catholic, lawless setting this would not sit well.

Minke is a heroine with the great immigrant spirit of the early twentieth century. What do you think it was like for a woman to start her life over—sometimes on her own—in those challenging times?

I'm awed by the number of people who left everything behind and started new lives in this country. Thousands went through Ellis Island every day. Women were not allowed to enter the country alone. They had to be part of a family who were already in the United States or on the ship with them. So Minke would have been able to enter, but without Sander's support she'd have been truly on her own with an infant to support. It took grit. In my own family, my grandmother was hired by the Misses Wiley as a seamstress, just as Minke is in the book. In real life, Mr. Wiley found a job for my mother, then age sixteen, at the *New York Times,* and she supported the family, having to give up a full scholarship at Swarthmore to do so.

How did your family react when you told them you were writing a novel based on your grandmother? What details did you change as Minke DeVries became her own character?

My family was not only supportive, but they were also able to fill in many of the gaps. As with many secrets, the things I didn't know were widely known by others. My second cousin told me about the dirt floors in my grandmother's house in Comodoro and the ever-present howling wind. She said Momée was so naive that once pregnant, she had no idea how the baby would come out.

Both Minke and Momée have a quiet strength and elegance, both are excellent seamstresses, and both are very wise. But I also gave Minke a hefty dose of my mother, who was a purposeful and ambitious woman. Momée used to exasperate my mother with her reticence. Even as a young girl, my mother would have to ask store clerks for things because Momée was too shy to ask.

In searching records at Ellis Island, I discovered that while Momée was quarantined in Holland with three little daughters during the war, her husband remained in New York and sailed first class to Cuba under the name Juan. He listed himself as Argentine and said his wife was my grandmother's sister. He did such a disservice to his real wife and children that I had no qualms about creating a wretch of him, even though I must say here that he never manufactured morphine and he never engineered a kidnapping.

All three of your novels are about secrets and lies, to some degree. What do you think attracts you to this theme?

I'm attracted to secrets and lies because there were quite a few in my own family. From the reactions to my first books, I would say everyone has them. What fascinates me is the way children make up whole logical scenarios to fill in the gaps of information. As a child,

I knew my grandfather was alive, although my mother would not even give me his name. I always pictured him out there somewhere. I imagined the reasons for his not being in our lives had to be monumental. Maybe he was too busy for us. Maybe he didn't like us. I never for a moment considered that he might be a bad man.

What are some of your favorite works of historical fiction?

J. P. Donleavy's *Ragtime* stands out. There were so many wonderful surprises in that book, my favorite of which was the appearance of the Little Rascals. I also liked Henry Roth's *Call It Sleep*. I don't read much historical fiction that predates the twentieth century, I realize now from considering this question.

What can your readers look forward to next? Will you return to historical fiction or suspense fiction, or try your hand at a new genre?

The next book will be about a group of sixty hikers encamped just outside Yellowstone who go in groups into the wilderness each day. There has been a mauling by a grizzly not far from the encampment. The story will revolve around three people—the director of the group, a young woman who has little experience with the out-of-doors, and the man whom she is stalking.

About the Author

Pam Lewis lives in rural Connecticut with her husband, Rob Funk. She is the author of the novels *Perfect Family* and *Speak Softly, She Can Hear,* and her short fiction has appeared in *The New Yorker* and various literary magazines. You can learn more about her on Facebook or visit her website at www.pamlewisonline.com.